Avant-Garde: Awakening

C. K. Stang

C. K. Stang

2nd Edition

Cover art and design by Lyndsey R. Stang / StudioArtHouse
Copy editing by Andrea H. Stang

The Idle Confessor
Visit and message me on
Facebook: https://www.facebook.com/The-Idle-Confessor
Email: idleconfessor@gmail.com

Check out my Star Wars Fanfiction Project:
http://royalroadl.com/fiction/1525

For my wife Lyndsey—
What can I say that I haven't already said a thousand times?
Thank you, for being that driving element in my life. You will always be an unstoppable force to be reckoned with, and I wouldn't change you for the world.

For my daughters Ella, Lainey, and Maisie—
Without you three girls, I would lack purpose, resolve, and love.
You three are my most valued achievements in life.

"I must not fear. Fear is the mind-killer. Fear is the little-death that brings total obliteration. I will face my fear. I will permit it to pass over me and through me. And when it has gone past I will turn the inner eye to see its path. Where the fear has gone there will be nothing. Only I will remain."

-Frank Herbert, *Dune*

CONTENTS

CHAPTER ONE: THE RUNAWAY TITAN

The room is uncomfortably bright and daunting. I shift in my seat, causing the leather cushion to squeal under my body. What was I thinking? Dispensation was not the answer, and yet here I am indulging my curiosity. My angst heightens as footsteps echo from the hallway and come to a silent halt outside the door. A moment later Odeza enters the room.

She glances my way and grimaces. "I thought we had gone through this once before," she says, studying the room's intricate details. "Although, last time you weren't so committed to the illusion."

I nod my head. "All I need is some clarity," I state, leaning forward and summoning a red oak desk with a cherry finish in front of her.

She bows her head in gratitude and promptly sits across from me. "First, let's start with the room. It's uncomfortable. Tell me why?"

"I guess I'm feeling overwhelmed, maybe a little anxious," I respond hesitantly.

Odeza leans forward, propping her elbows on the table. "And me, why did you make me into this?"

A feeling of frustration comes over me. "Can't you just play along?" Odeza scowls, pushing me to explain. "Ok, I feel more comfortable talking to—"

"An attractive woman?" she interrupts. "Or is it the need for human contact?"

"Neither," I say flatly. "It was your name."

Odeza gives me a curious look. "Explain," she demands.

"I imagine you looking like this, because it fits your name," I say, recalling my original image of Odeza. Almost everything had naturally fallen into place, from the dark brown of her skin to the curly poof of black glossy hair. Even the fitted gray business skirt and white button up shirt that accentuated every curve. Everything perfectly complemented her name, except for her eyes. Those damned emerald eyes didn't belong to her, and they never will.

Odeza stands and circles the desk, then leans against the front of it. "So you associate my name with this form? Intriguing."

"You're actually impressed?" I ask in a tone of disbelief.

"I digress," she quickly responds, pressing her hands along the front of her skirt and frowning. "Let's get back to why we're here." Odeza folds her arms in front of her. "How far would you like to go back this time?" Her tone was practically caustic with accents of irritation.

I pause, preparing myself for rebuttal. "All the way."

Odeza glares at me. "All the way!?" she growls. "John, you know we can't keep doing this. You can't change anything. The decision has been made!"

"I of all people understand that Odeza! I just—I need to remember!" I argue.

She scoffs. "For what? We took the memories for a reason. There was too much pain and suffering for you to do what you had to do!"

I jump to my feet, causing the room the tremor from my frustration. "I know what I have to do!" The room shudders more violently, causing the lights to flicker.

Odeza makes a smug look, waiting for me to calm down. "You know I'll have to talk with the Board about this," she says frankly, "But understand one thing, John. If they grant this Dispensation, it'll be the last time. No more of this clarity nonsense."

I cross my arms. "If you must." I didn't try to hide the disdain in my voice.

She shrugs. "Alright, give me a moment." She walks into an open area of the room and extends her arms, lifting her head up toward the ceiling. The room begins to shake and the lights become brighter until I can hardly make out Odeza's silhouette. A few seconds later everything returns to normal with Odeza looking at me, lips pursed into a tight smile. "Dispensation has been granted. Please take a seat."

I drop into the leather chair, making it creak. "They said yes, to everything?"

Odeza sits down at the desk. "Yes John, but like I said this is the last time. Now sit back and close your eyes."

I lean back into the leather chair and stare up at the ceiling. "Odeza," I say in a stern voice.

There are a few seconds of silence before she responds, "What is it John?"

"Please don't take them away again." My tone boasted a little more desperation than I would have wished but what's said is said.

The silence that follows is unnerving; some things should be left unspoken. No matter how much I wished, Odeza was not my friend. Finally, she clears her throat. "You know I don't have the power to make that decision."

"Yeah," I respond. "Thought it was worth a try." I let out a sigh. "Ok, I'm ready," I say, closing my eyes.

A few more seconds of silence pass before Odeza finally speaks. "Alright John, start by telling me everything you see."

*****

It's the same as always. I'm floating, weightless in space surrounded by unimaginable vastness dotted with the light of a billion stars. And I feel as though I'm at peace, as if my spirit has left my body to explore the endless space between all things. It's freeing really, knowing that I can escape the ravages of reality by embracing the absolution of sleep. I'll be honest though, it's a boring dream, but it is so real to me nonetheless.

After a while I find myself in the white room that is split in half by a glossy black wall that shimmers like a dark sea. I can see my reflection in the smooth wall— undoubtedly me but there is something different, something—off. And just like the countless times before I begin walking toward the wall. My shadowed reflection becomes more and more clear the closer I get, but no matter how long I walk or run I can never reach the surface of the glistening darkness.

As I get closer I feel a pressure beginning in my abdomen, at first nothing more than a nuisance but then growing in discomfort. I hunch over, still making my way toward the wall. But now the pressure has built to the point that I can barely breathe, causing my sight to diminish. I drag my body closer to the wall with my reflection copying my every move. I extend my arm as if to grab my reflection's hand as the last bits of air is forced out of my lungs. A dreadfully-cold feeling begins running though my body as I lose consciousness.

"Wake up!" A dull sting courses through my right check. I jerk awake coughing and gasping for air, realizing that the unbearable pressure on my chest wasn't from my dream but rather a drug addict named Tumbler kneeling on my sternum. He slaps me again, ensuring he has my undivided attention. "Where the hell is the Zeeklor!?" he yells pressing the cold carbonized steel knife against my throat.

"I—don't know!" I shout, trying to catch my breath.

His eyes fill with fury, pressing the blade hard against my throat; I feel the sting of the knife cutting into my flesh. "I'm not playing with you boy, I'll kill you!" he bears his teeth with drug-fueled malice.

Tumbler wasn't a very intimidating man, no more than sixty-eight kilograms. Pale skin covered with cold sweat, probably due to withdraws. His eyes were dark and sunken, his teeth yellow and neglected; he looked more like a skeleton with skin stretched over it. I could tell he was weak but desperate and willing to do anything for another hit of Zeek. I know better than to mess with people like Tumbler. But in my current situation I have little option otherwise.

I can sense Tumbler's growing impatience coursing from his hand into the blade. I comb the apartment with my eyes, catching sight of the cabinet just to the right of him. He notices my fixated stare and turns his attention to the cupboard, pushing himself upright then stumbling to the door and ripping it open as if life depended on it.

I slowly force myself to my feet, eyeing the apartment door just past Tumbler who was sifting through whole handfuls of junk at a time. The distraction isn't going to last long and there is no way I can get to the door without him noticing. I search the cluttered mess on the floor looking for something suitable to arm myself with. I grab a half-empty bottle and smash it against the coffee table, freeing a series of jagged glass edges.

"Where is it!?" Tumbler's shout makes me jump. Before I could respond his eyes shift to the broken bottle in my hand. "You have a death wish, boy?" he says with a sinister smile, lifting the knife in response.

I can feel my heart stutter as his eyes narrow like a predator's before attacking it's pray. Tumbler was ready to kill, and he didn't make an effort to hide it. I tighten my grasp around the bottle as he begins his advance, arm and blade outstretched ready to end me.

SNAP! The sound of a pulse revolver fills the small apartment. Tumbler freezes in mid-step, his face contorting in pain as he collapses to the ground with an echoing thud. Blood was gushing from a smoldering fist-sized hole just under his right shoulder blade. I look up at Jurin's smiling face and his revolver still trained on Tumbler.

"You alright John?" he asks.

"Yeah I'm good—thanks" I respond while Tumbler's corpse twitches on the ground in front of me.

"Good—" Jurin says unloading three more pulse rounds into Tumbler, causing his flesh to split open like a bloody canyon. "Such a shame, you know," he adds, grabbing a duffle bag and stuffing it with his personal effects.

"What is?" I ask, attempting to imagine a single person who would miss Tumbler.

Jurin stops stuffing the bag long enough to catch my attention. I look up noticing his twisted smile. "He was one of my best customers," he says with a laugh, "and I really liked this apartment."

Figures. Only Jurin would make a joke out of killing someone, but I can't fault him for saving me. He's strong, tall and cynical like me but his complexion was lighter, in fact everything about Jurin is opposite of me. He has intimidating grey eyes, whereas I have plain brown ones. He meticulously trims and combs his light blonde hair, when I could care less about the brown mess that resides on my dome. There was always something different about him even when we were growing up, perhaps a confidence I lacked. Whatever it may be, Jurin commands respect in all things, except for when it comes to people he cared about and for that I'm thankful.

I take another long look at Tumbler's ravaged body. The unfortunate truth is no one will care that he's dead. Here on Saturn's largest moon, Titan, commoners find ourselves conveniently misplaced from the rest of the Frontier and, like most things, we're out of sight and therefore out of mind. Left to squander under the rule of drug lords, corrupt mega-corporations, and overbearing militarized police. I wonder if there was a time when Tumbler was a normal man. He maybe had a family or kids. The thought of him having a whole life before he was Tumbler brought a significant level of sadness to me, useless emotions that'll get me killed. Besides it wasn't any easier for orphans like Jurin and me. At the age of eighteen we age-out, essentially ejected and left to our own devices. From there we become fresh pickings for Drafters who recruit people for various organizations against their wills.

It's hard to believe things weren't always like this. I glance out a window at the rest of New Horizon, the largest and last colony established on Titan. There was a time of prosperity once long before Jurin or I even existed. The Golden Age as the etexts call it, an entire era when humanity focused on common goals like expanding and colonizing, when we forfeited our differences for the common good and did things not because we could, but because we couldn't.

Of course that's all history now, thanks to the 110-year Great Civil War between the inner and outer solar system that never truly ended but rather reached a stalemate just about twenty-five years ago. Since then everybody's been trying to heal or forget the war ever happened. While places like New Horizon continues to suffer under the rule of outlaws, like the ancient Wild West. We were so foolish to believe that we had changed.

"John!" Jurin's voice whips me out of my head. "Hey, get your stuff. We have to go."

I look around for anything that I hold of valuable, but nothing really stood out. Then it occurs to me and I fumble through my pockets ensuring the only important thing I possess is still there. I nod, stepping over Tumbler's smoking corpse, and follow Jurin out of the apartment.

Tumbler won't be found for a while, probably only after the smell starts to spread, and by then I'll be gone one way or another. Though, it's not like we're worried about the authorities, other than the local slum lords, who couldn't give a crap about a lone drug addict. The Coalition Fleet doesn't meddle with locals unless their people are directly involved. For the most part, we all live and die by the wills of the wicked, just a population of expendable, lost souls. And luckily for me, Jurin is close to the king of these wicked people.

Chapter Two: The Baron of New Horizon

Cheever West is a megalomaniac, self-appointed Baron of New Horizon and absolutely not someone to cross. Jurin has been working for him as a Zeek runner since he aged out three years prior, and for some reason Jurin has impressed the insane bastard. Cheever is a member of the notorious Syndicate Builders Guild or SBG, a think tank of sorts. At least, that is how I have come to think of them.

The SBG has always sat at the forefront of engineering and planning, directly responsible for almost all the major engineering feats of humanity. It's once prestigious history culminated in a huge network of connections that reach beyond social and governmental jurisdictions. Cheever, while not being a genius, is well connected, and Jurin plans on using those connections to get me off Titan.

The problem is such arrangements take time, which I am in short supply of. It's been four days since I left the orphanage. And I've been hiding out ever since avoiding Drafters, but it is only a matter of time before they find me. Every Drafter promises a better life, but those deals come at a cost. In all honesty it's more closely related to slavery than work, and it's completely legal because some fat politician millions of kilometers away felt it would breathe life back into a dying community. I guess if you look at something from far enough away, it removes the moral obligation to be a decent human being. There is no hiding my disdain for it. Jurin and I have lost so many people to this drafting business.

Jurin stops at the front door of the apartment and starts riffling through his duffle bag, pulling a jacket out and handing it to me. "Here, put this on," he orders.

I take the jacket and give him a puzzled look. "How chivalrous of you, but I'm not cold," I say sarcastically.

"Ha ha, smartass. That's an Aug jammer. It will keep the Drafters from scanning you," he says. "I picked it up earlier."

I nod my head, wondering if the previous owner of the jacket had the same untimely end as our dear friend Tumbler, when Jurin grunts with laughter. "No, I didn't kill the guy who had it last," he says as if he had been reading my mind.

I slip the jacket on quickly and feel an immediate tingling sensation in my left arm, where my Biologically-Integrated Cybernetic System or BICS is located. Although most people call them Augments or simply just Augs, the BICS was a wartime development that has been integrated into all of society. Now, for the most part, every newborn has one installed right after they leave the womb.

The Aug has become a cornerstone of our culture. Not only does it record your personal data, including financial information and contact lists, but it also keeps track of your health status in real-time, even alerting hospitals hours before you feel the slightest bit ill. It has revolutionized our understanding of healthcare in the sense that we can finally predict life-threatening conditions and prevent them from ever happening, but it comes at a cost. Authorities have the ability to remotely scan people at their discretion. In fact, that's why the Drafters are so successful when hunting for new recruits. They simply sit back and scan entire crowds of people with little effort, sometimes even selling people's personal data for a little extra on the side. Because of this, criminal organizations and governments, sometime one in the same, have taken it upon themselves to develop Aug-jamming technology, and of course the average person couldn't afford such luxuries. I can't imagine what Jurin had to do to get his hands on one.

"Does it fit?" Jurin asks.

"Yeah—" I respond when the tingling finally stops. "Jurin, what did you do for this?" He gives me a grave look; I really need to stop asking questions I don't want the answers to.

Jurin pushes the door open. Rays of sunlight temporarily blind me. I hold up my forearm to block the brightness when the jacket starts to change color to match my outfit. "Pretty cool, huh?" Jurin says, "It reacts to light. It's like smart micro-weave tech or some crap like that."

"Kind of like a chameleon," I respond, watching the dark brown spread to the rest of the jacket. "It even feels like leather."

"Yeah, yeah quit drooling," Jurin says taking a deep breath and letting out a cough.

I look out at the rest of New Horizon. From a distance it looks like a beautiful, sprawling metropolis protected by a gigantic twenty meter thick dome. But the truth is its closer in relation to a festering sore. Like a giant organism that is already dead but the cells don't realize it yet. The northern quadrant is dedicated to the greenhouses and farms that used to produce enough food to feed hundreds of thousands. Now, the majority is used for drug manufacturing with just enough food being produced to keep the people barely fed.

In the east, plumes of water vapor emerge from massive industrial powers plants dedicated to water purification from Titan's subterranean oceans. Air manufacture from Titan's naturally nitrogen rich atmosphere and fuel processing from the liquid methane lakes that dot the surface of Titan's northern hemisphere. In a way, Titan was always a goal for humanity not only for the technological achievement but also for Titan's abundance of natural resources.

The southern district of New Horizon houses the majority of Horizon's one and a half million residents. Massive sky scrapers intertwined with other buildings of varying designs and materials— from a distance it would resemble a gorgeous formation of crystals emerging from the ground. But most of these structures were pieced together from scraps over the years as the population boomed without regulation.

Then there's the financial district in the west, the ticking heart of Horizon's commerce. Where the streets are adorned with filthy beggars, Zeek runners, Drafters and prostitutes. It's the true face of humanity's greatest colony. There, nestled between a pair of dilapidated store fronts, is a brothel named

Miner's Rest. It happens to be one of the many brothels owned by Cheever West and incidentally Jurin and my destination.

My eyes continue to pan over the landscape of Horizon as Jurin attempts to summon transportation with little success. My gaze comes to a rest on the tower at the center of New Horizon. If the financial district is the heart of Horizon then the tower is the central nervous system, reaching from Titan's surface to the apex of Horizon's protective biosphere. Run by a virtual intelligence, it's the tower that maintains artificial gravity, atmospheric conditions and even random weather generation. In fact, it's the tower that made all of New Horizon possible in the first place, and ironically it's the tower that allowed the freedom necessary for Horizon to become the cesspool it is today. No other Colony would have survived this level of neglect and disrepair, and now due to its success all the colonies have retrofitted their own central tower.

A shuttle falls out of the sky coming to a jarring stop just about a meter from the ground, kicking up plumes of dust in all directions. Jurin covers his mouth with his elbow, as he opens the shuttle's door and waves me in.

I run over and quickly slide into the transport with Jurin following closely. He latches the door behind him with a forceful pull, shrouding the cabin in darkness until a holographic display pops up showing a digital map of Horizon. Jurin leans forward and highlights a gray square in the financial district. The words "Miner's Rest" appear above it, along with the total cost of the fare.

He motions to pay the fee but I grab his hand. "I owe you enough," I say quickly, placing my left hand on the display. I feel a slight tingle in my arm as the screen flashes, confirming the payment went through. The shuttle jerks upward toward our destination. The words 'Thank you for your service" blink on the screen several times before disappearing.

The rest of the ride is uncomfortably quiet; Jurin sits with a holographic screen hovering over his lap playing some game where you have to match colored shapes in order to gain a certain amount of points before time runs out. I recognize it right away as the latest time dump for people with nothing more to do.

Instead, I bring up a vBook about the Great Civil War that I have been reading for a while. I was on the chapter about the Fall of Blitzkrieg, one of the last brutal battles of the war. I check the calendar, deciding to hold off on reading it until Blitzkrieg's anniversary in about a month and a half.

Jurin lets out a string of curses and closes the display with a violent swipe of his hand. "Game cheats," he mumbles under his breath, making me laugh. I return to my digital library scrolling through some of the ancient books from long dead authors, not seeing anything I'm really interested in. "Why do you read that crap?" Jurin asks. "I can't understand half of it."

"That's cause they were written with different dialects of English. It takes a little bit to decipher, but after a while it becomes second nature." Jurin gives me a skeptical look. We all speak Basic, which is directly based off ancient English.

He slightly tilts his head. "But they aren't interactive like modern vBooks." He scoffs.

I roll my eyes. Interactive vBooks are amazing, but there is a certain level of adventure when reading an ancient book. It's almost as if I'm living vicariously through the writer's written words, a romantic notion that isn't shared by many today. I continue to look through the library, finally succumbing to my indecisiveness and waving the display away with a simple gesture.

A moment later the shuttle comes to an abrupt stop. Jurin quickly opens the door and pulls himself out. A display appears, flashing the phrase 'Watch your step and have a nice day' as I crawl out of the shuttle, closing the door behind me. Without warning the vehicle shoots directly up, sending dust flying everywhere.

I take a second to adjust to my surroundings before noticing that Jurin was already making his way through the crowds toward a building with 'Miner's Rest' flashing on a massive holographic screen. I rush to catch up with him, avoiding puddles of God knows what. The ground was slightly vibrating due to the bass coming from the brothel. Several prostitutes were standing outside advertising their goods to passing bystanders, every now and then one poor sot would take the bait and be led into the wolf's den.

In all honesty there is nothing extraordinary about Miner's Rest. It's a decrepit, poor excuse for a whore house; Cheever has at least half a dozen that are a hell of a lot higher class. But for some reason he chose to make this one his main office.

Jurin gestures to the bouncer who nods and opens the door, allowing us to pass. The main floor of the brothel is no more than a mob of sin and ecstasy. Mostly crowded with over-worked and under-paid Jovian Mining Corporation employees either heading to the Kuiper Belt or on a return trip. Most of them are drunk, high, horny, and looking to spend their hard-earned credits for a few fleeting minutes of pleasure and Cheever is ready to deliver. As much as I may detest the Baron, he knows how to build and run a successful business.

Women surround the dance floor wearing little more than napkins, undulating to the electronic-beat that pollutes the air. The smell is a refined form of musk and sex that leaves one with a desire to dry heave. Every part of my body tells me to turn and run, but I find myself keeping up with Jurin, who seems to have adapted to this environment, weaving methodically through the crowd as if people weren't there at all.

After several close calls with some wasted miners, we come to a stop in front of another large bouncer. Jurin makes a subtle gesture to the guard, who nods and places his left hand on the wall causing it to open revealing a hidden elevator. We pile into the lift and the wall seals behind us. With a lurch, the elevator jumps upward making my nerves heighten with uncertainty; Jurin picks up on my angst.

"Don't worry..," he says in futile attempt to quell my tension. "Cheever will do this. He owes me that much."

What does he mean by that? Could Jurin have fallen further than I thought? Could he have been more use to killing people than I wanted to admit?

The elevator chimes and the doors slide open with a screech. Three guards immediately have us face the wall while they search us for weapons, removing Jurin's revolver from his waist band. With a gesture, the third guards lead us to the massive pair of wood doors with an ornate set of carvings depicting what seem to be the seven deadly sins in action. A chill runs down my back as the impression that we are about to make a deal with the devil plants itself firmly in my mind. The doors swing open, and Jurin confidently leads me through the point of no return.

Chapter Three: The Demon of Babylon

The room is gorgeously adorned with hand-carved wood and various masterpieces hanging on the walls. In the center is a massive fireplace where flames lick and leap from coals to wood and back again. There, standing in front of the fire with his back toward us, is Cheever. He is wearing a lavish black and navy-blue suit with gold and silver accents of jewelry. His jet black hair is slicked back and he is holding a crystal glass full of some form of liquor. Jurin immediately helps himself to a drink and plops down on the couch to my left. The room remains silent for several minutes, nothing but the sound of fire crackling in the background.

"Jurin tells me you're brilliant." Cheever's charismatic voice kills the silence.

"Well I suppose..," I say quietly.

"Do you suppose or do you know?" Cheever responds in a monotone fashion, still facing the fire.

I hesitate, trying to pick the correct words, then shoot a glance at Jurin for guidance, but he doesn't return the look. I guess I'm on my own here.

"Yes, I could say that," I state in the most confident tone possible.

"Jurin also asked me to do you a favor." Cheever pauses. "He has asked me to arrange for you to be transported off world. Is that what you want, John?"

"Yes, sir."

Cheever turns and we exchange glances for several seconds. From where I was standing I couldn't tell whether his eyes were dark brown or completely black. "Well, I happen to have a one-way ticket off world, but—" He smiles.

"But what?" I respond calmly, even though my insides are burning. Cheever's gaze penetrates so deeply that I feel like I've just been cut open and examined.

"But, I'm a successful businessman and businessmen don't become successful by giving things away." He walks to his desk and sits, gesturing toward the seat opposite him.

I walk across the room and sit while Jurin joins me, and I can swear he looks just as concerned as I feel.

"Hey boss, I thought we talked about this. I'll make up what he owes you—you know I'm good for it." Jurin almost stutters on the last words.

Cheever flashes a pleasant smile, bringing his right hand up and resting it on the desk. My heart stops, for it wasn't just his hand resting on the desk but also a large pulse gun.

"You know..," he says. "You are absolutely right, Jurin. We did talk about this." He stands and slowly makes his way around the desk in Jurin's direction. "Of course, that was before you lied about your little friend's talents!" He slams the butt of the pistol against Jurin's head, causing blood to spurt out. Jurin lets out a cry and falls to the ground. I quickly jump to my feet, but Cheever is already waiting with the gun trained on me.

"Why did you do that!?" I shout. Cheever rubs his temples with his free hand and glares at me.

"Because I hate liars and cheats. You'll find it's a pet peeve of mine." He lowers his gun and glances at Jurin, still unconscious on the floor. "All I ask; is for a little bit of loyalty!" he yells at Jurin, kicking him several times. "You disappoint me, Jurin—you're a damn disappointment, do you hear me?!" He points the gun at Jurin's motionless body.

"Wait, stop!" I take several steps toward Cheever, catching his attention. He jerks his whole body around, gun included, to face me.

I feel my body freeze in panic. I look around for anything that could possibly be helpful. But if I try to fight he will just shoot me. "Ok, listen don't hurt him. He was just doing what I asked him to do." I take a step closer. "This is my fault entirely—not Jurin's." One more step, the blue glow of the pistol grows more intense the closer I get. "I'm willing to work out a deal, as long as you don't hurt him." Not much further. I can tell he is willing to hear me out.

"What kind of a deal?" he asks.

"The kind that keeps us alive. The question is what do you want?" There's no way he could resist an offer like that.

Cheever is silent for several moments, and although the gun was still pointed at my face his skeptical look slowly fades into a more curious one. "What could you possibly offer me, the

Baron of this great city, that I can't get from some other random nobody?"

"First, put down the gun so we can talk freely." I avert my eyes, hoping he can't tell I'm bluffing, while I take another step closer.

"Sorry that isn't how the game works. You tell me what you can offer me, and I'll consider losing the gun." He smiles maniacally.

Well, I guess he isn't as dumb as I assumed. "Alright, I can get you access to the Coalition Fleet's Secure Network—"

Cheever pushes the gun against my forehead. "You think I'm stupid, boy! No one can do that!" he hisses.

I slowly move my hands up. "I'm serious, I can show you right now—I just need a net connection." I glance at his desk's terminal. "Let me show you—please."

Cheever smirks, finally removing the pistol from my head and waving it toward his desk. "You got five."

I nervously move around the desk and sit at the display. Exactly ninety seconds later I'm in New Horizon's First Church of the Star's network. Cheever was right. It's impossible to break into the Coalition Fleet's network without the right credentials or a quantum computer running a cracking algorithm nonstop for months. But he doesn't have to know that. I, on the other hand, am the one who set up the Church's network, which makes accessing it a breeze, a few simple banner changes and some falsified deployment data and like that the church's network looks like what I imagined the fleet's would. "There, come check it out," I say confidently.

The level of surprise and disbelief on Cheever's face meant he bought the ruse. He hustles around the desk setting the gun on the edge and hunches over to view the fake data I presented. The gun is well within reach now, and if I move fast I could have it in hand and pointed at Cheever's face before he even knew it. I can feel the adrenaline beginning to pump through my veins anticipating my next move. I begin edging my hand in that direction of the pistol, bit by bit.

Suddenly the door to the room flies open. Cheever quickly grabs the gun and points it in the direction of the guard.

"Sorry boss, we have a situation!" the guard screams both out of immediate alarm and self-preservation.

Cheever's face twists with frustration. "What is it!?" he shouts.

The guard takes a deep breath "Sir, there was a fight between some miners and fleet squids." He hesitates. "The miner pulled a gun on the officer and killed him, so now we have a delegation from the Coalition demanding to speak with you."

"Well you can tell this delegation to go shove it up their neatly tailored asses. I'm responsible for the location and the merchandise, not the costumers and their actions." He looks back down at the display but soon realizes that the guard has not left. "Was there something else?!" he says without looking.

The guard lets out a tense sigh. Apparently nobody likes to give the boss bad news. "Actually sir, the delegation will be here in few minutes. They have an armed escort—" he is cut short by Cheever slamming his hand on the table.

"You worthless pieces of shit are good for nothing." Cheever stands, tucking the pistol in his waist band and turns to me. "You stay put. After I finish with this we will continue where we left off." Then made his way through the door with his guard following him closely.

That was an unexpected and welcome reprieve. I look back at the display quickly bringing up the list of scheduled departures. Hundreds of names populate the screen so I adjust the search criteria to passenger vessels only. The display updates almost instantly with what looks like about a four-dozen general transports heading to various locations in Jovian space. I place my left hand on the virtual display and download the data to my Aug just as Jurin starts to come to.

"What the hell!?" he moans as I help him to his feet.

"Take it easy, you got hit pretty hard..," I say, using my jacket sleeve to wipe away some of the blood on his forehead.

"Where—did Cheever go?" Jurin asks looking around the penthouse.

"We still have a little luck on our side, but I suggest we leave now," I say, dusting off his shoulders. "You know another way out of here besides the elevator, right?" Jurin sighs loudly while lightly touching the gash left by Cheever's surprise pistol whip. "Jurin, focus we need to get out of here!"

"Alright, alright. Jeez, let me think!" He squints at the bookshelf behind the desk. "I remember Cheever told me there used to be a set of stairs that were removed during the renovation he did years ago."

I turn and study the bookshelf "Well, if I was a big time drug lord I'd have a secret escape route." We rush over to the shelf and attempt to move it, but it won't budge. "Dang!" I take a few steps back. "Maybe there's a switch or something."

Jurin shoots me a critical look. "This isn't one of your mystery books, John."

"Just shut-up and look!" I order.

We search the room for anything that would stand out as a switch, but nothing seems to beworking. Could we have been wrong about the secret passage, it certainly wouldn't have been the first time I overestimated Cheever and his cleverness—or maybe that's it; maybe I'm still underestimating the man.

I scan the room, finding my gaze gravitating to the fireplace. In this day and age there is no need for a fireplace; they have become something only afforded by the rich. What better way to conceal a secret passage than with the gaudiest object in the room, which is exactly Cheever's style?

I whistle at Jurin and point at the fireplace. We both run over and begin obsessing over every centimeter of the mantle when Jurin lets out an exciting yell. "I found it!" He engages the switch and the sound of gears immediately fill the room.

The fire place slides backward revealing a spiral stair case. Without hesitation we sprint down them as if Death himself was chasing us. The further we descend, the darker it becomes until we reached a dimly-lit tunnel.

I notice the sound of rustling at the top of the staircase and I can tell Jurin heard it as well because he begins racing down the tunnel with me closely following. We reach a split in the hall with one path leading upward and the other plunging even deeper into who knows what. Without thinking, I begin running toward the path that leads up to hopefully the surface, when I notice Jurin isn't beside me.

I turn, seeing Jurin forcing a cabinet open with a rusty piece of metal. "Jurin, what the hell are you doing?!"

The cabinet's lock gives way to Jurin's prying. "It's Cheever's get-away stash!" he exclaims, pulling out a pulse revolver and a credit chip. "Holy shit, this is a hundred thousand creds!" he shouts, running toward me.

"That's more than enough to get us both off world," I respond with unbridled optimism.

Jurin and I continue to follow the pathway when we reach set of double doors with shards of light from the setting sun piercing the dusty glass. I kick them open and gain my bearing. We aren't more than a hundred meters from the Miner's Rest as we exit through one of the abandoned store fronts that flanked the club.

Before I can fully catch my breath, Jurin has already begun running down the street. I struggle to keep up with him, shouting for him to stop when he ducks into an alleyway. "What are you doing?" I gasp.

"We need to get to the docking hub as fast and discreetly as possible," he whispers. "Before Cheever rips the city apart looking for us."

I nod my head, bringing up a map of the local area. "We are about one and a half kilometers from the Maranda Docking Hub; you think we can make it?"

Jurin shoots me a serious look. "Yeah; cause if we don't make it then we're dead."

"Ok," I say timidly. "Let's go."

CHAPTER FOUR: THE TITAN'S PAST

Night has fallen on New Horizon by the time we reach the entrance of the docking hub. In a way this was better because Horizon comes to life at night and more people mean better cover. Jurin and I make sure to stay out of the main streets, avoiding as much attention as possible. But even I am starting to worry that we have exhausted our life's allotment of dumb luck just getting this far. A sinking feeling starts to grow in my lower stomach when we walk past the Miranda Docking Hub entrance.

Thousands of people are coursing between various sized vessels known simply as skips. Every few seconds one or two of these skips jets upward through the energy shield protecting us from Titan's unforgiving environment and into space to rendezvous with their larger ships. The whole place is mesmerizing, and all I can think about is the growing pit in my gut as we begin to search for the skips that match the list I acquired earlier.

I attempt to keep up with Jurin while looking down at the list of transport skips, but I notice that he is getting further and further from me. I call out his name in a futile effort to catch his attention before I lose sight of him completely, almost as if the crowd has swallowed him. I close the list and start searching for him. After a while the pit in my stomach begins to ache as the realization that I'm completely lost comes to mind. Dread sets in and I stupidly begin running around aimlessly shouting Jurin's name at the top of my lungs.

I stop to catch my breath when a hand grabs my shoulder. "Hey! You're that kid from the orphanage!" the voice is stern and militaristic, which means one thing. I frantically look for Jurin, because he'd know what to do in this situation, but there is nobody there.

"I have no idea who you're talking about," I say flatly, attempting to shrug off the hand that remains firmly planted on my shoulder.

"Turn around and show me your papers!" the voice demands.

"Listen, I'm not the one you're looking for." I try to pull free of the hand, but it squeezes even tighter.

"I said turn around and show me your papers!" the man yells, pulling me around to face him. The pit in my stomach deepens as the Coalition Fleet Drafter grins. "Why can't I scan you, boy!?" he demands in a sharp rigid tone.

I shrug. "Maybe it's broken," I say sarcastically. "I've heard a lot of men have this kind of issue."

The man sneers, grabbing my left forearm with his hand. I feel a slight buzzing sensation and a holographic screen appears on the drafter's right forearm. He promptly reads the display, then a subtle smirk forms from his thin lips and he finishes before unclasping my arm.

"Turn around and put your hands behind your back," he demands, reaching for a set of carbon bands.

"You don't understand. I need to get out of here before some bad people come looking for me." I do my best to convey a sense of urgency in my voice, only for the Drafter to snort with amusement.

The carbon bands tighten around my wrists, slightly cutting off the circulation to my fingers. The Drafter takes me by the upper arm and begins leading me through the crowd toward a large skip with 'Coalition Fleet Standards' painted across its hull.

This is almost exactly what happened to Keida a little over a month ago. She aged-out and wasn't outside the church's doors for more than an hour before the Coalition grabbed her. That was the last I heard of her, as if she had never even existed. I didn't get to say goodbye and I probably never will.

Then there was Frang, a year before Keida. He was the genius of our little family back then. But unfortunately—instead of the Coalition—he was conscribed as a Sifter for the Jovian Mining Corporation. Basically long hours of toxic waste cleaning without the proper protection. And if, through some miracle, you survive two years of Sifting, then maybe just maybe you could be promoted to a position that didn't involve handling radioactive waste. Frang however, died on the third day because of a tear in his hazmat suit. But they didn't find him until the eighth day and by then there was barely enough of him left to identify.

The Drafter pushes me in line with about a dozen other draftees, some in cuffs like me.The others without cuffs probably volunteered, hoping for a better life I guess. Two soldiers were leaning against the back of the skip, probably exchanging tall tales of their various exploits. I look around, avoiding eye contact with the other miserable prospects, hoping to catch sight of Jurin, but he's nowhere. What the hell happened to him? Did he just take the money and run or was he looking for me? My thoughts continued to contemplate the possibilities for his disappearance.

Jurin was different from Frang, he was street smart. When he aged-out two years before Frang, he went directly to Cheever and vowed his loyalty to him. After that no Drafter would touch him without fear of reprimand from the Baron. Jurin's plan was simple; work long enough to get off Titan. But he soon realized that when you work for Cheever you don't quit until he is done with you. And when Cheever is done with someone, they typically end up dead.

That notion sent my mind into a downward tail spin leading to Genna. She was the first to age-out of our little family and was like a big sister to us all; she practically raised us. It had already been five years since she left the orphanage. Genna wasn't drafted. Like Jurin, she started working for Cheever, but sometimes I wonder if it would have been better if she was drafted instead. She was working as waitress for one of Cheever's more reputable businesses. However, it was only a matter of time before she succumbed to the appeal of money and power. Genna became hooked on Zeek and started selling her body in order to fuel her addiction. That went on for a few years, constantly in and out of rehab and attempting to get her life straight. She got close too. A year ago she told me she had found a way out and that she would leave and come back someday for us. But the very next day she was found beaten to death in an alleyway not far from the orphanage.

My mind continues to reminisce on the things I have lost and the truths I may never know, culminating with the question of how I ended up on Titan in the first place. My origin is a mystery. Unlike most orphans who were born to drug addicted prostitutes, I wasn't born here. I was found on the doorstep of the church's orphanage when I was three. According to Genna and the others, I didn't speak for nearly three months, and when I finally did I didn't know anything about my past. It was as if I was wiped of all my information. They checked my Aug and nothing was there, no name, no date or place of birth. It was like I just appeared out of thin air.

I shake my head, attempting to get my mind off the sadness. It was just Jurin and me now and there was no use dwelling on the past. I need to deal with the now. Another Drafter begins leading a few more recruits up the path toward the skip. One of them starts screaming about how he doesn't want to join and runs for the fence line. A few of the others begin to follow him when a single pulse round erupts from behind me, nailing the first runner in the middle of his back. The poor bastard flew forward hitting the ground and sliding about a meter before coming to a rest. The other recruits that were following him stop dead in their tracks, some falling to their knees in disbelief.

And here I was starting to think joining the fleet would be a good thing, At least Cheever wouldn't be able to get to me. Even a psycho like the Baron knows better than to pick a fight with the fleet. Neither side will ever admit it but they need each other. Cheever offers the wary, homesick squids certain amenities that their commanding officers cannot. Basically as long as the Coalition supplies Cheever with fresh new costumers then Cheever won't step on the fleet's toes.

The Drafters grab the few stragglers and return them to the line, leading them the rest of the way up the path. That's when I catch sight of Jurin.

"What the hell?" I whisper, as he flashes me a brimming grin.

"Oh, hey John. What a coincidence, right? Man, small solar system," he says sarcastically, joining me in the ranks.

I look at his hands and notice he isn't bound by cuffs. "So you volunteered?" I ask.

He smiles again, pointing across the docking hub to a small outdated skip. "That is our ticket out of here..," he says. "All we gotta do is get there in an hour—that's when they launch." He flashes me a hopeful expression.

I look at him, wondering when he'll get to the part about us getting away from the Coalition without being shot. But before I can ask, he shrugs and nods his head toward the two soldiers leaning against the back of the skip.

"But how?" I ask.

"No worries, I got this," he responds and begins walking toward the two soldiers.

As soon as he gets about a meter or two away from them, he puts his arms up. The soldiers point their pulse rifles at him and force him against the skip. At this point I can't see Jurin's face, but one of the soldiers lowers his rifle and glances my way, while the other begins walking toward me. He takes me by the arm and leads me to the end of the craft where the other soldier and Jurin are standing.

"Is this the one?" the soldier asks Jurin.

"Sure is—" he responds with a grin. "Now just as we discussed, a hundred thousand creds after you get us out of here—deal?" The two soldiers look at each other than nod.

They lead us to the other side of the skip and cut me free while one of the soldiers keeps an eye out waiting for the opportune moment to let us go.

"We need to hurry, Miller. A few more Draftees and we are on the up-and-out," the soldier closest to me says.

"Roger," the other responds, almost in a robotic manner. "Looks like we have an opportunity in thirty seconds," he adds.

I glance over in the direction the soldier is pointing; a single guard is walking the perimeter fence where there's a hole big enough for a person to slip through. I can feel adrenaline starting to pump as I slowly count down from thirty. The guard passes the hole and I feel a forceful push launching me from the cover of the skip. "Move!" one of the soldiers whispers. Jurin, the soldiers, and I quickly dash across the flight deck reaching the opening moments later. We wiggle through and begin sprinting toward the cover of some spacing containers.

We jog along the spacing containers, getting as far away as possible from the Coalition, and finally come to a stop between some stacked containers. The two soldiers point out the best route to reach the skip Jurin arranged for us without encountering any Coalition.

Jurin thanks them and hands over a credit chip loaded with Cheever's hundred-thousand creds. "There you go, try not to spend it all in one place," he says sarcastically.

We turn and begin walking when one of the marines stops me. "One more thing," he says. "We will have to report you're missing—nothing personal but it keeps our Commanding Officer from getting suspicious." He pauses and looks at his friend then back at us. "Don't worry though. We'll head in the opposite direction." He ends with a salute and the two disappear in the dark.

Jurin lets out a triumphant grunt. "Jeez, that really worked out, didn't it?" he says jabbing an elbow in my side.

"Yeah, I honestly didn't think you were capable of such ingenuity," I retort with a mocking tone. "So now that we're broke again, any idea how we're going to pay our way on that poor excuse of a skip you showed me earlier?"

Jurin smiles. I'm starting to get really worried when he smiles. "See, that's the beauty of it. I convinced the pilot that you and I are some expert maintenance men, so we will work our fare off."

He clearly feels very proud of his barging skills, so I won't be too rough. "Yeah that's great besides the fact we have never been on a ship before, so your plan is going to blow up in our faces." Ok so that was a little rough.

Jurin's smiles fades at the realization. "Well damn—looks like we will have to be adaptable."

Adaptable he says. What the hell? It takes years to learn how to work on Fusion Cores. One wrong setting or miss-configured containment field can spell disaster almost instantly. There is no way we could wing our way as part of a crew on an actual space ship. But from the looks of it, we have little choice. Either we lie and hope the ship's crew finds out long after we depart or we stay on Titan and get killed by Cheever or the Coalition Fleet. It's not every day you get both the Baron and the Fleet vying for your death certificate. So if we have to fake it, we might as well get a ride first.

I bump into Jurin who has stopped dead in his tracks. "What's the matter?" I ask, but he doesn't respond.

A familiar voice sends a chill down my back. "Remember when I told you I don't like liars and cheats? I bet you thought you got away—bet you felt you pulled a fast one on good old Cheever, huh?" I turn toward the voice as Cheever follows through with a punch so hard everything fades to black.

CHAPTER FIVE: THE DYING LIGHT

The feeling of raindrops shattering and splintering against my face pulls me out of the abyss of my subconscious. I blink several times attempting to clear my vision, caressing my left eye which is already throbbing and swollen from Cheever's surprise attack. How long have I been out? My strength is fleeting; I can barely muster the power necessary to roll onto my hands and knees. I try to judge my condition, determining whether my equilibrium is stable enough to stand, but I can't seem to focus on anything but the sound of the blood rushing through my veins. Everything feels numb, with only the wet ground keeping me anchored to reality. The sound of a distant voice echoes in my ear, but I can't make out what they're saying. Then someone grabs me by the collar and yanks me to my feet. It's Jurin and he is yelling something, but I can't seem to register what he's saying. I feel as though I'm in a trance, as if I'm in shock. Several pulse rounds fly past his head and he crouches a little before smacking me.

"John, what the hell?! We need to go!" he yells, shaking me frantically.

I feel my dulled senses begin to sharpen. "I'm—here, I'm good." A look of relief pours over him. He pulls my arm over his shoulder, and we make our way toward the skip and hopefully toward salvation.

Several more pulse rounds pass us as we reach the landing where the tattered skip was warming its engines getting ready to take off. Jurin drops me and runs ahead waiving his hands, desperately trying to catch the pilot's attention, but to no avail, the skip jets upward at surprising speeds. Jurin turns to me; his expression resembling one of a man with nothing left. I have seen that look before, but only on people who were broken—people who had given up. He looks to my left, quickly pulling the revolver from his waist band just as two pulse rounds pierce his chest and upper leg. Blood sprays across the pavement as the force of the impact makes him spin around on one leg like a dancer. I rush to catch him as he starts to fall, supporting his weigh with my body. I gently roll him on his back, his eyes looking all around trying to make sense of what just happened. A cascade of emotions flow across his face: fear, shock, regret and anger are just a few that I can discern. I put pressure on his chest in a futile attempt to slow the bleeding, but it is already too late. I know it and so does he.

I can feel him slipping away almost like he is getting lighter in my arms. "No!" I demand. "Hold on, Jurin!"

He attempts to grin, probably trying to make me feel better, lifting his hand to cup my face. "I'm—sorry." His hand goes limp and falls to his chest and I can almost see the light leave his body.

Tears of regret and agony overwhelm me. I'm alone—there is no one left to take, no one left to lose. And then a realization hits me: at this moment, this insignificant moment in the grand scheme of all existence, I am truly nothing. Not Cheever or Tumbler and even all of New Horizon can hurt me because there is nothing to wound. I don't care anymore. I wipe the tears away and let out a long sobering sigh closing Jurin's eyes. I feel Cheever's presence stooping over me. He grabs me by the cusp of my jacket and pulls me to my feet, causing Jurin's lifeless body to roll face first into a puddle.

"It's just you and me now, boy!" he says viciously, caressing my face with the barrel of his pistol. "I must say. You surprised me with your clever trick." He wears a sadistic grin.

Trick? "What are you talking about?" I ask flatly.

Cheever glares at me. "Don't act stupid, boy. That stunt you pulled cost me a lot of good men."

"There are no good men anymore," I say plainly, staring Cheever dead in the eyes. "Just kill me and get it over with or leave me the hell alone." I can see the rage boiling in his eyes. He really would love to squeeze the life out of me.

"You know, you got quite the mouth—" he responds "Maybe I'll cut out your tongue and force it down your throat. How does that sound?" He forces the barrel of his pistol into my mouth.

He searches my face for a reaction; fear or anything that lets him know that he has the upper hand. The sick bastard probably gets off to it, but I don't indulge him. Instead I continue to stare him in the eyes and for a moment I can see that he is the one afraid, but of who? It couldn't be me. I have done nothing to him. But now that I see hints of fear, I see other things as well: confusion and anxiety. Something really crazy must have happened after he knocked me out. Jurin must have really kicked ass before he—

Cheever removes the gun from my mouth. "You don't scare me anymore, Cheever," I say with an emotionless tone. "Just get it over with damn-it!" I demand.

He grimaces at my lack of enthusiasm, forcing me onto my knees and placing the pistol against my head. "You know," he says bluntly. "I'm going to enjoy this."

The micro vibrations from the pulse gun course through my body. In an odd way they relax me. Other than an annoying ache radiating in the back of my head, I find myself strangely calm. I had thought I'd be scared of dying, thought I'd fight or resist until my last breath. But now all I wish is for the pain to stop.

Cheever pushes the pistol hard against my head until I brace myself with my hands. Jurin's blood is starting to spread and mix with the water, making the ground a dark shade of crimson. I take a deep breath as Cheever pulls the hammer back on the pistol. I'm ready. I close my eyes, listening to the pounding of my heart.

"Cheever West!" a voice shouts over a loud speaker filling the atmosphere around us. "Drop your weapon and lay face down on the ground!"

I look up at Cheever studying his ruined suit that had been so perfectly kept just a few hours earlier. It makes me think about how everything eventually falls apart. How I have lost my best friend and how I had done so little for Jurin in return. Cheever's eyes don't hide his apprehension as a dozen marines in Heavy Armor Combat Suits step out of the shadows as if they were conjured from thin air.

"So what are you going to do now, Cheever?" I mock him with a low voice, so low that only he could hear me.

"Shut up!" he barks, thrusting the gun painfully against my head. "I'll kill you before they can stop me!" he adds.

"Cheever, it's over!" one of the marines says. "This is your last warning!"

Cheever turns toward the closest marine. "Do you know who I am? I'm the Baron of New Horizon. You can't touch me. None of you can touch me! You need—"

Cheever freezes in midsentence and falls to the ground. Two marines approach his body, kicking the gun away from his arm and cuffing his hands behind his back. "This is Delta Zero Two, the suspect has been shocked and apprehended, request further orders," a third marine says into the radio while two others lift and drag Cheever's stunned body away. "Understood, Sir," the marine continues before turning his attention to me. "Are you injured?" he asks while shining his pulse rifle's light into my eyes.

I glance at Jurin's still body and shake my head. Something seems familiar about him. I take a closer look at his name tag, Miller, one of the marines we paid off using Cheever's creds. "So what now?" I ask cynically.

Miller helps me to my feet, placing his hand on my shoulder while looking down at Jurin's body. "I'm sorry about your loss, but I need you to show me your papers." He extends his hand.

I reach out and grasp his forearm, and just as before there's a buzzing sensation followed by the holographic display. He reads for a bit, a look of discontent comes over his face as he breaks hand contact and engages his radio. "This is Delta Zero Two, I've reviewed the kid and he checks out."

The words reverberate in my mind and I stammer, "But—" The marine holds his hand up stopping me.

"Your friend wanted you to leave this place," Miller says, "It would be a disservice if I, let alone you, allowed his sacrifice go to waste." He turns and walks away, disappearing into the dark.

I fall to my knees. What the hell just happened? I look over at Jurin's lifeless body, half hoping that he'd jump up and say something sarcastically witty but he doesn't. I feel myself begin to cry, but I repress the urge long enough to recall some of the few good memories we shared. The rain finally stops and I can hear sirens in the distance, probably coming to clean up Jurin's remains.

I know I have to leave, that if I stay I risk being caught again. But it's too hard to say all the things I want to say, when nothing comes out every time I try. I finally gather the courage to stand up and walk away, taking one last look at Jurin and whispering, "Thank you. I'll miss you. But now I gotta go."

CHAPTER SIX: THE STOWAWAY TITAN

The Miranda Docking Hub is filled with people from all walks of life. There are children and the elderly. People of different races and ethnic backgrounds. They are all concerned with their schedules, peddling away at time that, at any second, could be ripped from them in a moment's notice. I walk among them but am not one of them; like a ghost, or a shell of a person aimlessly lumbering with only one thing left. I reach into my pocket retrieving the only important thing I have left and stare at it intensely. It is a torn section of fabric with a logo from some long forgotten piece of history and the acronym AIC scrolled across it. This is the only thing I was found with on the day I came to the orphanage fifteen years ago. That was also the first day I met Jurin, Genna, Frang and Keida. They were my friends, my family and now they are all gone. The marine was right. I need to do this not only for Jurin but also for everyone else I have lost.

I wonder around the various ships, scoping out the ones that I could possibly slip into unnoticed, when I come across a large skip that, for some reason, I can't stop being drawn to. About thirty people are boarding when I walk up and notice the maintenance hatch on the underside of the skip. I look around and not a single soul is paying attention, so I take it as a sign and quickly scurry up the ladder through the hatch. I find a somewhat comfortable spot under the main compartment walkway. I can hear voices and the sound of footsteps just overhead, and after a while I feel the skip begin to vibrate as the engines warm up.

"This is MDV-0425 requesting permission to launch and proceed to destination," the pilot says in a rehearsed fashion.

"Roger that, 0425. You have been approved for launch. Estimated time to thrust is approximately three minutes and thirty seconds. Happy flying and stay safe up there," the controller responds.

The hull begins to vibrate now more aggressively as the engines screech with anticipation. "Everyone please take your seats and fasten your belts—" a stern voice echoes through the compartment followed by the mass shuffling and moving of the passengers in response to the orders. "Nev, begin final departure checklist."

"Yeah, yeah already on it—pressurized seals—green, exterior sensors—green, hygithium-fuel cells—charged and ready, radiation shield—green. All systems nominal. We are up-

and-up. Let's get the hell off this rock," he finishes with a crude chuckle.

The skip begins to lift off, slowly at first but gradually gaining speed and pitch. The hull vibrates uncontrollably as I struggle to hold on to something. Then, just as I'm about to lose grip, everything falls silent and I feel the strange sensation that I have dreamed of since I was a child. My body floats up on its own, weightless. The hull stops vibrating so crazily, and I press my head against it to feel the skip's heartbeat flowing through my body. I hold myself steady with the walkway's brace, listening to the chatter of the passengers above. Man, I wish I was up there so I could see the vastness myself.

About fifteen minutes later, I hear several passengers gasp and the pilot start speaking "This is MDV-0425 on final approaching vector with MST-C: Idle Confessor; come in, Idle Confessor. I repeat, we are on final approaching vector. Respond. Over," the pilot says in a clear concise voice.

A few seconds later, "MST-C: Idle Confessor, reading you loud and clear. Proceed with docking protocol—" The voice pauses. "How you doin' darlin'? I bet Nev is driving you crazy by now."

"Hey I can hear you, jackass!" another voice, presumably Nev's, joins the fold.

"I assure you that was entirely my intention. Hey Lora, go ahead and drop the cargo off in hanger two. ETA five minutes. See you soon, Confessor out." The com falls silent.

The ship turns tightly, causing the hull to creek and whine under the stress, and before long we enter the hanger bay, or at least I believe we do, because my body falls under its own weight, indicating we have entered artificial gravity. The skip throttles down, coming to a soft landing, and the engines sigh in relief. I remain hidden under the walkway until the passengers have left, and then I wait even longer to ensure everyone has cleared out before making my way to the hatch and down the ladder.

The hanger was eerily vacant of life, with no evidence that there were people running around earlier. At this point my presence mustn't be known so I have to avoid others as best I can. Frankly this is a big ship, so it shouldn't be too hard to hide out for a few days. I run over to some crates and sit for a little bit, attempting the get used to the ship's feel. Just then the hanger doors slide open revealing two stout individuals, with meticulously-waxed mustaches, heading for the skip.

"Unload the skip," one of them mocks while the other chuckles.

"It's not like we aren't busy keeping the ship space-worthy, but now I guess we are also—" he stops mid-sentence.

"What is it, Don?" the other asks, while checking an inventory sheet on one of the crates.

"Ron, did Lora or Nev tell you that they were performing maintenance on the skip?" Don asks.

There is about a minute of silence. "Na, neither mentioned that they were going to do anything. Besides that is our job, so they shouldn't be messing with it anyway. Why?" He turns and looks at the skip.

It isn't until I take a closer look at what they are obsessing over before realize that I had forgotten to close the maintenance hatch after I exited the skip. Surely they wouldn't think much of a single hatch being left open—right?

"You'd better call them and find out if any of the passengers messed with the maintenance hatch," Ron says to Don, but he was already talking to Nev on his Aug's communicator.

Nev comes walking in several minutes later. "What the hell is it now? I was getting ready to sleep after—" he stops in his tracks, staring at the hatch wide open. "You guys messing with me?" he asks.

"No, it was wide open when we found it," Ron interjected.

Don lowers his left arm and faces them. "Just talked to Lora, and she didn't open the hatch either."

"Maybe it just opened during the flight," Nev suggests.

"Oh, it just opened—you hear that, Don?"

"Aye, I did Ron—it's amazing the captain lets him near the bridge with intelligent statements like those," Don says cynically.

"Alright, alright, you guys can go screw yourselves—" Nev responds contemptuously. "So, if it wasn't me or Lora then who opened it?" he asks.

I lean forward a bit to get a better view and catch sight of the twins standing in the same exact position with their hands situated just under their chins deep in thought. They glance at each other nodding almost simultaneously.

Ron turns toward Nev. "So, we talked about it—"

"And—we think there is a stowaway onboard the Confessor," Don finishes.

You've got to be freaking kidding me! Who are these guys, detectives? Nev's face scrunches into an odd combination of disbelief and confusion, which I imagine is what my face looks like at the moment. Well, there goes the plan to hide out for several days. Just then one of the twins turns in the direction of the crates where I am hiding. I drop to the floor as fast as I can, hoping, even pleading that they didn't see me.

"Really, a stowaway—how do you figure? Cause I'm not seeing it," Nev says in a skeptical voice.

There is a pause in which Ron and Don probably formulate a response that wouldn't confuse the likes of Nev; however I'd also like to hear how they determined the same conclusion.

"Aw, well the hydraulic maintenance hatches on the 0400 series of the Muti-use Drop Vessels lead to a spacious, although uncomfortable, area situated right under the walkway of the cabin," Don says.

"It is plausible for one maybe two people to sneak in and hold up in there for the duration of the flight, however," Ron elaborates. "It would be difficult for such individuals to simply hustle up that the ladder without being seen by someone, say the senior security officer of the vessel. So there must've been a big distraction in order to allow someone to slip past the likes of such a senior security individual—isn't that right, Nev?" He finishes with a cynical tone.

Now I don't have to see Nev's face to know he probably looks just as dumbfounded as I do. I have to give these twins credit. They really know their stuff.

"Yeah, but these are all assumptions—there is no way you could know without a doubt. I mean I might have looked away for maybe two seconds," Nev argues.

"You are completely right—don't you think, brother?" one of the twins says.

"Yup, yup, however we left one detail out—" There is a pause, probably deliberate to convey a sense of drama. "I think that if you take into account the information we just gave you in tandem with the fact that the stowaway is hiding behind the crates over there—you'll find that our assumptions are very well placed."

It takes a second for the information to sink in, apparently they saw me long before and were simply screwing with me like they were with Nev. I jump to my feet and begin to run for the door, but Nev was waiting for me with his pulse Pistol drawn and pointed at my face.

"Ok, ok hold up..," I say putting my hands slowly up. "There is no need for that—I'm not going to run. I have no place to go."

I can see Nev's face twist with anger "Or, I can waste you here and now, and call it a job well done."

"Nev—," Don says behind him. "We should really let the captain determine what to do."

It isn't much, but I'll take it. "Yeah take me to your captain—"

I expected Nev to look angrier, but he smiles from ear to ear, lowering the Pistol.

"Turn around!" he says, cuffing me with some carbon bands. "Oh and sorry."

I think for a moment about what he meant by sorry when a sharp pain shoots through the back of my head. Everything blacks out after that, and when I regain consciousness I realize I'm strapped to a chair in a room that looks similar to a bridge. Nev is standing off to the side near the door with the twins flanking him. In front of me is a large intimidating man. He approaches me, grabbing my face with one hand brandishing a pulse revolver in the other.

CHAPTER SEVEN: THE CONFESSOR'S SPIRIT

"My name is Captain James Rickard. I'm going to ask you a few questions. I suggest you answer them honestly and quickly or things will get progressively worse for you—understand?" he says in an unyielding voice.

The dull ache of my head pulsates through my neck as Captain Rickard lifts the revolver closer to my head. "I understand."

"Very good. First question: why are you on my ship?" His last words felt coated with acid, causing my stomach to churn.

"I—I needed to leave Titan." I struggle with the images of Jurin's lifeless face playing back in my head.

Captain Rickard looks at me coldly. "I asked you to tell me why you are on my ship not what compelled you to stowaway in the first place," he says irritably.

I study Rickard's features attempting to discern his intentions. He's in his late-forties or early fifties judging by the prominent streaks of gray flowing through his jet black hair and stubble. His skin is dark and weathered with faint scars across his arms and face. I can tell he has seen some combat and is probably a veteran from the war. Otherwise his light brown eyes reveal nothing other than a cold confidence and reserved strength of will.

I think for a while about his question, why did I choose this particular skip and not any of the others? I honestly don't know, but that won't be accepted as an answer. "I'm pretty much a nobody—less than that really, Titan took my family away from me, but when I saw your skip something inside told me that everything will be alright, that I had to get on that skip."

Captain Rickard looks at me, but this time there is more than just contempt in his eyes. There's also sorrow. "What's your name, boy?" he asks while sitting in a chair across from me.

"I was only three when the orphanage took me in. I didn't have a name so everyone started to call me John. Over the years it stuck."

The captain looked me up and down. "Last question. What should I do with a stowaway like you?"

Nev steps forward with a large smile on his face. "I say we throw him into the airlock and send him packing. He is a liability."

Rickard looks at me with his eyebrows raised. "And what do you think about Nev's idea?"

"With all due respect, I'd prefer something that doesn't mean I die," I say in a desperate tone.

"Listen kid, you sold your case when you told me no one will be looking for you. So what am I to do? Just allow a stowaway to wonder around my ship?" Rickard gets up and walks to the system chart, turning his back to me.

"I can help around here—I learn really fast. I'll work off the debt I owe you!" I frantically plead.

Rickard turns and glares at me. "I only have crew that I can trust. You have already betrayed every principle I hold. What makes you trust worthy, huh?"

I search my mind for anything that could possibly change his plan but nothing comes. Have I come this far just to be killed? So much for doing Jurin and the others' sacrifices justice. Now I'll be just another forgotten soul, one of billions, even trillions that have been forgotten almost as if they never existed in the first place.

Rickard sighs and motions for Nev to take me away. Nev steps up, a look of sheer glee on his face. The twins' faces don't hide a single shred of disdain for their captain's wishes. I try my best to accept my fate, but my spirit rebels against the notion of just accepting death again. "No!" I shout in the most powerful voice I can gather, Rickard looks up from his monitor and walks over to me, getting uncomfortably close to my face.

"What did you just say?" he asks in a voice so cold it could turn water to ice.

"I said no—" still maintaining my powerful tone.

"Bold words for someone tied to a chair; powerless to change his own fate," he retorts.

"Bolder than sentencing an unarmed, innocent kid to death by explosive decompression? Excuse me when I say go to hell. With all due respect—sir."

Nev pulls his pistol out but is stopped short by Rickard who instead places his revolver against my temple. "Give me one good reason why I shouldn't kill you."

Now is my chance. "I can give you a few. First, because you see something in me, something that reminds you of yourself. You may deny it all you want, but I can see it in your eyes. I remind you of your past; something you try very hard to cover up. Second, because you and your lackey are not murderers. I've seen murderers. You've killed before, but not because it brings you pleasure but because you are survivors like me. Then there is the last reason, and the most important one of all; the mere fact that you haven't pulled that trigger already because you don't believe it was simply coincidence that I got aboard your ship—"

Silence fills the room as if time has stopped all together. Rickard doesn't move; his eyes are still locked on to mine trying to read my thoughts. I definitely hit a nerve because I can see an avalanche of emotions hiding just past his hardened and practiced eyes. The question is will this change his mind or just piss him off even more? Then I hear the sound of the revolver's hammer being pulled back with an incredibly loud click. My heart stops as Rickard closes his eyes. This is it. This is the end—

CHAPTER EIGHT: GENESIS HAILING

"This is Lieutenant Commander Shultz aboard the Coalition Fleet Destroyer Class Warship: Genesis, hailing on all frequencies the Medium Standard Trade-ship Alpha Class Frigate: Idle Confessor. Your response to this transmission is required within thirty minutes. After that if no response has been issued, standard breaching and boarding procedures will be performed. This message will repeat every five minutes until the previously stated time threshold has expired or positive contact has been made. For the Frontier Lieutenant Commander Shultz, out."

Captain Rickard's eyes open he removes the gun from my temple and walks over to the display that's rapidly updating with new information. He turns to Nev. "Wake Lora then head to secure the cargo. I'll try to buy you some time here." Nev and the twins exit the bridge in a hurried panic.

Rickard then pulls a knife from his belt and walks toward me. I feel a shiver run through my body as he approaches me, reaches down to my bindings and cuts me free. I rub my wrists as the circulation returns to my fingers. The message plays again and Rickard acknowledges it and begins recording a response.

"Good day, Lieutenant Commander Shultz. My name is Captain James Rickard. I'm the owner of this Trade-ship. What can I do for you today?" Wow, he sure knows how to put on an act when he needs to.

Several seconds pass when another message comes in. "Good day Captain. I'm sure you are wondering why we are bothering you. I, along with most of the local CF authority, have standing orders to search any and all vessels leaving Titan. I apologize for the inconvenience. Please rotate four five degrees Starboard, lower your shields, and unlock your exterior hatch for our inspectors."

"Son of a bitch—" Rickard mutters under his breath as he hits the cargo's communication line. "How are we doing on the progress, guys? CF squids will be down our throats in a few."

Nev replies, "Captain we need more time. This much Zeek is going to be difficult to hide. We don't have enough compartments for it all."

"You guys are running Zeek?! That is why you were going to kill me, because you thought I was with the CF!" I shout. Captain Rickard turns to me, his eyes showing sad indifference.

"For someone claiming to have nothing to do with this, it sure seems rather coincidental. Don't you think?" he says in a low growl while hitting the reply button on the display.

"I'll be more than happy to host your inspection team, Lieutenant Commander. However, may I ask what you are looking for so I can better assist them in their search?" He hits the send button.

The respond is almost instantaneous. "Captain, nobody more than me wishes this to be done and over with as soon as possible, however I cannot elaborate on what my team will be searching for. I ask again for you to rotate four five degrees starboard, lower your shields, and unlock your exterior hatch for our inspectors."

"Damn—" Rickard spits while glancing at the live video feed of the cargo hold. "We don't have enough time," he says in a passive voice.

"What does that mean? You're giving up?" I ask.

Rickard hits the cargo com-link. "Nev report!"

The display shows Nev handing a canister to one of the twins and lifting another from the ground. "We need about ten more minutes, captain."

Rickard's face turns from the display as he mouths various obscenities under his breath. "I don't think we have five minutes. Get as much product hidden as possible and wait for the signal."

There is silence for a moment before Nev responds. "Sir, I don't think that would be wise—"

"I wasn't asking for your opinion! Just wait for the signal and handle it!" Rickard slams the 'end' button with a significant amount of force.

"You guys couldn't possibly fight your way out of this?" I say in a matter-of-fact tone. "I mean, it is a no brainer. This Destroyer is outfitted with a cocktail of weapons that can easily turn the Confessor into a heap of floating debris. Unless—" Rickard gives me a subtle grin "You've outfitted the Confessor with weapons!"

Rickard ignores me, instead hitting the reply button. "Commander Shultz, I apologize for the wait. I have several passengers that are very concerned with what it is you are searching my ship for and insist that I ask again. What will your inspection team be looking for? Remember I'm simply taking a few free civilians to Callisto."

"Captain, my proper title is Lieutenant Commander Shultz; please use it in all further transmissions," the CF commander says dropping his kind tone. "As to your inquiry, my reasons are that of the CF's. If you wish to resist then, you will be held in violation of Article Six of the Trade Act, commissioned by the Sovereign Republic of the Frontier and enforced by the various corporations aligned with the SRF. If you wish to continue down this path of disobedience, it will not turn out well for you and your crew. Now turn four five degrees starboard, lower your shields, and unlock your exterior hatch for our docking tube. For the Frontier Lieutenant Commander Shultz out."

"Insolent prick—" Rickard murmurs to himself, hitting a few controls that cause a warning to flash on the screen. He acknowledges the warning and proceeds finally hitting the reply button. "Lieutenant Commander Shultz, I have lowered my shields and unlocked the exterior hatch, however I sent my pilot down to greet your inspectors, so unfortunately I will not be able to rotate four five degrees per your request."

"Fine—" Shultz's voice sounded more irritated than before. "We will adjust to meet your position. ETA three minutes," he pauses looking around his bridge. "One more thing, Captain. For future reference, not all commanding officers will be as patient as me. Shultz out!"

Rickard closes the message by hitting the cargo hold com-link. "The Destroyer is docking with us in approximately two minutes. Get ready for my signal."

The monitor shows the crew standing abnormally, still watching the hatch as if a monster was getting ready to blast through. Then I notice Rickard seems oddly calm like the prospects of battle bring him peace. Several proximity alarms chime as the Destroyer's docking tube attaches to the Confessor. Two seconds later the hatch begins to open, revealing half a dozen fully loaded assault marines.

"What the hell?" Rickard gasps, watching the team rush past Nev, Lora and the twins leaving the cargo alone.

"Boss, they are heading for the passengers!" Don's voice comes over the display. "They walked right past the goods as if nothing was there."

"There was also a Lieutenant accompanying the team, probably heading your way captain," Ron adds.

Rickard glares at me, grabbing me by my collar and shoves me into a hidden compartment behind a panel, closing it right as the Maine Lieutenant enters the bridge. I find a small hole allowing me to see some of the bridge.

"Sir, I am Lieutenant Ilion. Please stay here for the duration of the inspection," she says in a tense voice.

Rickard nods. "Sure is a lot of security for a routine inspection, don't you think Lieutenant?"

"Not my place to question orders, sir," Ilion responds coldly surveying the room.

Rickard sits in the one of the chairs. "Listen, your commanding officer was less than helpful when it came to explaining why you're here so maybe—"

Lieutenant Ilion holds up one of her hands forestalling Rickard's sentence. "Just because I said that I didn't question orders doesn't mean you can—"

"Ma'am—" a voice cuts in over the tension that was building. "We found the passengers; none fit the description we are looking for."

"Roger that Sergeant. Standby for further orders," Ilion responds then turns to Rickard. "Are there any more people aboard your ship?"

"What do you mean?" he responds.

"Sir, I need to know without a doubt that there is no one else aboard your ship that is not with the passengers or part of your crew," Ilion elaborates.

Rickard places his hand on his chin. "None that I know of. Is this why you're searching ships?"

Lieutenant Ilion hesitates then sighs. "The fleet is searching for a person of interest that recently escaped from Titan."

There is no way she is talking about me; no one in their right mind would waste so many resources to find one draft dodging punk—right? Unless they are talking about Cheever, which would mean I'm dead because he probably wants nothing more than to flay me like a fish. My body shivers at the thought of Cheever hunting me to the ends of the solar system. That must be why there are marines in heavy armor.

Rickard shoots a fleeting eye in my direction, so subtlety that the Lieutenant didn't notice. "Do you happen to have a picture of the person? Maybe I can help," he says.

Lieutenant Ilion grimaces. "No, all we got was a description." She lifts her arm and rattles her fingers along her wrist, projecting a holographic display. "A male around eighteen years of age, approximately a hundred and eighty centimeters tall, with dark brown hair and brown eyes. Last seen near the Miranda Docking Hub."

Well there goes my Cheever escaped theory. But why would the CF go through the process of searching hundreds, possibly thousands, of ships just for me?

Rickard leans back into his chair. "That is very vague. You don't even have a name, right?" The Lieutenant nods her head in agreement. "So what did he do?"

Lieutenant Ilion frowns. "That's just it. They wouldn't tell us other than 'he is armed and extremely dangerous,' hence the state of the inspection team." She shakes her head. "Do you know anybody that fits the description, sir?" she asks.

Rickard leans forward. "Nope, no one on my ship fits that description. I'm sorry I couldn't be of any help."

She nods her head as she grabs her radio. "Sergeant, gather your men and return to the Genesis." She looks back a Rickard. "Thank you for your patience, sir. We will be out of your hair in no time." She stiffens and renders a pristine salute, then turns and leaves the bridge.

Rickard turns and studies the monitors as the marines again walk right past the Zeek then out the hatch. After several minutes the proximity warnings close. Rickard calls everyone back into the bridge, pulling me out of the compartment and sitting me down as they file in.

Nev is the last to enter, his face burning with a mixture of anxiety and anger. "Can someone tell me what the hell just happened?!" he yells.

"Yeah, that was not just an inspection team, sir," the blonde headed slim woman I recognize as the pilot from the skip says.

"Right you are, Lora," Rickard says confidently. "The Lieutenant and I had a little chat; apparently they are looking for someone."

Don steps up. "I don't know, Captain. I still think we should ditch the load. You know for safety reasons." He steps back beside Ron who is nodding his head in agreement.

"We are not going to dump the load!" Rickard barks. "The Lieutenant described someone that looks just like our little guest here." He points at me.

I flinch as everyone's eyes fixate on me. "I have no idea what they want."

"Oh bullshit!" Nev yells unsheathing his pistol. "Captain, I don't think we need any more reason to deal with this little prick." He presses the pistol against my head, panic shoots through me.

"No." Rickard's booming voice fills the room.

"But captain—" Nev starts. "The kid is a burden—"

"You'd better listen to your boss," I cut in like an idiot and Nev smacks me with the gun in response.

"I'm not going to lie; I am going to enjoy killing you," Nev says as he starts to pull the trigger.

Nev stops just short of the end as the sound of a pulse revolver's hammer being cocked back echoes behind him. "I said no." Rickard's voice sounds incredibly calm and soft given the situation.

Nev slowly lowers his gun and turns to face Rickard. "The kid is trouble, Captain," he says.

"Think Nev. If we kill him and the CF finds out we hid him, Zeek or not we're goners," Rickard clarifies.

I can almost see steam floating off Nev's head. "So what are we going to do?"

"We?" Rickard's lips twist into a smile. "You and the rest of the crew are going to clean up the cargo hold. I want every gram of the—product secured before we reach Threshold," he finishes. Nev gives him a long look then sighs before turning to the rest of the crew and gesturing. In seconds the bridge is empty and quiet with only Captain Rickard and me sitting in silence.

Now is a good time to say something, but what? A simple thanks isn't good enough. Not only did Rickard ignore a chance to turn me in, but he also kept Nev from killing me—again. I stand up, straightening the jacket Jurin gave me and I notice a little bit of dried blood on it. Jurin's final words flash through my mind causing an ache right behind my eyes which blurs my vision a bit. I blink through the pain noticing Captain Rickard standing in front of a display depicting the vastness of space.

"Listen—" my words shatter the silence as I take a few steps toward the Captain. "I never meant—" But I'm cut short by the jarring motion of being slammed against the display.

"No, you listen!" Captain Rickard says with so much spite I can feel it radiating from his body. "You have risked the lives of every single person on my ship. What did you think I saved you because we are friends! Nev is right. You are a goddamn liability; a liability I can't afford but at the moment I have to deal with!" He shoves his forearm higher into my neck. "Now I'm going to ask you just once, why is the CF looking for you!?"

I gasp for air, tapping Rickard's forearm until he eases up his pressure. "I swear on the stars, I'm just a draft dodger. My brother and I were trying to leave Titan when the CF picked me up. Jurin bribed some jarheads for my release. That is it." I rub my neck and look at Rickard; he has a skeptical look on his face.

"If that is so, then where is your brother?" he asks.

"He sacrificed himself so that I could get away." The memories in tandem with exhaustion begin to take their toll as a single tear falls down my face.

Rickard turns away, refusing to watch my shame. "Suppose I believe you," he says. "Suppose this is all a coincidence and the CF is searching for someone else. How am I supposed to react? You are a factor that changes the equation, John. What would you do if you were me?" he finishes.

"I would get rid of me as fast as possible," I respond in a dull tone. "It seems I have a knack for getting people around me in trouble; even if I didn't do anything but make what seemed like a simple damn choice."

Captain Rickard turns toward me. "Then it's settled. As soon as we get to Callisto you are off my boat, no questions. Understood?"

"Yes, sir," I respond.

"Now get to the cargo hold and help the crew—I will be engaging the ARAD as soon as we get to Titan's Threshold, and you'll want to be strapped into a chair for that." He sits down in the pilot seat.

I walk toward the door, stopping short and glancing back at Rickard. A part of me feels I should say something else, but what? There is nothing I can say to change his decision. Hell, I agree with his decision, but for some reason I know I want to stay on this ship. And no matter how unwelcome I am, I know that the Idle Confessor is where I belong. I resolve to say nothing and continue through the door and down the passage.

The hall is dimly lit with flickering lights every few meters. A holographic display emerges from the bulkhead as I get near it with a view of the hostile but serene environment outside the ship.

These displays function as a sort of window because actual windows on a space ship are weak points and as such most ships use a plethora of dynamic video systems to simulate windows. A seemingly luxurious feature at first has become a necessity because people hate feeling cooped up. Call it claustrophobia or what have you, but it has to do with basic human nature or instincts. I turn the corner catching a glimpse of a rare facing display showing Titan slowly shrinking in the distance with Saturn largely encompassing the view. I gasp in awe of its beauty, almost forgetting the hell that resided on Titan's surface. My thoughts return to the friends I have lost and how every second that passes brings me further from the oddly comforting place I used to call home.

I try my best to reject it, to vocally say what I cannot but the words are lost. I cannot say goodbye. I cannot renounce my title of Titan, as much as I hated the cesspool where I was raised, where I became a man, and where I met the people who matter to me the most. No, I will hold on to the memories of my past but I will not be haunted by them. I close my eyes and whisper a prayer, something I have not done for long time. Even though I know a few words doesn't make up for years of silence I feel as though a weight had been lifted, not much but just enough that I can breathe more deeply than before. I lift my hand and place it on the display; I feel a tingle in my shoulder as the image is saved to my Aug. I take one last look and head to the cargo hold.

CHAPTER NINE: THE CONFESSOR'S CREW

It's been four and a half days and six-hundred and forty-nine million kilometers since we left Titan's Threshold and engaged the Antimatter Rapid Acceleration Device, better known as ARAD. It was designed specifically for the purpose of rapid acceleration in order to reach velocities that the standard Ion Thrusters could not reach in a timely manner. This device can launch a ship from a steady seventy kilometers per second to a staggering speed of fifteen-hundred kilometers per second. The acceleration itself was more than enough to cause the contents of a ship without inertial dampeners to turn into a homogenous soup. However even with the dampeners the acceleration is still incredibly uncomfortable. The twins tell me after we equalize that the ARAD has the ability to go much faster but it has reached the 'Human' limitation.

Here's an interesting but decisive way to describe a limitation. For as long as humanity has been around we have had a set of overarching purposes. But one stands out above the rest: our never-ending quest toward transcendence. To constantly push the envelope of our limitation, never accepting failure and always coming up with new creative ways to solve problems that used to be impossible boundaries. We have a knack for breaking things just to figure out how they work and how to make them better. It is truly one of our redeeming features and at the same time will probably be our downfall as a species. I often think about these things, about how close we have come in the past and how many times we reach the proverbial crossroad that can make or break us and how, it seems, whenever we are on the cusp of total annihilation something changes inside of us. We take the road not known to us and the next thing we know we are freeing slaves, ending the rule of a tyrant, landing on the moon for the first time and spreading throughout our solar system. But even though we have achieved such amazing things it always seems like we regress to the more barbaric instincts that dictate us—we are a paradox.

A display flickers beside me showing Jupiter slowly growing almost as if it was consuming the space of the display. The estimated time of arrival updates to a little more than a day from Callisto's Threshold, where we will have to slow down to a more manageable velocity. I tap the display and it zooms in toward Callisto. I try my best to reassure myself that this looks like a better place than Titan. Of course the colonies on the last Galilean moon have been around a hell of a lot longer than New Horizon. I'll practically be in the heart of the Sovereign Republic, which means I'll have choices, options that where never afforded to me before. I'll get through this—on my own.

The last four and a half days have been more than my dignity can handle, let's just say I have worked my debt off in full. My one and only reprieve from Nev and his ever growing hatred for me are the twins, who amazingly took a liking to me, and a rather shabby tabby cat named Gremlin. The twins say that Grem just showed up one day out of nowhere and has since been a source of great strife, much like myself. I spend a lot of time with the twins and I find myself saddened by the thought of leaving just when things are getting somewhat better. But I don't want to tempt my four day streak of not having an gun pointed at me, so I'll try and leave quietly.

I let out a long sigh as my Aug begins to buzz annoyingly. I look down at my forearm where 05:00 is blinking incessantly. I immediately stop it with a simple flick of my finger. "Time to start another glorious day," I say aloud, rising to my feet and stretching.

I inspect the makeshift bed I threw together from some boxes laying around. The Confessor has space in the crew quarters for me, but according to Nev only the crew gets to sleep in the crew quarters and since I'm not part of the crew— So naturally I tried to sleep in the passenger quarters, but Nev snuffed that idea saying the passenger quarters are for paying customers and since I'm a worthless stowaway I don't get such luxuries. Prick. So instead I found a nice secluded walkway watching over the illicit cargo, which I have honestly considered destroying just to piss Nev off, but that would bring the wrath of Captain Rickard down on me, who in my so humble opinion, makes Nev look like a stud field mouse.

I crack my neck and grab the few toiletries some of the passengers were kind enough to share with me, making my way to the community locker room. It took me a few days to adjust to the Confessor, not because of Nev but rather the difference in living dynamics, such as water consumption and food stores. Things like that are important anywhere but on a ship one miscalculation could mean dangerously low food and water. Fortunately, modern ships operating systems calculate all of this in mere seconds. Not to mention the amount of bio-waste that the ship reuses. Like the water from showers and even human byproduct. At first it sounds disgusting that everyone is using and reusing the same water, but from a scientific prospective this was one of the greatest advances in space travel. Less storage needed for water means lest overall ship weight, which calculates into more energy efficiency. It's a domino effect that literally never comes to mind when you're on a terrestrial planet that has an abundance of resources.

The locker room doors slide open and as usual I'm the only one there. The lights turn on as I enter the space, revealing three rows of lockers and showers; enough space for fifty or so people. I walk to my usual shower stall and place my left hand on the wall, setting the temp to forty degrees Celsius. The water rushes out of the nozzle sending plums of steam billowing upward. I step under the warmth letting it flow over me and dull the pain of my left eye. I bring up a display of my reflection. The bruise is almost invisible at this point with only a yellow hue and some pain remaining. Four and a half days of scruff has formed and is starting to itch relentlessly, but I don't have a sonic razor available to remedy the issue. I tilt my head forward allowing the water to flow over my face and down the front of my body. I'm finding it hard to recognize myself in the mirror, as if everything that has happened in the last week has aged me far beyond my years. I'm so used to being reliant on someone else, but out here I'm alone.

I look at the clock, and it's five-thirty. Damn, I'm running late again. I finish cleaning myself and place my hand on the wall shutting the shower off, then grab a towel to dry my body on the way to the locker. I open it with a swipe of my index finger. The door unlatches and swings open. Several pairs of plain gray jumpsuits that the captain gave me are folded neatly toward the back of the locker. I grab one and quickly slip it on. I go to shut the locker but hesitate, taking a look at the jacket that Jurin gave me. There are still a few dried blood stains that I somehow missed. I reach out to grab it when my Aug begins buzzing indicating its five forty-five. I shake my head as I close the door and run out of the locker room.

No more than a minute and a half later I enter the cafeteria, quickly sliding an apron over my head as Lora, Don and Ron walk in. Lora, as always, is tall, beautiful and reserved. She has flowing dark blonde hair tightly pulled into a perfect bun revealing a petite face accented by crystal blue eyes. In contrast, the shorter, stalky twins have eccentrically waxed mustaches with wild unkept dark, reddish brown hair. Both look almost indiscernible from one another with only their color-coded jumpsuits being the difference. Don wears dark grey with a navy blue stripe along the arm and Ron, navy blue with a grey stripe. Everything about them screams mad scientist and incidentally that is what I like the most about them. They are talking nonstop about conduit manifolds and torque deafeners on Titan class ships. Lora shoots me a sidelong glance, slightly shaking her head and smiling. I let out a chuckle under my breath as the twins pry themselves away from what is obviously a riveting conversation and join me in the kitchen, donning their own flamboyantly-decorated aprons.

"Mornin' Einstein," Don says, smacking me on the back with an unnecessary amount of force.

"How'd the dreams treat you last night, Hawking?" Ron adds, also smacking me on the same spot his brother just christened.

I shrug off the sting and smile. "Hey guys, you know Nev doesn't like it when you help me," I say for the hundredth time.

"Nev who?" Don says in a poorly-sold sarcastic voice.

Ron laughs. "No worries, Tesla. Nev only looks big enough to smash you on the outside, but between you, me and this ugly bastard—" he points his thumb toward Don who makes an overly-insulted face. "We know that brains will always beat brawn." He smiles and winks, smacking me on the back again.

Man, I'm really am going to miss these guys. It's not their obvious humor or overly optimistic attitudes but the fact that they feel so real and kind. That is unexpected but much appreciated given the last few days. I kind of laugh a little noticing how incredibly alike they are.

Don starts tapping the spatula on the oven top. "Alright gents, let's get this food started. We have a lot of mouths to feed."

The three of us start cooking as several of the passengers begin to trickle in. Each one looks more and more cheerful now that we are almost at our destination. Then Nev Freeman storms in with the usual unpleasant look on his face. Nev only has several expressions. Most flaunt his hardened, steel-like scruff-covered jawline. He has grey hair but it isn't nearly as prevalent as the captain's, and he keeps his mane buzzed with only a light brown and grey wisp on the top of his head. In a way though he reminds me of Jurin, because he had the same grey eyes. Even though they seem cold and piercing I can tell there is a personality under all the rigidness. The only problem is Nev hates my guts—I guess he has a right to—and it's starting to get on my nerves.

He glances over at the twins who are knee deep in an argument about the physics behind scrambling or poaching eggs in zero gravity. "What the hell are you two doing?!" he shouts, causing several of the passengers to stop eating and look up.

Ron and Don turn to face Nev with looks of devilish mischief on their faces. "Oh, we were merely seeing if radiation can cook eggs just as good as any old stovetop," Ron says.

Don grins. "We thought you'd be a perfect subject to try out our new 'Rad Eggs,' patent pending of course, with a slight chance of, you know—cancerous death."

Nev, who had just filled his mouth full of eggs, freezes in mid-chew. "You're joking right?" he asks then turns to me. "They're joking right?"

I lift my shoulders and give him an apathetic look. "I don't know why you'd ask me. I've only been here for a few days. You should know them better than me." Nev darts his eyes from me to the twins, then promptly spits his eggs out and rushes to the bathroom.

"I swear, how does that man walk and talk at the same time?" Don says while gasping for breath in between his laughs.

Ron smacks his forehead. "One of the great mysteries of life."

"Hey, got any more of the Rad Eggs?" Lora says with a half-smile.

Ron and Don both stop in mid laugh. "Uh—well yeah, but—" Ron stammers.

"They aren't really radioactive!" Don shouts awkwardly.

Wow, that was smooth. Lora looks at me quizzically, and I shrug as I scoop some more scrambled eggs onto her plate. She winks and returns to her seat. I turn to the twins who are now completely focused on the sausage sizzling in front of them.

About an hour and a half later almost everyone on the ship has eaten breakfast except, of course, Captain Rickard who usually stays up most of the night to ensure nothing happens while everyone is sleeping. The twins prepare a to-go bag and hand it to me, giving me a look that screams 'This is your chance to impress the boss so you can stay on the Confessor and help us embarrass Nev!' I grin, hoping they really thought that.

I head down the winding passage toward the bridge located deep within the ship, a design that is standard in almost all ships for protection against cosmic radiation. At least it was a needed design before advancements in radiation shielding that are now on all modern ships. Even after decades we still design ships the same, just with shinier bells and whistles. Of course that was one of the many long talks the twins shared with me earlier on our trip. "We are creatures of habit, John, never changing things unless there's a need to change," Don had said.

I can feel the unease of nervousness growing inside me as I approach the massive door. We haven't really talked much since the inspection incident, and honestly he sounded pretty resolute when he said I'm gone as soon as we reach Callisto. So why bother with trying if it won't work out in the end? I look up and realize I have been standing outside the bridge for who knows how long. I really need to stop getting lost in my thoughts. I lift my hand to knock but hesitate before finally mustering the courage to just enter the room. Rickard is leaning so far back in his chair that my unannounced entry startles him and he almost falls backwards.

"Sorry Captain!" I almost shout as he glowers at me. "I just wanted to bring you some breakfast," I add, holding up the bag.

Captain Rickard reaches out and takes the bag from my hand. "Smells good," he says quietly.

"Thank you," I respond. I notice he seems more tired than usual, so maybe now isn't a good time to ask about staying.

"You can't stay, kid." Rickard's voice interrupts my thoughts.

"But, I—"

"My decision is final—you even said it, remember?" He looks up at me with a cold stare. I think back to my conversation mentally cursing my past self for screwing me over. "Thanks for the breakfast, but I need to you leave. I have to make some personal calls before we reach Callisto." I simply nod and leave. There isn't anything I could have said or done to change his mind.

I spend the next few hours finishing the menial and frankly degrading tasks that Nev assigned me, from doing the crew's laundry to polishing the walkway struts throughout the ship. I'm quite certain the latter was a bunch of crap. Noon finally rolls around and I return to the cafeteria to start lunch. The twins are already waiting there when I enter, their faces optimistically waiting for good news only to be squashed by my apparent displeasure.

"So what's for lunch?" I ask, tying the apron around my waist.

Don looks over his shoulder at Ron who is smacking the side of one of the food processors, shouting an undiscernible series of curses. "Ask the master chef," he says with a grunt.

Just then Ron yelps with glee as the machine begins humming loudly. "Hey, Don!" he shouts. "I have a real knack for fixing this dang thing."

"Yeah, Ron, you're the man," Don says gesturing for me to lean in. He pulls a remote from his pocket and flashes me an ornery grin. "We've had that thing for the better part of a decade and he still doesn't know it came with a remote," he whispers.

"You're an evil genius, you know that?" I whisper back.

Don sticks his tongue out and grins before quickly stuffing the remote back into his pocket as Ron walks up. "Who wants some chicken sandwiches?" he says as he puts a plate down in front of me.

There are many names for what Ron placed in front of me but chicken sandwich was the furthest from an accurate description. It was more like a pink-goo sandwich. "Uh, I've had chicken before and that is clearly not chicken," I say, pushing the plate away.

Don shoves the plate back toward me. "Just try it. You'll be surprised," he says with a smile. "This isn't a five-star cruise, kid."

I roll my eyes and grab the sandwich, quickly taking a bit and expecting the worse. "Wow!" I exclaim. "This is actually really good."

Ron throws his hand up in an overzealous show of accomplishment. "Settle down, Cujo." Don interrupts his celebration. "All you did was hit a button. That's hardly an achievement." Ron's arms fall to his sides.

"So what is this stuff?" I ask, pulling away the bun. "It even smells like grilled chicken."

Ron scoffs. "You've been cooking and eating this for nearly five days and you're just now asking?!"

"Well I assumed we had a freezer full of food and stuff," I respond

"Nope, everything we eat is essentially the same. It's a protein-based, vitamin-enriched, food substitute. That machine allows us to input what flavor, shape and even the texture we want it to be," Don says.

Ron flexes dramatically. "Yup, it's everything the body needs, baby!"

"So the eggs we had this morning?" I question. "And the meatloaf from last night?" Ron and Don both nod their heads in unison. "Weird."

"That's space travel, bub," Ron says while adjusting the processor's texture controls and producing something that looked a little more like chicken then pink goo as several passengers trickled in.

Before long lunch was finished and everyone, whether knowingly or not, was stuffed with the goo chicken, including myself. I took the time to tell the twins that the Captain was less than willing to let me to stay, and everyone took it seemingly well, except for the poor spatula Don broke in half. I attempted to shrug off my own displeasure for their sake. It was only fair. They didn't have a say in the situation and I didn't want them to think it was somehow their problem.

After we finished talking and cleaning I found myself with a little spare time so I headed for my cot. Hoping that maybe I could get some reading in before Nev came up with some other worthless job like cleaning the hanger deck with my sonic toothbrush or something. A few minutes later I was walking down the footbridge toward my makeshift bed, where Grem was sleeping. I flop down onto the covers causing her to jump and glare at me. But she changes her mind when I start scratching her chin, making her purr softly.

"Did you catch any mice?" I ask. She looks at me with her copper eyes and tilts her head, placing one of her red-haired paws on my arm. "Of course not. You're the worst mouser in the history of mousers, huh?" I add. She retracts her paw almost as if I have offended her and begins licking it profusely. Jeez, I am talking to a cat. I'm so pathetic. Grem props herself upright, sweeping her fluffy tail back and forth as she stares at me. "What?" I ask, but she continues to stare silently. I feel a chill run through me. "Would you stop staring at me?!" I demand. This time she meows in response but nevertheless continues to stare persistently.

We continue to silently stare at each other like a weird sort of contest when my Aug begins buzzing. I look down and see Don's face floating a centimeter above my arm. I tap my wrist and a holographic display pops up with Don's bust filling the screen.

"Hey Chaucer, we could use a little help doing some maintenance on the Fusion Core when you get the chance," he says.

"Me?" I respond skeptically "What would you need me to help you with?"

Don looks at something off screen as Ron's cursing roars over a loud humming noise. "Ron!" he shouts. "Don't touch that, it's—" before he van finish a loud electrical shock echoes over the communication, causing the lights in the room to shut off. "Forget it," Don finishes in a low voice.

"Is everything alright?" I ask.

Don looks at me and smiles. "Oh yeah—this sort of thing happens all the time," he says. "Just—get here as soon as you can, ok?"

Don closes the window before I could respond. I quickly jump to my feet, accidently sending Grem rolling onto her back. She attempts to play off the humiliation by playing with a stray string on the corner of my sheet. "Sorry Grem, but I think the twins are about to get us killed. We'll continue the staring match later." She doesn't look at me; I bet she won't know I've even left. I quickly hurry down the walkway toward the aft of the ship, where the twins typically spend most of their time.

CHAPTER TEN: THE GEMINI PRODIGY

When I reach the hatch of the conduit maintenance room, I can hear the twins talking to Captain Rickard.

"But Captain, you don't realize. The kid is brilliant. After only four days—" I presume Don says.

"He understands complex engineering as if he had been studying it for—well as long as us," Ron finishes.

"I already told you. He is gone as soon as we drop off the merchandise," Rickard responds "He's got the fleet squids after him for reasons that I think are beyond something as irrelevant as Draft dodging—you know we don't need that kind of attention!" he adds.

"But this isn't simply your decision, Captain. The first mate—" Don retorts.

"Excuse me!" Rickard barks. "All decisions are mine, because this is my ship. I don't give a crap if the universe sent him personally. He doesn't belong here on my ship!" he shouts.

"Captain—" the twins say almost simultaneously.

"Enough!" the hatch flies open and Rickard is standing there staring at me.

I try the say something but nothing comes to mind and before I can formulate a sentence Rickard is already passed me and down the corridor. I watch him go around the corner and then I turn and enter the room. The twins are standing on either side of a power conduit with a look of sad contempt on their faces. At first they didn't notice my presence probably because of the sudden loud buzzing noise emitting from the exposed coupling or because they were thinking about the conversation I had just overheard. Either way I stand silently for a few seconds watching them work efficiently together as if they know what the other is thinking.

Don looks up in my direction and smiles, tapping Ron on the shoulder. Ron glances up at me with a pair of large goggles magnifying his eyes. He also grins, placing the shielding panel back onto the coupling and removes his goggles.

"So what did you need my help with?" I ask.

Ron beams and nods toward Don who closes the hatch behind me. "We just wanted to see you off right," Ron says, while opening a panel on the wall and retrieving a bottle of clear liquid.

"You've had it rough these last few days. It's important to relax when you can or you will end up like Nev," Don says, pulling out three glasses from another panel then holding them up to Ron, who pours a generous amount of the unknown liquid in all three.

"Here you go, bud. Best if you try to down it in one gulp" Don passes me one of the glasses.

The glass is nowhere near my face and I can already smell the obvious alcohol. This isn't going to be my first drink by any means, but I have a feeling that this will be the strongest I've ever had. I lift the glass to my mouth and swallow the liquor in one swift motion.

The burning sensation that follows is damn near unbearable, causing me to cough and gasp. "What—the hell—is that—stuff?!" I ask in between coughs.

The twin's faces where bright red and twisted, no doubt fighting their way through the burn as well. "That—is—.our— home brewed—" Ron forces out between gasps of air.

"Degreaser—" Don finishes with a cough.

"Seriously?!" I say while wiping away the tears that involuntarily formed in my eyes. "If I didn't know you guys liked me. Then I'd think you're trying to kill me," I add, letting out a horse laugh.

Ron regains his composure "What? Once you get past the burn, it's quite smooth. Right?" He smacks Don's back, who nods his head violently in agreement.

Several minutes pass before we completely recover. Ron insists we do another shot, but Don and I convince him that one in a lifetime is more than enough.

Then silence fills the compartment, the type of awkward silence that causes everyone to squirm in their skin. It is the quiet that happens when something that should be said is left unsaid, like a nagging itch that you can't reach.

I take a deep breath and organize my thoughts, quenching the acidic burn raising my bowels from the degreaser. Alright, here goes. "I just want to say—"

"Stop," Ron interrupts in a stern tone I didn't think he could possibly muster. "We hate goodbyes," he adds in an equally-firm rasp with his face showing no hints of sarcasm.

"Ok then," I respond, hopefully lightening the mood. "Why don't you tell me how you came aboard the Confessor instead?" I ask both in an attempt to change the subject, and because I'm honestly curious as to how two individuals as gifted as the twins ended up in such a diverse crew.

Don's ears perk a bit like a dog's would after hearing the word treat. "Funny you should ask that. Ron I think it is your turn to start."

Ron smiles and retrieves an elaborate wooden plaque from behind another panel, then hands it to me. The plaque is heavier than I would have expected, undoubtedly made with the densest of woods and a glossy coat of varnish. In the center of the plaque is the Martian Science Academy's sigil with both Ronald and Donald Witman's names eloquently scrolled into the wood. Under their names was a short paragraph that I read aloud. "It is with honor that the Martian Science Academy and its affiliates present Ronald Alekrim Witman and Donald Malekrim Witman the MSA Solar Diamond award for their invaluable contributions to Applied Star-Ship Architecture and Engineering, which has undoubtedly changed the future of space flight as well as the future of human expansion in our solar system and someday the universe."

I studied the plaque a little more glancing up at the twins who seem to be lost in their thoughts. "Wow, you guys," I say. "I never knew you grew up on Mars, let alone went to MSA." I once read about the Martian Science Academy back on Titan. In all of the solar system there didn't stand a single academic structure that matched the prestige of MSA. Its halls cultivated the greatest minds the human race has seen and presumably will ever see.

"Yeah, that was almost thirty years ago," Ron says, taking the plaque and placing it behind the panel again.

"I still remember the day we got our acceptance. Mom was so proud. It was one of the best days of our life," Don added.

"So what happened next?" I ask.

Don smiles and leans against the conduit. "Well, we were the youngest graduates in the history of the school and during that time the Great War was still raging incessantly, so we did the only thing that two rational young boys could do—" he says while grinning.

"We joined the United Earth's Space Fleet Civil Engineering Corps," Ron continued. "We, being United Earths citizens, were raised in a time of war. It was considered an honor to fight for the good guys." He makes a sarcastic gesture. "Who would have thought the war would come to a standstill just few short years after we enlisted?" he finished.

"See, the war lasted so long and cost so much money and resources that both the United Earths of Sol and the Sovereign Republic of the Frontier couldn't maintain the conflict. So seemingly overnight we were separated from the fleet and we reallocated from the UES Ares Space Dock all the way back to mom and dad's basement." Ron and Don both chuckle.

"So just like that the war was over, huh?" I ask.

Ron's smile faded a bit. "Yeah, it was an interesting time for both the inner and outer solar system. A war that had ruled everyone's lives for decades literally just stopped so fast there wasn't enough time to adjust to the changes, like ripping a bandage off with one yank." Ron gestured. "It caused a lot of confusion, then soon after the governments began to fall under the strain. People didn't know who to trust anymore," he finished in a sober tone.

Don continued. "Entire economies throughout the solar system collapsed, millions of people lost their jobs. It was as if the war kept us afloat and ironically it caused our downfall. Soon after that the mega-corporations began calling in the huge debts that the governments couldn't pay, practically blackmailing the governments to allow the corporations to have more and more unrestricted control," Don added, flopping his hands down to his sides.

"I think that is about the time the Syndicate Builders Guild approached us offering promises of steady income and good work." Ron carries on. "At that time we were desperate—our father had passed away a year prior and our mother couldn't afford the house we grew up in due to the housing market's hyperinflation and outrageous tax increases. Then like that she got sick, so we took the deal in hopes that we could at least take care of her," Ron says.

The twins' faces show sadness and guilt, emotions I've never seen from them before and honestly never want to see again. I hesitate to urge them to continue, hoping that I didn't make a mistake for being so curious, when I catch Don's eyes. He smiles, almost able to tell that I felt bad for asking in the first place.

"It's alright, bud," Don says. "Life is full of sadness just as much as there is happiness. You can't have one without the other and honestly you truly cannot appreciate the happy moments in your life without a little sadness," he finishes with a smirk.

Ron clears his throat. "So where were we? Right. After we signed with the SBG, the bastards decided that we needed to move to the Jovian Mining Corporation's Odyssey Space Station, which incidentally meant we had to renounce our citizenship with the UES because the Odyssey is in the Sovereign Republic space."

"At first we were obviously apprehensive about the change, mainly because of war propaganda surrounding the frontier and the people who live there," Don says. "We almost stayed but mom passed away unexpectedly." The sadness returned to Don's face but only for a moment. "So we decided to leave Mars, and it was easier than we thought, mainly cause there was nothing left for us there."

Ron nodded his head in agreement. "We relinquished our citizenship, which seemed to be a growing trend amongst freelancers, traders and mercenaries at the time."

"But why did you have to drop your citizenship?' I ask.

Don walks to the bulkhead and brings up a holo-display showing a map of the solar system highlighting a large band between the inner and outer solar system. "You see this?" he points at the highlighted section. "After the war came to a standstill this was turned into a sort of a Demilitarized Zone. The only way for someone to be able to freely move between the inner and outer solar system was to hold no allegiance to any of the governing bodies in the solar system," he says.

"Essentially you become a citizen of the ship you are on. You cannot vote or exercise any of the rights a citizen has. You forgo one list of freedoms for another, this lead to the formation of the freelancer groups like the Syndicate Builders Guild and Free Trader's Union, and various mercenary groups. If you become a member of one of these groups, then you are afforded certain allowances in both the inner and outer systems," Ron adds with a gasp.

"So you guys are members of the SBG?" I ask, rubbing my temples trying to retain the vast amount of information the twins are dumping on me at once.

"Not quiet—" Don says. "No doubt you have heard that the SBG is a mere shadow of its former glorious self." I nod my head in complete and total understanding and agreement. "Well, we can attest to the validity of that statement. For years the SBG abused our gifts and overworked us to the point of insanity."

"And the worse part was we were powerless to change our fate cause we were incredibly indebted to the organization." Ron said callously "That, my friend, is when we met Captain Rickard. He had just finished a job that caused the Confessor a remarkable amount of damage; honestly he shouldn't have made it back. But yet here he was with the Confessor at his back. Don and I obsessed over her for ten days and nights fixing every single flaw," Ron says, slightly patting the bulkhead. "On the eleventh day Captain Rickard inspected the ship and was so impressed that he paid our outstanding debts and offered us the engineering job right on the spot."

"You're kidding me!" I respond. "That doesn't sound like the Captain I've come to know and love."

Don lets out a sigh. "Yeah well what did you expect? Men like Rickard have to be convinced that they need something before they commit to it, simple as that."

I think about that statement for a few moments. "So what you are saying is if I can convince the captain that I have skills he needs then I can stay—right?"

Ron laughs. "Sorry, bud. he captain won't be convinced at all, but—"

There is another uncomfortable silence where an obvious explanation needs to be. "But what!?" I almost shout while Ron and Don trade looks.

"But, if you can convince the first mate that you are needed on the Confessor then there may still be a chance for you," Ron says with a particularly impish grin.

A lot of good that piece of information does. "Nev hates everything about me. Why would he all of a sudden change his mind about me and furthermore convince the captain that the Confessor needs me?"

"Oh, dear boy. Nev isn't the First Mate," Don says with laugh.

How the hell did he—never mind. "Then who is?" I ask.

The twins hesitate again. God I hate it when they do that. Then my left arm begins buzzing. I flick my wrist without looking, a mistake I will certainly not be repeating in the future, because the next thing I know I'm blinded by Nev's angry glare.

"Where the hell are you, stowaway?!" he shouts, causing the holographic window to shudder.

"I—huh—"

"Forget it!" Nev interrupts "Just get your ass down to the cafeteria. We've got hungry costumers!"

Damn-it, I got caught up talking that I forgot about dinner. I look up at the twins who are trying to act like they can't hear Nev chastising me. "I'm on my way," I respond.

"You better damn well get your—" he says before I close the connection. I know that will make him even angrier but at this point I don't really care.

I smile at the twins then turn to leave when Don grabs my shoulder. "Why don't you let us take care of dinner? You could use a break."

"You don't have to do that."

Ron smiles while putting away several tools. "We know we don't have to, but we want to."

"Just go get some rest. I have a feeling tomorrow is going to be busy," Don says. "Not to mention, this gives us another chance to mess with Nev," he adds, nudging Ron, who flashes a wicked smile in response.

I smirk. "Thanks guys, I know you hate goodbyes, but I just want to say that these last four days have been somewhat bearable because of you."

That damned awkward silence returns to the room, this time not because there is something left unsaid but because something was said. The twins smile and nod almost perfectly in sync. Its crazy how truly alike they are. I bow my head to the twins and leave the mechanical room. For some reason the corridor feels colder than I remembered it from before, and I'm pretty sure it isn't the temperature that is causing the slow chill through my body. I hate goodbyes too; they are so final and abrupt.

The walk back to my ragged cot feels longer than usual, like every step I take is more anticipated, more thought out. It was as if I want to absorb as much of the Confessor into my memory as possible. It is still early when I reach my makeshift quarters, and Grem is sleeping on my pillow with her paws stretched out to the sides. She greets me with a passing glance, yawns, then rolls over to a more comfortable position. I drop down with a satisfying thump, causing Grem to meow with contempt.

"No worries my little Gremlin. I won't be annoying you for much longer," I utter in a low but soft voice as I scratch her behind the ear.

I glance at my Aug noticing three new messages from Nev. I promptly delete them without giving them a second notice, then I check the time. Wow, only six o'clock. Why do I feel exhausted? I roll onto my left side, bringing up the display showing Jupiter now completely encompassing the monitor and the Galilean moon Callisto several times larger than this morning. The ticker in the upper corner shows an estimated time of arrival being just a bit over thirteen hours. Once we reach an hour from threshold, the Captain will have everyone strap into a seat for deceleration. It's similar to the rapid acceleration experienced when engaging the ARAD. The sheer force of slowing down has the same uncomfortable result but not as uncomfortable as it would be if the inertial dampeners malfunction.

It's a wary subject to even think about, but yet my mind continues down the path with nothing more to do in the gifted time I have. I think about the utter amount of possible failures that can occur in space. One micrometer crack in a ship's hull could cause catastrophic decompression. A single fusion core shield failing completely could literally bake every organic thing on this ship in seconds. Not to mention the fact that a poorly kept fusion core could go nuclear at a moment's notice. So many ways we could die by so many little details that you couldn't see with your own naked eyes. It is enough to cause people to go crazy with anxiety; I imagine that is why some people have never left a planet's side. Those people who let fear dictate their action every minute of every day, who have to tell themselves that they are living without truly giving life a chance, I feel sorry for them.

The monitor shimmers, pulling me out of my trance. I let out a long sigh then tap Callisto and forcing the display to zoom in on the moon's night side. The designation Pilot hovers over the domed cityscape, population twenty-two million. The very thought is inconceivable when New Horizon had a population of about one and a half million and that place fell huge. How will I find myself in a place already so full of other people? I let out another sigh. This time though I can feel my eyes growing heavy. I take it as a sign and roll to my back, closing my eyes and focusing on the micro vibrations flowing through the ship. Before long I can feel myself slipping away into the abysses of my subconscious.

It is the same vivid dream as the one back at the apartment on Titan. But this time I'm floating above a planet covered in lights. It's odd because I don't recognize it. Then explosions begin to dot the surface of the unknown planet. The fire spreads and spreads and I begin to scream as all of the lights are consumed by the spreading fire of destruction and death. What's going on? What am I seeing and most of all why am I seeing it? Then as always I'm in the white room split by the black glossy wall. This time without hesitation I run to the wall. I'm determined to get some answers, to find out what this all means. I reach the wall but I cannot bring myself to touch it. It's not fear that compels me to avoid coming into contact with the wall. Rather it's a feeling of incompleteness like I am missing something that makes me whole and if I touched the wall than I would lose the rest. I resolve to simply stare at my shadowed reflection and try to determine what it is that makes it so completely different and unlike me. Then the most disturbing thing happens. My reflection grins and winks.

Chapter Eleven: The Confessor's Second

"Wake up!" The unpleasant sound of Nev's voice jars me back to reality. "Captain wants us to make sure everything is secured before we decelerate," he says, nudging me with his boot.

"Alright, alright!" I moan, slapping at his boot and sitting up, rubbing the back of my neck, which seems more tense than usual. "Where are the others?" I ask, noticing that Nev is alone.

"Just you and me this morning, stowaway," Nev says while brandishing a sadistic grin.

I let out a faint whine and rub my eyes, trying to erase the image of my dark reflection. Grem brushes against me, purring softly, and begins cleaning herself. She finally notices Nev leaning against the railing and begins growling and hissing. Nev grimaces and I let out a subtle chuckle that I thought was barely audible until Nev shoots me a glare.

"What the hell are you laughing at?!" he barks, pushing himself off the railing.

"Nothing, I was just wondering—"

Nev crosses his arms "About what!?"

"If pussy always acts like that around you." I let out a laugh, knowing full well I'll soon be paying for my remark.

Nev grabs me by my collar and lifts me to my feet, then shoves me against the wall with, in my opinion, an unnecessary amount of force. "Try to enjoy this as much as I'm about to you little shit!" he snarls, cocking back his free arm.

"Nev, what is taking so damn long?!" Captain Rickard's voice comes over Nev's Aug.

He scowls, letting go of my collar. I hit the ground with a loud thud. "Sorry boss, I was just taking out the trash." He glances at me, ensuring I knew what he meant by that.

I begin lifting myself up when Nev kicks me in the gut, causing me to lose my breath and crumple to the ground.

"Well, hurry the hell up; we don't have much time before we reach Callisto's Threshold." Rickard's voice fills the air once more.

"Sure thing, boss." Nev says, closing the connection then looking at me. "You're getting off easy this time, stowaway," he adds.

I glare at him, still catching my breath and rubbing my stomach. "You can be a real dick sometimes Nev!"

He smiles. "Go make sure the passengers are secure and then meet me in the cargo hold." He turns and starts limping down the walkway.

I watch him leave, wondering why he is limping but really I don't care. After a minute or two I finally gather enough strength to lift myself to my feet. I look down at Grem, who stops cleaning herself and looks up at me. "Where were you when I needed you!?" She tilts her head bit then returns to her grooming.

I take a deep breath, ignoring the ache in my abdomen, then start down the walkway for the passenger quarters. A few minutes later I'm walking down the corridor making sure everybody is awake and secured. Some look nervous while others are still groggy from the unwelcome wake up call. An overall sense of excitement can be felt in the air. After a few moments, everyone is strapped in and ready.

I head for the cargo hold, catching a display showing Callisto almost completely encompassing the monitor with Pilot's domed city covering a large portion of Callisto's hazardous yet beautiful landscape. The sheer splendor of it almost takes my breath away, causing a little part of me to feel excited, knowing that this is where I will soon be calling my home. I pry myself from the display and enter the cargo hold several moments later. Nev is kneeling by some of the illicit cargo, ensuring the carbon straps are secure. He looks up at me and grins. Making my abdomen ache. I grimace, sending him an obscene gesture. His smile widens as he begins limping towards me. I take a closer look at his left leg. It seems stiff and lifeless, with Nev almost having to swing his entire hip just to propel it forward, when I realize.

Nev stops in mid-step noticing my stare. "What are you looking at?"

"I had no idea."

Nev looks down at his left leg "Yeah, and you wouldn't have if the Bionic Module wasn't malfunctioning," he says drumming his fist on the prosthetic.

There was a moment where I finally understand Nev's prickly exterior and why he is so hard-up all the time. For that single brief moment I lose sight of all the bad blood between us.

"What happened?" I genuinely ask.

Nev looks up at me and for once his eyes don't show contempt but rather something else, like a sort of vulnerability I have never seen from him. "That is none of your goddamn business!" he barks, and like that the moment was gone.

"Sorry, I was just—" Nev sends me a chilling glare. "Never mind."

The uncomfortable silence that followed probably helped hasten the time it took to check the carbon straps on all the cargo, because we were done in no time. Nev gives me a nod, then limps to a row of seats bolted to the wall and begins strapping himself in. I follow suit ensuring I sit several seats away from him.

"Hey Captain—" he says, as soon as I finish buckling in. "The cargo is good to go and we're strapped in and ready for decel."

A few moments later Captain Rickard's voice comes in over the ship's intercom system. "This is the Captain. I hope everyone is having a good morning. We are about forty-five seconds from rapid deceleration. This will be similar to the discomfort felt when we engaged the ARAD, keep in mind it is completely normal and will last only several seconds. Thank you."

Forty-five seconds later the ship begins shuddering violently, Nev and I are forced against the backs of our seats as the Confessor wines and groans under the pressure. The cargo bay's lights flicker a bit as the vibrations start to subside and the force holding me to the seat relinquishes. We haven't completely slowed down but rather the inertial dampeners have over taken the blunt of the force caused by the rapid deceleration. Nev and I unhook ourselves and inspect the cargo once more to ensure the precious drugs didn't come to any harm. We finish right as the Captain calls.

"Nev, report." Rickard does little to hide the uncomfortable amount of angst in his voice.

"Everything is good down here, boss." Nev responds.

"Good, we'll be at the rendezvous in under an hour so have the kid get the passengers loaded on the skip," Rickard says with a little bit more ease in his voice.

"Roger, Nev out." He drops his left arm and looks at me. "Well you heard him. Get your ass to it!" he growls.

I shake my head, not bothering to indulge his obvious stab at me, and start toward the hatch. But right as I reach the door, I decide something needs to be said and I turn around.

"Nev—" I start, but before I can finish Nev holds up his hand.

"Listen, it happened during the war, ok." His voice was calm and sobering. "Now you know more than you deserve."

I nod my head. "I'm Sorry—"

"Don't. You don't get to be sorry cause you're just a damn stowaway. You're not even going to be here long enough for me to bother explaining it!" I take a few steps toward him. "Just get the hell out of here!" he yells, stopping me in mid-step.

I lower my head then turn and leave. Nothing more could have been said without making things worse. But in an odd way I understand Nev more than I had before. He is a hardened war veteran trying to deal with his past. The whole thing reminds me of Jurin. How much he had changed in just two years of service under Cheever and how I missed him, but most of all it reminded me of how small I am in comparison to the rest of the things going on. Nev was right; I'm not going to be around long enough to bother forging bonds and doing so would just cause more ripples, more agitation.

The passenger bay is bustling with anxious and excited people darting back and forth, gathering their personal belongings. Everyone is too busy to notice when I enter the bay and attempting to shout over the chaos would prove fruitless at best. I walk over to a terminal situated at the front of the passenger bay and place my hand on it. There is a slight tingle in my arm and I turn to face the mob of people who are still overly concerned with their own agendas.

"Ladies and gentlemen." The sound of my voice echoes through the intercom system, causing everyone to immediately stop what they were doing and look at me. "Please gather your belongings and line up in an orderly fashion. I will be escorting you the hanger bay for your departure."

For the most part everyone quickly finishes what they were doing and line up, except for an elderly grey-haired lady who seems to be frantically searching her bag for something.

"Ma'am, could you please get your stuff and get in line?" I try but fail to hide my irritation.

The old lady shakes her head and proceeds to dig through her bag as if her life depended on it. I let out a sigh and walk over to her. "What are you looking for?"

She looks up. Fresh tears cover her face and a look of absolute panic encompasses her stare. "I-I can't find it!" she stammers.

"Find what?"

"M-My Husband—I can't find my husband!" Her voice quivers and breaks a little as several faint but audible snickers rise behind me.

I tilt my head slightly. "Your husband? I don't understand."

She takes my hand. "His ashes. I was supposed to bring him home." She whimpers.

The snickers begin to grow louder when I turn around. Two low lives are laughing and mocking the old lady.

"What's so funny?" I ask but the two don't answer. "You know what happened to her stuff?" I almost shout, taking a few steps toward them.

"So what if we do?" the taller one says in a particularly smug tone while the short fat one laughs.

I look him in his arrogant face, thinking about how horrible my morning has already been and how I could really use this clown and his little friend as a good outlet for my anger, but I resist the urge.

"How about you just give the lady her stuff back so we can be done here!" The passenger bay falls silent and still.

The tall, overconfident prick leans forward still grinning like he knows a secret I don't. "Why don't you make me?" he whispers.

Well at least I can say I tried to be civil. He lingers near my face with a wide grin, a mistake he will soon regret because I immediately slam my forehead into his nose. The clown falls to his knees, quickly grabbing his nose as blood begins to flow down the front of his face. His pudgy sidekick takes a few steps toward me but changes his mind when I shoot him a glare.

"You! You broke my damn nose!" the bastard shouts. "You asshole!"

I grab him by his collar, pulling him to his feet and dust off his shoulders. "Now, where did you put this sweet old lady's husband?"

He moves one of his hands away from his face and points to a bag sitting at the feet of his sidekick, who retrieves the ornate urn and slowly brings it to the old lady.

"Good boy!" I say, slapping him on his exposed cheek. "Now get your ass back in line!" I shove him back toward the rest of the passengers.

I walk over to the lady who is holding the urn as if it were a newborn baby. She smiles at me, reaching out to grab my hand and nods. I smile back, feeling like I had just redeemed what was going to be a bad day.

I lead the passengers to the hanger bay where Lora, Nev and Captain Rickard were already waiting. The captain greeted everyone and thanked them for choosing the Idle Confessor for their traveling needs, then he practically pushed them into the skip. When the tall clown and his little friend walk up, Captain Rickard gives me a critical look and I shrug, causing an unexpected smirk on Nev's face. In moments every passenger is loaded and ready to depart, well, all but one. I look around hoping to see the twins one last time before I leave, but they must be busy doing something else. Lora walks up the ramp toward me, winking as she passes and I begin to follow her.

"Hey kid, what are you doing?" Captain Rickard's voice catches my attention.

"I thought I was leaving," I respond, trying to hide my surprise and excitement.

"Well you thought wrong!" he says grinning. "I mean, you were right about the leaving part but you aren't leaving with them."

My excitement turns to dismay at the revelation that I will not be departing the Confessor with the legal cargo but rather with the illegal one. I reluctantly nod my head in acceptance as the ramp of the skip raises up and seals. The skip's engines fire up and lift the vessel with ease, and before long it is a small streak of light shooting toward the surface of Callisto.

I turn toward the captain and Nev, expecting them to be leaving but soon realize that they are waiting for something. The captain seems on edge, not like I have ever seen before. Even when the Coalition was inspecting the ship he seemed calm, but now he just seemed worried. He wasn't the only one; Nev is showing signs of the same.

"What's going on?" I ask, but there is no response. Both are staring intently at a holographic display.

Then a woman's voice comes over the com. "Hey guys, sorry I'm late."

Nev and Captain Rickard let out an exhale. "Hey, you had us a bit worried here. What was the hold up?" Rickard asks.

A few seconds pass when the voice returns. "Aw, did you have to hold Nev's hand again? I'm late cause I had a little problem getting this good-faith gift aboard."

"Good-faith gift!?" the captain says. "There is no such thing."

"Relax, I think it will fit in our group nicely," the voice responds.

"It better not be another animal!" the captain retorts.

There is a significantly longer pause this time. "Oh, would you just stop?! You'll see for yourself in fifteen."

The display closes and Captain Rickard looks around the hanger. "Where the hell are the twins?"

Just like that, as if the captain has summoned them himself, the twins come flying in. "Sorry, sorry we had to fix a faulty plasma relay," Don says.

"Oh yeah, sure! Make it sound all fine and such, but I won't spare them the details of how close we all were to being vaporized!" Ron ripostes.

The twins laugh loudly. "So when will she be here, Cap?" Don asks.

"Little less than fifteen, then we will get the merchandise on the skip and wait for Lora to return form dropping off the kids," the captain says. "Then we get paid, gentlemen."

Nev claps his hands, gaining everyone's attention. "Not to mention we get rid of the stowaway!" He points at me.

"Oh shut it, Nev!" Ron shouts as Don nudges me in my side.

"Everything alright?" he asks.

I look at him realizing that have been silent for the last couple minutes. "Yeah, everything is fine."

But it isn't. I got so hopeful when Rickard didn't let me leave on the passenger skip that a part of me honestly believed I was staying aboard the Confessor.

"So who is this mystery woman?" I ask Don quietly.

Don turns to me and smiles. "You'll find out soon enough."

Man I hate it when he does that. But before I can press the matter, one of the several hanger bay openings begins flashing red as another slightly smaller skip enters the dock and lands. The anticipation and excitement of the Confessor's crew could not be hidden as the skip's ramp slowly lowers to the floor. A beautiful young woman no older than me with flaming red hair, porcelain skin and emerald eyes comes strutting down the ramp, smiling from ear to ear.

"My god!" I mutter, more or less involuntarily.

"I had a feeling you'd say that," Don whispers.

It wasn't the fact that she was absolutely gorgeous that caught me off guard, but rather the fact that I was completely and utterly infatuated with her from the moment I saw her. I have seen many beautiful women before but none that brought me to the brink of paralysis. My heart would not stop racing and my breath was shallow as if Nev kicked me in the gut again. I struggled to restrain my nerves, to control my emotions, but my mind kept racing. It became harder and harder to avoid imagining what her skin would feel like to my touch, the smell of her hair and the taste of her lips. I'm usually not one to indulge silly notions like love at first sight or even love in general, but I would be an idiot to ignore that something inside me yearned for her.

Don grabs me by the shoulder, saving me from my fantasies. "Come on, Cupid. Let me introduce you," he says.

We walk across the hanger deck toward Captain Rickard, Nev, Ron and the mysterious woman. As soon as she notices Don, she runs over and gives him a hug.

"How you doing, doll?" Don asks.

"I'm doing great. Happy to be home" she says with a smile and looks at me. "Who's the greenhorn?" Her tone changes from that of an angel to a slave driver in a fraction of a second.

Don grins. "This is John, He—well he hitched a ride with us back on Titan."

She looked me up and down, pausing every few moments to nod her head, and finally meets my stare with her stunning green eyes.

"Why wasn't he sent planet side with the rest of the kids?" she asks.

I open my mouth to speak but Nev beats me to the point. "Because he is a dirty damn stowaway!" he yells across the hanger.

The look on the flaming-haired woman's face did little to hide her surprise, and yet I could sense that she was a little impressed. "Is that true, did your seriously sneak aboard?"

I simply nod my head and look at the ground. She takes a step toward me. "You can speak, correct?" she whispers.

"Yeah, sometimes very well." I fumble on my words, making it apparent that this is not one of the very well times.

She smirks and looks at Nev. "So why didn't you just kill him?"

What the hell?! Why does everyone immediately think I should have been killed?

"It's complicated," Captain Rickard says before Nev gets a chance to respond. "I'll explain everything on the way to the bridge; I want to hear the details of this deal you set up," he adds, gesturing toward the hanger door.

She nods her head then turns toward the twins. "I got you guys a little present. Go take a look." Then she gazes at me. "And you—well you're probably not going to be here for much longer, but it isn't my style to not introduce myself." She holds out her hand. "My name is Avalyn but everyone calls me Ava. I'm the second in command on this boat."

I reach out steadily and grasp her hand with mine. I can feel a fire growing inside me just from merely touching her, but I suppress it the best I can. "You're the first mate?" I ask, sounding a little more skeptical than I wanted.

Ava's grin disappears and she retracts her hand. "You better remember it," she says in an authoritative voice, then turns and walks to the captain.

I honestly didn't mean to offend her. I can easily chalk that up to me being an idiot. But she is younger than the rest of the crew. I look at Nev who is shaking his head as if he could hear what I was thinking, then he turns and follows the captain and Ava out of the hanger.

"Great first impression, Casanova," Ron says after the hanger door closes.

I shrug. "I blame you guys. You didn't tell me that the first mate was a goddess."

Don scoffs. "We told you that the first mate wasn't Nev. That was enough of a heads up."

"Hardly," I say with a smile. "Now what is this good-faith gift she got you guys?"

CHAPTER TWELVE: THE SOUL BURDENED CONSTRUCT

Ron hustles up the skip's ramp, lets out a yelp of joy and turns toward us with the huge smile on his face. "Guys you're not going to believe this." He runs into the interior of the skip then begins dragging a large capsule out. "It pre-dates the war. I'd say it's at least a hundred and forty years old."

Don and I help Ron set the capsule down on the hanger bay floor. "This is a Syntech!" Don gasps. "And in mint condition!" he adds.

I look at the capsule window. "Is that a man?!"

Ron and Don both laugh. "This is a Synthetic, built by the Syntech Advance Robotics Corporation during the height of the Robotics Era," Ron says.

"No, I've seen Synthetics. They are nothing like this," I argue.

Don shakes his head "Yeah, you've seen modern day Synthetics. They're a mere shadow of what they used to be."

"I can't tell what Generation this one is part of," Ron says, obsessing over the exterior of the capsule.

Don looks at the capsule. "Looks like we'd have to open it up to check the hardware." Don drums on the capsule, looking at us for approval.

"Is that a good idea?" I ask.

“Hell no!” Ron yells, throwing his arms out. "That’s the dumbest idea I’ve heard! I don’t think the captain would take kindly to a rampant droid running amok around his ship!”

Don rolls his eyes. “We don’t know that it is a Gen8 anyways. All we’ve got to do is crack it open, determine what generation it belongs to, then—I don’t know, maybe turn it on,” he finishes in a hurry.

I look back and forth between the two brothers staring each other down. “I’ll be honest, I’m kind of curious, but there has to be a way to ensure it is safe, right?” Ron’s face lightens at the same time as Don’s and they both look at me.

“Right, I have a plan,” Ron says “But let’s get this thing out of here before the captain finds out. He isn’t too fond of Synthetics.”

“So where do we take it then?” I inquire.

Don and Ron exchange looks. “Well according to the capsule it’s a medical droid,” Don says. “Why not the infirmary?”

“When did we get an infirmary?” I say with a smile.

Ron opens his mouth, probably to pose an argument, but after a few seconds he shrugs and helps Don push the capsule.

A few moments later I find myself in an unfamiliar part of the ship. Well, unfamiliar to me at least. The twins can barely hide their excitement as we enter the infirmary and prop the capsule against the operating table.

Don turns to Ron. “Ok, so what’s your plan?”

Ron reaches into his pocket and pulls a pulse revolver out, handing it to me. "You know how to use it, right?" he asks.

I had almost forgotten how heavy these revolvers were. I hadn't shot one since Jurin taught me several months ago. But I'll never forget the feeling of the gun's micro-vibrations coursing through my hand. Then Jurin's lifeless face involuntarily comes to my mind, and I feel myself flinch.

"You alright, bud?" Don says, placing his hand my shoulder.

I jump and turn toward him, his eyes show sincere concern. "No, no I'm fine, really." I tighten my grip on the Pulse Revolver, checking the chamber where the Hygithium power cell was glowing cerulean. I lock it back into place then give Ron a confident nod.

"Alright, here goes nothing," Ron says while turning the locking mechanism. The capsule door springs to life with a loud click then the sound of hissing as air rapidly fills the vacuum sealed container.

The Twins grab either side of the capsule's hatch and remove it revealing the nude synthetic. Everything about this thing was realistic. They even made it look like it was in its mid-forties with veins of silver lining its dark hair and artificial ageing sculpted in its face. Then I hear the twins snicker from behind me.

"Looks like a little something is missing," Don says in a particularly childish tone.

It takes me a minute to realize that I was so concerned admiring its human-like facial features that I didn't notice a major lacking detail.

"Damn, that's depressing!" I laugh as the twins start cackling.

"Poor guy. I guess that isn't included in the basic package," Ron says between bouts of laughter.

Don hits the table with his fist, desperately trying to catch his breath. "I think before we proceed, we ought to get it something to wear," he says breathing hard. "That way it doesn't get too embarrassed when we turn it on."

"Turn it on?" Ron says. "We are not turning it on."

Don gives him a desperate look. "Oh come on Ron, it's in perfect condition."

"No, we agreed that we would only open it, remember?!" Ron retorts.

The twins continue to argue for a few minutes, but I can't keep my eyes off the synthetic. I take a few steps closer as Don begins yelling louder, causing Ron to drum on the table to try and drown him out. Its synthetic skin looks real, so real that I have to touch it. I place the revolver on the operating table beside the capsule and place my hand on its chest. It feels real, cold but real. I poke it a few times then a red light begins to glow under its skin.

"No!" The sound of Ron's voice rings in my ear.

I turn, meeting the twins' stares. "What?!" But they don't respond.

I hesitantly turn around where the Synthetic's eyelids have opened and are staring off into the distance. Oh shit! I reach for the revolver on the table. But just as I am about to grasp the gun, the synthetic begins screaming loudly. I cover my ears and retreat to the twins, who have fear painted on their faces. The door to the infirmary flies open and Captain Rickard and Ava enter, the captain immediately pointing his pulse revolver at the screaming synthetic.

"What the hell did you do!?" he shouts at the twins.

They look at each other, then at me. Ron steps forward. "Sorry, captain. I was curious," he says

"We were curious." Don follows, almost standing between me and the captain.

Why would they try to take the fall for me? They didn't do anything. "No," I say, stepping out from behind the twins. "I did it by mistake," I say in a soft voice, catching the eye of Ava and the glare of Captain Rickard.

The synthetic stops screaming and begins looking around the room, resting its gaze on the captain with his gun still pointed at it. "Oh dear, did I do something?" it says in a soft, calming voice.

Everybody including myself is rendered speechless as the synthetic turns to the rest of the infirmary. "I presume this is my new place of employment?" it says, taking a few steps forward.

"Stop there!" the captain shouts.

The synthetic turns to him. "Oh my. I apologize. Where, are my manners?" It looks down, gasps and attempts to cover itself. "Oh goodness, I am not decent and there is a lady amongst you. May I have something to cover myself?"

Ron slowly walks to the cabinet behind us and grabs a medical coat, then hesitantly gives it to the synthetic. Don places his hand on the captain's wrist and lowers his gun.

"Aw, much better," it says. "Now which one of you is the captain of this fine ship?" Everybody points at Captain Rickard almost simultaneously. "Very good. Hello," it says, taking several steps forward toward the group with its hand extended. "I am Synteck Model STG8MDA1."

"I don't shake hands with synthetics," the captain says coldly.

The synthetic slowly retracts its hand and looks at the rest of us. "Hello, are you all also medical technicians?" it asks.

"Umm, no," Ava says. "What was the last thing you remember?"

The synthetic thinks for a bit. "I was working in a hospital on Earth. My dear friend Robert had just received a message that upset him. He came in and told me that I would have to be deactivated for reasons he would not explain, but he kept telling me sorry."

"That must have been right after the mass recall," Don says.

"We need you to do a full diagnostic of all your systems," Ron states, taking a few steps forward.

"Don't be ridiculous. I did a full diagnostic last week and everything was fine," the synthetic said in a surprisingly irritated tone.

"That was a long time ago; you've been off for almost a century and a half," I say, almost sounding sympathetic.

The synthetic's eyes widen at this revelation then go blank. "Beginning self-diagnostics, estimated completion time: five minutes."

Everyone lets out a breath. "What the hell were you thinking bringing that thing onto my ship!?" Captain Rickard barks at Ava.

"I thought it'd be a nice addition to our marry bunch of miscreants!" Ava yells back in a cynical voice. "How was I supposed to know these idiots would turn the damn thing on?"

"Hey!" the twins, who are now inspecting every inch of the synthetic, yell.

"I meant it in the best way possible, boys," Ava says with a smile. "Besides does it really matter anyways? The thing is harmless. You need to get over your ridiculous fear of robots; it's not like it's a Gen8," she says in a spirited tone.

"Guys!" Ron shouts over Ava. "It's a Gen8!"

Captain Rickard lifts his gun again. "Are you sure?"

"What the hell does that mean?!" I yell, catching everyone's attention.

"Fifty percent remaining," the synthetic says in a monotone mechanical voice.

Ron rubs his temples. "The Gen8s' are the reason for the mass recall; they had issues with their personality cores malfunctioning, causing unwanted behaviors."

"So, as a precaution all the Syntechs were recalled and subsequently destroyed, presumably," Don says while pointing at the synthetic. "Then strict laws were established governing robotics and Syntech Advance Robotics was broken apart and bought by other companies.

"Ok, so what does that mean?" I ask.

"Twenty-five percent remaining." The synthetic voice fills the room.

"It means we've got to destroy this thing," Rickard says emotionlessly.

"Now hold on, captain," Don says, holding up his arms. "Not all the Gen8s' exhibited these flaws."

"Is that a risk you're willing bet your life on?" Rickard responds, glancing at Don.

"Yes," I say, assertively gaining the captain's attention.

"Your opinion doesn't matter; you're halfway out the door," he says in a bitter tone.

He was right. I am on my way out. "I'll take him, then." Maybe not my best idea but I'm stuck with it now. "I'll take him—it when I leave," I repeat with a little more confidence.

Captain Rickard lowers his gun and turns toward me "If you want to put your ass on the line for this thing then fine, but as long as it is on my ship it stays locked in here. Do I make myself clear?!" He looks around the room almost hoping someone would contest his authority.

"Ten percent remaining," the synthetic says.

"Great. Ava!" The captain's raspy voice makes her jump.

"Yes," she says in a high pitched voice.

"Stay here and make sure this thing doesn't kill anyone," Rickard says while walking toward the door.

"Yes, sir," she responds, regaining her cheeky undertone.

We wait in silence for a few moments after Captain Rickard left the room before we start to breathe again. "Man that was a close one." Don's voice finally breaks the silence.

"Great going, kid. Looks like you got yourself a souvenir for the journey," Ron says, slapping me on the back.

I ignore the sting as I meet Ava's stare from across the room. "You're kind of ballsy, you know that?" she says.

"Uh, yeah something I picked up from growing up on Titan, I guess." I fail to sound interesting and suave, but she grins and looks at the synthetic.

"All this fuss over something so weak looking," she says while shaking her head.

"I do hope you're not talking about me?" Everyone freezes as the synthetic begins talking. "I have the result of my self-diagnostic, I apologize for the wait." Don slowly nods his head. "Right, for the most part everything seems normal. There are a few parts that need a little adjusting, but I am more than capable of taking care of my own maintenance. Oh my, where did the captain go?"

"He had some other business to attend to," Ava says. "But I am the first mate if you have any questions."

"Well this is highly irregular, but it will have to do," the synthetic says. "Might I ask if I could have permission to interface with the ships data network?" it finishes.

"Why do you need access to the ships network?" Ava asks.

"Ah, excuse my rudeness. I wish to catch up on the last hundred and forty years I've missed, of course. If that is at all possible," the synthetic says. "It will also update my medical knowledge; you cannot imagine how excited I am to see how much we've learned in the last century." It finishes in an unnerving human-like tone.

Ava ponders for a moment. "Yeah, sure. Have at it," she says.

"Actually, that is probably not the best—" Ron begins, but his protest is too late. The synthetic has already begun downloading all the history of the last hundred plus years.

"Well shit—" Don says.

"What the matter?" Ava and I ask almost simultaneously.

Ron looks over at us. "A hundred and forty years! Did you happen to think about what major events have happened in the last hundred and forty years!?"

"How about a hundred years of bloody war, not to mention what has happened to his—its kind," Don adds. "These things malfunction cause they were made to feel, to understand human emotion, what do you think is going to happen when he instantly feels all the death and loss of the last hundred and forty years?" he finishes.

It was a realization that both Ava and I didn't think about. The last time this thing was on was during the end of the Golden Era, when the solar system was whole and peace had reigned for at least two-hundred years. The synthetic stood rigid in the room for a few more minutes. It seemed to take longer than it should have but just as I was about accept the fact that this thing was locked up it begins screaming and moving back toward the wall. Ava draws her pulse gun, ready to put it out of its misery when it just stops and falls to the floor.

"What the hell!?" I exhale.

"It must have shut itself down," Don says.

"It can do that?" asks Ava.

"It isn't supposed too," Ron explains.

All of us take a step closer to the synthetic. "So what now?" I ask.

"Beats me," Don responds, reaching down to roll the synthetic onto it's back and dusts off its face. Suddenly its eyes open, causing us to jump.

"Oh, I'm sorry. I didn't mean to scare you," the synthetic says while lifting itself to its feet. "My word, did I do it again?" it adds.

"Do what again?" I ask.

"My dear friend Robert installed a failsafe within my personality matrix that ensures I will not malfunction," It explains. "If I ever become encumbered by traumatic events, I go through a hard reboot. This allows me to process the information faster and in turn 'deal with it' as Robert put it."

"This Robert sounded like a smart man," Don states.

"Oh yes he is—was." The synthetic frowns for a second. "He was the designer of almost all of my generation," It finishes.

Ron's mouth falls open "You mean to tell me that your friend was Robert Brigman, the founder of Syntech Advance Robotics!"

"Indeed I do," the synthetic responds.

The twins and I spend the rest of the afternoon inspecting the synthetic and talking mostly about what it was like to have been around during the Golden Age. The synthetic was more than willing to indulge our curiosity, almost happy even. Then before long we are done with our inspection and just talk for hours. The way the synthetic talks seems antiquated compared to how most people talk in today's age. We explained how it would have to be locked into the room while it was on this ship, per the captain's orders and it seemed fine, almost as if it was just happy to be on and functioning again.

I take a look at the time and yawn. "Damn it's almost midnight."

The twins look up and chuckle, then frown and look at me. "You'd better get some sleep. You've got a big day tomorrow," they say.

I nod my head and shake their hands, probably for the last time, then look at the source of our attention for the last several hours. "I'll see you tomorrow Bot-Boy."

"Actually, I was wondering if you all could call me Thomas," the synthetic says in hopeful tone.

Don looks at it curiously. "You wish to go by a name?"

"Yes, well, I have found that people are more comfortable around me if I go by a name," it says.

The three of us look at each other and shrug. "Alright Thomas, have a good night," I say with a chuckle, surprised that calling a synthetic by name came so naturally.

By the time I leave the infirmary Ava had been long gone for several hours and although I was half hoping to bump into her on the way to my cot, I honestly didn't expect to. So I trudged wearily down the corridor thinking about what was going to transpire the following day. The notion of selling the drugs to all kinds of low-lifes like Cheever West caused a sour taste to percolate in my mouth. "Damn-it all," I mutter aloud for forcefully having to contribute to a system I loathed. But really, what was I to do?

"Do you talk to yourself often?" A soft familiar voice caught my attention.

I turn to meet those same beautiful emerald eyes that have been engrained into my mind. "Oh, hey. What are you doing awake?" I state in the most masculine voice I can muster.

"I can't find my cat, Gremlin. Have you seen her?" she says. "I swear, if Nev did something to her I will—" but she stops. "What are you smiling at?"

"Nothing. I just, well Grem has been staying with me for the last few days," I respond casually.

"Well, that cheating bitch!" Ava says with a laugh. "So which room is yours?"

I pause for a moment. "Room? I don't have one."

"What do you mean you—Nev!" she growls "So where have you been sleeping?"

"On the catwalk above the cargo hold." I look down, trying to hide my embarrassment.

"Well that can't be comfortable," she says with a smirk. "Why don't we go get your stuff and move it to one of these rooms? You deserve to sleep in a bed at least once before you leave."

Every part of me wants to scream yes, but when I open my mouth I say, "No, you really don't have to do that." I'm an idiot.

Ava frowned. "I wasn't asking and besides, I want to see Gremlin, remember?"

She walks past me emitting an aura of stubborn resolve and I have little to no option but to follow her. For the most part the short walk to my poor excuse of a bed feels long and awkward. I attempt to make small talk but quickly find that I can't say anything that won't make me out to be weird, creepy or both. So we walk in silence with nothing but the hum of the Confessor filling the space.

"Why are you here, John?" By this time I was used to the question, but Ava's query was completely unexpected.

"I thought the captain told you everything," I responded, slowing down my pace.

Ava stops and turns to face me. "Right, he told me you snuck aboard the ship and then the Coalition intercepted and searched the Confessor for someone with your description." Her eyes didn't hide a bit of animosity toward me. "And the Captain can't seem to figure out why we didn't get busted for the absurd amounts of illegally obtained Methozeeklor we have in our cargo-hold at this very moment." She continues while pacing back and forth. "The captain seems to think you are hiding something, something that you, according to the Captain, refuse to tell him. So, John—why are you here?!" she finishes with a huff and an intense stare.

Hundreds of words flood my mind but none form into a comprehensible sentence except for one. "I—I don't know who I am." I look at the ground and retrieve the scrap of cloth from my pocket. "This is all I have that could link me to my past." I hand the piece to Ava and she looks it over for a moment. "I swear to you, I'm a nobody. I don't know what the CF was looking for, but it wasn't me."

Ava hands the scrap of cloth back to me and looks into my eyes. "Come on," she says in a sober tone and begins walking down the corridor again.

We reach my bed several moments later where Grem has been lying about probably all day. Ava calls out and Grem rolls off my pillow and begins meowing incessantly. Ava picks her up and begins scratching her behind the ear, causing Grem to purr loudly. I lean against the railing and smile, realizing it has been well over a week since they've last seen each other.

Ava looks at me "Thanks," she says in an unpolished fashion. "For, you know, watching her and keeping her company," she finishes.

"Grem found me. I just woke up and there she was staring at me." We both laugh and an awkward silence fills the space between us.

"So," Ava starts "why don't you grab your crap—stuff and we'll get you a proper bed," she finishes uncomfortably.

I push myself off the railing and quickly grab the few belongings I have. We walk back to the crew quarters. Ava leads me to one of the many rooms that line the corridor, stopping at a door where we exchange awkward farewells. I enter the room and almost choke on the stale air; it is obvious that no one has been living here for a long time. As I sit on the bed, the springs squeal under me. It is still hard but better than the box I had before. I lay down, slamming my head against the pillow. My eyes are heavy and before long I'm slipping away. The image of Ava and her beautiful eyes, her wavy rosy hair and fiery disposition dominate my thoughts. Before long the endless tide of my subconscious inundates my mind and sleep takes me, but there are no dreams—not this time.

Chapter Thirteen: The Last of the Galilean Moons

Callisto, the furthest Galilean Moon from Jupiter was discovered in 1610 by Galileo Galilei, hence the moniker. It was named after one of Zeus's many adulterous lovers and it's one of the three governing bodies of the Sovereign Republic. Of its three major colonies, Pilot is the first and by far the largest of the other two. Also, Pilot was the second colony established in the Frontier with Galileo, Europa's largest colony, being the first and most populated of the Frontier. Every eight Terranean Standard Years the 'Big Three,' Europa, Callisto and Ganymede, vote for a new legislative congress as well as three executive heads—one for each moon. By doing this it ensures that each moon always possesses a third of the power, unlike the United Earths of Sol, which have one centralized government on Earth.

"Hey stowaway, quit screwing around and get your ass over here!" Nev's voice pulls my attention from the holo-display hovering above my forearm.

"Yeah, yeah I'm coming," I respond, closing the holographic screen with the wave of my hand, then grabbing a canister of Zeek from a crate and walking it up the skip's ramp.

The captain and Ava were already aboard checking the skip's systems with Thomas tied to the seat by several carbon straps, its face showing a mixture of disdain and confusion. Nev was standing in the middle of the walkway, his arms dangling from some hand loops attached to the ceiling of the skip and a grin on his face. I place the canister on top of the growing pile and step to the side as the twins push a cart into the mouth of the skip's opening with a dozen or so canisters neatly piled on. We begin unloading them and I notice the twins don't seem like their normal flamboyant selves. For the most part everyone is quiet except for Thomas, who keeps asking to be untied and explaining how this was not in the least bit ok.

We finish unloading the cart and the twins head down the ramp to grab another load as Lora enters the hanger. She still looks tired from the late return after dropping off the passengers, but even so her professional disposition isn't lacking. I greet her with a smile and she nods, walking past me, then up to Nev who is still occupying the majority of the skip's walkway. Nev stares at her for a few seconds as if he is expecting some sort of payment in order for him to move. Without a single word Lora slaps him, playfully, but enough to make him move. The Twins and I begin laughing as Lora struts past Nev, whose face is priceless.

Several minutes later every gram of illicit merchandise is neatly place aboard the skip and ready to brighten someone's day. I let out a groan and look at the twins who are nursing their lower backs.

"Youth isn't what it used to be, huh boys?" I say with a smile.

Ron scowls. "You hear that Don? 'Youth isn't what it used to be' says the one with an abundance of it—little brat," he finishes with a sarcastic grin.

Then the silence returns as the moment all three of us are dreading finally arrives. I look down at my feet trying to void direct eye contact, but then I feel a hand on my shoulder.

"Chin up kid, call me crazy but I have a feeling we will see each other again," Don says.

I look up to meet their stares and oddly I feel the same as if we were destined to see each other again in a weird kind of way. The thought of this lifts some of my grief and I feel better already.

I smile and extend my hand. "Well then, I'll see you guys later." The Twins smirk and return the gesture.

I turn and head up the ramp, meeting Captain Rickard on his way out. I don't expect much from him as he passes by but to my surprise he whispers a very faint "Good luck, kid."

Granted, he would never admit to such a thing but I think he was starting to warm up to me. I reach the bowels of the skip and sit by the increasingly frustrated Thomas, who has now resorted to threatening us with very long-winded written letters that it will surely be sending to the Organization of Mistreated Robot Workers about the poor conditions it is being kept in. Nev loses his composure on that one, almost crying from laughing so hard.

Ava takes a seat right across from me, and at first I don't realize I am staring at her until her gaze meets mine. I swear, no matter how smooth you are, you cannot play off the fact that you are caught ogling someone. I quickly turn my head away like I had seen a monster dart between the Zeek canisters, but I can see from my peripherals that she has a slight smirk on her face.

"Alright everyone, you ready for this?" Lora says as Nev straps in beside her.

The skip begins vibrating intensely and I can feel it lifting off the deck. I grab the armrest, catching the attention of Ava who seems overly calm. I force myself to relax right as the vibrating stops and the feeling of weightlessness comes over my body. We must have just left the Confessor's artificial gravity; my arms begin floating on their own, forcing me to hold them down. Ava lifts one of her eyebrows and I realize that I am beaming without knowing it. I ignore her judgmental expressions for the moment and instead bring up a display showing the vast beauty of space. It has only been several minutes and the Idle Confessor looks like a speck of dust.

Then suddenly the skip lurches to one side, whipping me out my thoughts; I grab the armrest so hard I can feel my hands ache. "This is your first time, isn't it?" Ava's voice pierces the veil of panic and doubt.

I look at her, still tightly holding the armrest. "Uh, what?!" I stammer.

"Your first drop? Back into atmosphere—" Ava clarifies.

"No, well yeah. I mean—" I force out awkwardly.

She smiles. "This is completely normal."

The skip lurches again and I can hear Nev curse. "Well, considering you're completely fine, I hope it is normal." My voice boasts an involuntary quiver.

"Pteromerhanophobia," Thomas chimes in over the skip's growing whine.

"What?" Ava and I ask almost at the same time.

"Fear of flying, that's what it means," Thomas adds with a charismatic smile.

"I don't have Pteromer—whatever," I argue as the skip makes another lurch and a loud buzzing noise starts from the cockpit area.

"Pteromerhanophobia," Thomas corrects. "My current assessments of your vitals tell me differently. You are displaying symptoms similar to an anxiety attack no doubt caused by an extreme fear of crashing." It continues. "Rightfully so as the chances of surviving a crash at this altitude are 0.001%."

"Thomas," I start. "In the future, please keep those kinds of facts to your damn self."

Thomas's head tilts a bit. "I apologize, did I say something inappropriate?"

"Don't worry about—" There's another hard lurch and this time one of the zeek canisters slips free of the carbon straps that were holding it still.

Without second thought Ava unbuckles and grabs the canister. The skip heaves again, causing Ava to fly across the walkway and into me. I grab her, unintentionally, around the waist and she glares at me.

"Sorry!" I let go and Ava scrambles over to her seat still cradling the canister.

"Five minutes till we reach the first drop site." Lora's voice bleeds in over the now screaming skip engines. I can feel that we must be getting close because I can sense an increase in gravity. "Looks like we have a lot of turbulence coming up. Hold on guys," Lora adds right as the skip begins shaking violently and jerking back and forth.

"Oh, God!" I gasp, slamming my eyes shut and squeezing the armrest even harder.

"John, what is your favorite color?" Ava's oddly timed question throws me for a loop.

I look at her; she is still showing a little frustration for the accidental grab in her eyes. "Uh, I guess red," I say hesitantly.

"No way! So is mine," she responds with a smile.

The skip shudders some more causing Ava to squeeze the canister tighter. "Why do you guys do it?" I ask while staring at the canister.

Ava looks down then back at me. "It keeps us alive."

"Growing up on Titan has taught me that Zeek does more damage than good," I say coldly.

Ava's eyes narrow. "What are you trying to say?"

"Two minutes till rendezvous," Lora's voice chimes in.

"Nothing, just." I stumble on my words. "Its bad stuff is all."

"So you think we're bad people?" Ava's voice overflows with contempt.

"No, I didn't," I try to explain before I make a bigger ass of myself.

"I'll have you know," Ava's voice stops me in mid-sentence "this drug you hate so much has saved millions and if it wasn't for misinformed people like you, then it would be a hell of a lot easier for those who need it to get it!"

"I didn't mean to offend you," I plead.

Ava's eyes are like lasers burning a hole through me. "Also, the majority of the drugs we run are practically given away to the free clinics here in Pilot. The rest we have to sell to the bad guys just to break even!"

I resist the urge to speak; nothing good would come of it anyway. I resolve to sit in awkward silence, which isn't so bad because we have already begun landing at the predetermined meeting point. Ava unlatches her harness and checks the Zeeklor, replacing the rogue canister where it belonged then extending the ramp. A gust of cool and refreshing air rushes in. I had forgotten how stale the air was in the Confessor after the first day of our journey; even then it was better than the stench of New Horizon. But here in Pilot the air was almost sweet and the view was breathtaking. We were perched atop a remote cliff overlooking the city. It was like nothing I had ever seen or even imagined before.

Fields upon fields of multicolored flowers rolled through the colony as transports darted through the air, heading to unknown destinations. The layout of the city was very similar to New Horizons, except everything seemed cleaner, new and most of all safe.

Nev smacks me on the back of the head, gaining my attention. He motions toward the canisters and mouths the words 'move it' without making a sound. I immediately start loading the Zeek onto a cart as four smaller transport crafts land several meters from the skip. Ava begins waving and shaking hands as if she was greeting old friends.

"Five minutes!" Lora yells to us as we wheel the cart down the ramp toward the group.

Ava grabs a canister and opens it for the four individuals to see. "As promised, one-hundred and sixty kilos of pure Methozeekloriforim powder."

One of the finely dressed men pulls out a device and takes a scoop of Zeek powder. A few seconds later he nods to the other three. "Test confirms, it's of good quality," he says in a flat voice.

Nev and I begin unloading the cart into the four vehicles with twenty canisters per vehicle. It doesn't take long before we are wheeling the cart back up the ramp. Lora has already begun ramping up the engines. Ava finishes shaking the gentlemen's hands and promptly returns the skip.

"That went smoothly," I say in an optimistic tone.

Ava glances at me then the remaining forty canisters. "If only the next one was so easy."

I open my mouth to inquire more about her comment when Nev shoves a duffle bag into my stomach "Here, put this on," he demands.

I let out a gasp of air. "What is it?"

Nev gives me a critical look and I proceed to shut my mouth and open the duffle bag. In it is a densely woven suit with a helmet and the letters HECS embroidered on the left leg.

"It's a Hazardous Environment Combat Suit," Ava says, while slipping into her own. "It'll keep you from freezing to death; the next rendezvous is outside the Pilot's protective dome," she finishes.

"Among other things," Nev says with a grunt.

"Current surface temp is negative one-hundred and sixty degrees Celsius," Lora says while looking at her display. "We will reach the destination in ten."

I finish squeezing into the HECS, then place the helmet over my head and lock it in place. My senses are muffled at first but then the suit begins to sync with my Aug. Information rapidly scrolls along my heads up display and the suit contours to my body as a tingling sensation runs through my arms and to my fingers. I look down realizing that the suit allows my fingers to feel through it as if I wasn't wearing gloves at all. I reach out and touch the bulk head; the sensation is amazing, then the words 'HECS to BICS Synchronization Complete' rolls across the visor.

"Wow this is awesome," I say out loud.

Ava looks at me and smiles. "Well your mic is working fine, how about you guys?"

Nev and Lora's voices fill my helmet almost simultaneously. "Good," Ava says standing in front of me. "Alright greenhorn, listen. This suit is made of nano carbon-fiber tubes, it is resistant to both ballistic and pulse rounds but it won't make you invincible. Also the suit acts as a sort of exoskeleton, slightly augmenting your physical strength. Don't get cocky though. This is an older model. You understand?" she finishes while tugging on the front of my suit.

I nod my head, noticing Nev assembling a pulse rifle. "Are we expecting trouble?" I ask.

"You can never be too careful," Nev says while handing Ava a pulse repeater and a pistol. "And those that can be too careful can't afford the consequences," he finishes with a grin.

"Got anything in there for me?" I ask, eyeing the gun case behind Nev.

Nev glowers at me. "What, like a gun!?"

"No, a hug, genius!" I retort.

He starts laughing. "You know what, you snide little shit? I wouldn't give you a gun even if my life depended on it," he says back.

"Can it, ladies!" Ava yells. "We've got to be professionals, damn-it, or these people will eat us alive!" She glares at us. "Get the Zeek loaded. The faster we're done the better."

"What about me?" says Thomas, who had been sitting quietly for so long that I had almost forgotten about him.

Nev looks at the synthetic. "What about you?" he says in a sarcastic voice.

Thomas looks around at everyone "Do I get a suit as well?" it asks.

"Why would you need a suit?" Ava responds. "You're not vulnerable to the cold like we are."

"You are quite right; however, I am very susceptible to high velocity projectiles," Thomas says with human-like apprehension.

"See—" Nev starts "this is why I don't like your kind. You're walking hardware with notions of self-preservation. Shit gives me the willies," he finishes with a shiver.

"Five minutes till rendezvous." Lora's voice reaches back to us.

Ava checks the chamber of her pulse pistol. "Sorry Thomas, but we don't have another suit and you are staying in that chair until we drop you and John off," she says while holstering the pistol. "You understand, it's for the best?" she finishes.

Thomas shows an uncanny look of sad content, then nods. "For the best," it repeats, almost like a chant.

The skip begins shaking again, forcing me to grab one of the loops hanging from the ceiling. Nev is still calibrating his pulse rifle with its blue hue changing in intensity, He looks up at me and grins excitedly. "Like what you see stowaway?" he says, grabbing his crotch. I shake my head, silently mouthing the words 'Fuck you' ostentatious enough so he can clearly see. He scoffs and returns to calibrating his rifle when the skip stops shaking enough for me to finish placing the remaining forty canisters of Zeeklor on the cart. Ava was not exaggerating when she said the suit augmented my strength because I lifted the entire eighty kilo pallet of Zeeklor with little to no effort and placed it on the cart with a satisfying thud. I look around to see if anyone noticed, but apparently I'm the only one that thought it was an amazing feat. I sit down across from Ava, who is carefully staring at a holographic screen. Her left leg is fidgeting and her overall stature seems tense unlike the cool composure that she usually vaunts.

"Two minutes!" Lora shouts. "Preliminary scans show we are the first ones here."

Nev stands up and looks at the monitor then back at Ava, but she is still staring at the screen hovering above her forearm.

"Everything alright?" I ask.

“Difficult to say.” Ava responds, not looking up from the display. “They should have been here by now.”

I bring up my own display, looking at the desolate ice wasteland that makes up the majority of Callisto’s un-colonized landscape. “What does that mean?”

“Could mean everything or nothing. Either way we need to decide to abort or wait," Ava says in a tense tone.

“No, no, no. We’re not waiting on these guys," Nev says. “I say we leave now. It could be a trap.”

I look at Nev then Ava. The silence is maddening. Then several loud buzzing sounds emit form the cockpit. “Incoming!” Lora yells as the skip begins shuddering violently. “It’s another skip—looks like they’re landing. I think it’s them," she says.

Nev looks back at Ava and shrugs. Ava closes the display with a flick. “Take us in but don’t land. I want to be in and out as fast of possible.”

I feel the lightness in my stomach as we descend at an astonishing rate, stopping just a few meters from the ground. Ava, Nev and I line up along the back of the skip I squeeze the handles of the cart when I feel a hand on my shoulder. I look back seeing that it is Nev’s hand. He doesn’t look at me but his eyes are focused and hollow as if he was staring through the skip and beyond that.

“Keep your cool, stowaway," he says in a low voice.

What does this mean? Nev has never acted like this toward me. I nod my head and he removes his hand. Ava hits the ramp control and in seconds a bone chilling gust fills the skip. In front of us, about fifteen meters away, are three well-armed and intimidating looking people. I feel a slight push on my back and I begin walking down the ramp with the cart of drugs leading the way.

CHAPTER FOURTEEN: THE GHOSTS OF CALLISTO

I don't quite know what I was expecting when I stepped down on Callisto's raw surface. Although it looks just like the snow I have read about countless times, it isn't soft under my steps but rather jagged and rough. The cart struggles to stay steady as I push it toward the three armed people. Ava walks ahead of Nev and me and holds her hand up letting me know to stop. She looks at the three individuals and clears her throat.

"One of you three is Vek?" she says confidently.

Arguably the largest of the three already enormous men looks around at his companions. "Honey, with a mouth like that you can call me anything you want," I assume Vek says with a chuckle.

"Charming," Ava responds in a flat tone, grabbing one of the canisters of Zeek from the cart. "Here, test it; I assure you it's pure."

Vek takes the canister from Ava and hands it to one of his men who runs back to their skip. He then looks us over stopping every now and then before finally resting his gaze on me. "It shouldn't take long, but you guys seem like you're in a hurry," he says leaning over to look at our skip still steadily hovering several meters from the ground.

"We have a few more things to do after this," Ava says.

Vek continues to stare at me. "Like what?" he asks. Ava opens her mouth to answer but Vek holds up his arm. "I was asking you," he says to me.

I look at Ava and Nev but both are doing a damn good job of remaining calm. I don't know Vek but I can tell that he is a killer, someone who enjoys screwing with people. "Business," I respond.

"What kind of business?" Vek's voice sounds like he is starting to get irritated.

I think hard for a moment about what to say, I have dealt with people like this before back on Titan. They are the types of people that thrive on intimidating others. "The kind of business that's none of yours." The line rattles off a little more acidic than I had meant for.

Vek takes a step closer to me. Although I can't see his face because of his tinted visor I can tell he is staring right into my eyes. I can feel the tension mounting but unexpectedly he begins laughing. "I'm just messing with you, kid," he says, punching me hard on the shoulder. I ignore the pain; I can't show weakness—not to this man. The guard returns from the skip.

"Looks good boss," he says, throwing Vek the canister.

Vek touches his helmet and his visor clears revealing his face. His eyes are completely black with only a blue florescent ring for irises; they are bionic and undoubtedly far more advanced than any biological eye. He looks at each of us, gauging our reactions. His light skin is covered in deep scars with a wisp of black hair dangling in his face. "Good, good," he starts in an upbeat tone. "Why don't you have your little friend here go and unload it on our boat while we talk price," he says pointing at his skip behind him.

"There is nothing to talk about. We agreed on five-hundred-thousand, no less," Ava responds.

Vek's smile fades. "Yeah, well I think we can agree on a lower price," he says "Something more in the two-hundred range."

Ava looks at Nev then back at Vek. "This is a waste of my damn time; if you're not serious then we'll leave." She gestures to me and I begin pulling the cart back toward our skip. But before I get far one of Vek's men grabs the cart.

"Hey what the h—?!" I turn to yell at the guy but the sight of his pulse rifle pointed at my face renders me silent.

Ava draws her pulse repeater, but Vek is already on her forcing the repeater up under her chin. "Now that is no way to negotiate," Vek says in a calm voice, sliding his hand along her body. Nev has his rifle pointed at them. "Tell your dog to lower his weapon nice and slow," he commands.

Ava nods at Nev who reluctantly lowers the rifle as the other guard takes it from him. "Very good," Vek says while groping Ava even more; the sight of it makes me want to kill him in the most painful way I can imagine. "Now tell your pilot to land and come out here."

Ava tries to pull her head away from Vek but he holds her still. "Lora," she starts hesitantly. "Land the skip and come here."

"Unarmed!" Vek hisses, yanking Ava's head back.

"Unarmed, Lora—" she adds in a painful tone. There was no response; Lora was of course watching everything helplessly on the skip's monitors.

The skip lands with a thud and the engines wheeze with relief. Then Lora walks out slowly with her hands up.

"Is there anyone else on the skip!?" Vek says, pulling Ava's head back.

I can hear her groan under the pressure. "No!" she shouts.

Vek smiles. "Now this is better, don't you agree?" He throws his free arm up. "Let me tell you what is about to happen. This piece of shit." He points at me. "Is going to unload the Zeek. Then after I'm going to beat him for being a smart ass." Vek glares at me. "Then I may take this fine piece of ass back to my skip for a little private negotiating." Vek laughs and continues to fondle Ava, pushing me over the edge.

"Knock it off!" I shout.

Vek's smile disappears and he turns toward me. "What, did you say?"

"If you touch her again, I'm going to fucking kill you!" The words flow out of my mouth faster than my mind can keep up.

Vek's face twists. "You believe the balls on this kid?" he says to one of the guards. "Your boyfriend doesn't like it when I touch you." He runs his hand along Ava's neck.

I take a step toward him but his guards are already on me forcing me to my knees. Nev and Lora move closer, only to stop after Vek discharges several pulse rounds into the air. "Now hold on!" Vek yells. "You apparently need to be reminded of who's in charge!" he continues to shout, whipping Ava about like a rag doll. "I'll start with the hero here," he says pointing the repeater at me.

Once again, I'm on the wrong end of a gun; just this time I'm sure Vek isn't going to hesitate. Damn my mouth. I lower my head and close my eyes as Ava pleads for Vek to stop. The snap of the pulse repeater echoes through the frozen wasteland. A few seconds pass before I realized I wasn't shot and I gather the courage to open my eyes. I look up realizing that Thomas has intercepted the pulse round intended to kill me. The synthetic stagers for a moment, regaining his stance then looks back at me and smiles.

"Thomas?" I mumble, both out of shock and appreciation.

The middle of his chest was split open and burnt with a light blue fluid slowly trickling out. "For the best," he says to me then looks back at Vek who is still surprised by what has just happened.

Vek yanks Ava's head back again. "I thought you said there was no one else!" he growls and punches her in the stomach and she falls to the ground. Then Vek kicks her across the frozen terrain. He looks at Thomas who is still standing between us.

"And what the hell kind of a Synthetic are you?" he demands. Thomas says nothing and Vek takes a few steps toward him. "Did you hear me scrap-bag?" he whispers.

Thomas turns his head to meet Vek's stare. "I won't allow you to kill my friends," Thomas says.

Vek smiles shoving his fingers into Thomas's chest cavity still oozing with blue liquid. "Does your kind feel pain?" he asks.

Thomas looks down at his chest where ice crystals are starting to form around the wound. "Our programming delineates damage as a threat to our service life and our sensors notify us when we sustain an injury, in a way that is the closest we come to fear and pain, with one major difference," Thomas finishes.

"And what's that?" Vek says with a scoff.

Thomas grabs Vek's hand shoving it further into his body. "We aren't crippled by fear and pain."

Vek immediately drops his gun and attempts to pull his hand free but Thomas is more than strong enough to hold Vek still. The guards that were holding me down rush to their boss's aid, allowing Nev and I to attack them.

"Lora!" Nev shouts. "Get the skip!"

Without question, Lora begins running for the shuttle. By then I was on top of one of the guards using all the strength I could to repeatedly slam his head into the solid ice over and over again until he stopped moving. I stumble to my feet, grab one of the pulse rifles from the ground and point it at Vek who had finally freed himself from Thomas.

"Come on kid, you can't kill me!" Vek taunts, waving his hands around. Nev is still fighting the other guard and Lora has just reached the skip. Ava, though, hasn't moved since Vek kicked her. I shuffle toward her, ensuring to keep my eyes on Vek.

"Ava!" I yell "Ava! You ok?" There is no answer, so I continue to move toward her.

Vek starts smiling manically when I finally reach her and begin nudging her with my foot. "Hey, come on." She begins to move and I let out a much needed exhale, but my joy is cut short but Vek's laughter.

"You're an idiot boy," he says.

I point the rifle at him as Ava attempts to stand. "A lot of talk for a guy who is about to die," I retort.

"Die? No you've got it all wrong; see I brought backup and you didn't." Vek says with an annoying amount of confidence.

Before I could fully comprehend what Vek meant, I feel a tug on my arm. I look at Ava whose eyes show nothing but dismay.

"Put the gun down and slowly turn around!" a voice shouts from behind me.

I throw the rifle on the ground without a second thought and gradually raise my hands, turning to see four of Vek's well-armed men standing there.

One of them pushes me to my knees. I can feel the cold from the icy ground seeping through my HEC Suit. Vek is pacing back and forth in front of us like a dog ready to attack.

"John." Ava's voice pulls my attention from the mad dog. Her eyes show resolve that one only gets through extreme discipline. "I'm sorry John," she says, losing a little bit of her practiced composure.

I force a smile and shrug as Nev gets thrown to the ground beside me. He looks at me with the same look of resolve, not from self-discipline but more of a resolve to kill every one of these bastards. I share the same sentiment. He nods and somehow I feel a little better. Then Lora hits the ground beside Nev. She lays her head on his shoulder and wraps her arm around his. Her face is pale and her eyes are red with tears. Then finally Thomas is placed beside Ava. Frost is starting to accumulate on his body and he has begun twitching, probably a sign the chest damage is starting to take its toll.

"Thank you, Thomas," I say, loud enough for him to hear.

"You're welcome," he responds—I just realized that I started calling it a he.

"Ladies and gentlemen, are you ready?" Vek's voice catches our attention. "For the most part we will try to aim for non-vital parts, that way you last longer—no need to thank me." His arrogant voice infuriates me. Why didn't I kill him when I had the chance?

I feel Ava lean against me as Vek orders his men to aim. A chill runs down my spine and I force myself to look beyond the firing squad. First the glacial mountains catch my gaze as they gleam perfectly flawless like that have for millennia. Then Jupiter, its massive body covering the sky, seemingly near enough to touch but actually so far away. Amazing, how could I have possibly missed this? That I might have left this existence without seeing such a wonder, this chaotic display of nature and yet a scene of serenity. I feel Ava grip my forearm, one last warm embrace before oblivion. I look at her and smile. Things could always be worse. I could be alone.

A single pulse round echoes through the canyon causing Ava and me to flinch. I look at everyone else and realize no one was hit. It becomes quiet for a second or two when one of Vek's men falls to the ground. Another pulse round flies past us and splits another guard's head nearly in half.

"What the hell!" Vek yells, looking around the icy ridge. "Spread out, spread out!" he shouts to his men as more pulse rounds begin to rain down.

"Now's our chance," Nev says, leaning forward and looking at Thomas. "Get us out of these bindings!"

Thomas nods his head and rotates his arms from behind him to the front in an astounding display of inhuman ability. He quickly undoes our straps as a barrage of gun fire inundates the valley.

Nev quickly grabs the rifles from the dead guards and throws me one. "We've got to move!" he yells as several pulse round begin flying past him. He pulls a device from the dead guard's duffle pack and slams it into the ground, suddenly a bubble of energy forms around us.

"It's a portable shield," I say, while reaching for the bubble.

Nev grabs my hand. "Careful, that will shock the hell out of you." I retract my hand as several pulse rounds hit the bubble and dissipate. "Ok," Nev begins, glancing at the device. "From the looks of things we've got about twenty maybe twenty-five seconds left before this shield shorts out." He explains, crouching. "Vek and his men are ten meters away behind some ice boulders and there is about thirty meters of wide open space between us and our skip." He continues, resting the butt of his rifle on the ice. "Here is what I'm thinking; we go for these boulders over here." Nev points at a pile of ice boulders that would put us halfway to our skip.

"But that will put us right in the line of sight for Vek and his men," Ava argues.

"Let me run for the skip, I can make it." Lora adds.

Nev shakes his head. "You won't make it; whoever is shooting at us is good enough to hit a moving target."

The device begins buzzing loudly and Nev turns to me. "Stowaway, you and I will lay down cover fire as we run."

Nev grabs my upper arm and looks me right in the eyes. "I got it," I respond as the device starts failing.

In seconds the chaos returns as several pulse rounds hit the ground around us. "RUN!" Nev shouts, shooting in the direction of the unknown assailants.

I follow closely, unloading several rounds toward Vek and his men, causing them to cower behind their boulders. About half way to the destination I run out of ammo. Nev was right, there was no way we would have made it to the skip. "Keep going!" I yell as Vek's men start shooting at us again.

Nev reaches the safety of the ice boulders, closely followed by Lora, Thomas and myself. I turn to help Ava but realize that she isn't there. I search the field, finding her on the ground. Oh God! I step out of cover to run for her but Nev pulls me back. I punch him in the visor, making him stagger. He immediately kicks me in the leg, knocking me off my feet and jumps on me.

"You won't make it!" he yells as I try and push him off.

I knew he was right but I didn't care. I force him off me and stand only to see that Vek's men were already pulling her from the ground and retreating to their skip. "I've got to do something, Nev!" I say, desperately.

Nev grabs me and slams me against the boulder. "Listen!" he barks. "I have no intention of letting her go, but we need to think before we act or we will die and that doesn't help anyone," he finishes.

I loosen up and he releases me. "So what then?" I do little to hide my contempt. Nev picks up one of the rifles and reloads it.

"Thomas, Lora and I will run for our skip, while you go after Ava," he says in a matter-of-fact kind of way. "That boat is a 0400 series just like the one you snuck aboard the Confessor with and I wager you know how to get on it, right stowaway?" he smirks.

I smile and nod my head. "Consider it done, but how will you guys find us?"

Nev brings up a holo-display showing me a digital map of the valley with several pulsating dots. "The twins made a tracking sub-routine for our Augs. If you're within five kilometers of us we'll find you." He closes the display and grabs my forearm. I feel a tingling sensation starting at my wrist and moving up to my shoulder. "Use it to find Ava when you land, we'll try and follow you."

I nod my head and grab the remaining rifle, quickly reloading it. Vek's skip is warming up. "We need to go now."

Nev looks over the boulder "The ridge is quiet, I don't see anybody." All of a sudden a pulse round pierces his shoulder and he falls to the ground; blood is spewing and freezing almost instantly.

Thomas immediately covers Nev's shoulder with some of the blue liquid from his chest, which solidifies within seconds of being exposed to the extreme temps. "We need to keep the wound covered from the elements!" he exclaims.

Lora helps Nev to his feet. "John, we're going!" she yells.

Another pulse round comes in from behind us. I turn and begin shooting; two armored men appear out of thin air and fall to the ground. "They're cloaked!" Nev shouts out in agony.

Then several more soldiers appear like ghosts. They were wearing what looked to be military grade heavy armor combat suits. Thomas takes Nev from Lora and they begin running for the skip as I lay down cover fire. The thing is the soldiers don't seem to be concerned with them almost simply letting them pass. I finish the clip and begin running for Vek's skip, which has begun to ramp up its engines.

The soldiers just stand and watch as I put the HEC Suit to the test, grabbing on to the landing gear right at the skip starts to jet off. I quickly climb up the ladder and into the crawl space situated under the skip's walkway. There is a hissing noise as the skip pressurizes and I remove my helmet.

Vek's voice reverberates through the skip. "What the hell was that!" he yells.

"I-I don't know," Ava's voice shudders with fear.

I move toward Vek's voice. "Don't lie to me!" he shouts.

I find a gap between the walkway and the seats where I can finally seeing Ava's face. "I swear, they weren't ours!" she says with more urgency in her voice.

Vek slaps her and I can feel hatred boiling in me. "You know what I'm going to do with you?" Vek grabs her face. She tries to look away but he forces her to look at him. "I'm going to rape you until you beg to be killed," he says in a low voice. "Then when I've had my fill, I'm going to sell you to the highest bidder." This time she looks him in the face and spits. Vek smiles and wipes his face. "You've got a lot of fight left," he says. "I like that in a woman." He stands and punches her, causing Ava to crumple into the seat. Vek begins laughing and walks to the front of the skip.

Ava's face is red and beginning to swell, it takes every bit of self-control to keep myself from going and cradling her. I desperately want her to know that I'm here that she is not alone but I can't risk being caught by Vek, so I decide to watch her. After a few minutes pass she awakes and lightly touching her face she finally lifts herself up off the seat. I can see several tears flow down her cheek as she looks around for anything that could be helpful. The skip begins to shudder violently and I can feel that we are about to land, but the question is where?

We touch down soon after and Vek drags Ava off the skip. I don't have much time but I can't leave yet, so I let the longest five minutes of my life pass before making my way out of the maintenance hatch, ensuring to close it this time. The building looks like a distribution warehouse with crates scattered all over, probably filled with illegal goods. I quickly find a door and run to it, pressing my ear up against it in hopes of hearing something, but there is nothing but silence.

I open the tracking program Nev gave me. It takes a few moments to update with a satellite view of the building. Two pulsating red dots appear. One is situated just beside a door while the other is in the middle of a room no more than twenty meters away. I watch it for a few seconds, but it doesn't move, leaving me with a terrible sense of fear.

I finally work up the courage and open the door. Behind it is a long hallway with what looks to be a security door at the end. I stand up straight and look at the screen again when I feel a sharp pain on the back of my head make its way down my spine. I fall to the ground and roll to my back. Vek s standing over me grinning.

"Hello peach!" he spits through his teeth. "Thought you'd save the princess out from under old Vek?" He hits me one more time and I lose consciousness, with nothing but darkness and the doubt that it fills me with.

CHAPTER FIFTEEN: THE FLAMING HAIRED VALKYRIE

The room is dark and my vision blurry; I blink away the haziness when a hand embraces my cheek. I jump when Ava's face comes into view.

She smiles as her eyes begin to water. "You're such an idiot," she whispers as a single tear runs along her swollen cheek then drips onto my forehead.

I lift my hand and wipe her cheek. "I'd do it again," I say softly.

She bites her bottom lip, attempting to stop it from quivering. "So what now?" she stammers. "I mean, are the rest coming for us?"

I don't know—the words fall heavily on my mind. The last I saw was Nev, Lora and Thomas entering the skip when I pulled myself through the maintenance hatch of Vek's shuttle, but Ava's eyes showed so much hope. "Yeah, Nev and the rest are coming."

Ava smiles as I sit up and look around the room. For the most part the walls are barren, no windows or vents. The only access in or out is the door which looked to be solid metal and the only light was from a single bulb that barely did its job; all in all it was stuffy, uncomfortable and worst of all hopeless.

I look down at Ava, realizing that she had a bandage poorly wrapped around her ankle. "What happened?!" I ask, examining the bandage.

"I got grazed by a pulse round," she explains "The HEC Suit took most of the impact, I should be fine." Her confident tone returns.

I remove the bandage to see the damage; fortunately the injury is minimal compared to what it could have been. Back on Titan it was common for drug dealers and crime lords to shoot people that owed them in the leg or arm, the damage was astronomical, even removing limbs at times.

"Will you be able to run?" It is simply an earnest question that Ava doesn't think is necessary because she gives me a sharp look.

"Yes, John. I can run!" she says, pulling her leg away.

I give her a puzzled look. What did I say? Did I hurt her pride, was I insincere or too sincere maybe? "You know," I start "you don't have to be a Valkyrie all the time," I finish sitting on the ground across from her.

She looks at me, pushing some of her flaming hair out of her face. "What did you call me?" Her tone was particularly caustic.

For a moment my fear of Vek is overshadowed by the prospect of Ava unleashing her wrath upon me. "Valkyrie," I state in a flat tone. "Warrior maidens of Odin?" Her look indicates that she is completely oblivious to what I'm talking about.

"Warrior maiden, huh? Is that what you're into?" She laughs.

I grin. "Yes, I'm into the girls that can kick ass, including mine." Her smirk fades a bit and an awkward silence falls over the room.

The silence persists for several minutes, but it feels like a lifetime. "Thank you," Ava whispers so faintly that it is almost inaudible.

I look at her and smile. "I didn't do anything but get caught."

"Even so, at least I'm not alone," she responds as tears begin forming in her eyes.

There she goes again, showing me this soft and vulnerable side. I understand her fear more than most people and I want to embrace her for it. "Yeah, I know what that feels like—to be alone."

Ava looks at me and wipes her eyes. "Tell me about growing up on Titan."

"There's nothing really to tell. I just appeared one day out of nowhere." The memories of Titan replay in my mind.

"You didn't have anyone?" Ava inquiries.

I shake my head, attempting to get my mind off the subject. "I didn't at first but then I met my family—I mean other orphans: Jurin, Genna, Frang and Keida. We were inseparable—more or less."

"What happened to them?" I can tell Ava's curiosity is getting the better of her.

I take a deep breath. "Uh, they're gone—all of them."

Ava frowns and averts her eyes. "That's why you snuck abroad the Confessor? You were running from all the sadness."

"Sort of." I begin to pull out the scrap of cloth from my pocket when the sounds of voices begin to come from the other side of the door.

I move closer, attempting to discern what they are talking about when the door swings open. The light form the hallway is blinding. I can barely make out what look like Vek and some guards.

"Time to go, meat-bags!" They put a dense cloth sack over my head and place some carbon bands on my wrists.

I can hear Ava starting to yell as they begin dragging me out of the room. "Leave her alone!" I shout repeatedly until one of the guards punches me.

She falls silent when someone lifts me to my feet and leads me down the hall. I can't help but worry about her. Why did she stop screaming? What were they doing to her? The more I think about it the more a burning sensation rises in my bowls. Finally after walking for several minutes they take me into room and push me into a seat. "Ava?!" I exclaim.

One of the guards slaps me on the back of the head. "Shut up!" he barks.

I hear the door open a moment later, followed by shuffling and then a loud thud beside me. "John?!" Ava voice fills me with joy.

"Oh thank God!" I gasp, provoking the guard to hit me again.

The room is quiet with only the panicked gasps of Ava and the throbbing of my heart keeping me company, then the door flies open "Vek this better be—" There is a pause then a slight huff. "Come on guys, these are our guests! Get that stuff off them." A moment later the cloth bag is removed from my face, and the light again is blinding.

"Boss, I don't recommend—" Vek starts.

"That is quite enough from you, Vek," an older man says while taking a seat at the desk in front of us. "Oh, where are my manners? I am Killian Orlan, pleased to meet your acquaintance." He stretches out his hand toward Ava and me, but we don't accept the offer. "Right, well I would like to apologize for any mistreatment you have received." Killian retracts his hand.

The gentleman is well dressed and kept. There's no doubt that he is wealthy and powerful. His light blonde hair is obsessively combed and complements his pale smooth skin. It is obvious he is conceited, the type of person who loves himself. However, the most striking thing about him are his neon green eyes that seem to change intensity at will. By the looks of how nervous Vek is in his presence, Killian must command quite a bit of loyalty and respect.

"What are you going to do with us?" Ava demands.

"Oh, I see why you like her," Killian says looking up at Vek. "Straight to the point. Good, well I am going to ransom you back to your captain. I believe his name is James Rickard, owner of the—" Killian touches his desk, bringing up a holo-display. "MST-C: Idle Confessor. What a charming name." He finishes, placing his hands together and staring at us.

"And if he doesn't pay?" I query.

Killian looks at me. "Well, we will just have to hope—won't we now?" He stands and circles the desk. "You see, we are in the business of—supply and demand." He holds up his hands. "And well, we are running a little low on a certain product that is very difficult to get." He looks at Vek. "The type of product you send your most trusted people to acquire." He walks over and places his hand on Vek's face.

Vek's eyes widen. "Boss, I told you they had back-up ambush us!"

"That is a damn lie. They weren't ours!" Ava screams.

"Quiet!" Killian barks. "You failed me, Vek." He brushes Vek's cheek. "And on top of it you decided to bring these two filthy vagrants back here!" Killian punches Vek several times, forcing Vek to fall to the ground. "Everyone out!" he yells. Several guards help Vek up and out of the room, closing the door behind them. Killian falls into his chair and rubs his temples before pulling his hair back out of his face. "I hope you'll accept my apology for calling you filthy vagrants," he says looking at us. "You understand right?"

Ava and I hesitate for a second. "I guess," Ava responds.

Killian smiles and pulls a glass and some liquor out of his desk. "You know it is difficult being the leader of a free-lance mercenary group and a senator of the Sovereign Republic. I'm sure you've heard of me." He pours himself a glass and offers some to Ava and me. We shake our heads and Killian shrugs. "Alas, it is times like these that make me question my choices. Do you ever question your choices?" Killian looks at both of us expecting an answer.

"I don't," I respond. "Everything I've done to get where I am has been for a single purpose."

Killian grins. "It is so nice to hear from this generation. I never get to have these types of conversations." He leans forward. "So tell me what your purpose is?"

That question, like so many others, has haunted me for as long as I can remember. "To find out who I am."

Killian smacks the table, causing us to jump. "Hell yes! The question we all seek answers to. The unattainable why." He takes a sip from his drink. "What about you, darling?"

Ava is quiet for a bit just staring off into space. "I just want to leave here alive." Her words are cold and unwavering.

Killian's grin disappears. "I told you, as soon as your dear captain pays up, you'll be released."

Ava looks at Killian. "Then why is it, Senator Orlan, that I don't believe you?"

Killian smiles again, gulping the rest of his drink and setting the glass on the table. "Well, I guess pleasantries are wasted on you both." He stands, leaning over his desk. "You're right, darling. You aren't leaving this place." He walks over to the door and opens it. "Take them back to the holding cell."

The guards trickle in one at a time with Vek heading up the rear, nursing the cheek Orlan chastised him on. They bind us again and lead us out of the office. The halls are mediocre at best, dotted with equally mediocre doors that lead to undoubtedly mediocre offices. There are no signs or markings that give clue to which direction we are going or even if we are on the first floor or the twentieth. I glance at Ava who is also studying every door and wall, hoping to find an exit that we can take advantage of. Then Vek grabs her by the back of the head and throws her into a room. I lunge toward him, but the two guards restrain me and drag me in after them.

Ava is still on the ground when Vek steps over her, pushing her head onto the flood. "It's time, little girl!" he whispers.

Ava screams and begins resisting, but Vek forces her legs apart staring at me the entire time. Tears begins to cascade from Ava's eyes, then she looks at me. All the fury, all the fight she had is diminished and for the very moment it seems she has lost hope.

"Don't do this Vek!" I shout.

Vek pauses a moment and grins at me. "After I'm done, the guards will have a go." Ava tries to lift her head, but Vek slams it back down. "And you will watch every bit." Vek's tone boasts his terrible cravings with little regard. "And there is nothing you can do about it."

I muster all my strength and begin fighting the guards, but they simply force me to the ground. Vek slowly undoes his belt and pants, taking his time and enjoying his power. My mind is flooded with feelings of anger, hatred, regret, remorse, defeat and helplessness. Everything all at once like a mob of people screaming at the top their lungs. My stomach turns and writhes with pain as Vek slowly pulls Ava's pants down.

Amongst the turmoil of my feelings, I sense my shadowy reflection smirking at me. What does this mean? The pain in my stomach begins to move to my chest and my head starts to ache. Vek leans forward and licks Ava's face grinning wickedly at me. My heart starts to pound so hard I can feel the ground vibrating, culminating in a single deafening shout.

At first I don't understand what has happened, but I recognize the feeling. It is same shell-shocked sensation I had after Cheever West knocked me out on Titan, but this time I am aware. I am on my hands and knees, the ground shattered beneath me. My senses are dulled and my head in a painful spin. I feel a steady drip on my hand, so I force myself to focus on it, realizing that it is blood. Initially I check my nose, but that isn't the source and the drip persists, so I look up. The two guards that were forcing me down are twisted and mangled, their faces contorted in a way that evokes pain at the very sight of them. Their bodies are so destroyed that it is almost impossible to think that I have done this—but I did.

The ringing in my ears is starting to disperse, when I hear Vek's voice. "What—what the hell are you!?" His voice can't hide his fear.

I look at him, lifting to my feet. The pain is dulling, but I can still feel the power coursing through me. "What's wrong, Vek. You're not afraid are you?" The words sound as if someone other than me has spoken them.

Vek's eyes widen with panic and dread as if the lion has fallen into an elaborate trap set by the gazelle. He pulls out a pulse revolver and fires. I throw my hands up, expecting the worst but there's nothing. I look at him, his eyes showing even more terror than before. He lets out another volley of pulse rounds, but none of them reach me. I can feel the pain beginning to return to the back of my head as each projectile bends around me.

Vek empties the revolver but continues to pull the trigger, and I feel myself grin. "It's time, little boy!" The voice is mine but the words don't feel like I'm saying them. It's almost like I have become someone else.

I raise my hand and Vek's body goes stiff and lifts from the ground. He tries to fight but he's helpless like we were just a few minutes ago. "Do you remember what I told you, Vek?" I begin slowly closing my hand, making Vek writhe in pain. "I said, if you ever touched her again that I'd fucking kill you!" I squeeze my hand into a fist.

Vek screams as his body is crushed with so much force that the floor and walls cave in around him. Blood and flesh flies everywhere and his ravaged body falls to the ground. I drop to my knees as an excruciating pain overwhelms my head. I can feel the warmth of blood flowing from my nose and I feel myself losing consciousness, I begin falling forward when Ava catches me.

"John!" She pulls me to my feet "We need to go!" she shouts, shaking me. But I can't seem to respond as if my body is in a mandatory reset. Ava throws my arm around her neck and walks me to the hallway.

The corridor is flashing red and an alarm is sounding. We turn a corner and Ava props me up against a wall and runs a little ahead looking back and forth, trying to find the best way out. The ringing in my ears starts to subside and I can hear an explosion in the distance with gun fire in between.

Ava returns and starts to grab me when I hold up a hand and say, "I think I can walk."

She looks at me and nods. Although she is focused I can tell she is shaken by the events that just took place. I don't blame her, because I'm still trying to make sense of it, but now is not the time for that. I follow her down the hall, darting left and right, but it seems like we aren't getting anywhere. The office building is like a maze. The gun fire gets closer and louder when we turn a corner and come face to face with six soldieries that look just like the ones from the canyon.

They turn and start shooting at us so we fall to the ground when one of them yells, "Cease fire!"

I feel an arm grab me and pull me to my feet pushing me against the wall. "My scan is bringing back static," one of the soldiers says.

"That's cause he is wearing a jammer," another responds pointing to my jacket.

The soldier holding me to the wall grabs my arm bringing up a holo-display on another soldier's forearm. "Checks out. This is our target. Let's get the hell out of here!" he yells making a circle motion in the air with his finger.

The soldiers bind Ava and me, throwing us over their shoulders and running us back to their transport. Before long we are jetting off from the office building that is smoking from several explosions.

After a while of silence, one of the soldiers touches the temple of his helmet. "Bravo team in transit with the package plus one, requesting further orders." A few seconds pass before another voice returns.

"Lieutenant, need I remind you that this was supposed to be a covert operation? There will be no witnesses." The voice cuts out.

The soldier looks at me and then Ava, who hasn't taken her eyes off of me since we entered the transport. He shrugs and pulls the pulse pistol out of his holster, putting it to Ava's head. I slam my eyes shut, feeling the pain return to my head as the sound of a single shot reverberates through the vehicle.

It's quiet for a second or two until the rest of the soldiers begin to panic. I muster the courage to open my eyes. To my relief, Ava is alive with a soldier's head lying in her lap, freshly split open by a pulse round. But that wasn't all that the soldiers were panicking about because their Lieutenant's head was completely twisted around. The solders pull their pistols on me as the numbness returns and my body goes limp.

"Shit! What the hell, man?!" one of the soldiers yells. "What do we do now!?"

"Shut it! We stick to the plan!" another soldier responds.

"Forget this, man!" he exclaims. "This whole damn mission is messed up!" His hand begins shaking with the pistol.

"Put it down, kid—remember the mission. Look at him, he's practically comatose," the other soldier demands. He was right. Although I could hear them perfectly, I couldn't move my body to save my life.

"Screw you, man. The Lieutenant is dead!" I can see him beginning to squeeze the trigger when the side of the shuttle explodes, sucking him and two other soldiers out.

The shuttle begins spinning uncontrollably as the ground and sky flash across the opening faster and faster. The engines wheeze and whistle under the stress as we tumble closer to the ground, finally coming to a shattering impact.

Chapter Sixteen: The Shadow Claim

I can only hear the echoing of Ava's voice in the darkness when I feel a sting across my face. I finally take a breath and see that she is relieved. We are surrounded by fire and smoke and Ava has blood running down her face from a gash above her left eye. I lift my hand to wipe some of the blood away and she helps me to my feet. We quickly find our way out of the twisted carcass that used to be the transport, reaching a clearing where we frantically gasp for air. Ava falls to the ground and begins coughing.

I crouch down and rub her back. "Are you ok?" She nods her head as she grabs my forearm and pulls herself to her feet.

"We've got to get out of here," she says in a raspy voice.

I grab her hand and turn to run as far from the wreck as possible when a soldier walks out of the smoke with his pulse rifle at the ready. "Get on the ground now!" he yells.

We put our hands up and get on our knees. The soldier starts walking toward us as he pulls some carbon bands out of his pocket. Several pulse rounds ring out from behind him and he crumples to the ground in front of me. Behind him is Nev, bandaged and bruised but somehow still deadly and I swear I have never been happier to see him.

He smiles and winks at us before bringing up his holo-display. "Lora, I found them!" The bandage on his shoulder shows a little blood seeping through, but it doesn't seem to bother him. He runs over and helps Ava to her feet. "Are you good, John?" This question is another unexpected surprise from Nev.

"Yeah, just take Ava," I respond.

A moment later the skip flies overhead and hovers just above the ground extending the ramp. Thomas runs out, taking Ava from Nev and carrying her back to the skip. Nev turns to me and for a second I worry that he is about to leave me, but instead he reaches his hand out. I take it without hesitation and he pulls me onto the ramp.

"Alright, let's get the hell out of here!" he yells.

The ramp shuts behind us and I quickly sit down and buckle myself in right as the skip shoots in a near vertical vector at astonishing speed. "Tracking multiple transports moving in!" Lora shouts.

"Everybody hold on. Those transports can't follow us in space," Nev says back to us.

The skip begins to vibrate wildly, so much so that it causes my body to ache. The engines are screaming so loudly that I wouldn't be surprised if they explode. Just when I think they are about to, everything becomes still and I can feel the weightlessness overcome my body.

"Enemies have cleared. We are homeward bound." Lora's relieved voice causes everyone, including Thomas, to cheer.

I unlatch my harness and float over to Thomas and Ava, pulling myself into the seat beside her. She looks at me and grabs my hand. "Thanks you."

Her words are so genuine that I almost lose all control right there. "You're welcome." She retracts her hand but doesn't stop staring at me. "So what do we do now?"

Thomas begins dabbing her head with a bandage but she waves him away. "What do you mean?"

"I mean what's going to happen now, after everything I just—"

Ava places her hand over my mouth. "Your secret needs to stay a secret," she whispers.

"I don't understand anything that just happened." My tone is overwhelmed with fear and uncertainty.

"You saved me. That's enough for now. We will talk about the rest later," she says.

Nev floats back holding the straps to stabilize himself. "Fifteen minutes till we reach the Confessor. The captain is pissed."

Ava looks up. "Rightfully so, but we can't do anything about that can we?"

Nev shrugs as he looks at Thomas twitching in the seat beside Ava. "You going to make it, Canner?"

Thomas looks up at him. "Efficiency is down thirty-five percent but my major functions seem nominal. I would like to be repaired as soon as possible."

"Yeah, wouldn't we all?" Nev responds, finally looking at me. "So what the hell happened after you snuck aboard Vek's skip?"

"They took us back to some office building like headquarters. Vek ended up catching me and then he tried—" I look at Ava who continues to stare at Nev.

"They were going to sell us to the highest bidder when those Soldiers attacked," Ava finished.

"Yeah, Vek was killed when they extracted us." The image of Vek's mangled body returns to my mind. "By the way, who the hell were those guys and how did you find us?"

Nev beams. "As soon as you slipped into Vek's skip, the soldiers left, as if we didn't even exist. We somehow managed to follow them back to the warehouse. I was getting ready to infiltrate when we picked up on your Augs in the IISF transport.

"IISF?"

"Integra Industries Security Forces," Ava says, still not looking at me. "Are you sure?"

"Damn right. I've never seen cloaking tech like that anywhere else," Nev responds.

"So, who are they?" I press the matter.

Nev rolls his eyes. "The IISF are like the best of the best, exclusively owned and operated by Integra Industries. These guys are covert-ops."

Ava glances at me then back to Nev. "What did they want?"

"I was hoping you would be able to enlighten me," Nev says. "I mean they were ballsy enough to assault the Vice Watch headquarters just to get you two."

Nev gives me a critical look. I open my mouth to talk when Ava cuts me off. "We weren't the only ones there. The IISF were taking a bunch of people." She looks at me and I nod my head.

Nev's stare is unwavering. "Well, I guess we will never know." The cynicism in his voice is unmistakable, but he shrugs and returns to his seat anyway.

I let out a slight sigh, then feel Ava's hand on mine again. "John."

The sound of her saying my name sends a chill through my body. "Yeah?"

"I just wanted to say—" She hesitates.

"What is it?" She looks away. Although she is beaten up and bruised, I can still feel the fire in me, yearning for her.

"Just—" she starts, but before she can finish the skip shudders violently and the lights flicker.

"Incoming!" Lora yells. "Unknown contact. Starboard. Same size as a destroyer! How the hell did we miss it?"

"They're firing at us!" Nev shouts as another violent shudder causes a hissing noise.

"We are losing pressure!" Lora's voice doesn't hide her anxiety.

"Hygithium cells at fifty percent!" Nev says while buckling himself in. "If we take another hit like that we are done!"

But the last volley doesn't come, only a message. "To whoever is piloting this Multipurpose Drop Vessel: as you probably already know, you are in no shape to run. If you agree to our terms you and your crew will live. If not then you will be reduced to rubble. Do I make myself clear?" The message stops and Lora looks back at Ava.

"It's the IISF," I say quietly.

"How do you know?" Nev asks sharply.

"When we were in their transport, one of the soldiers was talking to someone that sounded just like that guy on the message." I respond. "He made it clear that there would be no witnesses." The sight of the Lieutenant's head twisted around flashes through my head.

"Sounds like we are dead no matter what," Nev says matter-of-factly.

Ava unbuckles herself and floats to the front of the skip. "How close are we to the Confessor?"

Lora hits several buttons and a holo-display pops up. "Five minutes tops."

Nev looks back at me. "How about we find out what he wants first," he says.

His gaze is unnerving, but then I catch Ava's eyes also on me. I lower my head when she hits the respond button. "This is First Officer Avalyn, highest ranking crew member on this skip. Please transmit your terms." She closes the window.

Thomas leans toward me catching my attention. "I understand now may not be the proper moment, but I'm receiving several readings from your vitals that appear to be irregularities."

"What's your point, Thomas?" My response is a little more hostile than it should be but the situation is starting to wear on me.

"You see, if these readings are correct—which they can't be—then you should be undergoing what would be considered an epileptic seizure." Thomas finishes with a look of bewilder and concern.

"Damn-it, Thomas. We're about to be blown to hell and you're concerned about this?!" I grumble, but the sight of his face makes me take a moment and exhale. "It's probably because of your damage. We'll get you fixed up and then you can run every diagnostic test in the book on me." I force my tone to sound more genuine.

Thomas nods his head and leans back into his seat. I return my focus to the cockpit. However, I can't seem to shake Thomas's revelation. Epileptic seizure? That's ridiculous—right?

I'm pulled from my thoughts when a reply comes in from the IISF destroyer. "Greetings First Officer Avalyn. Our preliminary scans of your vessel indicate that there are four humans and a synthetic aboard, is that correct?"

"They could have scanned us without having to shoot at us," Lora states.

"We really don't have many options at this point," Ava replies hitting the display. "Yes, your scans are correct. Although, you could have simply asked for this information without threatening our lives." Ava sends the communication.

A moment later a message shows up on the display, Ava promptly accepts it. "I do express regret for our brazen lack of civility; however, a show of strength guarantees compliance with our requests. It has come to my knowledge that there is a member amongst your crew that is not what he seems. Our terms are simply that you will land your skip in one of our designated hangers and you will surrender this person of interest. Failure to do so will bring death to you and your crew. I'm sure I don't need to explain further. We patiently await your response."

Everyone is silence for several minutes with only the hum of the skips engines and a mild hissing noise in the background.

After a while Nev claps his hands together and laughs "It was you all along," he says looking at me "You lying son of a bitch!" he pulls a pulse revolver out and points it at me.

"Nev put the gun down," Ava says in a soft but serious tone.

I slowly raise my hands, "Listen, Nev. I don't—" He cuts me short.

"No, you don't get to talk! I'm not going to die for you!" he shouts.

"Think Nev!" Ava yells. "Even if we give John up, they will kill us anyways."

Nev's eyes dart to the side for a second then return to me. Meanwhile Lora brings up a display. "There may be a way we can get to the Confessor without doing what they want."

This time Nev looks away completely and studies the display. "If this doesn't work then they will just kill us. I'll take my chances with giving this asshole up!"

Ava looks the display over. "It will work if we time it right. Remember, they want John. They won't destroy us as long as we have him."

I don't know what it was that came over me. Either the situation finally pushed me to the breaking point or it was the fact that I was tired of other people deciding my fate as if I have no say. Whatever it was manifested and boiled over, leading to only one exclamation. "Will you all just shut the hell up?!" Everyone turns to me with a mix of surprise and anger on their faces. "I'm so sick and tired of everyone around me acting like I'm a damn fugitive or a piece of meat that they can determine what to do with!" I continue to yell. Nev opens his mouth to say something but I hold up a hand. "Shut up; I'm not finished!" He closes his mouth "I have been beaten, abused, threatened and all around treated with less human dignity than anyone deserves!" I unbuckle myself and float out to the middle of the walkway. "From now on I decide what will happen to me and for the love of God, Nev, put the fucking gun down!"

Nev looks at Ava and Lora whose faces show the same amount of bafflement as his, then finally lowers the gun with a huff. "So what now?" he asks.

I take a deep breathe realizing that I hadn't thought that far ahead when Ava opens a holo-display beside me. "We have two functioning Hygithium cells left; Lora insists that we only need one to make it to the Confessor." She looks around at everyone's faces. "If we jettison and overload one, the resulting explosion is enough to propel us and distract the IISF Destroyer."

"Yeah that is great and all but we are putting a lot of faith on the assumption that they won't kill us with him onboard." Nev narrows his eyes on me.

I ignore him for the time being. "What about sending a message to the captain?"

"Right now that's not a good idea because the IISF is most likely intercepting all transmissions we are sending. But once we start moving we will send him a message to get his ass over to us ASAP," Lora answers.

I study the display a little more and look back at everyone "Ok, I like it. What do we gotta do?"

Nev shakes his head while Lora and Ava both smile. "First we accept the terms then when we are about to land we initiate the plan." Ava hits the reply button. "This is First Officer Avalyn. We accept your terms. Please transmit where you would like us to land."

A second later we receive the landing approval and begin our landing process. Ava and I return to our seats and buckle in. Thomas has voluntarily shutdown to save his vital systems from further damage. His body sits rigid, still leaving me with an uncomfortable feeling.

"By disconnecting the Hygithium Cell we are going to lose all ancillary systems, including the Computer Assisted Guidance Systems," Nev says, giving Lora a critical look. "We'll be flying strictly by line of sight." He does little to hide his lack of enthusiasm.

The skip swings around facing its back toward the IISF Destroyer. Ava prepares a message to shotgun to the Confessor as soon as we overload the power cell. Everything becomes silent and still.

Lora twists her head releasing the tension in her neck. "On my mark, Nev." Her voice is sharp and focused. "Three, two, one, mark."

Nev hits a button and a loud cranking noise followed by a slight shudder spread through the skip's hull. Lora immediately opens the throttle and the acceleration causes Thomas's rigid body to lean over and pin me against my seat.

Nev holds up three fingers. "Cell overload in three, two, one."

At first there isn't anything that indicates the cell overloaded until the skip begins to shake uncontrollably boosting our acceleration and causing Thomas's body to crush me even more. Ava quickly sends the message as the skip starts moaning under the stress.

"Three minutes!" Lora shouts.

Sparks begin to fly from blown fuses as the vibrations continue to increase. The hissing noise from before is now more of an incessant roar. The notion that we don't much time left begins to form on the fringes of my mind. The displays begin flashing red with the words 'Critical Power Failure' in a continuous loop.

"We're not going to make it!" Nev yells.

The skip's temperature starts to drop rapidly and breathing becomes increasingly difficult as pressure continues to drop. Ava unbuckles herself and retrieves four masks from a panel, throwing one in my direction. I quickly place it over my face and take a long breath, forcing Thomas off me.

Lora begins hitting the flight controls in frustration. She turns to us and shakes her head. Her eyes betray the fact that we are dead. Nev places his hand on her shoulder and she begins to cry as the crimson words 'Target Locked' begin flashing. Ava looks at me, but not with a look of helpless defeat but rather one of hope. She nods her head, which can only mean one thing.

I straighten in my seat and close my eyes. I know I can do this but the question is how? I didn't really choose to use my ability the last two times; it just happened when Ava was in danger. Is that the secret to unlocking this—thing? The image of my shadowed reflection appears again this time clearer than before. The searing pain in my stomach moves up to my chest and the numbing pain returns to the back of my head. I can feel blood starting to flow from my nose as the image of the IISF destroyer becomes vivid in my mind. 'I've got you now,' a voice in my head says as I begin concentrating on the destroyer. The pain continues to mount beyond anything I've felt before as the exterior lights of the destroyer flicker and its trajectory shifts a little. 'Almost there,' the voice says. But by this point I can't keep my focus. My heart feels as though it is about to rip out of my chest and my head is splitting. I can hear Ava shout my name, but I can't seem to return to my body. My shadow reflection appears again, but this time he is not smirking. His eyes are narrow and I feel like he is disappointed.

"John, stop!" Ava screams as I start to breathe again.

I lean forward into her arms. "I'm sorry—I can't."

"Shut up—just shut up," she says softly.

I manage to wrap my arms around her. "This is it isn't it?" I ask.

Ava simply nods her head as the skip's incoming projectile alarm begins buzzing. A moment later the shuttle begins to shake and Ava squeezes me. This is it, I think and yet this is different than every other time I felt that I was going to die. I have never once feared death, always believing that death would come when it was my time. Instead I always feared how I would die. It is only now, in this very moment, embracing someone that I truly care for, yet barely know, that I realize how afraid I am of dying. To never know who Ava is and more so never experience what it would be like to love her and to feel her possibly love me in return.

"How's my timing, kids?" Captain Rickard's voice fills the crumbling skip.

It takes a moment for everyone to realize what is happening. Apparently the volley that was intended for us was intercepted by the Confessor. The shudder that we felt wasn't the impact of missiles but rather the Confessor's immense thrusters passing uncomfortably close to us.

Nev hits the respond button. "You beautiful son-of-a-bitch. I'm going to kiss you when we get aboard!" he shouts with excitement as he hugs Lora.

Ava smiles and looks at me. "John, we're going to make it!" Her hopeful words bring me so much happiness.

I open my mouth to respond but nothing comes out. The pain in my head continues to grow and my vision begins to blur.

"John!?" Ava says. "John, what's the matter!?"

Her voice sounds like it's far away as the pain continues to consume me.

"Nev, he's not responding!" Ava yells, shaking me violently.

My vision begins to tunnel and I feel myself leaving my body. Is this what death feels like?

Nev enters my line of sight. "He's going into shock. Ava, get the first aid kit and wake Thomas up."

Now I can hardly see them as the darkness continues to creep in.

"Oh God. He's not breathing, Nev!" Ava's voice is frantic.

I continue to drift away. My hands and feet begin to tingle. I like it here. I think I'll stay for a while.

Chapter Seventeen: The Avant-Garde

It's not like I'm unfamiliar with this sensation. Floating weightlessly in a sea of endless darkness has been a recurring experience for most my life. But this time is different. This time feels like I am on the cusp of something great, something amazing. The planet is here again, now lifeless with only the charred remains of the once great civilization that called it home. The pit in my stomach aches the longer I stare at the dead planet, so I turn away finding myself in the white room partitioned by the black glossy barrier.

I casually walk toward it but there is not reflection, just a void of light with the dead planet spinning in the background. I reach out and touch the wall for the first time. It ripples under my palm.

"I wouldn't do that," a voice—my voice says.

I look around for the source but find nothing.

"I'm right here," the voice says.

I turn to the glossy black wall and see my shadowed reflection materialize from the darkness.

"What the hell are you?" I ask.

The reflection smiles wickedly. "I am you, John, and you are me," he says openly.

"I don't understand," I respond "What is this? What's happening to me?"

The reflection rolls his eyes. "How many times do you ask the same question and not get an answer before you stop asking?" he say coldly. "I know as much as you do, maybe a little more, but in the end we are the same so you always know what I know."

I rub my temples, attempting to wrap my head around this situation. "So tell me, what do you know?"

The reflection smiles and gestures to the glossy barrier. "I have been here since we were a child, stuck behind this wall like a caged animal. I don't know who put it here or why, but I wager to guess that it was because of our little gift."

"Gift?" I ask sarcastically.

"What else is it other than that? You seem to enjoy the power," the reflection says rhetorically replaying the events of Vek's death on the black wall like a movie.

I turn away right as I smash him, causing the reflection to laugh. "It's not funny. I murdered five people."

"Murdered? You saved the girl. You saved the day. We're a hero." He begins playing the scene from Titan right after I had been knocked out.

Cheever West had brought more than twenty men with him. More than was needed for the likes of Jurin and me. I was only on the ground for a second when it happened, and the power was even more devastating than when I used it on Vek and his guards. One by one I slaughtered Cheever's men, ripping them into shreds and pulling their flesh from their bones. With every scream and shout of agony, a malevolent smile grew on my face; I was a monster. Then after I finished the last of Cheever's men, I approached him. He was on his knees, eyes wide with shock and terror, bowing before me begging for his life.

With a flick of my hand he flies into a spacing container. "I'm going to savor this one," I say. But Jurin grabs me and I collapse and the replay fades away.

"See," the reflection starts "for years I've been alone in the dark, until this happened." He hits the glossy wall it ripples violently. "Now it seem this barrier is getting weaker." He smiles.

"So what will happen then?" I ask.

The reflection shrugs. "Hard to say. We will be whole again, that's for sure."

"Whole again—" I repeat. A notion that sounds oddly fulfilling and yet it scares the hell out of me.

"It doesn't need to," the reflection says.

I grimace. "Need to what?"

"Seriously, we are the same; I can hear what you're thinking," he responds. "You're afraid that once I'm released we will go on some killing spree. Am I right?"

I nod my head. "Well stop," he says. "It's not like we are two different personalities here. I'm the aspects of you that whoever put me here felt would fight and resist control, your rebellious side if I may say so. Whereas you are all the other aspects that make you a good little lemming—judging from that outburst you had earlier, it sounds like this barrier is getting weak faster than even I anticipated."

"So what about this power?" I ask.

"This power is a gift; at least that is what we've been told from day one. A means to a new Golden Age for humanity, or some crap like that." The reflection paces back and forth. "Most of it is over here with me, apparently if we use it to much or too often it can kill us so it has been segregated, made to unlock in stages."

"So that was you? Every time I used this gift it was cause you let me?" I ask.

"Sort of. I don't quite understand it either, but it definitely has something to do with that fine morsel you got." He waves his hand and Ava's face shows up on the wall.

"Don't call her that!"

He throws up he hands. "Hey, hey remember I'm your primal urges. If you weren't thinking it, I wouldn't have said it, bud." He grins.

The headache returns. "This is a lot to take in."

"Yeah no shit." He responds, waving away Ava's image.

I turn my attention to the planet behind my reflection. "So what's that?"

He turns and looks. "Beats me. It just sits there replaying this massive genocide. It doesn't mean anything to me."

The planet glitches and resets. It's covered with lights and vegetation and just like before massive explosions begin to dot the surface. The pit in my stomach turns and I look away. "So, since you can recall things that I've repressed can you remember anything before I—we were three?"

This time he grimaces. "Only one thing, but you aren't going to like it."

"What is it?" I ask, now more curious than before.

The reflection sighs and waves his hand. A woman I don't recognize appears. She is covered in sweat and her hair is tattered. She is smiling at me and I feel—good. I float above her a little and I can see that she is wearing a medical gown.

"Oh my God!" I exclaim.

"Yeah, that's her," he responds.

It finally dons on me that this woman is my mother right after I was born. She reaches out for me, but whoever was holding me refuses to give me to her. Her mouth begins moving, but I can't make out the words and she begins getting angry, attempting to lurch forward to grab me. I can sense my infant-self beginning to cry as several nurses restrain my mother. She screams frantically, having to watch her baby being taken from the room.

My reflection lifts his hand, but I stop him. "Look on the wall!"

He glances up seeing the acronym AIC ornately painted on the wall. "What is that?" he asks.

"It's a clue. Is there anything else that indicates where this was?"

"That's it. Everything else is just static until we were found on the church's doorstep," he says.

The reflection waves his hand and the wall returns to its dark self. "Wait." He looks up at me "Can you show me her again? Please?" I request.

My reflection nods his head and with a wave my mother's face appears on the wall. She had black wavy hair and brown eyes that were kind and warm. Her smile causes a tingling feeling to course through my body as if I had been embraced for the first time in an eternity. I feel my eyes water as I reach out and touch her face.

"Thank you," I say.

My reflection looks at me and smiles. "My pleasure John." We both chuckle when I feel the pain in my head coming back. "Looks like it's time for you to go," he says.

"But I have so much more to ask you," I reply.

"Your time is up. You've got to return to the land of the living," he says as I start to be whisked way.

"Wait, what should I call you?" It was a question I should have asked him earlier.

He tilts his head a little. "It's kind of weird but you can call me Avant-Garde."

"What does that mean?" I shout, but he doesn't answer.

I turn to the direction that I'm being pulled and I can see a blinding light piercing the blackness. I can hear voices but they're distant and I can't make out what they're saying. At first they are a mere mumble droning on but as I get closer they start to sharpen.

"He is starting to wake up!" The unmistakable sound of Ava's voice catches my attention.

CHAPTER EIGHTEEN: THE FAUSTIAN PACT

I jerk upright, taking a deep breath like I haven't inhaled for weeks. The lights are blinding and painful.

"Give him some space," Thomas says. "John, take your time. Can you turn to my voice?" I squint and scan the room, finally seeing the silhouette of Thomas. "Good, good can you tell me the last thing you remember?" he asks.

"We—we were all going to die when the captain saved us," I stammer.

"Very good. You can go to him now," Thomas says.

Two soft hands touch my cheeks and I turn. Ava's face is almost completely healed; the gash above her left eye is barely visible.

"Hi," she says in a soft voice. "Is he ok?"

"Tip top, although I'd keep from doing anything too vigorous for a few hours," Thomas responds

"Good," Ava says looking at me and smiling. "John?"

"Yeah?" I respond with a grin.

She smacks me across the face. "Don't ever do that again!" she screams.

"That actually falls into the vigorous action I said not to do, Ms. Avalyn!" Thomas barks.

"It's ok. Thomas," I say waving a hand. Thomas returns to organizing various medical devices, muttering something about being glad he doesn't understand human emotion. "It is good to see you too, Ava."

"Good to see!? You almost died and that is the first thing you have to say to me!" she shouts. "You better stop smiling. I'm not playing with you."

"Always the Valkyrie," I say softly.

She opens her mouth to continue to yell but stops. The infirmary hatch flies open and the twins run in, both showing eager anticipation.

"We just heard," Don says gasping for air.

"And we got here as fast as possible!" Ron finishes.

I smile. "Guys, fancy meeting you here!" I say excitingly.

Don rushes over and hugs me while Ron smacks me on the back causing a sting to resonate through my body.

"Seriously, stop hitting the patient!" Thomas demands.

"Oh, keep your lab coat on, Thomas," Don retorts.

"Yeah, we are also here to check on our handy work," Ron says, pulling Thomas's shirt in the front and glancing down it.

"Do you have any concept of personal space?" Thomas says pulling away. "You must know everything is running fine considering I was shot."

"Touchy, touchy," Don says under his breath.

Ava and I start laughing as the twins move several objects around that Thomas had just finished organizing. The hatch opens again, catching everyone's attention as Lora slips through the entryway.

She stops in mid-step realizing that everyone is staring at her. "Is there something on my face?" She touches her cheek and smiles. Everybody chuckles and she walks over to me and gives me a hug. "I'm glad you're feeling better, John."

"Thanks, so where is Nev and the captain?" The question must have been loaded because the room fell silent.

Ava touches my forearm. "The captain is currently in a meeting and Nev was given strict orders."

"What kind of orders?"

"The kind that require me to take you the brig." Nev's voice startles everyone.

I start to laugh, but quickly realize from everyone's faces that he isn't joking. "What? Why?!"

"Captain's orders," Nevs says taking out some carbon bands and walking toward me.

Ron and Don step in front of him. "Now, you listen here meat-head," Ron starts.

"If you want him you've got to go through us," Don finishes, puffing up his chest.

"It's fine guys," I say, swinging my legs out from under the sheets.

"But—?' The twins say simultaneously.

I place my hand on Ron's shoulder. "I've caused enough problems for you all."

"See there, at least one of you has some damn sense." Nev walks toward me with the carbon straps.

I grab his wrist and he looks at me. "I'm going willingly so you won't need those." He pulls away and makes a motion toward my wrist. "What I meant by you won't need those is that you're not putting them on me, Nev." My voice boasts a level of calm authority that I never thought I could produce.

Nev looks at me twisting his face into a tense frown as he places the carbon bands back into his pocket. He turns and exits and I give everyone a quick look.

"Talk to you guys later," I say, following Nev out the hatch.

The walk is long and quiet. Nev refuses to look at me let alone say a word. Finally I formulate a sentence other than the typical, 'What the hell is wrong with you now?' I take a deep breath. "How is your shoulder?"

Nev rotates his shoulder as if he had forgotten that he was shot there and shrugs. "Better."

"That's good. I'm extremely glad it is better." The sarcasm is so blatant that a deaf person would have caught it.

Nev grunts, so I continue to push the envelope. "So, how long was I out for?"

"Five days," Nev says plainly.

"Five days?!" I exclaim "Where are we?"

"Are you going to talk the entire time?" Nev snaps.

"I don't know. Are you always going to be a hard-up asshole to me?" I respond.

Nev stops and turns to me. "Watch it, stowaway. You're treading on thin ice."

He turns and continues down the corridor. "See, I can't seem to get through to you. One moment we are all buddy-buddy and now you are treating me like yesterday's garbage."

"Stop," he says.

"No, I don't think I will, not until you tell me why you've got a problem with me," I demand, stopping in the middle of the walkway.

Nev turns and grabs me by the collar and throws me against the wall. The image of Thomas yelling about abusing the patient flashes through my head, causing me to involuntarily chuckle.

Nev's eyes glow red and he cocks his arm back. "Ok, good. Just get it over with cause I want to be friends." A part of me thinks that I need to knock the smart-ass remarks off before I really get hurt.

Nev hesitates, then punches the wall beside my head and releases me. "We're even now," he says.

"Even?"

"For Pilot. What you did," he responds.

I shake my head in confusion. "What did I do? I figured you'd be blaming me not thanking me."

"Do I really have to spell it out for you?" Nev grumbles.

"Apparently you do. That is if you can spell." I grin widely.

Nev glares at me. "It's that right there. You're so damn irritating!"

"And you're a stubborn asshole; so why did you owe me?" I practically shout.

"Ava," he mutters. "Because of what you did for Ava."

I get it finally. I saved one of his family. He hates me because I'm the cause of this, but at the same time he appreciates that I was able to save someone he cares for. Especially because he was injured and helpless. "Why is it so hard to think that I, a no good stowaway, can't be helpful? I want to be here, Nev. That's all I've ever wanted was to have a family."

He lowers his head. "You've been poison since you got here, but I'm thankful that you were here." He turns and walks down the corridor and I follow him.

It has to be the most remote part of the ship because it doesn't look very used. Nev leads me through a pair of heavy blast doors, then to an open room. He points to a spot on the floor and I stand there. He places his hand on the panel and an electric field generates around me.

"So what now?"

Nev walks over to a wall and leans against it. "Now we wait on the captain."

"You never answered me. Where are we?" I ask, but Nev doesn't answer. "Seriously. Are we just going to sit in silence for hours? We can at least talk."

Nev glares at me then sighs. "We're on the JMC Odyssey Space Station."

"You're kidding me." The realization that we are currently on the largest space station in the entire solar systems makes me smile with excitement. "Why?"

Nev scowls. "Those drugs we lost didn't belong to us. We're simply a small part of a massive Zeek distribution network."

"Meaning?" I probe.

"Meaning, we had to pay the manufacturer a percentage of the sell. Because we lost the product without the payment, we have to take responsibility for the loss," Nev says with a fair amount of disdain in his voice.

"Who was the manufacturer?"

"The Syndicate Builders Guild." Nev's voice cracks a bit.

The pieces finally start coming together. The reason the Idle Confessor was at New Horizon in the first place was to pick up the Zeek. I never understood why Cheever West was a member of the SBG until now. New Horizon must be the Zeek producing capital of the Frontier. That explains why such a small and remote colony gets so much traffic.

"That makes sense, but the drugs were produced on Titan. Why are we here on the Odyssey?"

"Because of Cornelius Firth." Nevs voice turns sour.

"Why don't you just assume I have very little knowledge of anything you're telling me, because it would go a hell of a lot faster," I respond sarcastically.

"Cornelius Firth is the leader of the Frontier's SBG Chapter. Everything the SBG does out here goes through him. He is one of the richest and most powerful people in the entire Frontier and we happen to owe him a lot of money." Nev spits on the ground in front of him.

"So how long has the captain been gone then?"

Nev looks at his forearm. "Three days in an hour."

"Three days?!" I yell, no wonder Nev is on edge. We have no idea if the captain is in trouble or not. Hell, he could already be dead, but I doubt that we would be left alone if Cornelius decided to kill us.

Nev's Aug starts to buzz. He glances at it, then jerks off the wall accepting the call. "Captain!"

"Nev," Captain Rickard starts. "Get everyone to the bridge. I'll be there in twenty minutes."

"Sure thing, boss. What do you want me to do with the stowaway?" Nev responds.

There are a few seconds of silence before the captain responds. "Is he awake?"

"Yes sir. I have him here in the holding cell just like you said," Nev says looking at me.

There is an even longer pause. "Yeah go ahead and take him to the bridge. We'll knock both things out at once. James out."

Nev closes the connection and looks at me. "What did he mean by knocking both things out?" I ask.

Nev shrugs and lowers the shield. "Guess we'll find out." His tone sounds more cheerful than before.

Almost exactly twenty minutes later Captain James Rickard enters the bridge with a sense of urgency surrounding him. "Glad to see everyone is healed up fine." He starts giving everyone a glance, finally resting his stare on me. "First off, sorry it took so long. There were complications to say the least."

"Complications? How so?" Ava asks.

"That's unimportant right now. We have been given a task that requires our urgent response," he says, tapping several controls on the panel.

"So we are doing a job for the SBG?" Don says.

"Since when did we march by their orders?" Ron adds.

Captain Rickard hits the panel with his fists. "We're up against a wall here, people. Some crazy things are going down between the SBG and the Coalition Fleet over some dispute they had." He turns to everyone. "Our options were very limited. Trust me when I say that I picked the best one."

Everyone nods and Captain Rickard returns to the panel. "So what is the job?" Nev asks.

Rickard brings up a display showing Europa's largest colony Galileo. "Apparently some company CEO is refusing to work with the SBG over some contracts." He highlights a set of coordinates. "Our job is simple. We go here and meet with another ship to pick up a prisoner. Presumably someone close to the CEO."

Ava takes a step forward. "You mean, we are kidnapping someone for extortion?!" she practically growls.

Captain Rickard glowers at her. "Essentially yes. We pick her up and hold her until the CEO signs a contract, then we return her. That simple. Nobody needs to get hurt and this will wipe the slate clear with the SBG."

"You mean all of the debt?" Don says in disbelief.

Captain Rickard nods. Everyone looks around in silence. "So who is the target?" I ask.

The captain looks at me. "You aren't coming."

"What?!" Ava and the twins practically shout.

"We are leaving you here on the Odyssey. That is final!" he says with a sharp voice.

"This is complete shit. We need him!" Ava says.

The captain looks at her "Is that so? You think you can be captain now?"

Ava hesitates. "He saved my life more than once back on Pilot!" she shouts.

"I've already been briefed on what happened on Pilot. If it wasn't for this nuisance!" He points at me. "None of that would have happened in the first place!"

"That's not true. Vek was a cheat. He was going to betray us no matter who was there. Tell him, Nev!" Her voice was cracking from the irritation.

Nev looks at me then Ava. "I could have handled it," he mutters.

"Bullshit, tell him the truth!" Ava snarled.

Lora steps forward. "If John didn't provide cover fire we wouldn't have made it to the skip. We wouldn't be here without him." Her cool attitude was a nice reprieve from the growing angst.

The captain opens his mouth when Don interrupts. "I say we vote." Ava, Ron and Don nod their heads.

"Vote?!" Captain Rickard shouts. "Did you forget who your captain is; this isn't a democracy. This is my ship and my rules!"

Ava opens her mouth, preparing for another volley when I decide to speak up. "I'll go."

Everyone looks at me. "What?" Ava ask in a low voice.

"I said I'll go."

Silence fills the bridge as the twins and Ava's face look as though I have betrayed them. I force a smile and turn toward the door.

"I'm leaving also," Ava says, following me.

"We're leaving too," the twins say at the same time.

"Guys come on—" I begin to say when Ava shoots me a vicious glare.

"So what now, captain? Either he stays or we all leave," Ava says unemotionally.

The captain leans onto the control panel with his arms crossed, silently staring at us. After a while he begins laughing hysterically. We exchange looks of confusion. "If you feel so strongly about him staying, then I guess he can stay."

The words were subtle and soft but the meaning behind them was beyond exciting. The twins immediately give me a massive hug, which I think dislocates some of my ribs.

Then Ava, still fuming over my brash move, reaches out with her hand. "Welcome to the Idle Confessor," she says formally.

I take her hand and firmly shake it. "Thank you for having me."

Lora pats my back, then walks over to Nev and flicks his chin so that he closes his mouth.

"Alright, alright." Captain Rickard's voice reverberates over everyone else. "We have about eight hours till we reach the coordinates. I want everyone to get some sleep and that isn't a suggestion."

Everyone begins walking out of the hatch when I feel a hand grab my forearm. I turn seeing Captain Rickard. "Did you want to talk to me?" I ask.

He nods his head as Ava begins walking past us, hesitating at the hatch. Rickard gives her a volatile stare and she frowns and storms out. The hatch closes with a loud clap and we are alone.

Captain Rickard walks to a chair and takes a seat. "I don't care if you are part of the crew," he says coldly. "If you ever threaten their safety again, I'll kill you myself." His voice is calm and deliberate.

"You were right," I respond. "About everything."

He gives me a quizzical look as I begin to tell him everything that happened on Pilot, including what really happened to Vek, his men and the IISF soldiers. I also tell him about the conversation I had with my reflection and the events that took place prior to me sneaking onto his skip. At the end I let out a massive breath as if I have just confessed to a life's worth of guilt. All the while James Rickard sits silently with his arms crossed as he stares at me.

Several quiet minutes roll by when I finally speak. "So, that's it. Are you going to say anything?"

He wipes his mouth, leaning forward and bracing himself on his knees. "Why tell me the truth now and not sooner?"

"Several reasons." I begin. "Because it is absolutely crazy. Because I didn't want to believe it myself. But most of all because you wouldn't have let me stay. You still don't want me to stay."

He looks up at me and stands, placing his hands on my shoulders. "You are right. I didn't want you to stay. You're unpredictable and dangerous. But for the first time since you've been here, you told me the truth." He turns and begins hitting various controls on the panel.

"That's it? All you wanted was for me to be honest?" I ask in disbelief.

"What else is there other than honesty? If you can't tell me the truth then you don't respect me, and if you don't respect me then I can't expect you to be loyal to me and the Confessor." The Idle Confessor lifts and exits the dock. James turns and faces me. "That's all that will ever matter. This crew is a family, and the Confessor is our home. If you want it to be your home you have to fight for it and its people with no excuses."

I nod my head. "I swear I will do whatever it takes to prove myself to you."

"Don't bother," James says coldly. "You've already done that. It's not every day that my crew threatens to leave because of a stowaway." He chuckles and shakes his head.

"I didn't know they were going to do that."

"Which makes it even more genuine." He holds his hands out. "I may be the captain but sometimes the Confessor chooses who she wants to stay and who she wants to go."

An antiquated notion that has been around since humanity manned wooden ships on Earth's oceans, is that a ship isn't just a ship but rather a living entity. Captain Rickard is one of a dying breed that believes in the old ways. I respect that, whether I believe it or not. The Confessor has felt like a home I never had and now finally I'm not just a guest anymore.

I look at him realizing that I had been silently lost in my thoughts for who knows how long. "Sorry," I say. "I'm still not all here from—you know."

James nods his head. "Why don't you get some rest then?"

Rest sounds like a good idea. Even though I have just been sleeping for five days, I can feel the wariness creeping in. I bow my head and walk to the hatch, soon entering the corridor. The walk back to my room feels good. I am familiar with the Confessor now, not losing my way as I did in the first few days I was here. The various displays popping up don't catch my attention as they used to and before long the hatch to my room slides open. The air is stale but it doesn't bother me. I quickly hop into bed and study the ceiling for several minutes.

My Aug begins buzzing. I glance at my forearm and accept the call. "Hey Thomas, can we talk later?"

Thomas's face doesn't hide a bit of his displeasure. "I was not finished running tests on you."

"We'll pick it up tomorrow. Right now I think I'm going to get some sleep," I respond.

Thomas's frown deepens. "I don't think that is a good idea. While you were unconscious I did several tests that came back with interesting results."

I sit up. "Interesting how?"

"Well, for one, they were like nothing I have ever seen before. I insist you come back to the infirmary so I can continue to do tests." He smiles with excitement.

"Thomas, focus. Am I going to be ok?" I stress the amount of urgency in my tone.

Thomas's smile disappears. "It's tough to say. My equipment is limited. Generally, you are in great shape. There are just anomalies that I can't seem to classify."

"Anomalies?!" My stomach writhes with worry.

"Also, as you know, I'm still learning about today's technologies. In particular the BICS or Aug as you put it." He grins awkwardly.

"That's right. You were made before BICS started to be integrated into society." Sometimes I forget that he is a synthetic, which may or may not be a bad thing.

"Well I decided to integrate with yours, so as to better understand how they worked and—" He stops. "Is something the matter?"

"Yes, Thomas you can't just integrate with people's Aug without their permission. It is a huge violation. And how did you get past my Biometric Encryption?" My tone reflected both aggravation and amazement.

"Oh my, I'm very sorry. No one told me I couldn't. I just thought—"

"It's fine. Now you know. More importantly, how did you circumvent my encryption?" I press.

Biometric Encryption was born from a fear that people's BICS could be hacked. It uses the uniqueness of an individual's DNA mixed with a quantum hash to create what is known in the tech industry as a Biometric DNA. Quite literally every human being has a unique Biometric DNA and is it impossible to break.

"Well," Thomas started "I'd recognize the Quantum hash anywhere because the creator was also my programmer. All I had to do was reverse engineer the other half from your DNA."

I could feel my jaw drop. Literally the safest and most secure security system in the solar system was undermined by an ancient synthetic that was simply curious. "Thomas, you weren't supposed to be able to do that. You can't tell anybody that you did." He nods his head. "So what did you find?" I ask.

"Oh, right." Thomas looks over to the right. "Apparently you have a significant amount of data partitioned as OS backup without reason."

"What do you mean without reason?"

"From the technical standpoint there is no need for it," he says with unbridled enthusiasm "Also, it was encrypted using an algorithm beyond even my comprehension," he finishes.

"Avant-Garde." The word slips out of my mouth involuntarily.

"What was that?" Thomas asks.

"Listen Thomas, you haven't told anyone else about this, right?"

Thomas is silent for a moment. "No, I take patient-doctor confidentiality. Very serious."

"Good, as soon as we finish this next job we can talk about it." I can see that this answer wasn't what he wanted, but the exhaustion was starting to take its toll. "Thomas, I need to rest right now. I promise we will talk about this."

"Ok, well let me know if you're having any problems. Sleep well." He forces a smile and ends the connection.

I fall back into my bed and place my forearm on my forehead. 'Unclassifiable anomalies, hidden partitions?' What the hell is going on with me? I want to continue to contemplate the reasoning behind these oddities but I find myself quickly slipping away into sleep. The subtle hum of the Confessor serves as my lullaby and before long I'm falling into my subconscious. There is a part of me that hopes to return to the white room and continue the conversation with my shadow self. But nothing of the sort comes, just darkness and eventually a knock.

Chapter Nineteen: The Emerald Encounter

At first I thought the knock was in my head, but after the second round I open my eyes. My room is dark. I lift my forearm up to see that three hours have already passed. I rub the stiffness from my neck when another series of knocks come from the door.

"Yeah, yeah. I'm coming," I say, stumbling to the door and opening it.

Ava is standing there, her blazing red hair just barely contained by a band that looks underqualified for the job. Her crystalline emerald eyes are more beautiful than ever. She is wearing a fitted jump suit that had seen better days, but to me it was perfect. At first she was looking at my eyes but then she glanced down and blushed. I was either still asleep or too enamored with her to realize that I apparently undressed myself while I was sleeping and I had just opened the door wearing nothing but my briefs.

Ava turns away as I quickly slip into my jumper. "Sorry—what's up?" I say, trying to hide my embarrassment.

She looks at me grinning from ear to ear, her cheeks still slightly rosy from my peep show. "I was wondering if you've seen Grem?" she asks softly.

"No I haven't seen her," I reply.

Ava frowns and looks down the corridor. "Ok, well." She hesitates, glancing at me, then taking a step away from the door.

I search my mind for something suave to say or anything that could delay her exit. "Wait—um—" I stutter.

"Yes?" she almost shouts, returning to the door.

"I—thanks." I force the words out awkwardly. "Um, for earlier back on the bridge."

She narrows her eyes as if I just reminded her of a repressed memory. "Why would you just leave without a fight?" she asks.

I was wondering the same thing, but the answer wasn't easy to explain. "I guess, because of you."

Judging from the look on her face she took my answer the wrong way. "What is that supposed to mean?!" Her tone was getting caustic.

I ignore her anger. "Because I'm afraid I'm going to get you hurt." The fury in her face melts away. "Because I don't know anything about you but for whatever reason, I can't help but—" I choke on the last words.

Ava takes a step closer. "But what?" she says, placing her hand on my chest.

I can feel the fire growing in me again. "But I want you." The words flow out of my mouth without a second thought.

She grabs me by the back of my neck and kisses me, slamming the door behind her. I caress her body, ensuring that I remember every curve. She shivers a bit when I reach her side.

"Sorry," I pant.

She laughs. "It tickles."

I touch her sides a few more times, forcing her to push against me. The fire inside is now overwhelming me and I'm sure she can tell because she moves her hand down in response. I gasp as she touches me. Ava bites her lip, staring at me with those beautiful emerald eyes. My heart starts to pound through my chest and I can't take it any longer. I pushing her against the door and she moans; for a moment I forget all the things that have been happening. All the grief, fear and unknown slips away replaced by sheer pleasure.

I start unzipping her jump suit, savoring every millimeter when she stops me mid-way, taking my hand and placing it on her bare chest. Her skin is warm and smooth and the anticipation is nearly unbearable. The whole time she is staring at me, slowly guiding my hand lower and lower. By the time I reach her abdomen she is grinding firmly against me. Then it happens, the moment our eyes meet time seems to stop. We are both completely and unequivocally captivated with each other.

Ava pushes me onto the bed, her eyes resembling a predator ready to pounce as she slowly finishes unzipping her suit and releasing her hair. She stands in front of me, her naked body practically shimmering under the dim lights, her crazy hair resting over her shoulders. I exhale, feeling my body weaken in her presence, she slowly crawls atop of me, never ceasing to break eye contact, finally leaning forward and whispering, "I want you too, John."

I have experienced so many moments in my short and trivial lifetime. Things that I can't explain, things that I wish I could forget, both noteworthy and insignificant. But this moment, lying next to Ava as she slowly falls asleep in my arms is not insignificant. Moments like these are defining and unwavering, the type that sends you a clear message. Is it possible though, to love someone so absolutely as if it was predetermined? As if the entire solar system came together in order for us to be with one another? I don't believe in love. I've never believed in it and yet when I look at her I feel that there is nothing more than love and I'm not bothered by that belief.

In no time I feel myself slipping into my subconscious. It is the most restful sleep I've ever had and without a doubt the happiest I'd ever felt.

My Aug begins to buzz incessantly pulling me from my sleep. I hit accept and Nev's face with his characteristic scowl pops up.

"Hey, stowaway," a voice from my wrist starts. "Get your ass up. We're almost at the coordinates."

I rub my eyes with my free hand, realizing that Ava is gone. I look around the room for her but there is no evidence that she had been here at all.

"Hello?" Nev's voice doesn't hide a bit of annoyance.

"Nev, thanks but you don't have to call me stowaway anymore. I'm part of the crew now." I let my tone sound as acidic as possible.

"Well, look at you, feeling like a big shot," he starts with a smile "You may be part of the crew now, but you'll never stop being a stowaway."

"Right." I flick my wrist, closing the connection and roll out of bed.

I shamble over to the sink and let the cold water run over my hands. I bring my face down to meet them, the water shocking me the rest of the way out of sleep. The events that took place only a few hours ago won't stop replaying like a video in my mind. I can feel myself getting excited again, so I force my thoughts into a different direction, noticing my reflection in the mirror. The sensation that it is not me creeps into the back of my mind as I rub my chin where a thick layer of stubble is now beginning to itch. I grab the sonic razor the twins gave me from the shelf and make little work of the growth followed by another cold splash of water, causing a shiver to course through my body. I take a moment to inspect bruises and cuts on my body. Some are almost completely healed while others still stand out against my completion.

I lean forward to take a closer look at the eye Cheever punched almost two weeks ago. So much has happened since then that it feels like months. Not even the bruise remains. But there is something else that's bothering me. Something has changed about my eyes. At first it is barely noticeable but the longer I study them, the more I can't deny the fact that they are different. There are what seem to be flakes or shavings of a blue and white metallic substance moving in from the lower edge of my iris. I continue to study them for several minutes, moving my focus from eye to eye, when my Aug begins buzzing again. I jerk away from the mirror, accepting the call. Nev's face, now boasting an even more irritated glare, shows up. I close the connection before he can say anything, quickly throwing on my clothes and leaving the room.

Chapter Twenty: The Unexpected Reunion

The walk to the cargo hold was faster than I expected. Undoubtedly because I was muttering to myself like a crazy person. I couldn't shake the idea that I was now physically being affected by whatever is happening to me. A surplus of questions started to run through my mind. What does this mean? Am I going to be ok? And what the hell is happening to me? These were just a few. Before I knew it Nev was standing in front of me, obviously fuming from my cavalier dismissal of his last call.

"What's up big man?" I ask, hiding my angst.

He raises his hands like he is getting ready to start yelling or singing, finally pointing at the twins and Lora. "Just go help them." He grumbles.

I look over at the twins who are waist deep in what looks like a riveting conversation about the plausible effects near light speed would have on a common potato. Lora, on the other hand, looks as though she is about to take a long walk out the Confessor's service hatch. All in all it is a sight that brings a smile to my face and makes me forget about my latest discovery.

I walk over and notice they are slipping into HEC Suits. "What are these for?" I inquire.

"Standard safety procedures. We don't want to get busted now do we?" Captain Rickard's voice catches my attention.

I turn, noticing Ava standing beside him. Her posture is straight and rigid and she refuses to make eye contact with me.

"I hope you've got some extra, cause Ava and I sort of lost ours back on Pilot," I say looking down at my feet.

"No worries," Don says.

Ron opens a black crate retrieving two brand new suits. "Got these for a steal on the Odyssey," he says, tossing them to us.

I quickly slip into mine. The new suit is much more updated than the old one I had. It even has the ability to change color, similar to my Aug jamming jacket. By no means was it as advanced as the IISF, but it definitely helped level the playing field. Once it finishes syncing with my Aug, Captain Rickard places his hand on the helmet.

"Can you hear me?" he asks.

"Loud and clear," I respond with a smile.

"Good, cause now you owe me eighteen thousand creds." He chuckles.

I feel my jaw drop. "Eighteen thousand?!" I stutter.

"Yup," he responds. "Oh, and this." Rickard walks over to the black crate pulling a pulse revolver and repeater out then hands them to me. "So that puts you at about twenty-three thousand—welcome to the crew." He pats me on the shoulder and walks away.

I look at the twins who shrug and return to their debate when the proximity alarms start to sound. Captain Rickard opens a holo-display showing a smaller ship beside us. "Looks like they're here!" he shouts.

Nev pulls his revolver as he walks over to the cargo hatch. "Have they sent a request to docking yet?"

Captain Rickard shakes his head. "It looks like they want to keep coms to a minimum because they're extending their tube now." He looks up from his display. "Nev, don't unlock the hatch 'til they formally request to dock."

I walk over to the twins who are studying a display of their own. They have a detailed view of the ship with the designation SST-A Hauser painted on the side.

Typically, I wouldn't question this, but judging from the twin's scrutinizing glare I have to ask. "What's the matter?"

"This ship is not what it seems," Don says.

Ron nods his head. "They're using a forged Ship Identification Code."

"How can you tell?" I ask.

"It's not unheard of for Small Standard Trade ships to have forged SIDCs, most of the time they don't have an ARAD so the Coalition Fleet doesn't pursue them like they would a Medium or a Large Standard," Don says.

"But, this one—" Ron starts zooming into the image of the Hauser. "Damn, Captain they're armed!"

I take a closer look at the image; there are several obvious additions to the hull that look like unnecessary plasma vents. "What are those?"

"Direct Energy Pulse cannons," Don responds.

Besides the fact that arming a civilian trade ship is absolutely illegal according to Article Ten of the Trade Act, we were now about to be tethered to a small ship that could do crippling damage to us because they were within our shield's threshold.

Captain Rickard runs over to look at the display. "Are there any heat signatures?"

Don rattles his fingers across his forearm and the image updates showing a chaos of colors. Rickard lets out an exhale as he pats Don's shoulders. "Keep an eye on it would you."

I look closer at the image. The fake plasma vents are a dark blue, indicating no heat. "If those start turning red we are in for a bad time," Ron says.

"It's surprising they have gotten away with this for this long," Don starts. "You know, with them being so poorly disguised and all."

"Well, they don't have that much room as it is, so hiding them would be difficult," Ron says. "Not like with us."

It took a moment to sink in. "So the Confessor does have weapons."

The twins look at me. "Oh right, you were unconscious," Ron says nonchalantly bringing up his display. "How do you think we saved you from that IISF Destroyer?"

He runs his finger along his wrist and the playback of the Confessor intercepting the Destroyer's missiles begins. The massive explosions gleam blue against the Confessor's shields with no apparent damage to the ship. Numerous panels on the Confessor lift revealing several large DEP cannons, a few Kinetic

Rail Guns and a plethora of long-range smart missiles pointed at the unsuspecting assailant. By then the IISF destroyer is moving too fast to change course. I can feel my body tighten in anticipation as I watch.

The Confessor unleashes her arsenal in a beautiful display of destruction slamming the IISF Destroyer head on and causing massive chucks of the ship to float off. The ravaged husk that remains careens uncontrollably, spitting escape pods in all directions. It continues to tumble weightlessly several times, resembling an intricate dance, when the husk begins to emit a bright blue light that encompasses the display. The recording shudders as the shock wave hits the Confessor. Several seconds later the blinding light dissipates and the IISF Destroy husk is little more than a floating field of rubble no bigger than my fist.

Ron closes the display and looks at me. "Pretty cool huh?"

"Cool?!" I exclaim. "You guys have outfitted a trade ship with enough weapons and munitions to decimate a Destroyer class warship in one volley and all you can say is 'pretty cool?!'" I exhale. The twins bite their lips, nodding their heads with controlled excitement. "Hell yeah that's cool!"

"Now that you are part of the crew," Captain Rickard interrupts "you'll find that the Confessor is unlike any other ship in the solar system."

"Yeah, upgraded armor, shields, oversized fusion core, advanced automated systems and of course the retractable teeth," Don says with pride.

"But isn't that a little much?" I ask mistakenly.

The cargo hold falls silent as everyone stops and looks at me. Rickard lifts his arm and opens a display showing the Main

Belt. “Do you know why the Trade Act was commissioned?” he asked.

“No, well I mean in school we were told that the Trade Act was needed to help protect and build the Frontier’s economy after the Stand Still,” I respond.

Everyone begins laughing. “The Trade Act was a means to control all distribution of goods in order to levy more taxes," Rickard says. “Before the Trade Act, Trade ships like the Confessor were able to have weapons for self-defense and also because the government could, in a time of extreme need, build a militia by commandeering privately own ships,” he finishes.

“But after the Stand Still the governments were weak and afraid of rebellion," I say flatly as if I had always known.

Rickard nods his head. “Exactly. With the existence of the Freelance organizations and their growing popularity, the government feared that the Freelancers could amass a fleet large enough to commit a coup.”

“But now that we can’t arm our ships, we’re easy picking for Skywaymen and the Brotherhood, who reside in the DMZ," Don says, pointing at the main belt.

Everyone had heard of the marauders and murderers that roamed the lawless DMZ. There are plenty of stories told to children before bed that warn of their attacks and even some that glorify them, but in truth they are just wandering killers that prey on the weak. The moniker Skywaymen is used when describing the criminals or low lives that rob unescorted trade ships. Apparently it’s a variation of the name used for ancient bandits that used to hold up something called stagecoaches before humanity reached industrialization. Given the romanticized nomenclature surrounding the ancient

Highwaymen, the name Skywaymen was most likely coined by the petty thieves themselves.

But the Brotherhood of the Stars is a different story. They are fanatical purists that believe humanity has arrogantly attempted to usurp God with trans-human technology and therefore we must die for our insurrections. Their beliefs are based off a pseudo-new religion that came about several hundred years ago: the Church of Stars. Similar to some of the more ancient religions, the Church of Stars believes in a sole omnipotent creator who simply left after creating all of existence. The Church believes that God left in order for us to grow and adapt to master the universe he created for us and that eventually we will find him after having transcended to a point where he greets us as his equals and no longer as his children.

It's a religion born of science and faith and during the golden age it was all humanity wanted, to reach for the stars and find our maker. Now humanity is lost, too concerned with trivial differences and precarious entitlement. And the Brotherhood is pompous enough to believe God charged them with exacting his retribution. If God could see us now, I wonder what he would say and think. I wonder if he would weep for his children. Sometimes I wonder how we have come so far, done so much and yet learned so little.

The cargo hatch sensors begin screaming as the Hauser's docking tube seals around the door. "Captain, they're not responding to any of our communication attempts," Lora says.

"Don't open that door, Nev!" Rickard orders.

I pull my revolver out and check the chamber, ensuring it is loaded, then I catch Ava staring at me. She quickly turns her head when she notices my curiosity.

"Kid, backup Nev. Lora, get to the bridge. We may need to get out of here quickly. Don, go with Lora. If you see those cannons start warming up, I want us gone!" Captain Rickard says confidently.

I walk forward and stand on the opposite side of the hatch from Nev as Lora and Don run out of the hold. Rickard opens a display and begins recording a message. "To the crew of the SST Hauser, this is Captain James Rickard of the MST Idle Confessor. We have repeatedly attempted to contact you with no response and still you have attached yourselves to our ship. You have thirty seconds to respond before we remove your docking tube with extreme prejudice."

Rickard closes the connection and looks at Ron. "Put us in attack posture, Mr. Witman."

Ron nods his head and bolts out the door. Several moments later the cargo lights go out and are replaced by red hazard lights. Ron's voice comes over the Confessor's intercom. "Charging DEP cannons. Waiting on your signal to deploy, sir."

By now the thirty seconds has more than come and gone, but we remain tethered to the Hauser. A display comes up on the exterior hatch. Five people are making their way through the docking tube to the Confessor and from the looks of it, one of them has their hands tied.

"What's the plan?" Nev says, but his question goes unanswered.

The captain begins pacing back and forth when a muffled knock comes from the exterior hatch. I look at the door display and one of the armored men is looking right at the camera, scribbling something on what looks like a glass tablet. A few seconds later he holds the tablet up facing the camera. The name Nalary Kross is scrawled across the glass.

We look at Rickard who is frozen. "Nev," he mutters "open the door."

Nev opens his mouth to protest, but the look Rickard gives him dissuades any further argument. A moment later the door opens and four armed individuals along with one prisoner enter the cargo hold with their guns at the ready. The one with the tablet scans the area with his gaze, finally stopping on Captain Rickard. He reaches up and removes his helmet, letting free his long gray hair.

"How the hell are ya, James?" he says in a raspy voice.

The room falls silent and for a moment I can't tell whether the captain is going to shoot the man or greet him. Thankfully, a subtle smirk begins to form on Rickard's face and he begins laughing loudly.

"Daniel, it's been too long?" Captain Rickard yells, pulling the man in for a hug.

Daniel looks around. "I had no idea this pile of scrap was still going, let alone with you in command."

"Hey, watch your mouth. She runs like a beauty," James says, tapping his foot on the floor.

Ava takes a few steps toward the two, causing the three other crew members from the Hauser to lift their guns again. In an instant, everyone pulls on one another except for James and Daniel.

"Bit jumpy," Captain Rickard says, placing his hand on Ava's forearm to lower her gun.

"Yeah, sorry. This job is—well you know," Daniel says, waving his hand at his escort. "We are guests here. You can relax."

The three lower their guns and begin removing their helmets. Nev, Ava and I do the same. I lift the helmet off and take a deep breath of fresh hair, wiping away the sweat on my forehead. Although the HEC Suit has advanced air filtration and circulation systems, it does start to get stuffy and hot after a while.

An audible gasp sounds behind me followed by a familiar voice. "Oh my god, John?!" A part of me didn't believe the woman's voice until I turned around.

"Keida?!" It has been just over a month since I last saw her being escorted from the orphanage by a Coalition Fleet Drafter, but she looks like a completely different person.

Before I fully recover from the shock, Keida has her arms around my neck and is kissing me passionately. She pulls away, smiling widely. "How did you get off Titan without being drafted?" she asks.

I quickly glance around the cargo hold for Ava, but she is nowhere to be found. Damn-it. Of all the people I expected to see again, Cheever was higher on the list than Keida. I'm not angry. It's just timing can be a real bitch. "Me? How did you get away from the CF?"

Keida's blue eyes gleam with excitement as she pushes back a stray lock of her golden blonde hair. She opens her mouth to respond but a hand rests on her shoulder. "Who is your friend, Keida?" Daniel asks.

"Sorry, sir. This is John. We grew up together on Titan. Remember, I told you about him." She sounded different, not like the little girl I remember growing up with.

I feel a sting in the back of my mind as the realization that she doesn't know about Jurin's death floods in, coupled with the string of emotions from my childhood that I had desperately tried to leave behind. It wasn't because of Keida. I mean, for all intents and purposes, I loved her. But I'm not the same person I was a month and a half ago. It was almost as if I was morphing into something else. And then the thought of Ava, not even twelve hours after we had sex. Having to see me kiss another woman. But what was Ava's problem? She left me in bed like I was nothing, like it meant nothing. Oh God, what the hell am I going to do?

I realize everyone is just staring at me. I feel my cheeks get warm. "Sorry, what?"

Captain Rickard shakes his head as Daniel smiles. "I'm Daniel Kross, Commander of the Hauser. It's good to meet you. Keida speaks highly of you," he finishes, extending his hand out.

I reach out and shake it firmly. "Thank you." I think a bit about the name he wrote on the tablet. "Who is Nalary?"

Daniel looks at Rickard then back at me. "She was my sister. We grew up with this ugly bastard and we were in the war together. I knew he would know it was me by mentioning that name."

A subtle frown forms on Captain Rickard's face, but only for a second before it returns to normal. "Alright, alright. I think we'd better get back to business," he says.

Daniel straightens and looks at the prisoner. "She's feisty, but we threw the Null gear on her and she calmed down." He points at a large helmet on her head that nullifies hearing and sight. Then he handed Rickard the glass tablet. "This is your itinerary. It's off the net and has a timed encryption. First you're heading toward Ganymede, but it will update you on your next destination before you get there. Once the CEO signs the contracts you'll be informed using the code word that the tablet will unencrypt for you in an hour."

Rickard takes the tablet and shakes Daniels hand. "Next time we get a chance we need to drink a few and catch up. First round is on me," he says.

Daniel grins. "Yeah, and maybe you can pay me back the fifty you owe me." He laughs, turning and walking toward the Hauser.

Keida kisses me again, grabbing my forearm "Here's my updated contact information. Send me an eVid. We need to catch up and talk."

I feel a prickle, indicating that I saved her contact information to my Aug. eVids run with a higher communication protocol and require the use of a Quantum Social Address. Similar to Biometric DNA, the QSA is a quantum string that is unique to everyone after they are graphed with their BICS. It allows people to communicate via eVids virtually anywhere as long as you have the correct string, unlike the live communicators, which have a functional range that varies.

I nod my head, still a little shocked, and force a smile as she turns and scurries back to the Hauser. I found myself standing there for several minutes, refusing to move because if I did then I would have to explain what just happened to Ava or deal with the confused chaos of emotions I'm feeling.

Captain Rickard snaps his fingers in front of my face. "You ok, kid?"

I shake my head and look at him. "Yeah it's just—"

"Hard to see people from your past? I get it. But right now we have work to do," he responds in an understanding tone I didn't quite expect.

Chapter Twenty-One: The Crimson Façade

I help Nev escort our VIP to the brig. The entire time I couldn't help but wonder why she seemed incredibly calm for someone that was being held hostage not to mention couldn't see or hear. I could tell Nev picked up on it as well, cause he kept giving me these sidelong looks that told me he had a bad feeling.

By the time we reached the massive holding compartment doors we were both more than anxious to get her behind the barrier.

"Once we get her in and the door is shut I'm going to remove this Null gear," Nev says, taking her by the upper arm and leading her in. "Be sure to have your visor tinted and your voice masked."

I shake my head in agreement. "What if she needs something?"

"We'll have food brought to us. Otherwise we talk to her as little as possible," Nev responds.

I look at him for a moment. "You sound as though you've done this before," I say flatly.

Nev grimaces and shuts the door behind us, then touches the side of his visor turning it black. I do the same and give him a nod. He proceeds to remove the Null gear, soon revealing the unfortunate victim. She squints and frowns, looking around the room until her stare reaches me.

"So they moved me to another ship. Smart, but you're still going to get caught for this," she says in an understandably irritated voice as she runs her hands through her messy brown hair.

Nev takes her by the arm and pushes her into one of the cells. He removes her bindings and I engage the barrier.

She rubs her wrists and looks around the brig, studying every detail. "A lot bigger ship. Probably a medium standard, maybe even a large. You guys planning on using the ARAD to get some distance?"

Nev and I remain still and silent, not reacting, because you can discern almost anything from non-verbal expression.

"Ah, you guys are good. Not like the last crew. I could tell you almost everything about them. One kept droning on and on about some guy." She stretches her arms and sits on the bed.

I feel warmth returning to my cheeks when a knock comes from the door. I walk over and hit the display to show the other side. Even though her visor is tinted I can tell it is Ava. I crack the door and slip out, no doubt to Nev's irritation, but I know he isn't going to act out as long as the VIP is watching.

Ava takes a few steps back as I remove my helmet and run my hand through my hair, hopefully making it look less like I was wearing a helmet. She remains still with the tray of food in her hands.

The awkward silences goes one until I clear my throat. "Hey, we should—"

Without warning Ava throws the food tray at me, which barely misses my head. It slams into the holding cell door sending food and utensils in all directions. That probably got Nev's attention. I look back at her but she is already walking down the corridor.

"Wait, Ava!" I run after her, grabbing her arm.

She pulls away and turns. Her visor is still blacked out, but I can feel her fiery glare. "There's nothing to talk about!" Her voice was masked by the suit.

She begins walking down the passage again. "Where did you go this morning, huh?!" I shout at her. She stops. "And then you won't make eye contact with me, like nothing happened."

This time she turns and stomps toward me, stopping at an arm's length.

"Who is she?!" Her voice, despite being masked sounded like a cocktail of hatred and frustration with subtle hints of jealousy and maybe even betrayal.

"Keida. She and I were together before she was drafted," I say in a low voice.

"Do you love her?!" the animatronic sound of her voice can't hide her overflowing emotions.

I think for a bit. "I—I don't know. I mean, I think I used to. But then you and all the stuff that has happened." My voice trails off, thinking about all that has changed.

Ava is quiet for a long time, finally turning and taking a few steps then stopping. "I didn't like you kissing her."

"Well, really it was all her."

"Shut up, I wasn't finished. I didn't like you kissing her, but I didn't like me not liking you kissing her more," she finishes, noticeably relaxing her shoulders.

I take a second to make sense of what she was saying when she removes her helmet and looks at me. Her eyes are still full of anger but also red and slightly swollen.

"I don't know what to do with myself, John," she starts. "Last night shouldn't have happened, but I'd be lying if I said I didn't want it more than anything," she finishes.

"I know, I feel it too, but what's the problem? Keida and I—so much has changed since then," I respond, taking a few steps toward her, but she keeps her distance.

"It's not that," she says.

I tilt my head, wanting nothing more than to take her in my arms and kiss her. "Then what is it?"

"I just—can't, John. It's complicated. There are rules!" she frowns, averting her beautiful eyes.

"Is it cause you're the first mate?" She opens her mouth, hesitates, then decides to simply nod her head. "Forget all that. I want you, Ava, and it scares the hell out me. I know you want me too, damn-it!" I rush forward, taking her in my arms and kiss her.

Ava's legs buckle and she wraps her arms around my head. Her lips are unbelievable, like a drug I can't get enough of. I push her against the wall and she wraps her legs around me. But then she stops, cradling my face in her hands, staring deep into my eyes as if she is searching for something. I can tell she notices the silvery-blue flakes in my eyes and a part of me thinks I should turn away, but her gaze has me in a trance.

"Ava!" Rickard's voice sounds on her Aug and we both jump apart as if he could see us.

"Yes, captain," she stammers.

"Is something wrong? You sound flustered," he responds.

I pick her helmet up and hand it to her. "No, I'm fine. Just finished dropping off the food." She looks at the aluminum tray with one corner crushed in from the impact and winces.

"Good, I need you back at the bridge as soon as you can. James out." She looks at me and bits her bottom lip innocently.

I can feel a fire starting in me, but I do the best I can to subdue it and put my helmet back on. She does the same and stares at me. "We'll talk later, okay?" she says.

"I look forward to it," I respond. She touches her visor and it goes black again, hiding her face from my sight, then she turns and walks away.

I pick up what was left of the food, mostly the sides that were vacuum sealed survived the unexpected impact, but I guess it's better than nothing. I walk over to the security door and type in the code. The door slides open and I take a few steps in. I was so distracted by Ava that I didn't notice the light were out.

"Nev?!" I call out, placing the tray on the table beside me and pulling the pulse revolver from its holster.

I take a few more steps, finding Nev's body on the ground. I shout his name but he doesn't respond. I make my way cautiously toward him with my revolver at the ready.

"Finally. I was starting to think you'd never come back." The voice of our not so helpless victim echoes through the room.

I open my communicator but the signal is jammed. "Damn-it!" I mutter through my teeth.

"Oh yeah, forgot to mention you're on your own." Her voice deepens with sinister intent.

My foot bumps into Nev and I nudge him a few times until he starts moving. "Nev, wake up!" I whisper.

He moans, rolling over to his back. His visor is shattered almost as if someone had punched it, which is insane because these visors can be hit by a small vehicle before they even crack. I start looking around the room frantically. This was a set up from the very beginning. That is more than evident now, but the question is why.

"Who are you?" I ask.

There is silence for a moment. "Let's just say I'm a friend of an acquaintance."

Nev, now on all fours, spits some blood out the front of his helmet and reaches for his gun.

"Be more specific. We have a lot of acquaintances," I respond, helping Nev to his feet.

"You'll find out soon enough." The voice lingers when the lights turn back on.

Nev and I search the room but there is nothing. Then I feel Nev elbow me and whisper "Infrared."

It takes a split second for me to react, hitting my forearm and updating my display. The view takes a moment to change, finally revealing the heat signature of a woman standing right in front of me grinning.

"Nev!" I manage to shout before being thrown across the room and into the bulkhead with a tremendous amount of force.

My display begins flickering and distorting when Nev hits the wall beside me. I quickly pull my helmet off and grab him by the arm, dragging him to the door. I start typing in the code when a stool shatters against the wall next to me.

"Where are you going?!" she growls "I'm not done!"

Panic, dread, fear—whatever you want to call it—grabs and squeezes me into a cowardly pulp. That is until I sense him, my other self, lingering on the fringes of my mind, and like that I lose all reservations. I drop Nev beside me and turn. The room seems empty but I know better.

"Ah, so the mouse found his nerve," the woman's voice says. "Let's see what your worth is, shall we?" The space in front of me begins to shimmer as the VIP, now looking completely different, uncloaks and strikes a pose. "What do you think?"

What stood before me was not a woman, well not completely, but rather the unholy offspring of cyber-bionics and a deranged mind. There was almost nothing natural about her from her four military-grade and-then-some bionic limbs to her continually changing skin, hair and eye color. She was created to be a master of infiltration and most likely assassination; I can easily tell that much but the most disconcerting thing about her was that she was obviously messed up in the head.

"Who are you?" I stammer.

She straightens and places her hands on her hips. "Where are my manners? My name is Nyla Crimm, but—" Her entire body turns crimson red. "Most know me as Crimson. At least they do before I kill them." She laughs as her body colors begin to change again. "Have you heard of me, mousy?" she finishes with pursed lips.

My throat swells with angst. Crimson is the infamous leader of the Triad Mercenaries. Everyone knows about her. She's like death incarnate and I'm staring right at her. "I have, but why are you here?"

Nyla tilts her head. "Why? Because of money and I like to have a little fun, mousy." She begins twirling around the room like a ballerina. "But first I have to cripple this ship, which I did about thirty minutes ago without you even realizing."

I feel an unsettling lurch and the Confessor's lights flicker. Nyla stops dancing and grins wildly. "What do you want with us?!" I demand.

Nyla looks at me and pouts "You of all people should know—right mousy? You have a little secret inside."

I lift my revolver toward her but she is already on me, landing a terrible punch to my lower abdomen. I cough and fall to the ground; the pain is agonizing even with the armor on.

Nyla twirls around me. "Hickory dickory dock," she sings, kicking me across the room.

I hit the wall and slump over, holding my side. The pain in the back of my head is starting to grow, but I can hardly open my eyes.

"The mouse ran up the clock." Nyla continues to sing, lifting me to my feet by my hair. "The clock struck one." I grab her hand and she slams the back of my head into the wall. "The mouse ran down." She tosses me into the control panel, causing sparks to fly.

I feel myself starting to lose consciousness as the pain in the back of my head starts overwhelming me. Nyla grabs me by my collar, sliding me up against the wall and cocks her free arm back like a loaded gun.

"Hickory dickory dock," she finishes with an ominous growl.

I wince in anticipation of the final blow but nothing comes. After a second I open my eyes. Everything has frozen as if time stopped. Nyla's face contorted with a mix of fury and pleasure. I lift my hand and touch her wrist with my index finger. Her arm explodes and time returns to normal. I slump back to the ground, bracing myself on the strut, as Nyla cradles the shattered remains of her left arm which was missing from the elbow down. She begins flailing around screaming obscenities hysterically.

I feel myself slipping away when Nev pulls me to my feet. "Not a good time to sleep, kid!" he exclaims, dragging me to the door and inputting the code. The door slides open and a blinding light hits us.

"This is the JMC Security Police. Do not move!" a voice yells.

Nev tightens his grip around me. "Whatever happens stowaway," he starts "I still freaking hate you."

I let out a chuckle that sends a shooting pain to my side. "I love you too, Nev." A slight smile forms on his face as several armored soldiers bind and gag us.

Chapter Twenty-Two: Gaining Clairvoyance

The Jovian Mining Corporation is the largest mining company in the entire solar system and also the strongest, considering their crown jewel the Titan Class Ship. Created for mining asteroids in the Kuiper Belt, they possess shields and armor that are an order of magnitude greater than the most advanced Battleships. Not to mention their assorted array of asteroid destroying 'mining tools' that can and have decimated entire assault fleets by themselves. Roughly three and a half to four kilometers in length, these super massive ships are the largest ships humanity has created since the colonial ships of ancient times and they are solely owned by the JMC. To keep their massive empire in check, the JMC employs the largest privately owned militia of any company anywhere, the JMC Security Police. With that being said, the Security Police are by no means as advanced as the IISF; however, their forces are not to be trifled with. It goes without saying that they don't answer to anyone, even the Coalition Fleet. Although, for the time being, it is mutually beneficial to stay civil with one another.

The twins always say that whoever controls a fleet of these asteroid-cracking behemoths, controls the solar system. It was a concept that I thought unbelievable until now. I'm sitting on the bridge of the Confessor under the control of the Security Police, approaching one of the dozens of docking bays littered across the side of the utterly massive JMC Flagship Clairvoyance. The sight of it reminds me of how truly insignificant we are and also the amazing feats we can accomplish with the right motivations.

The Confessor is not a small ship. It's able to sustain a crew of fifty, but if needed it could hold a hundred with reasonable comfort. The Clairvoyance, on the other hand, is the largest and most advanced of the Titans. For it, fifteen hundred is considered a skeleton crew with a maximum of thirty-five hundred for kicks. I shudder at the mere thought of it, and the Confessor does the same as she approaches the gaping hole, soon landing with graceful caution.

An elaborately dressed man opens his communicator. "Mr. Krane, this is Vice Marshal Riks, reporting a successful retrieval operation." There are several moments of silence where the Vice Marshal adjusts his collar.

"Very good, Vice Marshal," a charismatic voice responds. "This will reflect well on your next quarterly. Please prepare our visitors. I would very much like to greet them personally."

"Yes sir. Thank you, sir," the Vice Marshal responds, closing the display then snapping his fingers at several lesser officers who begin lifting us to our feet. The pain in my side returns, causing me to cringe as the Vice Marshal struts in front of us with a smug look on his face. "You are all about to meet the acting CEO of the Jovian Mining Corporation, Herman Krane. Suffice it to say you will be expected to act in accordance with the highest degree of respect you are capable of. Do I make myself clear?" he finishes and then waves his hand at the other officers.

They begin removing our gags, starting with Nev. Then it's me, Lora, Ava and the twins. Thomas was deactivated moments earlier, much to his dissatisfaction and outfitted with a lockout device, which makes it impossible for him to re-activate himself without someone removing the device first. We all stand there silently and patiently until Rickard's gag is removed. He stretches his jaw and looks at the Vice Marshal, gaining his attention.

"Excuse me," Rickard starts softly, prompting the Marshal to take a few steps toward him. "Is it at all possible to ask for a favor?"

The Marshal smiles with a pompous glint in his eyes. "Terms will be negotiated at a later time, but you are more than welcome to express your wants and needs now."

"That is good to hear," Rickard responds in the same soft tone. "Of course, if it is not at all inconvenient, I'd like to ask you to get the hell off my ship!" he shouts at the top of his lungs.

The Marshal takes a step back as one of the armed escorts hits Rickard in the abdomen. He falls to a knee, causing Nev to rush forward only to stop when the Marshal pulls a Pistol on him.

"I will have order!" he snarls.

Nev slowly returns to his spot as Captain Rickard begins laughing. "You guys are getting soft." He stands. "Either that or your boys hit like girls."

The soldier that hit him takes a step toward Rickard, but he stops when the Marshal shouts. "Enough!" He waves his hand and the officers place the gags back on us. "If you can't act like civil people, then you won't be treated like ones. Get them off this ship!" the Vice Marshal barks.

Several minutes later we are standing on the deck of the hanger marveling at its sheer vastness. A barely audible set of muffled gasps emit from the twins whose faces look as though they have died and gone to heaven. The Vice Marshal walks in front of us, stopping every few steps to scrutinize little details that ultimately are unimportant. It isn't hard to discern from his overall posture that he is extremely nervous. This must have been a career making mission, a fact that is proven when a large detail of ornately dress officers enters the hanger followed by a lavishly dressed middle aged gentleman and a younger just as extravagantly clad woman. He stops several meters from the Vice Marshal who has rendered a very precise salute.

"At ease, Vice Marshal. Or should I say Marshal Riks?" He reaches out and shakes the now bright red Marshal.

"Thank you, sir." The marshal stammers. "Here is the crew of the MST-C Idle Confessor as you requested, sir." He waives his hand in our direction.

"Very good," Herman says, looking back at the younger woman. "Ellabith dear, please join me."

"Yes, father." The timid and all around plain looking dark haired woman says, scurrying beside her father as he turns to address us.

"Undoubtedly you have many questions. That is understandable. Which one of you is the captain?" Herman says.

We all remain still until the Marshal snaps his finger at one of his subordinates, who removes Captain Rickard's gag. "Sir, if I may. This one has an attitude problem," Marshal Riks says.

Herman nods his head, looking at Rickard. "I assure you on my honor that no more harm will come to you, your crew and your ship. You see I, like yourself, have a certain amount of duties—"

"Cut the shit!" Rickard interrupts.

The hanger falls silent for several seconds when the Marshal lifts his hand, getting ready to order the gag back on when Herman stops him. "Alright then—" Krane pauses and drops the façade. "An associate of ours has requested I apprehend you for the Coalition Fleet. They are on their way to this location now."

Judging from everyone's face including Rickard's, the realization that we were betrayed by Cornelius Firth is both a surprise and somewhat expected. "Why?" Rickard asks.

"I wouldn't want to bore you with the details, and I doubt you would be able to understand, but in simple terms it all started when you picked up this boy." Herman points at me.

I feel an uncomfortable amount of eyes on me. There was no ambiguity in my mind any longer about what this was about, what all of this was about. I knew it was me from the beginning. I guess a part of me maybe wanted it all to be coincidence, but now—now I know that I'm not normal. Maybe I'm even special, but whatever it is, it's time to end the charades. The soldiers remove the rest of our gags.

"The boy is part of my crew. What business do you have with him?" Rickard's caustic tone falls on deaf ears as Herman walks up and looks me in the eye.

"To be honest, I want nothing to do with you. But I owe a debt to powerful people, the type of debt that can't be paid with meager credits. Our mutual friend has promised that the debt goes away if I do this," Herman replies.

"Then take me and let them go," I blurt out. "They had nothing to do with this. I snuck on their ship," I continue, ignoring the irritated glares of the twins and Ava.

"Admirable, and here I thought chivalry was long dead," Herman starts. "Unfortunately, my deal was for the Confessor and her crew so, alas, your efforts are wasted," Herman finishes, lightly slapping me on the face. "Take them to the brig until the CF gets here."

"Wait just one damn minute!" Nyla Crimm's hysterical voice echoes through the hanger. "He is mine!" she growls, walking down the Confessor's ramp.

"Who let you out of your cell!?" Marshal Riks yells.

Nyla laughs, flailing her bionic stump around, sending drops of blue fluid everywhere. "Did you really think your rent-a-cops could hold me? I'm Nyla fucking Cri—" Nyla freezes in mid-sentence, then collapses.

I look at Herman and a holo-display with the words 'Lock-out Protocol' hovering over his forearm. "I truly detest profanity," he says, closing the display. "Marshal Riks; see to it that she is off my ship immediately." Herman turns and begins walking out of the hanger, then stops just short of the door. "And make sure she is paid double. I don't want a scorned psycho on my list of enemies," he finishes.

"How did you do that?" I ask.

Herman glowers at me. "Power, my dear boy—" he turns and exits the hanger, followed by his armed escort.

It was no surprise that the brig of the Clairvoyance was more extravagant than most penthouses, but it didn't make the stay any less uncomfortable. I was placed in a cell of my own with the rest of the Confessor's crew in the cell across from me. For the most part everyone was silent, and I found myself wishing that I could read minds. Every now and then I'd catch one or two looking over at me with varying degrees of expression from Nev's unwavering look of hate to the twin's confused lack of understanding. Then there was Ava's face, showing concern and aggravation. For once the aggravation wasn't toward me, but rather the helpless situation and the apprehension that nobody was coming to save us this time. I felt alone, more alone than I did after Jurin died. But it was even worse now because six people—well, seven including Thomas—were at risk and it was my fault. And above all, I couldn't do anything to change it.

In the center of the brig was a massive display showcasing commercial after commercial depicting all the good that the JMC does for the Frontier, ending with Herman Krane thanking everyone for their hard work and dedication. After a few hours of that I would've rather had my fingernails ripped off than watch another reel of this pretentious crap. So I attempted to drown it out with my own thoughts, mainly of how to get out of this predicament.

It had occurrs to me several times to use my ability to spring us free, but the thought of what happens to me when I use it—how I kind of lose myself to it—makes me worry about hurting the wrong people. Besides, I haven't found out how to use it willfully yet. It always seems to show up at the very last moment I need it, when I'm the most desperate. The question is, how do I simulate that? How do I make it manifest of my own fruition? The power is undeniable. That much was surely true, and it would be more than enough to deal with whatever resistance there would be on the way out. I spend the next thirty minutes racking my brain for a solution but nothing comes.

"You're a liar, Rickard!" Nev's shouts pull me from my hopeless stupor.

I walk over to the barrier, noticing that Captain Rickard and Nev have begun fighting and exchanging punches. "What are you—" I start to say but Don catches my attention, shaking his head.

Genius. If they continue to fight, then the guards will have to get involved, possibly dropping the barrier, giving us a chance to break free. Granted, it may be a bit of a crude plan, but at this point it is the only one.

"So this is it, Nev? You think you can run things better than me?!" Rickard yells back, head-butting Nev.

Nev stumbles a bit, regaining his balance and rushed forward, tackling Rickard. "If you would have just pulled the trigger, we wouldn't be in this mess!"

Ava begins slamming her fists on the barrier yelling for the guards while the Twins and Lora attempt to break them up. A moment later, three guards run in with their weapons ready, screaming at the top of their lungs for them to stop.

"Help, they're killing each other!" Ava cries, selling the role of a helpless bystander incredibly well.

One of the guards runs over to the control panel and hits several commands, causing everyone to begin screaming in agony. "What are you doing to them?!" I yell as Ava collapses to the ground. The other two guards begin laughing as the third turns the pain emitting device on and off in a tortuous display.

"Turn up the intensity," one of the guards says, provoking the third to increase the pain. Lora begins vomiting in the corner as the twins start to convulse and tears begin to flow from Ava's face.

"Stop, damn-it. You're killing them!" I scream, slamming my fist into the barrier. The familiar pain starting in my chest and moving up to the base of my head brings a smile to my face.

Knowing that the tables are about to shift in our favor, I continue to slam my fist into the barrier.

"Looks like this one needs some attention also." A guard says motioning toward me.

The pain hits like nothing I have ever felt before, like my insides are being ripped apart then sewn together then ripped apart again. Although it is excruciating it is enough to throw me over the top. "I said enough!" My voice was booming and I could feel the power emitting from me like an explosion. The entire electrical system in the brig halts for a millisecond, causing the pain device to short out and eject sparks everywhere.

Ava and the rest immediately stop screaming and look at me as the three guards lift their weapons. For what seems like a minute or two there is silence with only the annoying music from the commercial, until the feed stops and the image of a hooded figure walks into view.

"Hello, brothers and sisters," the hooded figure begins in a deep voice. "For too long we have not been walking the path predestined for us. We have grown weak and dependent on the companies and governments that whittle away at our rights and freedoms. It is now time for you all to wake up." The display updates with an image of Europa's largest colony, Galileo. "What you see is ignorance embodied: three billion people fruitlessly living and dying without purpose. The Brotherhood has come to issue you our lord's righteous judgment. The tool of our retribution is none other than the same false security you've invested so much into, the Jovian Mining Corporation's Flagship Clairvoyance."

The three guards immediately open their communicators, but every connection is dead. They discuss what to do for a few seconds before running out of the brig as the video continues.

"The Clairvoyance has twenty-four Kinetic Rail Guns which launch a two-hundred metric ton tungsten slug at a fraction of the speed of light. According to the inventory database there are a thousand of these currently aboard, along with the ability to refine and manufacture more."

The sound of gunfire echoes in the distance when Herman Krane enters the display window, blood running down his face from several gashes. "And here is our key, your chosen false prophet who would rather sacrifice three billion than face martyrdom. You have been lied to." The hooded figure pulls out a blade and slashes Herman's throat. Blood squirts from the cut as Herman desperately attempts to stop the bleeding. The camera zooms to his hazel eyes as life begins to fade from them, leaving nothing but terror in its wake. He collapses and the hooded figure returns to the display. "In one hour we will unleash death upon Europa, beginning with Galileo. Then we will move on to the rest of the Frontier. Judgment awaits all those without faith." The displays changes, showing a timer counting down from sixty minutes. The brig falls silent with Nev and the others slamming their hands vainly against the barrier.

After ten solid minutes of futile labor, exhaustion finally sets in and the direness of the situation becomes a reality. Lora begins crying softly, holding Ava who also begins to lose her composure. The twins are arguing with each other over how to get out of this situation. Nev continues to beat the barrier every few minutes, taking brakes to catch his breath. But Captain Rickard seems calm, staring into the distance, deep in thought. Then there is me, watching my friends suffer as I have for most of my life, helpless to do a damn thing, even with this power I have.

"You are weak and worthless," a voice in the back of my head taunts. "I mean look at you. You're giving up without a fight, just like they always have," the voice continues. "Like the good little boy you are, always playing their games—"

"Stop-it!" I shout and everyone looks at me.

"Oh, there you go. But it isn't enough. You have to get angry," the voice continues.

"Shut up, shut up!" I scream, slapping my hands over my ears. I ignore everyone's looks of concern and close my eyes, seeing the blurred image of my reflection.

"You know what you must do. Embrace me. Make us whole again, save your friends, save billions. Just take—my hand—John." My reflection extends his hand.

I look around and I'm in the white room again, the glossy wall rippling violently. My reflection fades as I quickly run to the wall and begin hitting it. Waves emit from my fists, growing more and more intense until a visible crack forms. I begin frantically clawing at it, pulling small chunks of the blackness off and throwing it to the side when my reflection materializes in front of me.

I stop and look his eyes. They are white with blue metallic flecks swirling around and a sort of ethereal aura is visibly radiating from him. He reaches his arm through the hole I created and grabs me by the throat lifting me off my feet, bringing me close to his face. "Finally—" he hisses as his mouth twists into a grin.

Chapter Twenty-Three: Judgment Awaits

Absolute power corrupts absolutely, or does it? Power has been the obsession of the powerless for all time. It's the first thing we seek to have over those we deem lesser and history shows us that the ones with power often abuse it. But maybe it isn't the power that corrupts but rather the people that corrupt power. Maybe we are the source of all our strife and maybe I'm the answer. I won't lie; this power—this gift is exhilarating. I can feel it coursing through me like a raging river unbridled by shores of limitation. I snap my fingers and the holding cell barriers overload and discharge with a loud crack. Everyone is staring at me as I step down onto the walkway.

"What's the matter?" I ask, tilting my head.

Ava takes several steps toward me her mouth partially open. "What's happened to you John? Your eyes are—"

I hold up my hand. "I'm finally awake, Ava. And I'm getting you all out of here." My words seem to reverberate and echo through the ship. I can feel it—I can feel everything.

Ava takes a few more cautious steps toward me, reaching out with her hand and touching my cheek. "It's still you—right?" her voice cracks a bit.

I take her hand in mine and look her in the eyes. "For the first time in my life, I can say that this is who I really am." Ava tilts her head, pulling away when I grab her hand. "I'm here, Ava. I've made my choice, and you have to know that."

Ava smiles, fighting back tears. She looks back at the rest of the crew. "Let's get the hell out of here."

The Clairvoyance is in a state of chaos. Systems are malfunctioning everywhere. However, what we end up finding is much worse. Signs of fighting are evident all over the place with fresh scorch marks littering the walls, but it isn't until we reach one of the main common areas that we see the true effect of the Brotherhood.

The silence is maddening. The sight of dozens of dead bodies strewn about with little to no regard. Some were shot while others looked to be chopped or stabbed to death. It is gruesome, but I feel nothing but anger and an undeniable desire for revenge.

I look back at everyone. Various looks of shock and disgust paint on their faces. The twins are gasping for breath from our elevated pace, while Nev is attempting to get his Bionic leg to cooperate. "Let's take a break, everyone," I say in a low but poised tone.

I glance at the captain, who sharply nods and begins maneuvering through the victims, trying not to disturb them. I do the same. Unfortunately there is no time to spare for respect, no time to give the dead the dignity they deserve.

I finish stepping over the remains of an elderly woman when a holographic man emits from the ground in front of me. "H—H—Hello. My—My—My name is Trevor," the holograph's voice echoes through the common area, causing everyone to jump. "I am the on board Virtual Intelligence. How may I be of service?" The holographic program flickers erratically in front of me.

Ron and Don stumble over, fresh sweat stains covering their jumpers. "This must be the VI. Each Titan is outfitted with one. They help manage almost every aspect of the ship," Don says in-between breaths.

"Qu—Qu—Quite right! You must have done your re—re—reading," the VI responds.

"What's the matter with it?" I ask.

Ron grabs his chin. "I believe it's been corrupted." He takes a step closer to the hologram. "Trevor, could you tell us what's happening?"

Trevor looks at Ron and smiles. "Absolutely sir, we are cur—cur—currently going through an active shooter and hijacking scenario."

"Scenario?" I respond, looking at the twins.

They both shrug. "It must be how they're circumventing the automated security system. The VI believes this is just an exercise."

"Right you are, sir. Would you like to hear the current stan—stan—standings?" the VI asks. "Of the two-thousand, three-hundred and thirty-eight people on this ship, two-hundred and ei—ei—eighty-eight are showing no vitals while three-hundred and forty-one are ranging from minor to major injuries. In accordance with the scenario protocols, I have disabled all automatic security systems and loc—loc—locked down all escape pods and hanger bays."

"My god," Captain Rickard's says. "There is no way to evacuate the ship and they're going to kill everyone."

Ava steps toward the VI. "This isn't an exercise Trevor. Look around, there are dead bodies everywhere!" she yells.

Trevor flickers a little, staring at her. "My scenario protocols indicate that—that—that—" The hologram closes and the lights flash.

Nev looks at his forearm. "Forty minutes. Guys, how much further?"

"Didn't you hear the VI? All the hangers are locked," Lora says with a hopeless ring in her voice.

"So we get to the Confessor and use her arsenal to blast our way out," Nev retorts.

Don shakes his head. "The shockwave from the DEP cannons will absolutely kill us and the hanger door is so thick that it probably wouldn't even dent it."

Nev throws his arms up. "Well, I'm not ready to give up yet. There has to be some—"

Rickard places his hand over Nev's mouth and everyone gets quiet. The sounds of pulse rounds fill the air. We quickly run through a pair of doors into what seems to be a maintenance room. I crack the door just enough to see about a dozen heavily armed men enter the large common area sweeping it for survivors.

A sound in the back of the room grabs our attention and we whip around, seeing a woman and two kids crouching behind some machinery. Lora shushes them, smiling at the kids as the group of men move closer to us.

"Nev," I whisper. He quietly crawls to me. "Is there a back door?"

He looks at the twins, who are already studying the schematics for a way out. "Judging from their faces, we're stuck," he responds.

I look back at the group of fanatics. They're smiling and dancing around the corpses that litter the area. Then a man runs out from another door and falls to his knees, I can't hear what he is saying but I can tell he is begging for his life. The Brotherhood circle him like a pack of wild animals would. One of radicals slings his rifle and places his hand on the man's shoulder.

I try to look away because I know what is going to happen, but I can't. For some reason I have to see this. The three fanatics behind the man unsheathe machetes and begin hacking him to pieces. The man lets out a single shriek as blood flies everywhere but they continue to chop at the man's corpse until there is nothing left but a heap of flesh and bone.

It was too much. I couldn't stand by any longer. Before I knew it I was out the door and walking toward the group, ignoring the sound of Ava's protests as several of the blood splattered bastards notice me. I'm calm, even though I shouldn't be. I can feel my heart beating slowly. The pain that was so characteristic with my gift before is non-existent as the three machete wielding extremists' start running toward me. Their mouths stretch into wild grins, bearing their teeth with uninhibited excitement. They feel nothing from killing these people. They enjoy it, and I hate them for it.

I've seen this before, back in that apartment on Titan, Jurin's apartment. Tumbler was coming at me with a knife, with the same deranged look on his face as these unholy radicals. But this time no one is coming to save me, no Jurin with a pulse revolver. I feel myself grin with anticipation, lifting my left arm and sweeping across the front of me, affectively cleaving the three men in half without ever touching them.

They fall to the ground with shocked looks on their faces. They're already dead, but their minds haven't registered it yet, still denying the inevitable. I step over them as one begins screaming in agony. I crush his skull with the snap of my fingers and take a deep breath before looking at the other nine.

"Well?" My voice sounds weird to me but I ignore it. "Who would like to go next?"

It always amuses me how, when someone is about to die, they show what kind of a person they really are. Whether they'd fight to the last breath or cower in the face of their own demise. For the most part I wasn't surprised. Five of the remaining nine begin running in the opposite direction, attempting to flee their punishment. I understand it, really. They just witnessed me kill three of their people without touching them, but they didn't get far nonetheless. A simple flick of my wrist and their bodies twist and contort in such a way that they look more like rag dolls than people.

Of the remaining four, three are so terrified they can't move. Their faces are locked in a state of pure horror. I can't decide whether to show them the mercy of a fast death or indulge my curiosity. Ultimately, I simply chose to crush them in the same manner as I did Vek.

Then there's the last one—the one that was willing to fight for his life. He has been attempting to shoot me since I finished the first three fanatics, but the pulse rounds simply shatter against an invisible barrier half a meter from me in a spectacular display of blue light and white plasma. I can't help but think that at least he tried, unlike his spineless companions. He deserves my unbridled attention.

I lift my hand and his body goes rigid, he begins incoherently mumbling what sounds like a prayer, so I rip out his tongue. "There's no salvation for the wicked, not while I'm here," I growl. He shrieks as blood runs down his chin. I can feel his heart pounding and I can sense his panic. "It's so different now isn't it? When you're on the other side of the blade. Can you imagine how they felt?" He attempts to shake his head and close his eyes. Tears are starting to run down his cheeks. "I want you to look at them," I demand but he refuses to open his eyes. "I said, look at them!" I shout so loud several lights bust and send sparks in all directions. He opens his eyes and scans the room. But I can tell that even now, on the verge of his own death, he feels little to nothing for them. No remorse or guilt, just fear.

The anger inside of me begins boiling over at the sight of his complete disregard for the actions he's committed. I lift my other hand and slowly begin ripping him apart, an ordeal that takes a little more than a minute. The whole time in the midst of his screams, I make sure to keep him from passing out with my ability. I can sense that I'm enjoying causing him agony and deep down there is a part of me that is disgusted, but even then I don't stop. In the end there is barely anything left of him, just little bits and pieces of meat and bone scattered across the floor.

I take a breath, feeling my heart starting to pound. A sort of fog is lifted and the situation starts to sink in. I look down at my hands. They're completely clean, but I know better. I killed these men—and I enjoyed every bit of it. I unleashed everything onto them and barely broke a sweat. Is this—what I am now? I hear the sounds of gasps from behind me, and I turn to see everyone standing with various expressions of shock and fear on their faces. I go to say something but the words escape me when Rickard breaks the silence.

"We have to keep moving. Don, how close are we to the Confessor?" he says in a sober voice.

Don hesitates for a second, slowly bringing up a display. "Ten minutes, but we still can't—"

I hold up my hand to forestall him and everyone freezes in fear. "Sorry! I was just—" I lower my hand. "I can end the lockdown," I finish in a low voice.

Everyone begins breathing again. "What do you mean?" Ava asks.

"I mean, you all get to the Confessor. Take whoever you can find with you and I'll end this," I state with confidence. Ron opens his mouth to offer a counter augment but I interrupt him. "I was meant do this. I know that now. Just trust me. I can stop this before anyone else gets hurt."

"You don't have to do that, John. Just come with us," Ava protests.

"It's already too late, Ava." I point at the woman who holds the two children close to her, covering their eyes, shielding them from the horrors around them. "I can save them, and I can save all of you. Besides, you guys are afraid of me now."

"Well, look around. It's pretty freaking obvious why," Nev scoffs, cleaning blood off one of the pulse rifles and checking the magazine.

I shrug and nod my head, taking a few step away from the group, but Ava persists. "So that's it, huh?!" She takes a few steps toward me when Rickard grabs her arm.

"He's right, Ava," he says flatly, looking me in the eyes.

"No!" she pulls away. "I'm not an idiot. You're going to die and you want me—us to just accept this and let you do it." She looks around at the others, but no one steps forward to back her up. "Don, Ron, come on!" she yells, tears visibly forming in her eyes.

"Sorry, darlin'. It's the only option," Ron says.

"And it sounds like John has made up his mind," Don adds.

I tilt my head to both of them, taking as few more steps away. Ava grabs a rifle off one of the dead fanatics. "Fine! Then I'm going with you." She starts walking toward me.

I take her cheek in my hand and smile. "Always the Valkyrie—" She looks at me as I brush away a tear. "But you can't come with me, Ava." I feel a chill run down my spine as Ava passes out in my arms.

"What did you do to her?!" Captain Rickard shouts as he and Nev rush toward me.

"She is just sleeping." I pick her up and hand her to Rickard, who looks exceedingly worried. "She will wake up in about five minutes. By then I'll be gone and you will be too." Captain Rickard nods, returning to the group.

Nev lowers the rifle and smirks, placing his hand on my shoulder. "Give them hell, stowaway." He turns and follows Rickard.

Lora walks up and hugs me. "You better not die," she whispers. "Ava will kill you if you die." I let out a quiet laugh.

Behind her are the twins, both averting their eyes. "Well, I guess I'll see you guys lat—" I start when they both hug me tightly, causing my side to hurt again. "You guys are—hurting me." I gasp.

They release me and grin. Don brings up a display showing the Clairvoyance with three marked spots. "These highlighted spots are the bridge, the main engineering deck and the location of the VI Core. We don't know how many of the Brotherhood are here, but to take a ship this size a few hundred and some change would suffice. I know that doesn't evoke a lot of confidence, but it's the best we can do."

"Most of them will be concentrated near these three locations. As long as they control these, they control the ship. Teams like the one you just—dispatched will likely be all over, clearing out the place," Ron continues.

"Thanks, guys. Be sure to tell Thomas goodbye for me." The thought of saying goodbye to a synthetic brought a smile to their faces but they understood me.

Then there was something else that we realized. Verbally admitting that I'm probably going to die made me shudder, and I can tell the twins didn't like that idea at all. Ron grabs my shoulder. "You'll tell him hi when you get back. Ok, kid?" he says.

They turn and walk back to the rest of the group. Every part of me knew I should be going with them, but I remained, still just watching them move further from my sight. "It's better this way." I try to convince myself. I look at my forearm. There are a little over thirty minutes left until hell is unleashed on billions of people thousands of kilometers away. Thirty minutes to stop the worse mass murder in the history of humanity.

I let out a sigh. What a way to turn up the pressure. A tingling sensation starts at the base of my skull, but I pay no attention to it. First thing's first, I need to go for the beast's head. I select the bridge as my destination and it updates with the fastest route to take. The course has me using the tram system, which would undoubtedly be under the control of the terrorists. Two birds, one stone? I think to myself. If I free up the trams, the evacuation will move a lot faster, so why not.

I take another long sigh and a glance at the ravaged corpses I created just moments earlier. Even though they deserved it, a part of me feels guilty. I guess that's the difference between me and them, at least I hope it is. Who knows how much I'll succumb to the bloodlust before this is all said and done. Yet, I feel a disturbing amount of excitement at the thought of killing these monsters. I feel my lips twist into a grin. That's it—I'm just another monster, killing monsters.

Chapter Twenty-Four: Of Monsters and Men

I've lost count of how many fanatics I've killed. Well, more like I have stopped counting. There is something oddly inspiring about their level of mindless devotion, even as their comrades are being flayed alive around them. It's starting to become a game for me. Just remove some flesh here or there and watch as they run about screaming and cursing. Then, when I get annoyed or bored, I pop their heads off like a cork on a champagne bottle.

It doesn't take long before I finish with the last of the Brotherhood on the tram car. Human remains are scattered everywhere, I take a moment to reflect and maybe I got a little out of hand this time. The blood haze, as I'm now calling it, is getting a harder for me to see through. I knew that I'd lose myself, but I never thought I'd actually begin toying with these radicals like a cat does with a mouse. The all too familiar tingling in the back of my head is starting to ache incessantly. I crack my neck in an attempt to lessen the pain but to no avail.

I glance at my forearm, twenty-three minutes left, which should be more than enough time—right? The thought of billions dying made my stomach ache, not just because of the action but the way they would all probably die. The impact of twenty-four, two-hundred metric ton shells moving well over three thousand kilometers per second will kill hundreds of thousands, maybe even millions instantly. They, however, will be the lucky ones. The rest will die slowly, clawing at one another out of a desperate need to survive. People will be trampled under thousands as the bio dome collapses and the atmosphere that sustained billions gets siphoned into space; faster than anyone can get away from but slow enough for them to realize what is happening. The temperature will drop at an astounding rate. In all reality, that would be the biggest killer. Most will freeze to death before they suffocate. A sour taste comes up from my stomach. I won't let this come to pass; I swear it.

The tram bell chimes as it comes to a screeching halt at the bridge terminal. As far as anticipation goes, I didn't know what to imagine but the furthest thing from my mind is the utter lack of guards at the bridge. I cautiously step out of the tram, expecting an ambush, but nothing happens. I feel my Aug start to tingle. Twenty minutes left. The words reverberate in the back of my head, and I run the rest of the way, entering the bridge a few seconds later.

I feel my heart drop into my stomach; there were no guards here because the bridge has been pillaged. I take a few steps in. Sparks are flying everywhere, parts of the control panels are littered all over and it is obvious that there was nothing I could do from here. I feel a sense of hopelessness overwhelm me. The Brotherhood is smarter than I assumed. They must have created a mobile command and control suite and hid it somewhere else on the ship, having all the perks of being on the bridge without actually being on the bridge. I punch the table, causing the holographic space map to stutter. Then the hooded man comes into the display's view.

"So you must be the hero," he says in a raspy voice. "I've enjoyed watching you—work."

He brings up a recording of my latest slaughter. I avoid looking at the video. "Why are you doing this?"

"Why? The question everyone asks. The why is unimportant. It has always been unimportant. Why is the lie sold to us from the moment we are born, in order to feel better about the truth of our existence," the hooded man responds.

"And I assume you know the truth of our existence?" I retort.

The man smiles. "The truth is, there is no why. There is no purpose, no destiny predetermined for each of us. We live, we die and that is it."

"Careful. You sound more like a non-believer than a religious fanatic."

The man laughs. "More useless titles and categories—let me enlighten you. There is no why for the individual, but there is a greater destiny of all of us together. What you see as senseless murder is nothing, because we don't matter. The one true why is transcendence, seeking our place beside God. We are blinded by our greed, our overwhelming concern with the unnecessary. It has crept into us like a degenerate rot, steering us away from the truth."

"And you think killing innocent people will achieve your goals?!" I shout, feeling the anger growing inside of me.

"We have grown too many. Trillions of voices talking all at once, so much to say with so little meaning. Our cup is overflowing with it—nonsensical babble. It's everywhere—and it's time to dump it out and start anew." The hooded man clasps his hands together in front of him.

"You're insane—and I'm going to enjoy killing you."

He grins. "Kill me and another just like me will take my place—I'm only a means to an end and a beginning—"

I scoff. "That's good cause I really do enjoy killing fanatic terrorists. I mean it's like God blessed me with this divine destiny," I say sarcastically.

The hooded man stops smiling. "Your purpose, John, is far greater than mine and the rest of the human race."

"How do you know who I am?" I demand.

The man continues. "I've known of you for a long time, John. You are the catalyst, the true reason I have come here today."

"What do you mean? Who are you working for?"

The man removes his hood, revealing a nasty looking scar on the left half of his face and a dead eye that is light gray and shrouded in a milky haze. His other eye is blue but seems to be lifeless and empty when it stares at me. "My name is Brother Calon and I work for no worldly man. I am the Lord's hammer, His justice personified." The camera zooms in on his face. "But you—you are His Shepard, His harbinger. Your apostles will be here soon and I will make you worthy of them."

The connection closes and I punch the table again, using my ability to rip it out of the floor and throw it across the bridge. I start screaming at the top of my lungs, feeling my anger overflow and causing the power to jitter. Suddenly I feel a buzz coming from my Aug; I look down and notice that it's Don.

I open the connection. "Don, thank God!"

"It worked," he responds. "John, we are on the Confessor with about thirty people."

"That is great to hear. Did everyone make it fine?"

Don looks off to the side. "Yeah more or less, no casualties though. Listen, John, I don't know how long we have this connection. But we need to get out of here now."

I bite my lip. "I can't stop the bombardment. They destroyed the bridge, and I don't know what to do."

Don gives me a grim look. "You did your best, but we still have an opportunity to save the people on this ship. Go to the VI core and force it to reboot. That should reset the systems."

I blink back some tears. I know what needs to be done, but it still isn't enough. The connection flashes. "Don, what about—"

"She's ok, a little hurt, but you did the right thing," Don interrupts.

The connection fails before I can respond, and I continue to stare at the blank screen for a few seconds hoping that Don will return but nothing happens. I swipe away the display and bring up the map of the Clairvoyance, selecting the VI core as my next destination. Don is right; I can't dwell on the things I can't change, but that doesn't make it easier to deal with.

The map updates with my new route and I start walking to the bridge door. There is a moment where I hesitate right before I enter the hallway, looking over my shoulder at the destroyed panels. A part of me thinks that there has to be something left for me to do and not to accept the seemingly inevitable fate that is coming to pass. But the moment leaves as fast as it comes, so I continue out the door and through the corridor.

Hopelessness is a dreadfully powerful emotion and even more dreadful when a powerful person feels hopeless. That fact became evident when I encountered a group of the radicals guarding the VI Core. Instead of simply killing them like I had before, I maim them. I rip their insides apart and let them suffer. And as they lay before me bleeding out from every orifice, I sit and watch, sating my suffering with theirs.

I come down from the blood haze and feel the last remnants of life leave the radicals—except for the young boy. He looks no more than ten with a future of infinite possibilities stolen from him by the Brotherhood's indoctrination—and me. I immediately feel him, the fear, the pain and anger but most of all the lack of understanding of what is happening. It all overwhelms me; clouding my mind and making me hurt. There is no justifying this, no reasoning away the fact that I had just killed this boy. Tears begin flowing from my eyes and I fall to my knees.

"I'm so sorry!" I sob uncontrollably.

The other men were already gone. There was no way I could end their suffering, but the boy was still holding onto life, staring at me with his beautiful sapphire eyes. I am no different than the fiends I killed. I've become what I hated the most—the powerful that plays God with the weak and helpless. It is in this moment that I know I am a monster and that there is no going back. I crawl to the boy, taking him in my arms, begging for him to forgive me. He mumbles something in a language I don't understand, placing his hand on mine. I cup his face and put him to sleep; his breath is shallow and strained, his pulse weakening. I can feel it coursing through me, making me ache with self-loathing. I put my hand on his chest and slow his heart down until it stops beating. The silence is unnerving. After he is gone there is nothing on this ship that is a threat to me, and yet I am afraid of being alone with myself.

My Aug begins to tingle, indicating that there are ten minutes before Brother Calon's judgment begins. But there is a part of me that doesn't care any longer, part of me that wants to just stay here and die. The soreness in the back of my head is now beginning to throb as my despair deepens. After a minute or two I lay the boy down, placing his hands across his chest, and turn toward the VI Core.

I take a few steps toward the mainframe when Trevor materializes. "G—G—Good day sir. How m—m—may I help you?"

I wipe away the remaining tears and gaze at the program. "We need to do a system wide reboot. Is there a way for you to do that?"

The holographic intelligence lags a bit. "I'm so—so—sorry sir, only a system admin has the ability to reset my systems. Besides we are cur—cur—currently in the middle of a scenario. Would you like to hear the up-to-date stan—stan—standings."

"Not really—so Trevor, this mainframe is magnificent. What kind of disaster recovery systems do you have, say for overheating?"

The hologram smiles. "Thank you, my quantum com—com—computing core is quite a feat of engineering. I can assure you that every po—po—possible failure has been considered, specifically the possibility of ov—ov—overheating." Trevor gestures to several large pipes leading to the core. "Those pump three-thousand liters of coolant every ei—ei—eight seconds."

"Interesting, and what would happen if those pipes stopped pumping coolant? Figuratively speaking, of course."

"Ab—ab—absolutely sir. If there is a coolant pump failure, there is a backup forced ventilation system that will sustain my major systems until the pumps are fi—fi—fixed." Trevor opens a schematic, showing a large array of fans situated under the VI Core.

"Now theoretically speaking. If that were to fail, what would you do then?" I say, placing my hand on my chin.

Trevor gives me a quizzical look. "It is highly improbable that that would happen, sir."

"I understand, but tell me anyway."

Trevor makes a displeased face. "I wo—wo—would have to do a system wide shut down until one or both of the co—co—cooling systems are restored."

"Great, that is what exactly what I needed to hear." I smile and it nods its head in response.

I take a moment to think about how I will be doing this. I know I have to ability to stop the pump and the vent fans. It's the delicate nature of it that I'm worried about. I'm not the best when it comes to being tender and I don't want to destroy the Core just for it to reset. I take a deep breath and close my eyes; I can feel the coolant raging through the pipes with surprising speed and pressure. I follow the current with my mind, back through the ship until I find the central pump. A massive turbine is the source of the power. I reach out and begin slowing it down. I can feel the back of my head radiate with pain as the turbine comes to a halt.

I can hear several alarms sounding from the core few seconds later, then the sound of the vent fans spinning up. I shift my focus while still holding the pump turbine to the large ductwork of vents now forcing large volumes of air to flow through the mainframe. I can feel myself losing grip as the pain starts to spider out from the back of my head when I attempt to stop the vent fans. My frustration mounts and I inadvertently twist the vent fans just a millimeter too much in one direction, causing a catastrophic series of failures. In a moment, high velocity shrapnel starts flying everywhere. "Damn-it," I spit through my teeth, attempting to shield the mainframe from the destruction.

A numbing sensation starts to creep up from my legs. Just a few more seconds, I think to myself as more alarms begin to scream. A red glow starts to emit from the mainframe as the temperature continues to climb. Finally, the core shuts down and the lights go out. I release the pump turbine and the coolant starts to rush into the mainframe, causing steam to fly. I fall to the ground and attempt to get control of my breathing. Not yet—I can't stop yet. I look at the boy, forcing my sight to focus on his face. My breath slows and I can feel my strength returning.

A few seconds later, the mainframe boots up and Trevor reappears in front of me, his face showing a mix of disappointment and disdain. "Tracking multiple system vulnerabilities—assessing ship damage—issuing evacuation orders to all passengers—" The sound of alarms can be heard in the distance. "Opening all Hanger doors—unlocking all escape pods—ship security compromised, engaging automated ship defenses"

I feel myself smile as I lift my Aug and contact Don. His face pops up a second later. "The hanger doors are opening. All we need is you and we can go," he says with a smile.

I look at the boy again, feeling my stomach turn. "I'm not coming, Don."

He frowns. "But the lockdown is lifted—"

"Don, I've—" Damn-it. "I've done something—" I choke on the words. "Something I can't come back from." Don opens his mouth, but I stop him. "Tell everyone goodbye for me—and tell the Valkyrie I'm sorry." I close the connection before he can respond and turn toward Trevor.

"Detecting unauthorized access to mining equipment—attempting access refusal—" The hologram falls silent for a few seconds. "Mining systems shutting down—" Trevor brings up a display of the Clairvoyance, showing twenty-four green blips slowly turning red one after another. An uplifting sensation washes over me as the last few blips turn red. "All Kinetic Mining systems shut down—filing incident report with Jovian Mining Corporation Headquarters."

I let out a much-needed breath. "Way to go Trevor. You just saved three billion people." I look at my Aug. "And with three minutes to spare."

Trevor looks at me but doesn't smile. "Ship navigation protocols corrupted—new destination selected." The Clairvoyance twists and turns faster than it should. I stumble, bracing myself against a wall.

"Trevor, what's going on?!"

The hologram looks at me. "The ship has been set on a collision course with Galileo. My systems have been either corrupted or overridden. I cannot stop it."

Just when things were looking good. "Is there anything I can do?"

The program shakes its head. "Not from here, but you could control the ship manually."

"But the bridge was destroyed. I can't control the ship from there," I respond.

Trevor opens a window on my Aug, showing a green highlighted area in the bow of the ship. "I intercepted a navigation command from this area before I was locked out. Most likely that is where they are."

Hovering over the highlighted area were the words 'Central Observation Deck.' Of course. What better way to watch your judgment than from an observation deck? I select the destination and the route updates.

I look back at Trevor. "How much time do I have?"

Trevor shudders "I was able deactivate the ARAD before being locked out. With just the Ion thrusters it would take twenty-five minutes to impact. However once the Clairvoyance is caught in Europa's gravity, well the thrusters won't be strong enough to escape it."

"So how long before we reach the point of no return?" I say in a bleak tone.

Trevor hesitates. "Fifteen minutes. Give or take."

I update my Aug with the new information and look at Trevor. "You've been more than helpful. Thank you."

"My pleasure, sir. Once this is over, please fill out a quick survey in regards to my service. Once completed you will be entered to win your choice of three vacation packages," the hologram finishes with a smile.

I shake my head. Just when I was starting to like this thing. I head for the door, taking another long look at the boy, ensuring I never forget his face. I feel a tinge of pain run through me. I can't stay. I know this, but I don't want to leave the boy's body. I end up forcing myself to leave, reaching the tram moments later.

Chapter Twenty-Five: Razing Clairvoyance

The tram comes to a halt at the Central Observation Deck's terminal five minutes later. As expected there are heavily armed members of the Brotherhood waiting for me. They immediately begin unloading hundreds of pulse rounds on me, overpowering me with superheated plasma. I can feel the overuse of my ability starting to take its toll. I need to finish this fast before I can't go any further. I slam my foot onto the deck, causing a massive shock wave that throws the zealots in every direction. I kill the lights, shrouding the area in complete blackness. Even though I can't see, I can easily sense the Brotherhood's hearts beating and the sound of their blood coursing through their bodies, almost painting their pictures for me in the dark.

I feel a malicious grin form on my face as the blood haze starts to take me. The room fills with screams as I go from one terrorist to another, ripping their hearts out of their chests with little more than a flick of my wrist. The lights return and the terminal is covered in blood. One of the fanatics is still alive, looking around at what I had done. His eyes widen with horror. He falls to his knees, begging me for forgiveness. I tilt my head, reaching down and retrieving a pistol from one of his dead Brothers and walk to him. He cowers as I get closer to him, cringing when I drop the pistol in front of him.

"You want forgiveness?" I start. "There it is." I point at the pistol. The man takes it in his hand and looks at me. I turn and walk out of the room as a single pulse round rings out, followed by the sound of a body slumping to the ground.

I'm almost there. The thought brings a great amount of pleasure to me. The nightmare is almost over. At this point I have fully embraced the blood haze, killing monsters left and right as I make my way to Brother Calon. There is nothing on this ship that could stop me from killing him. My Aug updates with seven minutes remaining.

I reach a heavy metal door that seems to be wielded shut. I place my hand against it, sensing the other side. I close my eyes and see the images of five people. Three were the Brotherhood but the other two—ah yes, one is the good Marshal Riks and the other, Ellabith Krane, daughter of the late Herman Krane.

One of the terrorists takes Ellabith by the hair and throws her against the table, pulling her dress up, preparing to take her forcibly. The Marshal attempts to intervene but he gets pistol whipped by one of the other terrorists and falls back to the ground unconscious. They're confident that this door will keep me out—too confident. I take a step back and breathe in deep. The more I focus on the door the more I sense the very matter of it, trillions of atoms holding on to each other. I throw my hands out in front of me and the door explodes off the frame, smashing one of the assailants against the wall.

I walk in and snap the other guard's neck before he realizes what is happening. The monster that was getting ready to devastate Ellabith's body attempts to flee, but he trips on his pants. He turns, holding up his arms. I can feel his fear emanating from him. Ellabith crawls to the Marshal, shaking him awake. The monster continues to scoot backwards until he hits the wall.

"What are you afraid of?" I ask, but he doesn't answer. I slant my head a little. "Surely it can't be me—you're kind isn't afraid of death," I mock as he shakes his head, attempting to pull his pants up. In a swift motion, I break his arms and legs. He lets out a cry of agony. "I said, what are you afraid of?" He begins to cry and shake his head.

I let out an annoyed sigh, and then glance at Ellabith and the Marshal who are watching me with the same amount of horror as the monster. I walk over to them. They also flinch when I get near and I shush them, undoing their bindings.

"Why are you doing this?" Ellabith asks, rubbing her wrists.

"Because you're a good person," I say, looking at the monster then back at her. "Don't ever stop being good." She hesitantly nods her head, lifting the Marshal to his feet and then helps him out the door.

I look back at the fanatic still sobbing in the corner, mumbling a prayer to himself. I let out an irritated exhale. The least he could do is have a bit of dignity in his death. I walk toward him and he recoils, letting out a pathetic squeal. I feel myself smile at his misery. Beside him is the last staircase to the observation deck and Brother Calon's death.

I shake my head at the sobbing mess on the ground before turning and walking up the stairs. I can sense his panic subsiding as I walk past him. He truly believes that I'm going to let him live. To his dismay, however, as I pass him I reach out with my ability and remove his phallic member. That way if he somehow lives from the blood loss, he will never threaten another person with it. His screams fill the stairway as I climb closer to salvation.

The light of the observation deck pierces the darkness and causes me to squint. Galileo, in all its glory is in front of me, getting closer with every second. Makeshift equipment is everywhere spewing sparks, causing my frustration to mount. Brother Calon is standing in the center of the deck, facing Europa with a hammer in his hand.

"I trust you realize now how folly your efforts have been," he says in a ponderous voice.

"It doesn't change a thing," I respond.

Calon drops the hammer. "It changes everything!" He turns to me. "You can't stop the ship, John. My judgment will be administered." He takes a few steps toward me. "And you—you can't redeem yourself." He opens a display showing me maliciously torturing the group of fanatics from the VI core, including the boy.

I feel a shot of numbing pain course through my body. My Aug updates with three minutes until Galileo's fate is sealed. "You're right. I can never redeem myself." My words cause Calon to grimace. "The moment I realized that was long before you declared it." He pulls a machete from his cloak. "No, Brother Calon. I'm damned for what I am—for what I've done. I never intended to leave this ship alive." Calon's eyes get wide with anticipation as he lunges at me with his machete cutting the way.

I close my eyes, focusing on the ship's micro-vibrations and following them with my mind back to the source, finally reaching the three oversized Fusion Cores. The blue light radiates from them, pulsating rhythmically. This is it, I think to myself, feeling the pain spread from the back of my head to the rest of my body. One more time—one last trick; I focus on one of the cores, causing the shields to fail. The subsequent blast overwhelms my mind, whipping me back to my body.

Brother Calon is coming down on me with the machete, but I'm ready yet. The ship is crippled and on the way to self-destruction, but the Clairvoyance is still moving toward Galileo. Time slows down and I sense myself outside of the ship, floating in front of the mass of steel moving tens of kilometers per second. I give everything I have, letting the ship hit me, hundreds of thousands of metric tons of pressure being absorbed by my body. I feel warm blood flowing from my nose as the pain takes me and the darkness starts to creep in.

The ship lurches forward, throwing Brother Calon and I forward to hit the observation window with bone breaking force. I fall to the ground, my body ravaged, every muscle strained beyond the failing point. I stare at Galileo, three billion lives saved by a man they will never know. I feel myself smile when Calon's face enters my line of sight, blood flowing down his face from a fresh wound above his eye.

"Looks like I win this one, huh Calon?" I force out a chuckle.

His anger is brimming as distant explosions echo through the ship, causing the deck the shudder. He grabs me and forces me onto my knees, placing the machete against my neck. "Your apostles are almost here," he starts. "I will make you worthy of their attention."

"This was all a test?!" I force out. "For what?!"

"My cause would have been benefited with either outcome." He leans in. "But you haven't fully awoken yet, Avant, and I shall make you worthy of the title," he whispers.

"How do you know that? What role do you have in all this?" I demand as he presses the blade against my throat.

"Death comes for you, sinner," he hisses.

Peace—that is what I feel. The pain is still there, but it doesn't bother me anymore. I know I would die here and my thoughts don't rebel against that notion except when Ava comes to mind, with her beautiful red hair brushing against my cheek, the taste of her lips on mine. I take solace in the thought of her in my last moments.

Brother Calon lifts the machete high above his head, a mixed look of absolute insanity and calming resolve painted on his face. Then, like a guillotine, the carbonized metal slams into my neck with tremendous force. But there is nothing—no pain, no death, just the sound of metal shattering and before I know it I am holding Brother Calon by his face. His good eye is staring at me with nothing but pure dread and excitement. He tries to free himself from my grip, only causing me to tighten it around his head, making him to scream with pain.

"It's time for my judgment, Calon." My voice is deep and raspy, my vision blurred.

"Kill me!" Calon shouts. "I will be greeted in the afterlife as a saint and the Avant will ascend as the apostles wished it!"

I squeeze his head even more and he squirms and thrashes at me. "No Calon, you and I won't be going to heaven. There's a special place for people like us and I'll see you there." I flex my arm, blasting Calon's head away in a mist of blood, flesh and bone. His body flails about before falling to the ground.

I look down at my hands, for the first time they have blood on them, but I know it's been there all along. I take a few steps before the exhaustion takes me again and I collapse. My breath is shallow and my body broken, but my thoughts are calming. More explosions can be heard in the distance, making the Clairvoyance rotate off course. No time to get to an escape pod, no way to make it out— not this time.

I feel my Aug tingle, forcing myself to look at it to see Ava's face and accept the call. "Wh—what are you doing?!" the tone of her voice brings me an odd sense of uneasy comfort.

I force a smile, trying not to lose consciousness. "Hey, fancy seeing you here."

Her face turns red with rage. "That's it—Damn-it, John!" Her words hurt in a way that can't be explained.

"Always the Valkyrie—" I force out, feeling the darkness starting to move in.

Ava notices my decline, putting aside her frustration. "John, stay with me. We're coming to get you."

I shake my head as my vision tunnels. Ava says something, but I can't make it out. Another loud explosion causes the deck to violently shake. "I'm sorry, Ava." I muster the rest of my strength into closing the connection. I can't let her see me die, not like this. I can sense my reflection's presence as the darkness consumes the rest of my vision and I drift away.

Chapter Twenty-Six: Demon of the Past

The barrier is still standing when I reach the white room, but there is no sign of my reflection. "Where are you?!" I shout, running to the wall and slamming my fist into it, causing ripples to cascade along its glossy surface.

The planet was still slowly rotating in the distance, barren and scarred from the latest round of genocidal destruction.

"I can't say you made the best decisions, but I have to say you have style." My reflection materializes in front of me.

I step away from the wall. "Style?! You're a sick bastard!" My tone is caustic.

The Avant-Garde points at himself outrageously. "Me? What the hell are you talking about?!"

"You made me into a monster!" I shout. "If it wasn't for you—"

"If it wasn't for me, my dear friend, you along with three billion people would be dead. Besides, there is no such thing as you and me. Remember? We are the same person. If you don't like it and you want to blame someone, then look in a damn mirror!" The barrier shudders.

"That's a lie. We aren't the same! I would never kill or do what I did."

"Oh, you're blaming me for this?" He waves his hand and a replay of me torturing the boy begins. "Look that is who we are." He speeds up the replay to the point where I am cradling the boy.

"And this is the same person as before." He waves away the replay.

"It doesn't make sense."

"It's duality. Every person has the same amount of potential to be either a monster or a saint."

"Then what am I?" I ask sarcastically.

The Avant smiles and shakes his head. "We're human, responding to human stresses with superhuman abilities. Think about it. You said yourself you're just a monster killing monsters, right? But does this look like what a monster would do?" He brings back the image of me cradling the boy, asking for his forgiveness.

"So what? I tortured and killed him. I can't justify that. I can't make it right by just saying I'm human."

My reflection scoffs. "You're doing it now. Remember, you're the one having a conversation with yourself. I get it. I really do. We are about to die and you want your conscience cleared before then." I hesitate, then nod my head. "See, I think that right there has some say. Do you think a child killing insects feels remorse?"

"That's not the point!" I retort.

"Of course it is! The gift we have puts us above everyone else. It's that simple. But even then, you feel remorse. Even when we are justified, we're wrong. But ask yourself, honestly. Would that kid have felt remorse if he had killed us? His mind was poisoned by a group of people that, in the end, don't deserve to be part of the human race." My reflection smiles because he knows he is right. At least I know I was right. Not once did I feel a bit of remorse from anyone of the people I slaughtered—even the boy.

"That doesn't make it right," I say in a somber tone.

"It doesn't—but none of that is going to matter because we are about to die anyway," my reflection responds.

The stars dotting the blackness behind my reflection start to disappear. "What's happening?"

"Don't know, maybe the end?" the Avant responds.

I feel a pulling sensation in my abdomen as a shroud of darkness starts to consume the white room. "I'm scared." The words escape my mouth before I realize.

"I know," my reflection responds, fading into the darkness.

A sense of anxiety grips me as the last bit of light is consumed, I feel cold and weak. Is this how it is to die? Alone in darkness with nothing. A chill runs down my back with that very thought as the pulling sensation in my abdomen moves up toward my chest. My breath becomes strained as the sensation starts to ache relentlessly. I fall to my knees, grasping my throat as if I'm drowning.

"Clear!" I hear a voice shout, shortly followed by a jolting sensation in my chest. I take a deep breath, lunging forward. Someone grabs and forces me back down onto the steel operating table.

"He's stabilizing," another voice says. By now my eyes are starting to adjust to the overhead light.

"Where am I?!" My voice is panicked.

At first there is no response, then a female synthetic walks over and places its hand on my chest. "You're in good hands. Try to relax." The robot then secures my arms and legs before attaching something to my head.

I take a few deep breaths, feeling my heart starting to slow down. By now my eyes have adjusted to the bright room. I know I'm in an infirmary on a ship. I can feel the micro vibrations coursing through the hull, but judging from the room's layout, it is not the Idle Confessor.

Several minutes pass. The synthetic nurse checks my vitals and my binding again. Every now and then it would glance up at someone behind me, the second voice I imagine.

The synthetic finishes and nods to the person. I feel a hand on my shoulder as an elderly man comes into focus above me. "Good day. You had us scared for a second." He smiles.

"Where am I?" I ask again.

He pats my shoulder "You're in good hands, I assure you. My have you grown. It must have been fifteen years and all the while you were living on Titan of all places."

He walks out of my line of sight, giving me enough time to let his statement sink in. "You know who I am?" My voice quivers.

"Well, you were only three the last I saw you—but you could say that I was a friend of your parents." He returns to my view and checks my eyes with a flashlight.

"My parents—" I stumble to find the words.

"Yes, your father was a colleague of mine and your mother—" he pauses and lets out an exhale. "Your mother was incredibly beautiful—I see a lot of her in you."

I feel my heart start to beat faster as I recall the images of my mother. "Who are you?"

The old man was quiet, most likely contemplating the ramifications of telling me who he was. "Excuse my rudeness. My name is Doctor Ellis Baker."

"Ellis Baker—where am I, doctor? Where are we going?"
He hesitates; scanning the room for a few seconds before opening his mouth to speak when the infirmary door slides open.

Dr. Baker quickly straightens up and moves away from my view. I can feel the other person's eyes on me. They take several steps toward me, stopping at my head but still out of my range of vision. I then feel two hands rest on my shoulders. They were big hands, strong. Something about them makes me feel uncomfortable. I try to move my head up to view the unknown person, but they keep me planted on the table.

"Dr. Baker?" My tone boasts more angst than I intended but there is no response.

I feel the unknown person crouch beside my head, their warm and steady breath hitting my ear. "Remember when I told you I don't like liars and cheats?"

The sentence brought more panic to me than was rational. I immediately start to hyperventilate, attempting to pull myself free from the carbon bands that held my body. I feel the hands on my shoulders force me down with so much force it didn't seem human.

"Let me go!" I shout, causing the man to laugh and release my shoulders.

He walks around the table, entering my full view and smiles. "Be honest. Did you miss me, kid?"

Cheever West stooped over me like a wolf getting ready to sink its teeth into the jugular of its prey. In that moment there wasn't a word that could describe the amount of apprehension I was feeling. My throat closed, my hands began to sweat and my heart was about to bust out of my chest. The spider had me in his web and there was nothing I could do—except.

My head is still in an absurd amount of pain; however I know I have to do something before Cheever gets his way with me. With a mere thought, I have Cheever against the bulkhead. The pain is on the verge of unbearable, but I have enough strength left to finish him. A sudden shot of lightening pierces my skull and brain. I let out a scream, immediately releasing Cheever who falls to the ground.

He begins laughing maniacally. "Like that little toy, don't you?" He stands up and tilts the operating table up, so I can face him completely. "It was created just for you." He raddles his finger on the apparatus mounted to my head. "It works similar to a shock collar. If you use your little ability, it'll shock the hell out of you." He laughs again, taking a step back. "How long has it been, John—since I killed your little friend? What was his name?"

My hatred for him reaches a level I thought was impossible "His name was Jurin," I say through my teeth.

He grins, "Oh, right, Jurin. Sorry, these modifications can cloud your memory." He strikes a pose, showing off his new augments. "Completely state-of-the-art, all paid for by the IISF just to catch you." He quickly grabs me by the jaw. "And when they're done with you, I'll get to rip you to shreds bit by bit."

Cheever was a murdering, psychopath before, but now he's a murdering, psychopath with some of the most dangerous cyber-bionic augments available at his literal fingertips. He can tell I'm terrified and that he has all the power, just the thing he gets off to.

"So why wait? The old Cheever would have killed me by now!" Taunting him wasn't a good idea, but in the midst of all my agony I really didn't care what anyone did to me.

He punches the steel table beside my head. "Don't test me."

"That is quite enough, Mr. West." A familiar voice sounds behind me. "Does the device work?"

Cheever straightens up. "Yes, the device works perfectly. He's no more dangerous than a baby." He shoots me a snide glance.

"Brilliant." The man walks around and stands in front of Cheever. "Hopefully Mr. West's display of barbarism wasn't too off putting." Cheever grimaces but remains silent.

That voice. I remember that voice, but from where? "Have we met before?"

"Once but not in person. I believe you recall the events at Callisto?" the man says with subtle hints of annoyance in his tone.

"So you're the leader of the Integra Industries Security Forces?" I ask, remembering what had happed to the unmarked destroyer.

The man smiles. "You humble me, sir. I am merely a minor executive. My name is Timotheus Bernard. I have been tasked with securing you."

Timotheus was a man of small stature, obviously enamored by his own exaggerated legend. He stood there with his hands in his pockets, jet black hair slicked back and oblivious brown eyes.

"And what is it you want with me?" I ask as Dr. Baker begins checking the apparatus on my head.

Timotheus laughs. "Surely, you know why we've been after you." He takes a step toward me, looking into my eyes. "There is something we want in your head and from the looks of it that thing is starting to come out."

"I get that—but why am I the way I am?" I figure if I can't get away then maybe I can get some answers.

Timotheus looks at Dr. Baker then back at me. "We aren't—qualified to tell you such things, but I can assure you. All the answers you seek are close."

Not qualified? What does that mean? "Then can you tell me where we are going, or at least what ship this is?"

Timotheus scoffs, "You are very curious aren't you?"

"It's a bit of a bad habit—but is it really so much to ask?"

He leans in close to my face. "More than you know." He looks and nods at Dr. Baker, who pulls a syringe out of his pocket.

“This is a mild sedative. It will help you relax for the trip,” Dr. Baker says, bracing my arm.

“Wait," I say, quickly searching my mind for something to forestall the injection. “What happened to the Clairvoyance? How did you save me?”

Timotheus frowns, “Disappointing. We would have never enabled Calon if we’d known his true intention.”

“You’re the apostles?!”

Bernard gives me a quizzical look. “Apostles?”

I shake my head. “Calon killed hundreds. He almost murdered billions, and it’s your fault!” I shout.

“Like I said. The events on the Clairvoyance were—unfortunate, Calon was unstable, but he did do his mission by delivering you to us.”

“You and your employer are sick!” I hiss. “What was the point of it all?”

“I don’t ask questions. I only do as I’m told. Integra Industries has already sacrificed so much for you,” Bernard elaborates.

“But why?!” I yell.

Timotheus scowls and motions to Dr. Baker, who injects me with the sedative. I pull and yank at my straps as the drug rushes through my body, causing a sense of euphoria to flow over me. “There ya go, kid.” Cheever’s pompous voice echoes in my ear, “I’ll see you when you wake up, buddy.” He finishes with a sinister smile as I slip away into the blackness.

CHAPTER TWENTY-SEVEN: THE GOOD DOCTOR

"Wake up!" I feel two hands shake me hard, jarring me out of my drug-induced sleep. Dr. Baker's face looks frantic.

"Wha—what's happening?" I muster out in a slurred voice.

"No time to talk. We have to go." He unstraps my hands and starts working on my leg straps when the lights begin to flicker.

He glances up for just a second then goes back to undoing the strap. By now I am almost completely awake, attempting to undo the carbon band holding my head to the table. The sounds of alarms start ringing in the distance when he frees one of my legs.

"Why are you doing this?" I ask.

His anxiety is undeniable. "There are things—that I've done, that I'm not proud of. I know that now."

He fumbles with the last strap on my other leg, cursing under his breath. "What do you mean? What aren't you telling me?"

He hesitates, leaving my leg and moving to look me in the eye. "I did it for the science, to unlock the secrets of the universe, to find God." He was in a panic. "But it went too far. By the time I realized what was going on it was too late."

"What? Doctor, what happened to my parents?!" I demand. He opens his mouth but freezes when the infirmary door slides opens.

Dr. Baker looks up right as a pulse round pierces his shoulder. He spins and falls to the ground with a shriek. Cheever walks past me holding the pistol on the doctor. "Now what do you think you're doing, doctor?"

I start frantically pulling at the strap wrapped around my head; I can't use my ability until I'm free from this thing. Cheever looks at me, his eyes burning with sadistic intent. He quickly pistol-whips me, causing blood to flow from my nose.

"Cheever!" Dr. Baker musters out, pulling himself to his feet. "You don't know what you're doing." He's holding his shoulder, attempting to dam the blood but failing.

Cheever finishes binding my hands, tilting me upright again. "No. See, that's where you're wrong doctor." He places the pulse pistol on the counter. "I know exactly what I'm doing." He brings his cybernetic arm up, staring at me the entire time, as a long black blade extends from his forearm. "You know, doctor, when I was young I wanted to be a surgeon."

I know what's about to happen. Cheever has a flare for showing off. "Cheever, stop!" I shout but I fear my words only fuel his malice.

Dr. Baker moves back against the wall, still clutching his shoulder. All the while Cheever is slowly making his way toward him. "Please—" Dr. Baker begs.

"Don't do that, doctor. Have some dignity!" Cheever snaps. "As I was saying, I always wanted to be a surgeon. I used to play doctor with this girl I lived by. What was her name—aw well we can call her Val. Come to think of it, isn't that the name of your daughter?" He continues one slow step after another. "I'll have to visit her after this—someone will have to tell her that her daddy died. No need to thank me, doctor. It's my pleasure," he finishes.

"You will never touch my daughter!" Dr. Baker says in low, rough tone.

"The old dog still has teeth, but it's rude to interrupt," Cheever says. "So one day Val and I are playing our usual game of doctor. Now she was always the patient. But that day she was being a bad patient—you know constantly wiggling and refusing to listen to what her doctor was trying telling her." He glances at me and grins. "So I did what any rational doctor would have done—I applied anesthesia. After Val stopped wiggling, I returned to my work. I quickly found out that I don't have the steady hands that a surgeon needs. I made a real mess of it. There were parts and tools everywhere." By now he was only a few steps from the doctor. "Imagine my parent's disappointment when they found out that I couldn't become a doctor. Society tends to frown on child killers becoming successful doctors. Don't you think, kid?" He looks at me.

"I think you're a sick son-of-a-bitch," I respond, trying to sound unaffected by his terrible acts.

He stares at me for a moment. I can tell he hates that I'm not reacting the way he wants. The doctor notices and begins sneaking around toward the pistol still sitting on the counter. The lights flicker again and the sound of another alarm can be heard.

"I like to think of myself as an artist," Cheever responds.

I search my mind for something to say, something that will hold his attention while the doctor gets the gun. "An artist, no. You are a disgusting excuse for a human. Your entire existence is to hurt and murder at will. What's the point?!"

Cheever scowls and grabs my face. "You—I will break you!" he hisses. "I will take everything from you—I will hurt you until you beg me for death! You will be my Masterpiece, my Magnum Opus! Everything you are, everything you could be will be mine. And only then, when my legacy is written in your blood and flesh and bone, will I allow you to die."

His eyes are cold and unwavering. For the first time, I truly see Cheever for what he is and it terrifies me in a way that I have never felt before. How has a man like this come to existence? To kill with so little regard and so much pleasure? I realize he's not far from me when I succumb to the blood haze. Then I realized that I'm not afraid of Cheever as much as I'm afraid of being like him. We are two sides of the same coin, bound by our similarities and yet separated by what?

The audible sound of a pistol cocking pulls my attention away from my thoughts. I look over at Dr. Baker, holding the pistol with one shaking hand. "Get away from him!"

Cheever makes an amusing grunt, retracting the blade and extends his hands upward. "Very sneaky, doctor."

"Shut-up!" he shouts, wincing from the pain in his shoulder.

Cheever seems too amused to be at a disadvantage. I look back at the doctor. "Shoot him!" Cheever looks at me and frowns. "Doctor, you have to shoot him now!"

Dr. Baker hesitates, attempting to steady his hand before finally pulling the trigger but nothing happens. He drops the gun and holds his arms up as Cheever grabs him and faces him toward me. Tears begin to fall down Dr. Baker's face when Cheever pierces his throat with his blade from behind. The doctor's blood runs down the front of his lab coat turning it from white to a deep crimson in mere seconds. The blade retracts, causing more blood to spurt out and hit my chest. The doctor collapses, eyes wide from shock, desperately holding his neck in a futile attempt to stop the bleeding. He thrashes his legs around as the blood starts to spread from beneath him.

Cheever casually walks over to the pistol and picks it up. "Biometric safety—" he says with an amused huff, discharging several rounds into the doctor then looking at me.

"I don't care what it takes, Cheever. I will kill you. I swear you will suffer."

Cheever smiles, placing the gun against the side of my head. "Talk is cheap."

The infirmary door flies open and Timotheus enters with half a dozen armed guards. He looks down at Dr. Baker's lifeless corpse. "What the hell happened?!" He looks at Cheever "Why haven't you secured the cargo?!" he yells.

"I walked in on the good doctor attempting to free the cargo." He kicks the corpse. "He resisted."

Timotheus paces the length of the room. "And how the hell and I suppose to explain this—huh?!"

I can tell Cheever is getting frustrated. "Who cares? He was a traitor—"

"Shut up just shut up!" Timotheus interrupts. "Just get the boy to an escape pod. Surely you can manage that without killing anyone else!"

The lights flicker once again, followed shortly by a tremor. "What's going on?" I ask.

Timotheus looks at me. "It has become apparent that we need to keep closer eye on our perceived allies, because Doctor Baker installed a virus in the ship's operating systems that would cause catastrophic failures throughout the ship!" His tone was a mix of annoyance and fear as another shudder is felt through the ship. "I've issued evacuation orders and a distress signal has been sent to our nearest allies. The doctor's plans have failed."

Another tremor shakes the ship. This time it's so violent that Timotheus grabs one of his guards for balance. He quickly regains his composure and storms out, followed by his escorts. Cheever mumbles an insult under his breath and looks at me. "Time to go, princess." He grunts, tilting me back to the horizontal position and rolling me out of the infirmary.

The ship is in a state of disorder, with people running everywhere. The power keeps fluctuating, overloading in some places and causing sparks to fly. In the midst of all this Cheever seems calm and at home.

"I have to say, Cheever, your new master seems like a real dick." I mock but he ignores me. "Does he understand that you're the Baron of New Horizon?" Still no response, but I can tell I'm getting under his skin. "Then again, the Baron would have disemboweled him where he stood—"

"Shut up!" he says quietly yet aggressively.

"It's cool man, you're the lackey now. Cheever do this, Cheever do that, Cheever you idiot—" I push the envelope.

He punched the steel table between my legs, uncomfortably close to my testacies. "Keep talking!"

I remain quiet for a minute or two, contemplating whether or not Cheever can see through my manipulation, when we enter the main escape pod bay. Just as expected every pod has been launched. Cheever rips a set of fastened benches from the deck and throws them across the room as if they were no heavier than a feather. He walks over to a terminal and places his hand on the screen, when another wave of tremors cause the hull to groan.

"Looks like there are three left on the starboard side," he says. "They're undergoing maintenance by a tech named Albert Hawking."

Albert Hawking? That name sounds familiar, yet I've never heard of it. Then I remember overhearing the twins arguing about their favorite theoretical physicist of old. Don was enamored with a man named Albert Einstein while Ron preferred the teachings of Stephen Hawking. There could be no possible way the twins—unless Dr. Baker. I feel my heart flutter with excitement but do my best to hide my joy from Cheever.

"Well, aren't we just the luckiest," I respond in the flattest tone I can muster.

I can tell Cheever is unimpressed by my cynicism, but I really don't care. If what I think is right, he's in for a hell of a surprise. Cheever pushes me out of the pod bay and through the corridor. The ship seems lifeless at this point. Every stride Cheever takes echoes throughout the passage, making it sound like an army marching out of step. It all brings an odd and uncomfortable feeling, as if something horrible is about to happen.

A moment later we are flying through the door to the starboard pod bay. Cheever lets go of the surgical table and I roll into the walk with a loud smack, causing the device on my head to slam down and split the bridge of my nose. He runs over to one of the pods and attempts to disable the lock out, obviously to no avail because he begins cursing and punching the wall repeatedly.

He runs over to me, taking my head in his hands. "How do I make them work?!" he snarls.

"Hell if I know, and even if I did—" he slams my head into the table.

"There's no one around to tell me what to do." He slams my head into the steel table again.

My vision gets blurry as he lifts my head again. "I—" He slams me again, this time causing me to black out for a second or two.

"Tell me how to fix it?!" He begins squeezing my face, causing me even more suffering.

"All you need is the code," a voice says. Cheever drops my head and looks up. "You must be Cheever. I'd appreciated it if you'd stop hurting our friend."

It takes me a moment before I interpret what is going on, and then Cheever kicks me and the table to the side. "And who the hell are you?"

"We're his family. Now step away from him!" There was no mistaking. That was Nev's voice. I look over, only seeing the burred outlines of four people plus Cheever.

My eyes are heavy but I attempt to blink them awake. The pain from Cheever's repeated blows are pushing over the limit when I feel a pair of soft hands on my face. Ava! I jerk awake seeing her wild red hair first, then her rosy lips and perfect cheeks.

"Have you come to take me away, Valkyrie?" I mutter.

She scoffs as a single tear shatters against my face. "You're such an idiot."

"You can make up later. Get him out of that thing!" Nev shouts.

Ava begins undoing the straps on my chest while the twins start on my legs. Nev, on the other hand, is holding Cheever at gunpoint. I am still recovering from the Clairvoyance as well as Cheever's abuse, but my senses are starting to clear.

"Nev," I say softly. "You have to kill him, now."

"You got it kid," Nev says, letting out a volley of fire without hesitation.

CHAPTER TWENTY-EIGHT: THE SACRIFICE

The sound of Nev discharging several pulse rounds gives me a sense of relief. My legs and hands are free at this point, but I still have the apparatus on my head. I am hopeful that things are going well until Nev's pulse rifle flies across the room, shattering against the wall. I look over to see Cheever holding Nev by the neck with one arm. Ava pulls out her pistol and unloads several rounds into Cheever, but they splinter on his chest in a flash of blue plasma. He looks at her and grins as several armor plates extend from his armor to cover his head. He throws Nev at Ava, smashing into her and knocking the table onto its side.

Ron and Don were still trying to free me from the table. "Guys, get this off my head!"

They crawl over and start undoing the device keeping me from using my ability. I can't see what is happening but judging from what I could hear Nev and Ava aren't going to last long against Cheever and his modifications. Ron undoes one of the straps and I can feel the apparatus loosen. Then there is a hesitation like time has stopped. I feel a warm liquid on my face. I strain my head to look over only to see Ron leaning over the table with Cheever's blade through his chest.

The air escapes my lungs and a knot forms in my throat. Oh God, no—Ron's eyes are wide and scared. I can feel it. His mouth is half open and quivering. He squeezes my shirt so tight I can feel his pulse. Then Cheever throws him across the bay, making a bone crushing noise against the wall. Don lets out a blood-chilling cry, grabbing Cheever by the neck; he overloads his Aug, shocking Cheever and causing his arm to burst into flames.

Ava grabs me and says something, but I'm still in shock. It is happening all over again. First it was Jurin, then Dr. Baker and now Ron. Cheever had single-handedly killed everyone who tried to help me. The apparatus was still firmly attached to my head, but I didn't care. The pain was nothing anymore. I let out a shout, focusing all of my power on the infernal device. It begins shocking me, but I don't let up. I can't let another person die for me. I feel tears running down my face as the image of Ron, like the boy and Jurin are burned into my memory. Then I feel something like a runner's high. There is pain but I have reached a point where I'm in a sort of trance. The apparatus increases its intensity. My brain feels as though it is being flayed by a thousand knifes, but I don't stop. I can't stop. I let out another agonizing yell before the device finally fails, causing a shock wave that throws the surgical table against the wall.

I look at Cheever, who was still recovering from Don's quick thinking. I can't see his eyes, but I can tell he's afraid. The dread is radiating from him. It is the same fear he had when we were back on Titan, only now I know why. He quickly stands and attempts to impale me with his blade, but it shatters against my body. I grab his forearm and use my gift to throw him. He flies into the a pod door with enough force to cause the door the crumple around him, I look at my hand, where his severed bionic forearm was still firmly in my grasp, then toss it to the side and take another step toward him.

"John!" Ava's voice cuts through the blood haze. Nev is dragging Ron into one of the escape pods. He isn't dead but he is in shock, hyperventilating with Don putting pressure on his brother's chest. "John, we have to go!" Ava shouts.

There is no hesitation. I know time is running out, so I sprint to the pod and help Don put pressure on his brother's wound. Nev is holding him in his arms and telling him to stay awake. Ava runs over to the terminal and inputs the launch code, but just as the Pod door is closing, Cheever grabs her by the hair and pulls her out. I run over to the window where he has her by the throat.

"Open the door!" I yell, hitting the terminal, but the pod is sealed with a countdown to launch initiated.

"If you want her back alive," Cheever starts in an arrogant tone "you'll have to go to where you began." The pod launches and I'm forced against the glass as Ava and the ship shrink in mere moments.

I slam my fists against the door, feeling my stomach turn with agony. "Ron! Come on. Don't do this, Ron!" Don's quivering voice brings me back to the moment. "Someone do something!" he screams.

I crawl over and place my hand on Ron's chest. His pulse is very slow and he has lost a lot of blood. We all know it, but we won't accept it. There is just nothing we can do.

I take Don's hand. He looks at me, eyes swollen and red. "I'm sorry. I'm so sorry."

Don begins shaking his head. "No, no damn-it. Ron, wake up!" He hits Ron's chest with his fists. Nev tries to stop him but Don pulls away. "Stop! He's fine—Wake up—he's fine!" he leans forward onto Ron's chest and begins sobbing.

The pod remains silent for what feels like hours before Nev's Aug starts buzzing. He hesitates, finally binging up the connection. Captain Rickard's face appears and it only takes a few seconds for him to determine that there is something wrong. "What's happened?"

"We need medical—Ron um—" Nev chokes, looking down at Don still holding his deceased brother. He looks back at the captain and shakes his head.

There is a moment of silence before the captain responds. "ETA five." Then the connection closes.

This—all of this is my fault. Everything I touch dies. I look down at the blood on my shirt and attempt to wipe it away, but there no getting rid of it. Even when it's clean the blood will still be there. Then there is Ava. My mind wonders about the atrocious things Cheever could be doing to her as I sit here and wait to be picked up. I'm nothing but a corrosive acid eating away everything. My self-loathing reaches an all-time high as the Confessor finally intercepts us.

Several minutes later the pod door opens and Lora enters, first gasping at the sight of Ron's lifeless body. Tears immediately form in her eyes as she looks at me, then Nev and finally Don. She crouches down and rubs his back. Thomas follows, pausing a moment to assess the situation. Nev stands and walks out when Thomas and Lora attempt to pry Don away from his twin. And despite having one arm, Don resists them while screaming and crying the entire time. Thomas ends up having to sedate him to relax him enough to transfer him onto a medical bed.

Then it is just me and Ron, his eyes frozen in a state of fear and pain. The very sight of it made me hurt, but I couldn't look away. I need to atone for this somehow. I deserve to be punished for everything I've done to this crew. They accepted me and all I've done was bring death to them.

Something brushes against my hand and I look down where Grem is rubbing against my open palm. I don't know what happens to me next, whether it is my mind finally catching up with the events that have just taken place or the simple gesture of an oblivious cat. I began to cry a violent cry, one that hurts my chest and stomach. That is where I stayed for almost an hour, holding Grem and crying like a baby desperate for the touch of his mother.

By the time I regain some semblance of self-control Thomas has returned to collect Ron's body. He steps in and sits next to me, silent and stoic. "What do you want, Thomas?" I was being rude for no reason, but all I wanted was to be alone.

"Your vitals—"

"Leave me alone!" My tone could melt steel but Thomas didn't move.

"I know what you're going through," Thomas says, staring at Ron.

"How—how could you possibly know what I feel like? How could you understand what's going on? You're just a machine, nothing more than a series of protocols with flashy bells and whistles!" I respond in a way that isn't me, but I hurt so much that I can't stop.

Thomas remains silent for a few minutes. "Do you know why they were scared of us?"

The question was random, but it offered an opportunity to get my mind off the now. "Why?"

"Because we feel. You all just see a machine without a soul, but I feel everything you do. That was what we were created to do." Thomas shakes his head. "We were created to care for you, to love you and in time become more like you. That scared people because in reality you're scared of yourselves."

Thomas was right. We often fear what we don't understand and we often don't understand our own very nature. But for Thomas it was more than that. Ever since we reactivated him, he has been struggling with the realization that his kind was killed—not just decommissioned. He could very well be the last Gen8 Syntech to exist. How utterly lonely that must be, and yet he still finds the motivation to move on. "You're right, Thomas," I respond in a soft tone.

"When I was first commissioned I was assigned to a mobile hospital ship. The purpose was to provide free medical services to people who were less fortunate than others," he starts while staring at Ron's body. "There was this young girl. She was so malnourished and frail, but she had the most beautiful blonde hair I had ever seen." Thomas looks down at his hands. "She had Heterochromia, which caused her to have green and blue eyes, but what I remember most was a stuffed rabbit she always had with her that she called Thomas." I look at him and he gazes back at me. "She was diagnosed with a rare form of Restrictive Cardiomyopathy which is virtually unheard of now days with the advent of proto-genetics. But alas, she required a heart transplant nonetheless. Now at that time I had done three-hundred and sixty-five successful heart transplants in less than a week. I was able to perform surgeries seventy-three percent faster than a human and I would never tire, never need sleep. Fatigue has no hold on me." Thomas looks away. "But even then with all the gifts my makers gave me she still died from unknown causes."

"My God," I utter under my breath.

"The technician said my personality core suffered from a catastrophic failure due to a power flux. The only thing that saved me from permanent damage was a failsafe my designers built in for that exact reason."

"You tried to self-terminate, didn't you?"

Thomas freezes for a second or two before responding. "I had failed. There was no other purpose for my existence other than saving people," he replies. "In the end, I realized that I'd rather not live knowing I can't save everyone." He finishes and gives me a profound look.

"What happened next?" I ask.

"I was sent back to Dr. Brigman for subsequent reload and reimage."

I think for a moment. "Wait, so how do you remember all this?"

Thomas hesitates. "I manually wrote it into my firmware. That way I can never forget that little girl."

Thomas is more human than most humans are. There is no doubt about it now. "Thank you Thomas—and I'm sorry for earlier."

Thomas bows his head and stands. I help him take Ron's body to the infirmary where Rickard, Nev and Lora have been waiting with Don while he slept.

I walk over to see how Don's doing when the captain turns and punches me so hard I fall to the ground. "I should have killed you when we found you back on Titan!" he yells, kicking me in the abdomen.

I wasn't mad, or remotely angry at the captain. For all I care, I deserve whatever I get. "I know."

"Shut up!" he shouts, punching again and again. "You killed him—you did!" Tears were starting to form. "And—" He stops and bits his knuckle, pulling his gun out and pointing it at me. Nev and Lora take a few steps toward him but I hold up my hand stopping them.

"Listen, I know I deserve this, but I can also fix it." I get on my knees and hold my hands up.

"How? Ava is gone—my baby girl is gone," he says with a tear falling down his cheek.

Baby girl?! "Ava is you daughter?!" I exclaim. The captain covers his face with his hands and sobs quietly. "I had no idea—" I stand up, only for the captain to punch me again.

"That's enough, captain!" Nev shouts.

"I swear. I will do anything to saver her," I say in a solemn tone. "Cheever told me that if I wanted her back I had to go to where I began."

The captain points his gun at me again. "What does that mean?!"

"I'm not entirely sure, but I think the people that are after me are the same people that know where I came from. If we can find out where I was born, then that's where we go."

I think for a bit while the captain finally holsters his gun. "I'll be on the bridge. Let Nev know when you have a destination." He walks past me and out of the infirmary. Finally, I start to breathe again.

I nurse the fresh welts on my face, looking at Nev. "Can we track Ava's Aug to find out where they're going?" I ask.

Nev shakes his head. "No, we're too far away for that—" He looks at Don and Ron lying side by side. "Don might have been able to, but I don't think his Aug works anymore."

I curse under my breath. There has to be a lead on this. I stick my hand into my pocket and pet the torn fabric. I know this is the key but I have no clue what AIC stands for or how to search for an answer I look over at Thomas inspecting Don's left arm when something finally clicks in my head. "Thomas!" I exclaim.

He glances up at me with a puzzling stare. "What's the matter?"

I rush over to him, retrieving the torn cloth from my pocket with the AIC printed on it the same acronym that was painted on the wall of the room my mother gave birth to me in. All this time Thomas, this hundred-and-forty-year-old Syntech, has unknowingly held the keys to my past. I should have put it together when we first activated him. "Most databases don't have this acronym in it for some reason. For as long as I can remember it seemed really peculiar but given everything that's happened so far it's starting to make sense that Integra Industries had all the records expunged."

"Well, all but one," Lora says looking at Thomas.

I hand Thomas the torn cloth and he stares at it for several moments. "This is the insignia for Averratech Interstellar Conglomerate. They owned a lot of mining stations in the Main belt while I was active."

"What happened to those facilities?" I ask, but Thomas shrugs.

"They were abandoned," Nev says. "The United Earths' Fleet couldn't defend them so the stations were mothballed during the war."

"This is it. I was born in one of these facilities eighteen years ago," I say. "That is what Cheever meant by go to where I began."

The room falls silent when Lora lets out a gasp. "Ceres, Oh my God."

"You have to be shitting me!" Nev adds. "But with all this weirdness I guess it could be possible."

"What?" I ask.

Lora looks at me "When did you say you were found at the orphanage on Titan?"

"I was three—so fifteen years ago." I respond directly.

"It matches up—the captain is going to hate this," Nev says running out of the room.

"Can someone please explain this to me?" I demand as Lora follows Nev out.

Thomas and I silently look at each other for several minutes when Don's monitor starts beeping. Don slowly lifts his good arm and reaches around looking for something to grab.

I walk over and take his hand; he opens his eyes a moment later and stares at me "Ro—Ron?" he forces out in a horse tone.

"No, it's me, John," I reply and Don smiles.

"Hey Einstein, I had the worst dream," he responds.

I look up at Thomas then back at Don. "I have something very important to tell you, Don." He grimaces and glances at the medical bed beside him where his brother's body quietly rests.

CHAPTER TWENTY-NINE: THE CERES INCIDENT

Don sits quietly for a while, staring at his twin's lifeless body while Thomas inspects his left arm. "I didn't know it was possible to overload a BICS like this," Thomas says, inspecting the burnt flesh.

"It's not supposed to be, but when Ron—" he chokes "was younger, he found out how to modify them."

"Why would you need to do that?" I ask.

Don looks at me. "Mostly so we could communicate with our own systems or write our own sub programs—it wasn't too fancy at first, just a bunch of party tricks and what not. But later we realized the true applications of being able to alter one's BICS."

"Like what?" I query, causing Don to look at the floor.

"Twins have always been something of an enigma to doctors and scientists. Did you know they used to think twins could communicate telepathically?" I shake my head. "Of course, there was never scientific proof of it, but for as long as I've can remember Ron and I could almost read each other's thoughts. It wasn't until we started tampering with our Augs that we realized we could send signals to one another with a simple thought." Don looks down at his left arm. "BICS are completely integrated into our Nervous Systems. Although they don't directly send input to the brains because of safety reasons, they do receive output from it. We changed it so that we could receive and send data directly to and from our brains."

It made sense, how many times had I been surprised by their ability to finish each other's sentences and work so well together without saying a word. They had networked their brains, combined into a shared intellect and now it was gone. But it wasn't just that connection that was lost; the twins had been inside each other's minds for so long that the silence in Don's head must be maddening. "I am so sorry—if it was because of me—"

"Stop it." Don's words are sharp. "This wasn't your fault. Ron knew the risks just like I did."

"But if I was only—"

Don grabs my shoulder. "Ron died doing what was right for someone he cared for. Given the opportunity again, even knowing the outcome, he would have gladly sacrificed himself."

His eyes start to water. "I would do the same." He blinks, attempting to hold back the flood.

"But why—how can you say that?" My voice cracks.

"Some people are worth giving your life to protect. Ron and I both knew from the moment we saw you that you were destined for something important. You gave Ron meaning in death." A single tear falls down his cheek.

"But why me? In the end, aren't the people who are willing to sacrifice for their friends the ones you want to live? It's not fair to carry a burden that everyone I care about has to pay for." My throat dries and my voice goes horse.

Don looks at Ron again. "Such is the nature of life. Remember what I told you? Happiness doesn't mean anything without sadness. It's the balance that's important."

How could he do this? How could he sit there and comfort me when he lost his brother? Yet here he is making me feel better about it. Don winces and flinches away from Thomas's prying instruments.

"My apologies," Thomas says, placing the tool on the tray beside the bed. "So what would you like to hear first? The good or bad news?"

Don looks at me then at Ron again and shrugs. "I guess the bad."

"Right, well the worst of it is that if we don't install a replacement BICS soon then you will lose all functionality of your right arm." Thomas finishes in an uncharacteristic up-beat tone.

"Great, so what's the good news?" Don says in a subdued voice.

Thomas hesitates. "Aside from the obvious second degree burns there is no major internal damage, along with an interesting burn pattern that all the cool kids will be jealous of." Don and I glower at Thomas's poorly timed joke. "Sorry, just thought I'd try."

"So the good news is—what exactly?" I inquire.

Thomas gently lifts Don's arm, pointing at a network of dark red burn lines stretching across Don's arm and hand. "These are cyber-bionic circuits." He points at an open square shaped sore on Don's shoulder where all the paths collide. "And this is the BICS command module. When you are born you are immediately injected with millions of microscopic robots that essentially build the BICS over the course of your life. These circuits run through your entire body feeding data to the command module." Thomas pauses and looks at my blank expression.

"What he means is I should be dead but I'm not—that's the good news," Don clarifies.

"Exactly. For some reason the overload you initiated stopped at your shoulder and didn't hit the rest of your body," Thomas adds.

"Then why is he going lose his arm's functionality? Wouldn't the Aug repair itself?" I ask.

Thomas softly puts Don's arm down. "The BICS, for lack of better classification, takes on the role of a mutualistic symbiotic parasite. It continues to spread through the body, eventually replacing the nervous and immune system as life goes on."

Thomas notices the horrified look on my face. "No, no this is a good thing. People who have been born with nervous and immune system defects are cured now because the BICS not only replaces but also perfects the human condition. In the distant past people had to get shots to boost their immune systems and help them fight diseases. It was affective, albeit rudimentary at best, but it didn't help with genetic diseases. Now with the BICS, you simply download your immunizations."

"Of course if you fry the system, it's about the same as a setting fire to every nerve ending in your body," Don says sarcastically.

"It could repair itself," Thomas starts. "But only if the command module survived and in this case it didn't."

"So where do we get a new one?" I ask directly.

"There are clinics that specialize in BICS; I took the liberty of looking up the closest one to our location and it's a medical ship three days away. Unfortunately, even if we left now we wouldn't get there in time." Thomas frowns and the room falls silent.

"What about Ron's," Don says in a soft voice.

Thomas pauses. "Are you serious?" he starts. "Technical difficulties aside the ethical violations are numerous and obvious."

"What would the technical difficulties be?" Don retorts.

Thomas thinks for a minute. "We aren't going to do that. Ron's BICS has his entire life on it. His memories and his consciousness. Everything that makes him who he was is stored on it."

"I didn't ask about that—" Don responds, getting out of the bed and walking over to his brother, placing his hand on Ron's cheek. "I asked if it was possible."

Thomas looks at me for support, but I offer nothing. "It is possible for me to remove Ron's command module and place it in you. Theoretically the nano-bots should start repairing the connections immediately. But there is no telling what would happen once the connections to your brain are fixed."

"Will I be able to use my arm?" Don says, wiping away a smudge on Ron's cheek.

"Maybe, but I don't recommend—"

"Do it." Don looks at Thomas.

I can tell Thomas doesn't think it is a good idea, but instead of pleading he simply shakes his head and motions to the surgical table. "It will be a little while, John. Why don't you go and get some rest."

"But I don't—" I start, but Thomas gives me a scowl that tells me 'your vitals indicate you need rest' and I nod my head and leave the infirmary.

I don't know what it was but the walk back to my room was more of a trudge, with every step rebelling against me. I was tired. Thomas had that much right, but I didn't want to go to sleep. I guess a part of me was afraid of what would happen next. Ava comes to mind. The thought of her in danger makes my stomach hurt. I can't imagine how the captain feels, I shake my head. Why didn't Ava tell me she was the captain's daughter? No wonder she was so hesitant about our feelings. I'm such an idiot; the signs were there all along.

I look up, realizing that I have been walking aimlessly for a good five minutes. I'm not far from the bridge. A part of me wants to go talk to the Captain, while another doesn't want to get hit again. But it seems that even as I'm contemplating whether to go to the bridge or not my feet seem to be heading there regardless. Before long I come to a stop outside the hatch. I pause for a second, listening to the ship's hum before finally mustering the courage to walk through the door.

Instantly three pairs of eyes greet me as I close the door behind me. Nev is hunching over a terminal with a holographic image of Ceres hovering above it. Lora looks as though she is in mid-sentence when I interrupt and the captain is sitting with his back facing me.

I take a few more steps into the room when Nev waives me over. "Show the captain the torn cloth."

I pull the cloth out and flash it toward the captain. He glances over and frowns. "Have you ever heard of the Ceres Incident?" he says in a deep, calm voice.

I shake my head. "No, it doesn't ring a bell."

Captain Rickard sits up in a swift motion that makes me flinch. "Right after the Stand Still an organization calling themselves Humanity United bought the Averratech facility on Ceres. They retrofitted it as an Advance Medical and Research Clinic with the catch phrase 'Forging the future for the betterment of Humanity.' Some of their goals were to start rebuilding relations between the inner and outer solar systems. But they weren't what they seemed," the captain finishes.

"Fifteen years ago Humanity United had to abandon Ceres because there was what they claimed a disaster that made the facility unstable." Nev continues where Rickard stopped. "Right after the Ceres Incident the organization was disbanded."

I look at them both. "What does this have to do with me?"

The captain stands and walks to a display. "Humanity United was illegally experimenting on people. For what reasons and purposes, we don't know. But an informant within the organization leaked some information about their illegal activities." I frown, imagining Dr. Baker was that informant, but still not understanding where the tie-in is when the captain continues. "Remember when you first came aboard the Confessor and I asked you why you were on my ship?"

I think back to that first encounter with the captain. So much has happened since then and yet the memory is vivid in my mind like it had just taken place yesterday. "Yes, I remember I didn't know why but that something told me to pick that skip."

"What if I told you that you have been on the Confessor once long ago?" He responds, still staring at the display. "What if I told you that Nev and I have met you before?"

I understand the words he's saying but they just don't make sense to me. My head gets light and my knees buckle. I quickly rush over to a seat before I pass out. "What—but that's—"

"Impossible?" Nev interrupts. "Yeah that's what we thought, but we were there fifteen years ago during the Ceres Incident. We picked up a kid, no more than three and delivered him to an anonymous contact on Ganymede. That boy was you."

I begin hyperventilating as my stomach starts to move to my throat. Lora comes over and places her hand on mine. "I don't—how?"

The captain turns and sits in the chair across from me. "We were contracted by the unknown benefactors. They hired the Confessor along with about a dozen ships to infiltrate and retrieve you from the facility on Ceres. At the time I was just the first mate. Nev had a lot less gray hair and my wife and child—Ava—were on board."

"Wife—you mean Nalary Kross, don't you?" I interject.

The captain adjusts in his seat "She was Nalary Rickard then but I called her Nal—Ava looks more and more like her every day and they share the same fiery disposition." Rickard smiles, but only for a second. "We were ambushed by a cloaked unmarked fleet when we arrived at Ceres. Many of the ships that were hired were destroyed very soon after that."

"I. along with a strike team, entered the facility to find you while the ships were fighting outside," Nev says. "I didn't realize then but these forces had the IISF written all over them."

"What were they doing?"

Nev shrugs. "There were so many children from infants to five years, but we didn't have time to save them all." Nev's face has a solemn expression on it. "We found you in this white room separated by a black glass wall."

I feel my jaw drop. It was the room from my dreams. "I remember that," I say with an exhale.

"But here is where things get interesting." Nev continues. "After we secured you the attackers just left."

"Yeah, it seemed like the moment we got that message the unmarked fleet retreated," the captain adds. "The mission didn't go without casualties though. The Idle Confessor was heavily damaged with the crew either dead or seriously injured," The captain pulls his shirt collar down, revealing a large scar. "Our old captain was killed by shrapnel. I would've died if it wasn't for him pushing me out of the way. We took on whatever survivors we could find and dusted our tracks. I searched for Nal and Ava but I couldn't find them anywhere and when I did—" The captain wavers under the memory. "Ava was by her mother's still body. From what I could tell Nal shielded Ava from a blown power junction."

The room turns quiet. "All those people—your wife—they all died for me?" The words left a sour taste in my mouth.

"They died ending whatever tests the IISF were doing on Ceres," the captain responds in a flat tone, as if he had to repeat that to himself just to justify the sacrifice.

"But I was the reason? Why else would they send you in to save only me?" I insist. I don't really know what I am trying to prove. Maybe I want the captain to blame me, but in any case I blame myself—again.

The captain doesn't respond and the bridge gets quiet again when Lora chimes in. "What's the plan?"

The question is a welcome distraction. Nev returns to the holographic map of Ceres. "We can assume they will be up to the same tricks as last time."

"Yeah. We aren't falling for that twice," the captain responds. "We will stop here and use this asteroid as cover. From here we will deploy drone sensors all around us." He updates the holographic display with his plan. "The sensors will act as an early warning system for anything that gets near."

"The drones can sense stealth ships?" I ask.

The captain makes a sad expression. "The twins made them. They don't actually sense the ships, but they do take advantage of the way light refracts when it hits the stealth fields." He updates the display, showing a bubble of sensors around the ship. "The sensors create a network with one another. If a stealth ship breaks that boundary, the sensors will record the light refracting and update the ship's flight computer with a rendering of the approximate size and shape of the ship."

"The only problem is after they leave the sensors they can change their course and we wouldn't see it. Ideally we'd want the sensors far enough away to give us ample warning but if we wanted to fire at them the sensors would need to be within the range of our weapons—which puts us in range of their weapons," Lora adds with a technical flare.

"Why don't we make a mesh of the sensors instead of a sphere?" I say, updating the computer model. The display flashes and the sensor bubble disappears and is replaced by a webbing of sensors reaching out from the ship to just past our affective weapon range. "This way we can track the stealth ships within the sensors."

The captain grabs his chin, scrutinizing the display. He looks at Nev who shrugs then at Lora who spins the virtual image of the Confessor, inspecting every angle. She smiles and nods her head. "It works," the captain says in an unexpected optimistic tone. "Now that we have our plan of attack, how are we going to get Ava and escape unscathed?"

Nev begins talking about infiltrating the station by using me as a decoy. "The stowaway is who they want, right? So I'll hide on the skip, then when he lands I'll slip out and find Ava. The kid uses his creepy, murderous voodoo magic to destroy the facility and the people in it, then we all go home and have a drink," he finishes with a devious grin.

The captain looks at me, then at Lora. "Please, someone come up with a better plan—" he says bluntly, causing Nev to pout.

I think for a moment. There has to be a way to guarantee not only Ava's safety but also the crew's and the Confessor's as well. "Me!" I almost shout. "Nev, you're a genius!" Nev lights up as if he has never been accused of being a genius, while the captain and Lora give me a critical look. "It's so obvious. You said they stopped attacking when you had me all that time ago. When we were on Callisto the soldiers never shot directly at me. They won't do anything that would put me in danger."

Captain Rickard smiles and looks at Nev. "How many grenades do you have?" he asks. "You know the ones I told you not to have—"

Nev straightens up, looking at the captain with a side-long stare. "If I knew what you were talking about I would say that there are possibly eight," he finishes in an impish tone.

The captain looks back at me. "Ok, kid. What's your plan?"

Chapter Thirty: The Fall of Blitzkrieg

The vest is heavier than I expected. Nev smacks me on the back, causing a miniature panic attack. "Damn-it Nev. What the hell is wrong with you?!"

"I should ask you the same question!" he responds with a laugh. "Remember, it was your idea to have eight thorium grenades daisy-chained to your body." He smacks my back again.

"Do you have a death wish?" I say in a low voice.

He laughs again. "These things are stable as hell. There's no way—"

I lift a large spacing container behind me with my ability. "I wasn't talking about the grenades."

His face is a mix of fear and astonishment, but only for a second before he begins smiling again. I drop the container and we both start laughing when the hanger door opens and the captain walks in.

"Is everything working?" Rickard asks.

Nev looks at the harness he's rigged with the explosives. "Yup. I installed a timer and a remote trigger. Plus I made a false dead man trigger for the ship." He grins.

The captain nods his head, bringing up a holographic space map. "We're stopping for some supplies at the Kelasoran Space Station." He updates the display and it zooms in on a modestly-sized space doc with hundreds of ships either docked to it or floating around it. “From there it will take three or four days to reach Ceres.”

Nev and I nod our heads and I pull the suicide vest off and gently set it on a pallet. The Kelasoran Space Station is the last remaining bastion of the Kelasoran Defense Array. It is only a cog in a network of about three dozen that used to defend the Frontier from attack. Now the station has been retrofitted as a rest stop for ships leaving or going through the Main Belt. The rest were dismantled by either the government or scavengers looking for quick creds.

Captain Rickard continues to go over the plan, now including the explosive vest which I will use to threaten myself with. If everything works as planned, it’ll bully the IISF into giving us Ava and letting the Confessor leave without being destroyed. I feel a chill run down my spine with the thought of carrying that many explosives for so long. I’ll have the detonator with me, but as Nev said there is also a timer. If the shit hits the fan, which is very likely, then I will do my best to destroy the facility with the vest and escape using my voodoo magic, as Nev so eloquently put it. The plan is solid. We know what needs to be done, but as far as it being sound, well that’s a different story.

The captain finishes his briefing and gives us a serious look. Everyone knows that something will come up. The unpredictable will happen. But the captain and the crew of the Confessor are relying on me to make this a success. Unfortunately, I know that Integra Industries will never stop looking for me and they have nearly unlimited resources. Destroying the facility may bring closure to the captain and Nev, but for me this is only the beginning.

Captain Rickard closes the display. “We are about eight hours from the Kelasoran.” Then he looks at me. “You should get some sleep, kid. You look like hell," he says frankly before quickly leaving the hanger.

He is right. I crack my neck, feeling the fatigue of an utter lack of sleep weighing me down. I look at Nev who is standing near the skip I used to gain passage onto the Confessor.

"Hey Nev, I'm going to get some shut eye!" I yell across the hanger.

Nev doesn't move or say anything until I turn and start heading for the door. "It happened at the Fall of Blitzkrieg." His words echo through the hanger.

I turn and stare at him "What happened?" I stop and look at his bionic leg. "You said the Fall of Blitz?"

He slowly tilts his head and looks at me. "Have you heard of it before?"

Everyone knew about the Fall of Blitzkrieg. It was one of the final battles of the Great War and also the bloodiest. "I assumed you served but I didn't know—" I stop when Nev gives me the same look he had on Callisto, as if he sees through me.

"The captain was also there. He was a Lieutenant and I was a Special Forces Officer. We were on the Blitzkrieg." His voice trails off.

The Blitzkrieg was a Titan Class Ship much like the Clairvoyance but even more deadly. It was the flagship of the renowned Vanguard Armada, whose sole purpose was to maintain the border between the frontier and the inner solar system. The Vanguard was a fraction of the size of a normal fleet, which allowed it to respond to incidents quicker than the main fleet could. Despite its size, the Vanguard boasted the Frontier's deadliest capital ships as well as the most renowned soldiers the war had seen. That is, at least from the Frontier's prospective.

During that last few years of the Great War, it became less of a war and more of an arms race with both sides building up their military strength. There were fewer battles but more casualties. Basically most of the souls lost during the entirety for the war happened in a time frame of a decade or so. The iconic 'Fall of the Blitzkrieg,' as the texts puts it, happened right before the Armistice Concord was signed. To many lecturers and academics it was this very battle that brought the notion of a ceasefire to the table.

Stories of the Blitzkrieg's valiant final stand have been exaggerated and told to little kids for as long as I can remember. I couldn't help but feel honored to not only know one, but two of the legendary ship's few surviving crew members.

"What happened?" My question ends the silence.

Nev's shoulders drop a little. "We were doing our rounds. It had been months since we had seen the UE Fleet, so apathy had started to take hold." His voice was flat. "Then they were on us before we could react, two fleets from two directions using asteroids for cover."

"Yeah, the history vids say that the United Earths' Fleet attempted to breach the Main Belt by splitting their main armada into two smaller tasks forces." I respond and Nev nods his head.

"They had us surrounded and outnumbered. We were just barely able to send a high-band distress signal out before they jammed our coms. But it took two days for the rest of the Sovereign Republic Frontier Fleet to respond. By then over half of the Vanguard's hundred and ten ships were destroyed, including all of the Supplemental Fleet Support Ships." Nev continues in the same sober tone. "The UEF took a lot of casualties as well, but that was mainly due to the fact that we had Titans. But it wasn't enough. With all of the Support Ships destroyed we had no way of resupplying our weapons and fuel."

I can feel my mouth drop, trying not to recoil in wake of Nev's vulnerability. I knew what happened next I had seen dozens of videos and documentaries about the Fall of Blitz, but I wanted to hear what Nev had to say. "What then?"

"When the SRFF finally showed up, the UEF made a blockade, effectively cutting us off from the rest of our fleet." Nev sits on one of the pallets. "The UEF was still larger than our entire fleet. There was nothing we could do. It was a hopeless situation." He pats his hand on his prosthetic leg. "Then that bastard Ferguson did the unthinkable!" His voice goes scornful.

"Ferguson—you mean Vice Admiral Typhon Ferguson? The legendary Fighting Ferguson?" I say in an incredulous tone. Typhon Ferguson was a hero even before the Fall of Blitzkrieg.

Nev picks up on my excitement and gives me a grave look. "Ferguson was a piece of shit that cared more about his legend than the people he was willing to sacrifice!" Nev's words were piecing. "The legendary Vice Admiral attempted to surrender to the UEF right after the ambush."

A part of me feels offended. Jurin and I each used to pretend that we were Ferguson leading the Blitzkrieg in an epic battle against the dishonorable UEF. Nev's words cause that memory the crack. "What do you mean he attempted?"

Nev looks around as if he was about to share something that was not supposed to be spoken aloud. "Captain Rickard and the other Lieutenants—relieved the Vice Admiral of his duty right after the battle started."

The truth shattered the remnants of my childhood memory. "Then the captain—"

"Commanded one of the greatest space battles in the history of the war," Nev says matter-of-flatly.

"And the decision to ram the blockade?" I ask.

Nev grins. "It took Rickard quite a bit of finesse to convince the rest of the Vanguard that it was the only option."

I let out a huff, shaking my head and grinning. "Crazy son of a bitch!" I exclaim.

At the bleakest point of the battle when the Vanguard was pretty much defenseless, weaponless and on the verge of being annihilated by the UEF, one crazy act turned the tide and solidified the Blitzkrieg in history. What was thought to be Admiral Ferguson's last great act was really Captain Rickard's decisive thinking. The remaining Vanguard Armada formed a wedge and rammed the main mass of the UEF, essentially beheading the beast and ending the battle in a stalemate. But, unfortunately the Blitzkrieg sustained critical damage and exploded soon after without warning. Only five percent of the Blitzkrieg's three-thousand-five-hundred crew lived. It was this sacrifice that inspired the namesake 'Fall of Blitzkrieg' and also the speech 'Remembering the Blitzkrieg,' which is read every year on the anniversary of the battle.

Nev sat silently, letting me process the information when he finally broke the peace by clearing his throat. "The truth is the Blitzkrieg didn't fall from the damage."

"What?!" I respond in disbelief.

Nev frowns. "It was set to self-destruct." His voice was sobering. "By Ferguson himself."

"I don't understand," I say, shaking my head.

Nev stands. "The Breach Authority was a protocol given to every commanding officer of a ship. During the war it was forbidden to allow your ship to fall into enemy hands. The Breach Authority was a self-destruct command hardcoded in all of our ships, especially the Titans."

It was a detrimental truth that could turn the SRF's crown jewel into a horrible stain that would never come out. "Ferguson initiated the Breach Authority after you rammed the UEF. He killed everyone that knew he failed, all to protect his legacy."

Nev bows his head. "I lost my brothers in that battle, among other things." He places a hand on his bionic leg.

"I'm—so sorry Nev." My voice quivers, realizing that this is the true Nev. That he has finally let me in, that I have finally been accepted. "But why are you telling me this?"

He shrugs, looking off to the side. "I guess—I've been a real asshole to you." He looks at me. "The Blitzkrieg's anniversary is coming up soon and in light of everything that's about to happen, I thought you should know. You've done good by us, John."

"No I haven't," I retort. "You were right all along. You all should have killed me when you first found me on the Confessor."

Nev drops his hand on my shoulder with an unexpected amount of force. "I never told you about what happened when we brought you onto the ship all those years ago."

I search his face for an indication of where this is coming from, yet nothing but his unwavering stare meets mine. "What did I do?"

Nev smiles. "We lost so much to get you off Ceres. We were surrounded by death and I—I was an alcoholic haunted by the sins of war. I was low, lower than low. Everywhere I looked I saw the people I lost and I hated you for it. You were just this little three year old that couldn't understand a damn thing that was happening, but it didn't matter." His eyes were starting the well up. "So there I was at the bottom of a bottle, sitting in the ruins of the Confessor contemplating whether I should kill you or not. When you just walked up and placed your hand on my cheek." He blinks, freeing some tears to roll down his cheeks. "And the weird thing is I felt better, as if you cleared out the dark. You didn't know what you were doing, but something about your stare made me not feel so alone anymore."

There are no words to say. I'm shocked. Nev had held this moment for fifteen years with such a high regard. I now realize this whole conversation—everything Nev is telling me—is the most elaborate show of gratitude as well as an apology. I search my mind for something to say. "Thank you, Nev."

He smiles and smacks me on the cheek. "Yeger."

"What?"

"My real name is Yeger Marsh. After I deserted my post, I changed my name to Nev Freeman—like Never Freeman. I'm clever like that." He lets out a laugh.

"Yeger, huh?" I mock.

Nev grimaces. "Hey that was my father's name, be nice."

I shrug. "Well, if it is all the same to you I prefer Nev over Yeger."

Nev lets out a small chuckle, patting me on the shoulder. "Get some shut eye, stowaway," he says in his characteristic coarse tone.

I nod my head, feeling the fatigue rushing in again. "Yeah, sleep sounds good."

The ship is eerily quiet as I approach the door to my quarters. I look at my Aug. Damn, it's already three in the morning. No wonder I feel so tired. I place my left hand on the door, hearing it unlock a moment later. I am almost through the door when I notice something moving in the dark corridor. I hesitate halfway in my room, searching the darkness for whatever its hiding. A disturbing feeling that I am being watched comes over me and I feel a slow chill run through my core.

Then something moves within my peripheral. I whip my head to see what it is, only for it to be Grem sitting and grooming herself, oblivious to my anxiety. She pauses in mid lick and stares at me for a second before stretching and sauntering into my room. Then, without hesitation, she hops onto the cot and makes herself comfortable on my pillow.

"Who do you think you are?" I say, flopping down alongside her. She jumps and scowls at me. "Don't you look at me in that tone of voice," I retort as she returns to grooming herself.

I nudge her to the side and lay down onto my pillow. Grem lets out an annoyed meow in protest. There is so much in my mind that I need to process, so much that I have to deal with but I'm too exhausted right now. I rest my arm on my forehead, staring at the shadowed bulkhead. Before long I feel Grem purring against me. I play with her fuzzy ears, making then twitch. A few hours of sleep couldn't hurt. God knows I need it. I close my eyes, feeling the Confessor's hum flowing through me. Just a few hours of sleep, then I can deal with all this.

SECTION 31: NULL

My Aug begins buzzing incessantly, pulling me from my self-imposed coma. I let out a groan, sitting up and glancing at my left arm. Nev's face is hovering a few centimeters above my wrist, waiting for me to receive the call.

With a flick I accept the call. The small display expands and all I see is Nev grimace. "Stowaway, get your ass up and come to the bridge. We've reached Ceres."

What the hell is his problem? "Yeah, ok I'll be there soon."

Without another word, he closes the connection. I shake my head, attempting to clear out the lethargic sludge that clouds my mind. Then I recall what Nev told me before I went to sleep. How the hell are we at Ceres? I look at my Aug. According to this, it's only been five hours, when the captain clearly stated it would take three to four days to get there.

I bring up a display showing Ceres in the distance surrounded by thousands of asteroids. What is going on? I rub my eyes before mustering the motivation to roll out of bed and walk to the sink and mirror. I splash some cold water on my face, giving me a chill and look at my reflection. My eyes have changed back to brown from the crystalline blue that they have been since the Clairvoyance. I let out an amused exhale when my Aug begins buzzing again. It was Nev wondering where I was. I choose the ignore option and head for the door, when I realize that Grem is nowhere to be found.

I search the room for her but there is nothing, odd considering my door was closed and there is no other way out. My Aug begins buzzing again. I let out an annoyed growl and leave my room, entering a corridor but it seems unfamiliar to me. It's as if I'm on a completely different ship. In fact this entire morning has been weird with nothing but inconsistencies surrounding it, even going as far as to say that I'm not me or something like that.

I feel a headache starting to percolate just behind my eyes. Ultimately I need to get to the bottom of this and the first place to start is the bridge. I begin down the corridor, quickly coming to the conclusion that the ship is a different layout then the Confessor. Within a few moments I find myself lost and for some reason panicked. It's almost like the ship doesn't want me on it. Even the micro-vibrations from the hull make my body ache. My Aug begins to buzz again, making me curse in frustration. What is going on here?

It seems like an hour has passed since I started aimlessly wondering the ship. Every turn yields a new corridor that looks the exact same as the last. By now my headache has formed into a numbing migraine and for the love of God my Aug will not stop buzzing. Just as my frustration is reaching its peak, I finally see the door to the bridge. I let out a sigh of relief when I approach the door. It's time to get some answers.

I place my left hand on the door and it slides open. Don, Lora, Nev, Thomas and the captain are all standing and looking at a large display showing Ceres in the background.

"Can someone please explain to me what the hell is going on?" I say in a demanding tone. But there was no answer, no reaction. Everyone just stands there staring at the display. I take a few more steps in and approach Don, noticing his left arm is completely healed. "Wow, Don, your arm looks great," I say, reaching out and touching it.

Don moves away from me and glares. "Don't touch me, stowaway," he barks.

Stowaway? "Don, what's wrong. Is this about Ron?"

"What about me?" Ron's voice causes me to whip around.

"Ron?! But how?"

Ron walks over and scowls at me. "Why do you care, murderer?"

Murderer? The migraine is starting to pulse and my Aug begins to buzz again. "Ron, I don't understand. What is going on?" I look around the bridge. "Guys, please. What is happening right now?"

Captain Rickard turns to me. "We're doing what we should have done long ago—Nev."

Nev pulls his revolver out and points it at me while Ron and Don force me into a chair. "Why are you doing this?!" I shout "Thomas, what's the matter with you?"

Thomas turns and tilts his head. "It's for the best—for the best."

Everyone repeats it almost as if it was a chant over and over again. My Aug begins buzzing once more. "What are you going to do to me?" my voice trembles.

Ava walks out from behind the captain, also pointing her pistol at me. "We are going to hand you over to ArchDyme. What they plan on doing to you after that is really none of our concern."

"Ava?! Where did you come from?" I can feel my gut twisting.

"I never liked you, John," Ava says in a cold tone and everyone repeats. "You were just a job all along."

I begin to hyperventilate when the proximity alarm begins to sound. The display shows a ship that looks like nothing I've ever seen before slowly dock with the Confessor. "No, it can't be—we had something."

Lora comes around and smacks me across the face. "Murderer!" she shouts and everyone repeats.

"Murderer!"

"Murderer!"

"Murderer!"

Tears start to flow down my face. "Stop, please stop it!" My Aug begins to buzz again.

The Bridge door opens and Cheever walks in but he isn't alone. Behind him are Jurin, Vek, Brother Calon, and the boy from the Clairvoyance.

They begin chanting with the rest of the group when brother Calon unsheathes his machete and hands it to Cheever. He points the blade at me and everyone goes silent. "Everyone will get their chance, starting with the first person you killed."

Jurin walks up and takes the blade from Cheever. "Jurin! Don't do this!" I beg.

He approaches me, grinning spitefully. "You were my brother—and you let me die."

"No it wasn't me. It was Cheever. I didn't—" I feel the air leave my lungs as Jurin sinks the blade into my gut, freeing my blood.

He removes the blade and hands it to Vek. The blue neon of his augmented eye gleams against his pale face as he approaches me. "It's time, little boy," he says in a malicious tone. "And you thought you were so strong."

I am still trying to catch my breath when Vek stabs me and I let out an agonizing scream. "Please—stop!"

Vek smiles and twists the blade, making me writhe, then removes it and hands it to the little dark-haired boy. "I was an innocent little boy. You don't even know my name and you tortured me."

“I’m sorry!” I weep. “Please don’t—” The dark-haired boy slashes my chest open with the machete. I feel the warmth of my blood gushing down my chest and resting in my lap. And all the while I can still feel my Aug buzzing.

Next Brother Calon steps forward. I can feel myself starting to lose consciousness. He smacks me. “No, no, no. You don’t get to sleep through this—my judgment awaits,” Calon says with a sinister grin.

“Fuck—you,” I force out when he cleaves my neck open. I begin sobbing uncontrollably. Why am I not dead yet? Why is this happening?

The captain goes next followed by Nev, Lora, Thomas and Don. Then Ron walks up; at this point there wasn’t much of me left of me, just a pile of flesh, bone and blood, but still I was somehow alive.

“Ron—” I force out in a gurgled voice, holding up my left hand. “Pl—please.”

Ron frowns and takes my hand, leaning forward just enough so only I could hear him. “Try to enjoy this, you killer,” he hisses, forcing the machete into my chest so deep I can feel it scrapping my spine.

He leaves the blade in when Ava walks up. “Oh, you poor, poor baby,” she mocks, cupping my head in her hands. “You want to screw one more time before you die?” She mounts my broken body and plays with the machete’s handle. “Oh baby, it’s so big," she says with a smile.

“I—” speaking is extremely hard after Nev slit my throat, but I still force out the words. “I—Love—You—Ava.”

Ava pouts. "Oh that's no fun," she says, pushing the machete so that it severs my spine. My head slumps forward. This is it, I think to myself. Finally I get to die. Then Cheever grabs me by my hair, lifting my head so I can see him. "Now it's my turn. ArcheDyme only needed your head after all." He pulls the machete from my chest and takes his time practicing his swing.

"What the hell do you think you are doing?!" Time freezes and my dark reflection appears in front of me. His eyes are glowing blue and he looks as though he is otherworldly with a white aura surrounding him. "Seriously man, what's happening here?" I open my mouth to speak, but only the sound of blood bubbling comes from my throat. The Avant leans forward. "Do I have to do everything for you?"

He straightens and snaps his fingers, restoring time. My Aug begins to buzz again. Cheever takes another swing when the Avant taps his shoulder. "Excuse me, but can you stop killing me?"

Cheever stubbles and falls to the ground. "No!" he shouts. "It's impossible!"

The Avant smiles, lifting his arms while staring at me. "This is what true power is," he says.

Unbelievable. That is the word that comes closest to describe what the Avant does to the people who were killing me. In a single moment they are reduced to nothing but piles of tenderized flesh and bone. My friends and my enemies meet the same gruesome fate. It all brings a disconcerting amount of pleasure and disgust to me. I'm so conflicted by everything, and I still don't understand what is happening.

The Avant finishes his work with a satisfied grin, dusting his hands off. "Well you are welcome." I attempt to say something but nothing comes out. "Jeez, pull yourself together, kid. You're embarrassing us." He lets out a narcissistic chuckle. But when he notices I'm not laughing he frowns. "Ah well, let's see what the doctor thinks." He lifts Thomas's severed head and floats it in front of my face, contorting his mouth like a puppet. "You're screwed, huhuhu." The Avant lets out a bellowing laugh, but I'm still not amused. "Damn, I really thought that one was funny." He sighs and places his hand on his chin, tossing Thomas's head to the side. "You know," he begins after a while. "You really are weak—maybe I should finish what these worms started. Would you like that?"

I try and force my head to shake, only managing to slightly wiggle as the Avant lifts the machete with our gift. "N—No." I force out as my Aug begins to buzz again.

"What was that?" He uses the ability to grab my head, nodding it up and down. "Yes, please end my suffering," he says in a cartoonish voice. "Well if you insist—" He snaps his finger and the machete flies forward, imbedding itself into my face.

*****

"Odeza!" I shout "What are you doing?!" I was surrounded by darkness, but I could feel her presence.

"We lost harmonization—your reality is becoming unstable, John." Odeza's voice echoes through the void. "You're committing too much to this. We need to stop!" Her voice is panicked.

"No, we keep going!" I yell.

"John, it's too much for you. This is part of the reason we took your memories! We have to stop before the damage is irreparable," she pleads.

"I said no, Odeza!" I scream, causing the dark void to waver.

CHAPTER THIRTY-TWO: THE REQUEST

I jerk awake, gasping for air and clutching my chest where my heart is about to rip out. My Aug is buzzing. I look down to see Nev's face hovering just above my wrist. I reach to accept the call but hesitate. What just happened to me? Then Grem rolls over and glares at me. I finally catch my breath and tap my wrist.

Nevs face wasn't annoyed, but rather concerned. "John, is everything ok? I've been trying to get ahold of you."

"Yeah, sorry. Just—never mind. What's wrong?" I respond, trying to hide my anxiety.

"Don is awake and wants to see you. The surgery was a success," he says with a half-smile.

Finally some good news. I place my hand on my face. "That's great, I'll be there soon." The display closes and I collapse onto the bed.

Grem stretches and hops off the cot to scurry to the door of my cabin, lightly pawing at it and looking back at me. I let out an exhale and roll out of bed, shambling to the sink and splashing my face with some cold water. I study my reflection closely. My dark hair is starting to get long. I'll have to get a haircut soon. I run my hand through it, attempting to force the tangled mess against my scalp, but after a while I give up. My gaze rests on my still blue eyes, leaning forward to take a closer look at them. It's crazy how I don't miss my brown eyes any longer. It's almost as if this is who I really am now. I grimace at the thought.

Something weaves my legs and I look down to see Grem's annoyed face. "Alright, alright bossy paws—" I respond to her glare, letting her lead me out the door.

The atmosphere of the infirmary is surprisingly high-spirited when I entered several minutes later. Nev and Lora are both smiling. Thomas is shaking his head with disapproval. The captain, however, retained his signature stoic expression and rigid stance.

I see Don peek at me from between Lora and Nev. "Hey Einstein," he says with a brimming grin.

"Hey, how you feeling?" I say, returning his smile.

Don half shrugs. "Heh, you know me, none the worse for wear." He lets out a half snicker.

Don's left arm was bandaged from his shoulder to his hand, then tied closely to his body. "How long?"

"A few days to a few weeks. It's hard to say how the nanites will react to this much damage," Don responds in a serious tone.

Nev frowns. "We have some Zeeklor. One dose of that stuff and you'd be healed in hours rather than weeks."

Don opens his mouth but is interrupted by Thomas. "If he heals before the new Aug takes, then it could cause permanent scaring and nerve damage. Unfortunately, Mr. Witman, will have to wait until the nanites do their job."

"Bummer—" Nev says under his breath.

"It's really not that bad," Don says, attempting to sit up.

Thomas places his hand on Don's chest and forces him back down onto the bed. "What you need is rest. That is the best thing for you now."

"No, I'm pretty sure I rested enough, mum. What I need now is to get back to work—and maybe have a stiff drink." He lets out a painful grunt. "Better make it two."

Thomas rolls his eyes and begins muttering to himself, returning to his equipment. Don finishes sitting up and looks over at Ron's body on the table beside him with a sheet over his head.

Captain Rickard places his hand on Don's good shoulder. "We'll take care of him. Just tell us what you want us to do."

Don looks at him and smiles with tears forming in his eyes. "Home, He—Ron would have wanted to go back home, to be with mom and dad."

The captain bows his head "Ok then, Mars it is." He looks at me, Nev and Lora. "But after we finish this. Is that alright?"

Don nods his head. "You make those bastards pay."

I feel a wave of angry sadness hit me at the thought of Cheever and all that he has taken. Soon I will be the one doing the killing and with that comes a disconcerting level of exhilaration. There is no doubt that Cheever deserves whatever he gets, but I'm afraid of how inventive I might get with him. Even with this mixed cocktail of emotions I feel my heart skip a beat with anticipation.

"I look forward to it," I say in a low voice, causing everyone to look at me.

I feel my cheeks getting warm. I didn't mean to say that out loud. I'm starting to sound like a psychopath. I attempt to laugh it off but the words have already been spoken and the uncomfortable quietness persists until Captain Rickard begins walking toward the door.

"John," he says right before he reaches the door. "I have something I want to talk to you about."

I hesitate when he opens the hatch and gestures for me to go though. A few seconds later we're walking down the corridor, heading for the bridge in complete silence. Captain Rickard is several steps ahead of me with his hands clasped behind his back, and even though he is slowly gliding through the corridor I can sense urgency with every step he takes.

I clear my throat, causing an echo through the hallway, and open my mouth to speak. "So what's up?" I ask in a non-affirming way.

The captain stops and looks at me. His eyes are piecing and cold. “What is the extent of your involvement with my daughter?”

His words are clear and resolute but I stumble on them nonetheless. “I—we—” I waver. “What do you mean?”

“Don’t play dumb, John. Ever since you’ve been here I’ve noticed a change in Ava," he says in another sharp but calm tone.

I do my best to maintain my composure. “I won’t lie. I have feelings for her.” I feel a sting in the back of my head. “But whether she feels the same about me—” I shrug.

Rickard turns and begins walking down the corridor again. “She is everything I have left. Do you understand?”

“Yes sir,” I respond almost instantly.

“Then you understand that I’d do anything to keep her safe.” Rickard stops again and shoots me a disturbing stare.

“Absolutely, but know I would never do anything to hurt—
”

“You already have,” Rickard interrupts, turning to face me completely. “I believe that you would never hurt her intentionally, but it is obvious that whatever is happening to you doesn’t care.”

I feel my stomach turn. “That’s not true. The first time I used my ability, it was to save her. I swear I’ll protect her.”

“Then what about now? Don’t mistake me, John. I count you as part of my crew, but honestly ask yourself if you are the best thing for Ava, for the Idle Confessor, and for the rest of us.

Everything that has happened since Titan is because—" Rickard pauses.

I feel another sting penetrate the back of my head, while my chest tightens, making it hard to breathe. "Say it!" I shout. "Just say it's all my fault!"

The captain looks me in the eyes. "It is." He doesn't hesitate or flinch. "You have everyone else convinced that you are some goddamn savior! Hell, you almost had me convinced, but look at what you brought with you."

"You don't think I know that?! You don't think I feel regret for everything?! I hate myself—is that what you want to hear, captain?!" My frustration mounts and I fight back against a flood of emotions. "And even then, when everyone should be blaming me, they don't—they just keep trying to make me feel better about what I am." I choke. "My best friend was killed helping me get here and then Don lost his brother because of me! And what you told me yesterday about hundreds that died for me—your wife, your captain and crew!" I hit the wall with my fist, causing the lights to flicker through the corridor. Captain Rickard takes a few steps back. "I've killed people, captain, murdered them in the most horrid ways!" The boy's tortured face flashes through my mind. "And it doesn't matter if they were good or bad, I'm still a monster!" I shout. "But—here, I know I'm meant to be here. And I will do anything to fix this, to bring back Ava and end this nightmare, but I need you to believe in me now!"

Rickard just stares at me for several seconds, cold and emotionless, before finally exhaling. "I believe you, John. Even when the better part of me says I shouldn't. But after we save Ava—" He pauses. "I want you to leave."

I feel my heart drop, leaning against the wall to steady myself. "Is that an order?"

"No, think of is as a request—for the people you care about. You and I know that Ceres isn't the end for you. Integra will never stop hunting you. How many more will die before you find a way to end this?" Rickard takes a few steps toward me.

He is right. I know he is, but just for a second I wish it wasn't true. I push myself off the wall and the captain takes me by my shoulders. "I understand."

Rickard smiles, but I notice a slight flash of sadness in his expression. "We'll take you as far as Mars. After Ron's funeral, you can sneak away. I'll pull some strings and find you a good crew that will help you track down your past. This is for the best, John."

I look at him and nod my head. "Yeah, for the best."

Rickard nods his head. "We're coming up on the Kelasoran, why don't you go get some food and take a shower. It'll make you feel better."

"Yeah," I start, avoiding eye contact. "I'll see you in a little bit then."

I turn and walk away, holding back my sadness until I break the captain's line of sight. A few minutes later I enter my cabin. I don't know what comes over me but I immediately fall to my knees and lose my composure. What is it that I'm supposed to do? I'm more lost than ever before. I gain enough self-control to slide into the shower and let the hot water flow over my face and body. A few minutes later I dry off and wipe the steam from the mirror. My face still shows the signs of the Clairvoyance and Cheever with the bridge of my nose boasting a large red scab from where the device split it open. My body is covered in bruises and cuts. I look as though I've been through the grinder and somehow made it out with all my parts. But everything is worn down and sore and I feel my spirit is in the same shape.

I finish scrutinizing my beat-up body and quickly throw on a fresh jumpsuit. I go to leave my room but hesitate, looking back at the jacket lying on the ground. It was gray and drab, almost reflecting my mood perfectly. I pick it up and slide it on. My Aug begins to tingle immediately as it conforms and changes color to match my light gray jump suite. I feel a little better now, almost as if the jacket has become synonymous with the comfort a child feels with their blanket.

I leave my room and head to the cafeteria. It feels abandoned since the passengers left. For the most part everyone eats on their own, when they find the time of course. I don't remember the last time I had a full meal and my stomach reminds me by aching loudly as I walk through the double door and smell grilled chicken. I feel a wave of grief hit when I walk up to the food dispenser and remember Ron smacking it over and over again without realizing that Don was messing with him for years. I quickly configure it to produce what looks to be a form of fried rice and ham. Despite the look, the food is delicious. I eat it faster than I had planned, causing my stomach to whine.

In a weird way the captain was right. I sit silently for a few minutes letting the food settle and I feel this uplifting wave come over me. I hate feeling better, like I am forgetting everything bad that has happened. But I'd be lying if I say I didn't need it, especially now, because my work isn't done. I still have a mission to complete and Rickard needs me on my top game.

CHAPTER THIRTY-THREE: THE KELASORAN EMINENCE

The Kelasoran Space Dock could have been held together by duct tape and look safer than it did. Its massive steel frame is littered with makeshift add-ons that resemble malignant tumors, and yet it spins elegantly in a dense cloud of debris. The Idle Confessor's proximity alarm sounds as we fly through the debris, with chunks of metal being vaporized by the Confessor's Proxy Shields. We come to a steady halt just about a kilometer from the space dock.

"Kelasoran Space Dock. This is the MST-C: Idle Confessor requesting permission to dock." Captain Rickard's tone reflects his resigned composure.

A few seconds later we receive a response. "We read you, Idle Confessor. Please proceed to Dock forty-three Charlie."

The display updates, highlighting a path to a curled up, structurally questionable docking arm. The captain whips the Confessor around and heads toward the dock. A moment later the arm attaches itself, causing the ship to shudder. The captain lets out a string of curses under his breath, then unlatches his harness and opens a communication link.

The grizzled face of Daniel Kross enters the frame. "What took so long?" he asks. "I was worried when I got your eVid. I rushed here as soon as I could."

The captain looks at me, then back at Daniel. "We had some complications. I need your help with some—supplies. Think you can manage?"

Daniel's face scrunches into an uncertain frown. "I might be able to muster up some stuff. Let's meet at the rec center on level fifteen."

Rickard nods his head, closes the connection and turns toward Nev, Lora and me. "Nev, kid you're coming with me. Lora, keep an eye on Don. We'll be back in a few hours."

Lora responds with a simple head nod while Nev and I follow the captain out of the bridge and toward the exterior hatch.

I look at Nev, nudging him to get his attention. "What are we doing here?" I whisper.

Nev shrugs. "To get supplies."

"But we don't have time for this." I glance at the captain, who is several steps ahead of us.

Nev cocks his lips into a smirk and shrugs again. "Maybe it's another plan the captain is cookin' up."

"But—" I start when the captain stops and looks at us.

"You two schoolgirls know I can hear you, right?" he says in an annoyed voice.

"Sorry, captain, I'm just wandering—" I start when the captain pulls a data tablet out of his pack and gives it to Nev.

"Nev, go get these supplies. We will need them to get through the Main Belt after Ceres. Just put it on the Confessor's tab," he says, refusing to look at me. Nev nods his head and starts down the walkway. The captain watches him until he disappears in the thick crowd then he looks at me. "I'm going to try and get you a place on the Hauser with Daniel. He is one of the few people left that I trust; I have no doubt that you will do well with him."

The captain turns and begins walking down railed walkway. "But didn't they betray us?" I ask.

The captain continues walking. "Chances are they didn't know that she was Crimson, or that the entire thing was a setup without their knowledge."

"Really, cause it sure didn't seem—"

The captain shoots me a critical stare. "Daniel Kross is one of the best people I know. He would never betray his own blood. Do I make myself clear?!" I nod my head feebly.

I must have hit an obviously sensitive nerve with my prying questions and accusations. Maybe the best course of action is to keep my mouth shut and follow the captain. At least it wasn't unnervingly silent like it would have been on the Confessor. There has to be at least several thousand people either living or working on this space station at any given time. In a way it reminds me of New Horizon but with more of a stale taste in the air. I was well adapted to this overcrowded environment, able to flow through the currents of the crowd with little resistance and best of all with little attention being drawn to me.

After several minutes of weaving though the masses of people, we reach the entrance to the rest of the space station, modestly known as the rec center. However, in all reality, it was a one-hundred-and-ten story tall core that connected all the docks through massive walkways and lifts. We were on level forty-three and needed to reach level fifteen. I look up at the seemingly free floating skyscraper being held together by hundreds of walkways that look like nothing more than tethers holding it in place. I let out an involuntary gasp at the sight of this wonder gaining the attention of an older man walking beside me.

"First time on the Kelasoran?" he asks.

I look at him and grin. "One of many firsts in that last few months."

"Ah, to be young and experience things for the first time again." The old man grunts with amusement, looking up through the glass. "But I guess one never really gets used to a view like this."

"Have you done a lot of traveling in your life?" I ask as the doors to a massive lift open in front of us.

"Oh, you know. Here and there, mostly in and around the Core planets." We squeeze into the lift and the doors seal behind us. "Have you ever been?"

"To the core planets? No, but I'll be heading there after this stop," I respond still gazing out the window.

"Is that so—where too?" the old man continues.

I get ready to respond when I notice the old man is now staring at me with all of his attention. "Uh—you know, hit all the sights."

"You travelling alone, kid?" he follows up almost instantly.

"Nope." I attempt to hide my suspicion. "Traveling with a large group."

"You must be on a large ship to accommodate a large group of people for that long of a trip," he says with an open-ended tone.

Damn, I fell for the bastard's tricks. This kind of thing happened all the time on New Horizon. People would show up unfamiliar with the area and because of their vulnerability they would naturally trust the first person who shows them any kindness, but in truth these kind people were simply getting as much information out of their potential victims as possible. Where are you heading? How many are you with? What type of ship are you traveling in? These are just a few of the questions they ask. Then when the kind people get the whole picture they have their fellow kind people take everything from the unsuspecting tourists. Sometimes it was just to rob them blind, but other times it involved human trafficking. It got so bad on New Horizon that the tourist market virtually disappeared.

I realize that I have been silent for a little while noticing the old man's smile. I glance around the lift, catching several other glances in my direction. It is hard to tell how many of these people are in on the ruse. I avoid looking at the captain, fearing that I'll pull him into my mistake. I quickly think for a moment. The typical next step in this process is to try and get the mark alone. There is still a chance that the old man's plans will fail if I avoid doing what he wants me to do when the lift stops. But how much did he already know about me. First of all he knows we are docked on level forty-three, I wish I would have seen what else was docked there. If the Confessor is the only Medium-sized ship then I just give away that information by telling him we have a large group. The lift comes to a stop on Level fifteen and the captain begins walking without giving me a glance.

I look at the old man who now looked a bit confused. "Well it was nice talking to you, but—" I start to say while walking at a higher than normal pace.

"Hold on, I know this restaurant not too far from here. I'd love to hear more about this trip you're going on. It brings me comfort talking to you young people." He smiles again.

Damn he is a good actor. Most of the people from the lift have passed us. When I look back at the captain, he hasn't noticed I'm not following him yet. I smile back and think about my response. "No, I don't think so, but nice try."

The old man's contorts into a confused gesture. "Excuse me?"

"Knock it off, old man. I know you've had me marked since we entered the lift. And from the looks of it you have about three guys waiting to mug me as soon as we are alone." I feel my heart beating faster with excitement for having caught the old man in the act.

The old man scoffs and gives me a very different stare. "Well done, boy. There is just one problem with your little observation." The old man snaps his fingers and five men walk out from the crowd. "I've got five men not three."

I let out a chuckle feeling the all too familiar tingle starting to rise up from the base of my head. "Listen, I could have just walked away, but I was worried that, in my lapse of judgment, I might have given you a little too much information about myself," I say in a confident tone. "I have one simple request for you and you patsies just forget about it, ok?" I turn and start walking away when the old man clears his throat.

"You believe this boy? He has the balls to walk into my house and order me around. Hey! You don't tell me what to do!" The old man drops his façade completely. "Get him!"

I feel a grin creeping across my face, knowing that I'm going to hurt someone soon. I turn right as one of the old man's thugs is about to hit me with a metal rod. I stop the rod a few millimeters from my head and flick my finger, throwing the thug against the railing and shattering the glass. The other four look at each other and hesitate, questioning whether they have just seen what they had just seen.

"He must have slipped," I say in an amused tone as the other four rush me.

I take a deep breath, repeating in my head that I mustn't kill them as if it was a mantra. With a wave of my hand, one of the thugs hits the railing and slumps to the ground. Another, I throw down the walkway, sending him rolling into a kiosk vendor. The last two stop and look at the other three muggers before the old man yells and they resume their attack.

I grab the rod from the first one and place my hand on his head, resisting the urge to scramble his brain, settling instead to simply put him to sleep. I feel a tinge of pain in the back of my head not from over using my ability but rather for not indulging the blood haze. In the moment it takes me to regain my self-control the last thug gets a solid hit across my face with a metal rod. I stumble and let out a painful shout that shatters the rest of the glass on the walkway. I can hear screams from people who stopped to see what was going on. The rod didn't hurt as much as the urge to murder the thug. I can feel heat rushing to my face as I turn and look at the criminal who quickly dropped his bar and fled.

The old man was the only one left, a look of sheer terror painted on his face. I continue to resist the urge to turn him inside out, causing more pain. "What are you?" the old man stammers as I slowly walk toward him.

"I'm the culmination of your sins, old man. You could call me your judgment or your punishment," I say in a low echoing voice.

The old man trips on one of his thugs legs and falls backwards. I desperately try to rein in my homicidal urges as I get closer to the old man. But then he does the unthinkable by pulling a gun from his jacket and losing several rounds.

I never expect to see a ballistics weapon in space. It's not only stupid but extremely dangerous, as asinine as that notion may sound. Handheld DEP or pulse technology was developed because it wasn't powerful enough to puncture the hulls of ships and stations, making it a safe but effective weapon. Whereas ballistics weapons have a bad habit of going through the intended target and possibly hurting or damaging whatever is behind it. In the old bastard's panic he must not have been thinking—panic that I caused.

Everything was a blur after the old man let off four shots, I didn't fully comprehend what had happened until I had the old man by his throat. I look back, replaying it in my head. None of the rounds reached me thanks to my gift but unfortunately I couldn't just stop them like with pulse rounds. I remember deflecting the first two and they imbedded themselves in the walkway but the other two i curved around me hitting two innocent bystanders in the leg and shoulder. And there was something else, I had lost control of my blood haze and was beginning to squeeze the life out of the old man. I was about to kill again and I really didn't care, when a hand grabs my forearm.

I look over seeing Captain Rickard glaring at me. "Let him go!" he says in quiet but assertive tone.

"He doesn't deserve to live!" I hiss.

"Maybe not, but it isn't up to you," Rickard says. "Now let him go!"

I look at Rickard, then the old man. I can feel his pulse surging through me. All it would take is a simple twist and he would be gone, never able to hurt another person again. I look back at Rickard, who shakes his head and I can feel myself regaining control. "I'm— not a monster." I mumble to myself, feeling the blood haze slip away. I drop the old man, who falls to his knees gasping for air.

Rickard pats me on the shoulder and we start walking away when the old man starts to yell in between gasps. "You're dead—you and your crew!" he shouts. "Yeah I know about your ship—the Idle Confessor!"

I stop and look at the captain. He shakes his head as I turn and walk back to the old man. He cowers when I approach him. "You don't know anything." I reach down, placing my hands on his head and face. The captain shouts and grabs my jacket collar when the old man starts to scream.

A few seconds later I release his face, his eyes wide, looking up through the walkway's ceiling. "Wow," he gasps, looking at me and Rickard "have you seen anything so amazing in your life?" The old man begins laughing hysterically.

I look at Rickard. He has a look of disappointment on his face, the kind a parent has when their child acts out in public. I ignore his frustration. "Let's go."

We easily slip into the crowd before the local authorities reach the scene. For some reason no one was willing to tell them about us.

We were quietly walking until Rickard catches my attention with his stare. "What the hell, John?!"

"He was threatening us," I explain.

"That is beside the point. You can't just keep using this thing whenever the opportunity presents itself," he lectures. "You could've—"

"Killed someone. Yeah, I know. I wanted to, but I didn't!" I retort.

Rickard glowers at me, grabbing my arm. "Now I'll admit, you have done some good things with this power, but you need to control it. Do you understand? You put everyone at risk every time you use it without reason," he finishes.

I'm still coming down from the haze, and I get a sudden unsettling urge to throw him, but I suppress it. "Why do you care?" I pull my arm free from his grasp. "You want me gone. That's why we are here, isn't it? So let's go." I turn and begin walking again.

"John—" Rickard starts in an unnervingly supportive tone.

"No, I'm not interested in being lectured to by the likes of you. You don't understand what I'm going through and you've made it clear you're not interested in helping me, so after this mission you're not my captain and the Confessor—" I pause. "The Idle Confessor isn't my ship."

Rickard straightens and squares his shoulders. "Well ok then—"

CHAPTER THIRTY-FOUR: THE TITAN'S HEART

Five minutes later we enter a room where Daniel Kross and Keida are waiting. The captain and Daniel greet each other with a firm handshake than the captain looks at Keida. "I thought you were coming alone?"

Daniel grins. "She insisted on seeing the kid."

Keida had already wrapped her arms around my neck. "I'm so glad you are ok, John," she says. "We had no idea that she was Crimson and then what happened to the Clairvoyance right after—" She looks at my face. "Oh my God! What happened to your eyes?!" She pushes away, studying my eyes, then looks at the rest of my face. "What happened to you?"

"You guys can go catch up. James and I need to talk," Daniel says, pointing at the door.

Keida takes me by the hand and leads me out of the room. A little while later we are sitting at a restaurant and she is telling me how she escaped the Coalition Fleet a week after they picked her up. "So I was hiding from the CF when I stumble on Daniel and some of his crew all shot to hell." She continues, "I didn't ask questions. I just started to patch them up and the next thing you know Daniel wants me to join his crew as a medic," she finishes with a smile.

God, I remember how much I missed her cheerful disposition. She never lost hope when we were growing up. She used to volunteer at the local clinics. She's always loved helping other people. "Why were they shot?"

Keida rolls her eyes. "They were tracking this bounty and things went sour, you know?"

More than you think. "Wow, Keida that is pretty amazing," I say with a smile.

She places her hand on mine. "Enough about me. You look like you have a story to tell. How did you get out of New Horizon and end up with Daniel's friend?"

Where do I start? How could I start? There was so much—sorrow to tell her, and my power—how do I explain that? "Jurin, helped me." I recall the look on his face right before he slipped away in my arms.

"Yeah, did that big oaf cry when you left?" She smiles.

I feel everything building up. Being around Keida was too much. She reminded me of everything that I have lost. "Keida, I have to tell you something very important." My words are cold and feel distanced.

She frowns, squeezing my hand. "Ok?" She was studying my face for anything that reminded her of the boy she loved on Titan, but I'm starting to think that boy doesn't exist anymore.

"Jurin—died helping me get off Titan." My voice cracks on the words. Kieda gasps, placing her hand over her mouth as tears start to trickle down her face. "It was because of me. He was so desperate to keep his promise and it cost him his life." I look down, refusing to see her face. "I'm so sorry, but that's not everything."

Keida's eyes refocus. "What?" Her voice quivers, and it makes me ache

"Something is happening to me, Kei. It started right before I left Titan." I struggle with the words. "My eyes are blue because of it."

Keida wipes away some stray tears. "Is it life threatening?" Her genuine concern makes my shame hurt even more.

"As a matter of fact, it is—but not necessarily for me," I respond.

"I don't understand." Kei's eyes narrow, not out of suspicion but rather out of knowing me better than anyone else. She could tell I was struggling to tell her something.

I let out an exhale. "This is going to sound crazy, but I can do things with my mind that no one else can."

Keida gives me a confused look. "Like what?"

"Almost anything—I think."

"Really?" she says in an annoyed tone. "So, you decided to tell me that Jurin is dead right before you tell me that you have super powers—"

"Now that I think of it. I could have said it differently." Although I don't know how.

"You think?!" Keida stands and starts walking away.

"Wait, Keida." I get up to follow her.

She turns and points at me. "And to think that I was so excited to be seeing you again. But looking at you now—I don't see you anymore, John."

Keida turns to leave, but I use my ability to lift several chairs in front of her. She stops and looks at me then back at the chairs then me again. "I'm not lying, Kei."

She calmly walks back to her chair and sits, staring off into the distance. "I want to know everything!" she demands.

I sit down across from her and let out another long breath. Then I proceed to tell her everything that has happened from the moment I woke up in Jurin's apartment to the first time I used my ability. About the dreams and my shadow self, about how the IISF, the CF and the SBG are all hunting me. I told her about the Clairvoyance and how I murdered people and killed the young boy but somehow saved billions. Then I told her about Cheever West and how he not only killed Jurin but also two great men. I told her how I'm afraid of my power, of hurting people, of being like Cheever. And finally I told her about Ava, how I've never felt that way about anyone, how helpless I am knowing that she is in the hands of a madman and how utterly sorry I am that I cannot love her the same way I do Ava.

Keida sat silently and motionless as if she was a statue. I feel horrible for her. I honestly wanted to hold back but as soon as the flood gates opened I couldn't stop talking. She's one of the few people I trust so wholeheartedly and confide in, but this might be a little too much. Finally after what felt like a solid thirty minutes of quiet she places her hand on the table top and stares into my eyes.

"I'm sorry I wasn't there for you John," she says in an uncharacteristically sober tone.

This time I couldn't stop the tears from gushing down my cheeks. She walks around the table and embraces me, like a mother would with an upset child. "I'm—a—monster," I force out between sobs.

Keida hushes me. “You are not a monster. You are a good person who has lost their way. Do you hear me, John?” I nod my head, regaining some semblance of restraint when she runs her fingers through my hair. “God, you need a haircut," she says in an upbeat tone, making me laugh.

We sat there holding each other for a while, two young souls forced to grow beyond their years. I can see myself loving Keida again, maybe growing old together in some lost forgotten nowhere, but that was a past life now. There was nothing left of the Titan she fell in love with. I am something much different now and even more volatile. Keida’s Aug begins to buzz. She accepts the call while I wipe my face, removing the evidence of my weakness. “Hey, you all done with your friend?” she says in an innocent manner.

“Yeah, all done here. What about your little playdate?” Daniel responds sarcastically.

Keida blushes. “Just catching up. We’ll be on our way soon.” She closes the connection and looks at me. “If it is any consolation, the blue eyes look real sexy on you.”

I let out a scoff and follow her out of the restaurant when my Aug begins vibrating. Captain Rickard’s face pops up. “Hey kid, I’m heading for the lift. Better hurry before it takes off," he says.

“Sure thing captain, on my way,” I respond in an unusually good tone. I can tell the captain notices before I close the connection. I guess that is the effect that Kei has on people.

“Well then, this is goodbye again.” Keida’s voice sounds sadder than I can bear.

"I'm sure we will see each other again pretty soon." I open my arms and she hugs me, resting her head on my chest.

"You smell the same," she says after taking a deep breath. "I've missed it."

The hug was rapidly feeling less like a friendly one and more like an intimate one. "Kei—"

She quickly pushes away and looks at me. "I know, I know, Ava—but you need to know that I don't plan on giving up. I love you John, and at this point we are all we have left so I don't care how long it takes. I will be waiting for you."

Before I can respond she kisses me passionately and walks away. I stand there for several minutes feeling the tingle of her essence on my lips. Why am I so conflicted by all of this? My Aug begins buzzing and I look down seeing it is the captain again. I select ignore and head for the lift.

"How did it go?" Rickard asks as we walk across the broken glass of the walkway I destroyed earlier.

"Good, I think," I respond, still trying to figure out my feelings. "How 'bout you?"

Rickard rubs the back of his neck. "He made no commitments but he did say he'd meet us on Mars—that is if we get that far."

I chuckle "Yeah—no such thing as guarantees." The lift doors close and we begin our decent toward the forty-third level. "Captain."

Rickard looks at me "Yeah?"

"Sorry, for getting angry at you earlier," I say, causing one of his eyebrows to twitch. "You're right. I need to learn to control my—urges. I guess I've been keeping everything inside since the Clairvoyance and what happened to Ron. I never said thanks for getting me out of there."

The captain was quiet for a minute or two. "It wasn't me," he finally says. "Ava made the call to get you."

I give him a quizzical look. "Ava?"

The captain nods his head. "I wanted to leave you behind, let you die with the Clairvoyance and be rid of you." His expression is that of an old man who regrets so much. "Ava and the rest of the crew demanded we go back." He pauses for a second. "I'm sorry John, you deserved better from me."

The lift chimes and the doors open. For the most part we were quiet the rest of the way to the Confessor until Nev gets our attention.

He is encumbered by the supplies the captain had him get, tripping and tumbling all over the place like one of those ancient gag reels. "Little help!" he shouts, finally noticing that the captain and I are watching and laughing with the crowd.

We each take a portion of the supplies and head the rest of the way to the Confessor. It is nice to be back home in the comfort of what I was familiar with. The Confessor's vibrations are as part of me as my own pulse now. After unloading the supplies, Nev, the captain and I head to the bridge where Lora is playing with Grem.

"How many times have I said I don't want that cat on the bridge?" The captain barks.

Grem lets out a low growl as the captain walks by. Lora and I chuckle but the cheer is short lived when the captain shoots us a glare, pressuring Lora to take Grem out of the bridge.

The captain detaches the Confessor from the Kelasoran and heads for the Main Belt's checkpoint. He plots the course to Ceres and the estimated time updates to just over three days. He looks at me with unexpected worry. It's been almost two days since Ava was taken captive. These next three days will be terrible without knowing how she is.

I force a confident look and he nods his head. "Everyone strap in. As soon as we get past the checkpoint I'm engaging the ARAD," the captain says over the ship's intercom.

There is a lengthy line leading into the DMZ. We have at least fifteen minutes of waiting before we can reach the gate, which is really just a massive ship scanner. Everyone is quiet like we are on the verge of something new. The anticipation is thick and oppressing. I attempt to hone my thoughts on how I will fill my time for the next three days to keep me from going insane, but nothing comes to mind. I'll probably find myself with Don and Thomas killing time with long talks about any and everything that keeps me from thinking about now. I feel myself zoning out and staring off into the distance when Lora's hand touches mine.

I look up and she smiles. "Almost lost you there," she says. "Captain wants to know if you're ready."

I look around the bridge. Both Nev and the captain are staring at me intently, waiting as if they are relying on my confidence. Am I ready? I repeat in my head several times, almost as if I'm trying to conjure an answer. It's not like I have a choice otherwise. We are rapidly heading to the end of something and I have to be ready for it or more of the people I care about will die.

I can't afford to doubt myself now. I feel my gut twist at the thought of losing more people. I can't let anything happen to Ava or Don, Lora, Nev, Thomas or the captain. There is no excuse anymore—either they live or I die.

"I'm ready." My words are confident, and for once I believe them.

CHAPTER THIRTY-FIVE: THE PRODIGAL CHILD

Helplessly waiting is truly a form of torture. It can nurture the embers of doubt into roaring flames of uncertainty. Three and a half days of waiting, of not knowing if Ava is alright. Eighty-four hours of obsessive planning and worrying with no real results. Five-thousand-forty minutes of slowly falling into guilt-riddled insanity, and if that's not enough, every second that passes seem to compound the collective angst that now makes up the Confessor's crew. The high I felt three and a half days ago is long gone, with little to show it was ever there.

The display updates beside me showing Ceres eerily still in the distance. The IISF is undoubtedly tracking us now that we are a mere hour from threshold. I feel the weight of fatigue from the last couple days starting to let up when my Aug begins buzzing. I've been expecting this call, and honestly I'm surprised it didn't come earlier. I let it go a few seconds before accepting it. Captain Rickard's face pops up.

"Hey, kid," he says in a monotone voice.

"'Bout that time?" I fake an upbeat voice.

The captain nods his head. I sigh and then close the connection. Grem looks at me. "Well, my little Gremlin, I guess this is goodbye." I run my finger down her spin, causing her to lift up her backside. I gently put her on the ground and head through my door toward the hanger.

Nev is waiting for me when I enter the hanger. He seems very calm and present as he fastens the thorium suicide vest around my chest. He finishes with a light pat on my shoulder, then we strap in to the seats running against the wall. As soon as we are secure he informs the captain that we are ready for rapid deceleration. Moments later the familiar uncomfortable feeling of extreme inertia forces us against our seats, the lights flicker and just like that the feeling is gone. I quickly unlatch myself and run for the smaller skip as Nev brings up the display showing the network of stealth sensors fanning out in front of the Confessor.

"The sensors are up. You've got this stowaway!" Nev shouts as I run up the ramp of the skip and fasten myself into the pilot seat.

Moments later I'm lifting off the landing platform and heading for Ceres. A display opens up beside me showing Rickard's face.

"In five minutes I'll contact the facility, I'll tell them that you are on your way. After that you're on your own," he says.

"Got it. I'll send Ava as soon as possible," I respond.

The captain hesitates, catching my attention. "Good luck kid." He closes the connection before I can respond.

God, waiting is such torturous hell, even with the skip's Pulse engines are at full throttle it takes twenty long minutes to reach the inner threshold of Ceres. Not enough time to do a damn thing but think about everything I shouldn't be thinking about. What if Ava is hurt? Or worse, what if she's dead? The thought of it makes my skin crawl and yet something deep inside me gets excited at the thought of killing every single soul on that installation for laying a finger on her. I rebel against the notion when my control panel lights up indicating a high band text message from an unknown source.

"Starboard, Hanger 4 Bravo. Lower shields and follow the green lights."

I close the message and bring up my navigation display, selecting Hanger 4 Bravo. A virtual path arks across open space and to the now green lit hanger. I manually lower the shields, feeling the skip lurch immediately after as if an unseen force takes control of the shuttle. I attempt to open a connection to the Confessor, but all I get is static. The captain was right. I'm on my own now. I feel a distinctive shiver start at the base of my head and run through the rest of my body as the massive hanger doors open and a blinding light hits me. I feel the skip land a minute later and the engine winding down. The light is still blinding me when the ramp automatically descends, followed by the sound of footsteps running up it.

I turn to see who is there but my eyes are still blurry from the light. "I—I have a bomb!" I shout, holding up the detonator.

The footsteps stop, leaving silence in their wake. I continue looking around but I don't see anyone, when it dawns on me that they are probably cloaked.

Finally after a solid minute of our quiet stalemate, a soldier speaks up. "Step forward five paces!" he demands.

"Show yourself!" I retort.

There is a pause and then one of the soldiers appears about five meters in front of me with a pulse rifle pointed at me. I feel the back of my head twinge with painful glee but I repress the sensation.

"Come forward now!" he demands.

I wave the detonator in my left hand, ensuring he can see it and also the eight thorium grenades attached to my chest. "Whatever you say," I respond, taking slow and steady steps toward him.

I can sense that he isn't the only soldier in the skip. The others must be cloaked as well. I come to a stop in front of him, looking at his tinted helmet. "Do you have any other weapons or devices that we cannot see?!" the soldier barks.

"You mean besides the bomb?" I pause for a moment. I have a pulse revolver in my waistband, but they don't need to know that. "Na, I think the bomb is enough." I can tell the soldier doesn't appreciate my sarcasm.

"Turn around and keep your hands were I can see them!" he shouts.

I lift my arms slowly and turn. "Now what?" Next thing I know, someone places a harness on my head followed by a set of spikes that embed themselves into my scalp. I lunge back hitting the soldier's visor and causing him to stager. "You bastards!" I shout, attempting to remove the harness with my free hand but as soon as I touch it I feel a shock pierce my skull, forcing me on my knees. Four more soldiers appear out of thin air. They pull me to my feet and drag me out of the skip.

Cheever is standing against the wall with an irritating grin on his face. "Ah, the Prodigal Child returns. Welcome to Ceres—but then again you've been here before, haven't you?" he says with his arms outstretched. "I must say. I didn't expect you to be packing." He takes a few steps toward me and taps one of the thorium grenades. "Tricky little fucker."

"What's wrong, Cheever. Were you hoping I'd be easy?" I mock.

He smiles. "You know I had hoped, but I would've been disappointed any other way. Besides, I've been busy with—other things." His eyes narrow.

"Where is she? I swear, if you hurt her!" I pull my arms free from the soldier flashing the detonator.

"Oh, you'll kill us all?" Cheever laughs. "That seems kind of counterproductive, don't you think?"

"I'm sure your employer doesn't want any harm to come to me." I pull a pulse revolver from my waistband and shoot two of the soldiers flanking Cheever.

The two unfortunate guards' slump down with blood escaping the gaping holes in their chests. The other IISF draw their weapons and train them on me while Cheever begins clapping his hands. "Look at you, so strong now, so in control. Nothing like you were on Titan. You remind me of a young, less attractive me."

"I'm nothing like you!" I jeer.

Cheever looks at the fresh corpses on either side of him "Really?" He cocks his eyebrow.

I feel my heart flutter with exhilaration. "Just give me what I want and I'm yours." I lower my revolver and drop it on the ground at Cheever's feet.

Cheever lets out an excited exhale. "Bring her in," he says in a lustful tone.

The door slides open behind him and two guards walk in dragging Ava. I rush forward and take her in my arms. It looked like every part of her body was covered in bruises or small cuts. I push her hair to the side and place my hand on her face. One of her eyes was swollen and her lip was split.

"Ava, baby. Come on," I say, tapping her cheek. I hear a faint laugh come from Cheever. "What did you do to her!?" I shout feeling the back of my head ache.

"Me? Wha—I did nothing!" Cheever taunts.

"You son-of-a-bitch!"

"Ah, watch it. By now you've guessed that thing on your head is the same as the one from our last encounter. But this time I assure you it'll break you before you break it," Cheever says coldly. "She'll be fine. She should be coming out of the sedation soon."

Just then Ava's eye open. She starts screaming and flailing around. I grab her arms and force them to her side and she finally begins to calm down. "John!" she cries. "John, but—" she looks around the hanger, taking in the surroundings. "You shouldn't be here," she whispers as a tears fall down her cheeks.

I wipe them away. "I couldn't leave you."

Ava's eye dart to Cheever then back to me. "You don't understand," she mutters. "This is what they wanted."

Of course it is what they wanted I've been the fixation of this place, these people for two decades. But something tells that wasn't what Ava meant.

Cheever takes a few steps toward us. I lift the detonator, stopping him in mid stride. "If your little reunion is quite over," he says holding up his hands, "I have a schedule to keep."

Schedule? "I don't care about your priorities!" I state, lifting Ava to her feet.

I can tell Cheever is losing his patience. He usually isn't one to ask nicely. "You said you'd be mine if I gave you the girl!"

"You've been waiting this long," I snap. "What's another five minutes?"

I help Ava up the skip's ramp and into the pilot's chair. She places her hands on my face, "You can't stay. Please." I can feel her worry overwhelm me.

"I have to. I need to finish this." I latch the belt around her waist. "Will you be able to fly?"

Ava shakes her head. “I’m not leaving you.” Another tear rolls down her cheek. “They’re monsters, John.” She whispers.

I crouch so I can meet her gaze. “I know. I was born here, Ava—” Her eyes widen. “The captain, your father, has a lot to tell you about me. I wish I could. But for now you have to leave.” I lean in and kiss her on the cheek.

I quickly stand and begin walking out of the skip. If I stayed any longer then I wouldn’t be able to leave her. I walk down the ramp, ensuring to flaunt the detonator for all of the IISF guards can see.

"Alright," I say to Cheever. “As soon as she and the Confessor are safe I’ll disarm the bomb.”

Cheever had his arms crossed and was leaning against the wall. “You really have changed, like you found your balls or something.”

“Spare me your complements and let her go,” I demand.

Cheever shrugs, looking at one of the guards and nods. The guard opens a display and unlocks the hanger door. The skip powers up and moments later it is nothing more than a white streak against the blackness of space.

I let out a sigh. “Ok, Cheever," I say in a low voice. “I’m all yours.”

Cheever smiles. “Follow me.” He walks out of the hanger and down the hall.

I follow closely. The facility feels familiar, almost like a distant dream or déjà vu but even then it is remarkably mediocre for being the place where cutting edge technology was developed and tested.

Cheever glances back. "You know, I always knew you were something special, ever since I first met you."

I glare at him. "Is that what we're going to do now? Reminiscing about our past like old friends?"

Cheever stops at a window, facing the interior of the facility. "You're right, boy. I hate you and want nothing more than to slowly kill you, but look at what has come from this." He lifts his prosthetic arms. "I was powerful before, but now I realize that wasn't real power." He looks at me. "You and I are same, the ying and yang if you will. Don't you see what we could do—together?"

I feel my stomach writhe with disgust. "I might still detonate this bomb if you keep talking like that." I hold up the detonator.

Cheever scoffs, "You're not going to do anything because you, like me, want to know the truth. Honestly, boy—you think I did this to myself just for revenge." He faces me fully, gesturing to his additions. "No, I did this because he showed me the truth."

"Who?" I ask.

Cheever smiles again, nodding his head toward the window. "See for yourself."

I take a step forward and look out the glass. I feel the air escape my lungs. The entire core of Ceres was hollow. I could see lights in the distance from the other side of the dwarf planet. And in the middle, suspended, was a massive series of disks slowly rotating. Blue energy was emitting from the center, warping and bending all the light and space around it.

"How is this possible?" I ask, taking several steps back from the glass.

Cheever lets out a laugh. "Beats the hell out of me." He turns and begins walking down the hall again.

"Wait!" I shout. "What is that thing?"

Cheever stops at a massive door. "I'm not the one to answer that." He waives his hand toward the door.

I hesitate, faced with the unknown. My entire life has culminated into this one moment. I know the answers that I seek about my past, about this gift, are just behind this door. I step forward and place my hand on the metal. It lights up and slowly slides open. The room is dark. I look at Cheever, but he shows no emotion, no hint as to what is inside. I take a deep breath. I feel as though I've been here before, as if I'm about to pass through the point of no return. I look at Cheever and it dawns on me this whole thing was set into motion the moment I walked into Cheever's penthouse. I feel a strange sense of—balance as if this moment was the close of a long, unraveling misadventure. I finally work up the courage and enter the room. The door slides closed behind me with an echoing thud, followed by silence.

Chapter Thirty-Six: The Avant's Beginning

I've never been one to shy away from the dark. But the blackness of this room is unnerving to say the least.

"Hello."

"Welcome home," a voice in the darkness responds.

"Who's there?"

There is no answer but instead a clicking noise that subtly gets louder and louder. Then a bright light begins emitting from the walls. I squint, attempting to get used to the light. In front of me I can just make out a figure so I begin walking toward them, and end up hitting a wall. I blink my eyes, bringing the room into focus and I realize that I'm in the white room from my dreams. I take a step back from the glossy black wall to look at the figure that is actually my reflection.

"What is this?!" I demand, looking around room for the exit.

"This is an Axiom, a tool use for many purposes. Yours was in order to help you control your gifts," the unknown voice said.

"Where are you?" I ask.

There a pause. "Go to your reflection," the voice requests.

I walk over to the glass and stare at my reflection. Typically this is disconcerting to me, but this time I don't feel my shadow-self's presence. My reflection begins to warp, starting with my forehead, then moving down to my cheeks. I touch my face, ensuring that it isn't me that is warping. Then the glass separates and the blackness flows into the room like a dense smoke forcing its way into my lungs, causing me to cough and choke. I fall to my knees, bracing my chest and focusing on my breathing. Then I hear footsteps in front of me.

I look up and the smoke is gone. In front of me is a middle-aged man wearing a fine suit. His hair is neatly trimmed and combed and his stance is confident and strong. He has the look of a man with a purpose and the conviction to pursue that purpose.

He waits for me to regain my bearing before smiling. "Enough smoke and mirrors. The Axiom responds differently to everyone," he says.

I look at the all-around average room before meeting the man's stare. "Who are you?"

The man jumps as if I have startled him. "Oh, sorry. You were only three last time I saw you." He reaches out with an open hand. "I'm Jensin Reach."

I ignore his hand. "I have questions."

"Of course, of course," Reach says. "There is so much to tell you."

I tilt my head, "I not sure—"

"Where to start?" Reach finishes. "That's understandable. How about we start with your parents."

I feel my heart skip a beat. "My parents? Who are they? Are they here?!" I rattle.

Jensin puts up his hands. "Everything you need to know about yourself has been with you all along."

"What?" I respond, but then I think about it. The partition within my Aug. It was there the entire time—my life, my past, everything.

Jensin stretches his hand out again. "You have no idea how nice it is to see you again, John"

I take Jensin's hand and I feel my Aug begin to tingle, and just like that the encrypted partition unlocks, giving way to a flood of information about my life. I begin hyperventilating and I feel myself smiling. "My parents—their names are Benjamin and Anissa Markus." I gasp, feeling tears flowing down my face. "My last name is Markus." I sob.

Jensin walks around me. "What else?"

"My birthday is July twenty-eighth—I've actually been nineteen for the last two months!" I say with a laugh.

"And your name?" Jensin probes, "I think you'll find it as ironic as I did."

I search through the information, separating the two lives as best I can. "My name—is still John," I say with a surprised tone.

"In fact, you were named you after your grandfather, Jonather," Jensin says. "Your legal name is Jonather Henrik Markus."

I shake my head. It was all too surreal, being reunited with a lost part of myself. My journey for answers has come to an end at the hands of the same people that willingly killed for me. I look at Jensin. I know he is the person I've been fighting this whole time, but a part of me wants to trust him.

"Why did you do all this?" I ask.

Jensin scrunches his face. "I know what you must think of me, John. I won't lie to you. We've done horrible things."

"Why?" I respond. "What could possibly justify what you've done?"

"The simplest answer is for all of us, humans," Jensin says flatly. "Think of it like this. Of all the other creations in existence that started on Mother Earth, why is it we were chosen?" He hesitates. "It was because we possessed something that no other creature did. Do you know what that is?"

I shrug. "Intelligence?"

Jensin smiles. "Innovation. If it wasn't for our need to understand God's work and make sense of the chaos around us, then we would have never made it to where we are today. But despite all our gifts there is something wrong with us, something flawed. Deep down we are and always will be nothing more than animals, killing one another for whatever we hold more valuable than a person's life." His face for the first time shows the burden of his decisions. "You know it's true. The Axiom has told us that you agree."

"So you kill people, in order to stop us from killing people?" I retort.

"There is so much more to it," Jensin says.

I look down at the detonator in my hand. "Then tell me. But first I want my crew's safety." I lift the detonator.

Jensin brings up a display showing Ava's skip just reaching the Confessor. "I promise no harm will come to them, if you would just listen to me."

I look at the display. I know that everything he says and shows me could be a lie but I choose to believe him. I deactivate the detonator and remove the suicide vest. In a few seconds the Confessor will get a warning that the vest was removed but they won't know the reason. Hopefully they don't do anything stupid.

"Tell me everything," I demand.

Jensin brings up a large display on the wall in front of us. "In the early twenty-third century, miners on the moon found the remains of an ancient unknown civilization." A series of photos begin playing, showing a massive temple on the moon. "It was evident that these ruins were built by something human-like, but no one could explain how it was possible."

"This happened over a thousand years ago. How did no one know?" I interrupt.

Jensin looks at me. "We have been around since the beginning, orchestrating events behind the scenes. You know us as Integra Industries, but we've gone by hundreds of names."

"Like ArchDyme?" I respond, remembering the dream I had.

Jensin tilts his head. "Indeed, ArchDyme was the first non-government corporation to colonize the Moon, and because of the technology reverse engineered from these ruins they became the first to colonize and terraform Mars and Venus. Because of ArchDyme we were able to have a Golden Age."

"So, your predecessors decided that it was better for humanity as a whole to be ignorant to the fact that we weren't alone in the universe?" I ask.

"What would have come from it?" Jensin retorts. "We would have killed ourselves with this knowledge, and frankly we still would."

"But it wasn't your responsibility—"

"It is only our responsibility!" Jensin snaps. "We do what we do because it is necessary. Because Humanity must survive. If we have to sacrifice hundreds, thousands, or even millions for the whole species, then so be it!" Jensin loosens his collar. "You have no right to judge. Look at what you have done with your gifts."

The room falls silent, with only the slide show rolling on with images of similar ruins found on Mars, Venus, Mercury and every other place that humanity is now living flashes in and out.

"What were they?" I finally ask.

Jensin sighs. "We've called them many things, but as of recent they are simply known as Antecedents."

"And that thing floating in the center of Ceres?" I ask.

"A relic, one of many throughout the solar system. What we think we know is that there was a cataclysmic event or war that destroyed most of their civilization," Jensin ponders.

I recall the planet from my dreams covered in genocidal flames. "War, I'm sure of it. And I'm starting to realize where I fit in here."

Jensin looks at me. "You were the only one that could bond with the Antecedent DNA. We tried thousands, but you were the only one."

A part of me knew all along. That there was something in me that wasn't human. And Jensin just confirmed it. "Huh," I let out. "I thought I'd take that differently." I look at my hands and think about what I have done with my ability. It would be so easy to say that it wasn't me. But then I would be lying to myself. This is who I am. "I'm not human."

Jensin grabs my shoulders. "No, you're something more. You're our future. The next step in our evolution. Don't you see?" He brings up a display showing our reflection.

"All I see is a monster and his creator," I respond coldly.

Jensin frowns. "You are our only way ahead. You will lead us all into another Golden Age that will never end." He brings up an image of an ornate metallic tablet with intricate caricatures scrawled across it. "This is a prophecy we found here on Ceres. It foretells that there will be one who is chosen, called the Avant-Garde that will awaken and begin a new cycle of rebirth," he says with his hands up. "You are the Avant-Garde and as it was foretold, you are here to usher in a new era. It is your destiny."

"And that thing out there has something to do with it?" I say matter-of-factly.

"That is the doorway to the stars. When we found it there was so much work to do. It took hundreds of years to repair it. And now you are here, so you can open it." Jensin grins.

A quantum wormhole device. That is what Jensin just described. Even in this day and age such a thing is still merely theoretical at best, and he says they have had one for hundreds of years. "Why didn't you open it yourselves?"

"We tried. That was before we deciphered the texts and realized only the Avant-Garde could open the door," Jensin responds.

Everything that has happened has led to this moment. It goes beyond me to over a thousand years of advancement and growth all guided by this organization and secret society just for this one titular moment. I was created to be a key, to save the human race from itself. It was all so inspiring seeing the amount of effort that was put forth just to reach this precipice. And yet I feel a sense of wrong doing here. Everything was built on a foundation of human sacrifice and misguidance. An entire existence based off lies that freewill doesn't exist. And here I am enamored by this man who represents a future for humanity but at the cost of what makes us human. I can't do it. Humanity should be left to reach these conclusions on its own. If we fail, it is because we don't deserve to live, because we couldn't get over our petty ways. Who gives Jensin Reach the authority to take on the responsibility of humanity?

"Everything that I've been through—all the killing and death that has surrounded me my entire life—was so that you could use me to open a door to God knows where?" I say bluntly.

Jensin narrows his eyes. "I was hoping after what I just told you that you'd reach that conclusion on your own," he says, placing his hands behind his back. "That you'd see the silver lining of all the bad."

"Millions of people. Maybe billions over the course of a thousand of years have died for your dream, and they didn't have a choice. Hell, they didn't even know what their deaths meant. Did you orchestrate the Great War as well?" I probe.

Jensin grimaces. “Who cares? Most of them cared only for their own agendas and we’ve fought petty wars for lesser causes, committed worse sins for petty reasons. All these sacrifices have led to this. It would be a disservice to their memory not to assume your destiny.”

“It just seems—wrong. I’m not qualified to lead an entire race! And I’m sure if the solar system knew about this they wouldn’t want to be manipulated by you or your organization.” I slowly step back from Jensin. “It’s too much.”

Jensin looks at me in a way he hasn’t before, as if I was threatening his very life. “I’m sorry you feel that way," he says coldly. “I misjudged you. I hoped you’d be convinced—I imagined this going so differently.”

“I’m sorry to disappoint you," I say directly. “We should be left to come to these conclusions on our own. It’s the only real way we will deserve that future.”

“No!” Jensin shouts. “If you will not see reason, then we will have to do this the hard way.” He brings up two displays, one showing the Confessor and the other showing a man and a woman dressed in what seems to be prison attire. “I take it you recognize the ship, but the other two people, well they are your parents.”

“What?!” I reach out, placing my hand on the image of my mother’s dark hair. “What are you doing!?”

“You will assume your destiny.” Jensin says “Or we will kill every single person you hold dear.”

“You promised!” I shout.

Jensin frowns. "We've waited centuries for this! You may be the most important person to have ever existed. You think a mere promise will end a thousand years of meticulous planning. No, Mr. Markus—you will assume your destiny or you will lose everything!"

"If you kill them, I will never help you!" I feel the back of my head starting to tingle. "I don't think you understand. I would sooner kill myself then let you hurt them."

"You mistake me as someone who negotiates." Jensin's voice is cold and lifeless. "We've been doing this for so long that it doesn't matter what you say, and in the end you will do what we want. Your choices are simple: open the gate now or we kill everyone and then you open the gate."

I open my mouth to argue, but before I can say anything Jensin targets the Confessor and launches a volley of missiles toward it.

"Stop!"

Jensin sighs. "You have three minutes." The display updates with a timer.

Damn-it, Reach was right. I have no power here. Even if I killed myself and destroyed this facility, how much difference would it make? I'd be dead, the people I care for would be dead and I would have only delayed this plan by maybe a few decades. Two minutes left till the Confessor is obliterated. By now Captain Rickard would have seen the missiles and attempted to evade them but the ship didn't move. Probably something else was keeping them there. Maybe the same tech that took control of the skip from earlier.

"Ok!" I shout frantically. "I'll open the damn gate, just stop the missiles."

Jensin clasps his hands and smiles. "I'm glad we reached an accord," he says, rattling his fingers across the display, destructing the missiles with only fifty-eight second left. "You won't regret this, Mr. Markus!"

CHAPTER THIRTY-SEVEN: THE TITAN'S END

Regret, one of the few insecurities universal to all people. No matter what we do, we regret things that range from unimportant to detrimental. I won't regret this, Jensin says to me as if to reassure me. To make me feel that what I'm about to do is for the best. But I do regret. I wish I hadn't been born and none of this would have happened. I wish that I had the power to fix my mistakes instead of causing them to become worse. Because the truth is simple and yet we refuse to see it: nobody lives without regret. All those people that say they do are lying to everyone, including themselves.

Jensin closes the slide show and the room returns to normal lighting. He looks at me and smiles. "You should really look at all this in a different light."

I glare at him. "What should I be feeling? Honored? Righteous? Blessed? Or should I be happy knowing that I've literally fallen right into your plan?"

He frowns at my lack of enthusiasm. "You know this moment will be remembered for all time. You should be proud to be leading it." I simply nod my head. There is no point resisting the inevitable any longer. Jensin walks over to the door and opens it. "Mr. West, would you be so kind as to escort Mr. Markus to the Viewing Platform." He looks at me. "I'll catch up. I need to make some arrangements before the big moment," Jensin finishes.

I walk out of the room and meet Cheever's stare. "What?"

"Pretty impressive, huh?" he asks.

I cock my head to the side. "I'm still wondering what part you have in this, now that I'm finally here."

"All in due time," Cheever responds, walking down the hallway in front of me. "After you do this, I finally get what I deserve."

"And what is that?" I ask.

Cheever glances back at me and smiles wickedly. "You."

I start laughing. "You're such an idiot. We both are." Cheever stops and faces me. "They're not going to give me to you. In fact, you're nothing to them now. I've agreed to do what they want. Your purpose has been served and like every tool without a job, you'll be discarded."

Cheever sneers. "But, they promised—"

"They lied—that's what they do. I bet if I asked them nicely they'd let me kill you myself," I retort. "Wouldn't that be quite a twist?" I can tell Cheever is starting to get angry. "You know it's true. You were a tool for them all along, like me. Just cogs in their machine, only I was the real prize. And that means I'm the one that lives, Mr. West," I mock. Several guards show up and surround us. I look around before locking my eyes on Cheever's glare. "To the Viewing Platform."

Cheever turns and begins walking down the hall again with the guards following closely between us. Cheever is uncomfortable. I can feel it emanating from him. He knows that his time is up and everything I just said is true.

We reach a large lift at the end of the corridor and pile in. The door closes and I can feel the elevator starting to rise when Cheever begins laughing manically. This goes on for thirty solid second before two blades extend from Cheever's forearms and he begins killing the guards in a whirlwind of death. I back up against the wall as he purposely savors the kills, reminiscent of how I was dispatching the Brotherhood on the Clairvoyance.

The lift comes to a screeching halt at the top of a large platform where scientists and IISF soldier alike stop what they're doing and look at Cheever with varying levels of horror painted on their faces. Cheever is covered with the bloody remains of half a dozen guards and breathing heavily while staring at me.

"I will have you!" he roars, forcing me to my knees and placing the carbonized blade against my throat.

It's morbidly funny how symmetrical this situation has become. How Cheever and I started and ended the same. I let out a faint laugh, gaining Cheever's attention. "Remember what happened last time you had me, Cheever?" The memory of New Horizon quickly flashes through my mind.

He grimaces and presses the blade against my neck as several solders approach. "Stay back! Or I swear I'll cleave his head clear off!"

"Mr. West, that is quite enough." Jensin Reach's calm voice echoes across the platform.

Cheever glares at Jensin. "You promised I'd get to kill the boy! I let you tear me to pieces for him!"

"We rebuilt you—made you stronger and better than you were. Whatever reasons that motivated you to join us are superficial now. Forget your vendetta. There are much greater things to be done," Jensin says.

Cheever drops his shoulders and lowers his head toward he floor. "Cheever," I whisper. "You'll never be in control again. No matter what you do, they will see you as nothing more than an expendable tool. Face it, the Baron of New Horizon died the moment you agreed to help them."

"Shut up!" he shouts lifting the blade high above his head. "I'm the one in control!" he slams his arm down with surprising force.

I shut my eyes, refusing to see the end. How ironic is it? Dying here of all places at the hands of Cheever West. But the end never comes. I open one eye and see that Cheever is frozen with his blades a mere centimeter from my throat.

His face is contorted and tightly furrowed. "What—are—you—doing!" he forces out through his clenched teeth.

I look at him and smile, playing with the point of his blade. "It wasn't me," I whisper, tapping the device embedded in my skull. "Remember?"

I can see the frustration overtake Cheever as he tries the move his body. From behind him I can see Jensin Reach with a display hovering over his forearm. "Are you alright, Mr. Markus?" he asks.

"It's just John and I'm fine," I respond and lean in so only Cheever can hear me. "You were so close," I whisper, placing my hand on his cheek. "I can't even imagine how that must feel."

Cheever contorts his face out of frustration, spitting, drooling and cursing under his breath. "I take it you'd like to do the honors?" Jensin asks, running his hand along the display.

A seconds later the device on my head detaches and falls to the ground. I wipe away the fresh blood running down my forehead and give Cheever foreboding look. "Goodbye, Mr. West," I say lifting my hand.

Cheever's eyes widen with dread as I lift him off the platform and begin ripping his bionics apart piece by piece. I won't kill him until I see the real Cheever, the one who killed my friends. I feel an exhilarating sense of satisfaction as I remove his augmented limbs one at a time. Finally, I tear his breastplate off and let it fall to the ground with a loud thud. All that remains of Cheever, the Baron of New Horizon, is his fleshy torso with faded tattoos scrolled across his skin. He is so vulnerable and afraid that I can feel his pulse racing. This is for everyone he has hurt—Jurin, Dr. Baker, Ron and the countless others he has tortured and killed on New Horizon. I reach out with my ability, following his pulse to the source, his heart pounding against his rib cage. I feel myself grasp it with my mind, slowly squeezing. Cheever begins squirming and convulsing with panicked agony. Blood begins bubbling up from his mouth as I tighten my grasp. His heart is getting weak and his body is starting to shut down. My breath quickens with every second and then it's over. His body becomes still with his face frozen in a state of fear. A warm sensation flows over my body—closure at last. I release his body and it falls to the ground. In the end Cheever West was just a man who though himself a God.

I look at Jensin who was grinning with his hands held firmly behind his back. "What's so amusing?" I ask.

"Seeing your gift on video is nothing compared to experiencing it in person," he responds in a satisfied voice.

I shake my head, feeling the high from killing Cheever dissipate. "You're sick."

Jensin frowns. "Don't be rude. We are all here to see your greatness."

"Then let's get this over with," I respond coldly.

Jensin's frown deepens. "Very well." He motions to a panel situated in the middle of the platform.

I walk over to it. The tech was unfamiliar to me but it seems to come alive as soon as I approach it. The platform begins to lift as the ceiling opens, revealing the massive gateway in its glory. Blue energy reaches out and touches the platform, warping the space around it. A dull hum echoes from the center that vibrates me to the core and makes my body ache.

Jensin walks up behind me and places his hands on my shoulders. "Beautiful, isn't it? This is the moment that changes everything. All you have to do is turn it on. It's what you were made for," he whispers.

What I was made for. The words echo in my head. I am just like Cheever to them, just a tool that they can control. The rotating discs of the gate combine into one large convex plate facing the platform. The blue energy is flowing from a black sphere hovering in the center. I suspend my hand over the controls; this is it, the moment that'll define everything.

But for some reason I hesitate, a sense of dread comes over me and I look at Jensin. "Something's wrong," I say. The image of the planet from my dreams lingers on the fringes of my mind.

Jensin glares. "Nothing is wrong, open it!" he hisses.

"No, I can't," I respond, the dread overwhelms me and I realize that I was never worried about Jensin or Cheever but rather this gateway all along.

Jensin slaps me. "Open the gate!" he shouts.

"It's going to kill us all," I say without hesitating.

Jensin bares his teeth. "If you don't open it everyone you care for will die!"

"If I open it everyone everywhere will die," I say without understanding why I'm saying it.

Jensin brings up a display showing the Confessor. "This is your last warning."

Just then the gate lets out a loud glass-shattering moan. I feel my head being ripped apart as the gate's center begins to expand. I fall to my knees, the tremors lashing out from the device feel as though they were tearing me apart. Bolts of blue energy start to whip out and destroy parts of the facility.

My eyesight starts to blur "Run!" I shout, but it is already too late.

The gate lets out another reality-bending howl, causing several solders and scientists to collapse and convulse uncontrollably. Jensin grabs me by the collar and pulls me to my feet. His voice is mumbled, but I can make out the words "Stop it now!" before he looks at the gate behind me.

His eyes become wide and his jaw drops. Behind him several soldiers and scientists stop fleeing and also look at the gate. One points and begins shouting about something coming through the gate. There is another deafening ring, so strong it throws Jensin Reach off the platform.

I crumple to the ground, unable to move. I'm either paralyzed by pain or fear and at this point they might as well be the same thing. The sound of distant screams echo, the type of screaming I know very well—the sound people make when they are torn limb from limb. The gate groans once again, causing the platform beneath me to shake violently as an overwhelming presence forces me against the ground. I feel my body throb as if every cell is being torn apart. The pain is both indescribable and unbearable like nothing I have ever felt before. I cry out in agony before my vision and consciousness finally give way.

And so it is like the countless times before—I am floating, weightless in space, surrounded by the unimaginable expanses of nothingness. There are no stars or planets. No feeling of freedom or contentment. No dark reflection maliciously staring at me. There is just silence, oblivion and me.

About the Author

Clinton K. Stang is an aspiring new author, born the youngest of three in Wichita, Kansas during the month of May in 1990. It was evident at an early age that Clinton exhibited the unmistakable signs of an overactive imagination. By the time Clinton turned into a brooding teenager, he was fully self-diagnosed with an irrefutable lust for exaggeration and storytelling. Alas, things do not always work out the way they were destined. Upon graduating high school, Clinton joined the Kansas Air National Guard and eventually married his high school sweetheart, who then further entrapped him by blessing Clinton with three beautiful daughters. It was at the age of twenty that Clinton finally realized that he could no longer deny his need to write and for the next three years he honed his talent while struggling to find the conviction necessary to fulfill his lifelong dream. This struggle culminated into his first novel, *Avant-Garde: Awakening,* and will hopefully grow into a wonderful adventure.

For my Readers...

First, I thank you, nameless reader! Not only for enduring my work but also for making my dream come to life. Every word you read, sentence you recited in your head, was labored over by myself, and I hope that I conveyed my passion and love through my words to you. It is in all of your hands that my success will cultivate and grow, not mine. You have reached the end of the beginning and I wish for you to continue this crazy ride as I figure out the controls. Please give me your feedback and help me become better at what I know is exactly what I was meant to do.

Thank you, Your Idle Confessor—C. K. Stang

Made in the USA
Lexington, KY
06 June 2017